Beyond & Within
LATIN AMERICAN SHARED STORIES

Speculative storytelling from
many voices. Edited by V. Castro.

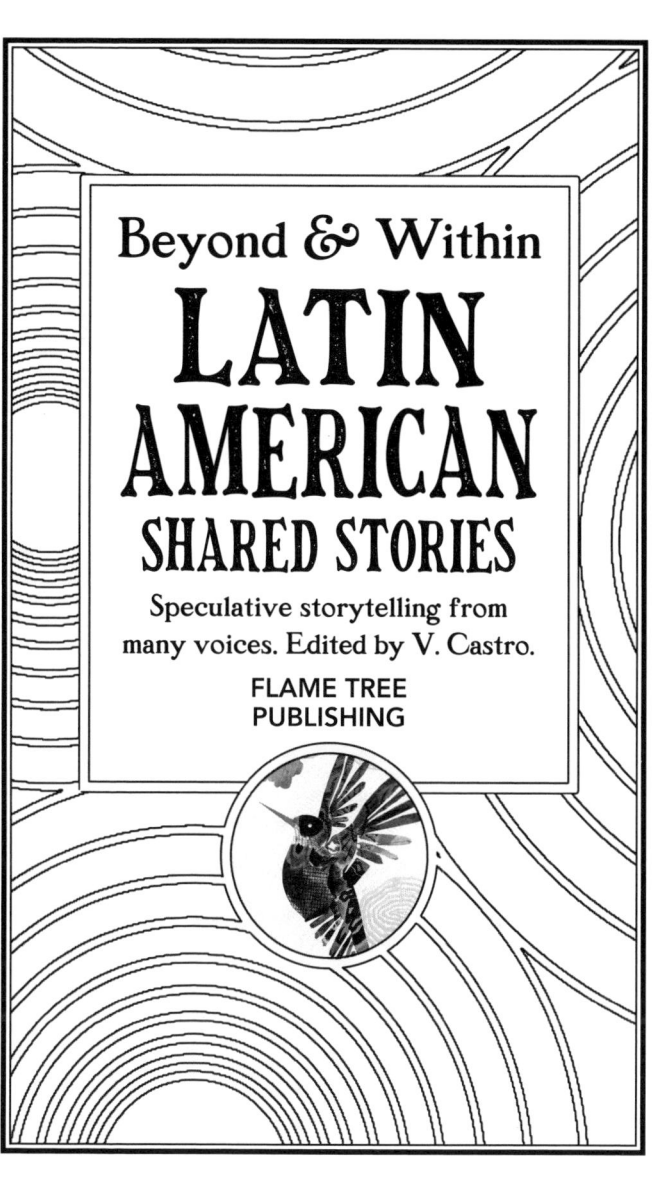

Beyond & Within

LATIN AMERICAN SHARED STORIES

Speculative storytelling from many voices. Edited by V. Castro.

FLAME TREE PUBLISHING

Publisher & Creative Director: Nick Wells
Senior Project Editor: Catherine Taylor
Editorial Assistant: Simran Aulakh

FLAME TREE PUBLISHING
6 Melbray Mews, Fulham,
London SW6 3NS, United Kingdom
www.flametreepublishing.com

First published 2025
Introduction © V. Castro 2025.
Copyright in each story is held by the individual authors.
Stories by modern authors are subject to international copyright law,
and are licensed for publication in this volume.
Volume copyright © 2025 Flame Tree Publishing Ltd.

25 27 29 28 26
1 3 5 7 9 10 8 6 4 2

Hardback ISBN: 978-1-83562-305-3
ebook ISBN: 978-1-83562-306-0

All rights reserved. No part of this publication may be reproduced,
stored in a retrieval system, or transmitted in any form or by any
means, electronic, mechanical, photocopying, recording or
otherwise, without the prior written permission of the publisher.

Publisher's Note: This is a work of fiction. Names, characters, places, and
incidents are a product of the authors' imaginations. Locales and public
names are sometimes used for atmospheric purposes. Any resemblance
to actual people, living or dead, or to businesses, companies, events,
institutions, or locales is completely coincidental.

The cover is created by Flame Tree Studio. Frontispiece illustration and
cover detail is © *Hummingbird* 2025 Jorge González.

A copy of the CIP data for this book is available from the British Library.

Printed and bound in China

Table of Contents

Introduction
V. Castro 8

From Parts Unknown
Hector Acosta 12

Sucker
Alyssa Alessi 33

Southward, Then Upward
Gustavo Bondoni 45

Whispering Shards
David Bowles 62

Listen to This
Arasibo Campeche & Carra Flowers 82

*Mestiza Death: How the Spanish Grim Reapress
Morphed into Mexican Santa Muerte*
Dr. R. Andrew Chesnut 99

Belinda Matos & The Bronx River Wishing Stone
Angel Luis Colón 115

Maternal Instinct
Rios de la Luz 131

Taíno: An Untold Story
Ivette N. Diaz.. 147

The Mother of Canals in Dade County
Laura Diaz de Arce 163

Eaten Alive
J.F. Gonzalez 181

El Puente
L.P. Hernandez... 185

Night of the Nagual
Pedro Iniguez... 199

La Diablada
Ruth Joffre 208

The Stained Walls
S. Alessandro Martinez... 225

The Snake God's Wake
Juliana Spink Mills.. 252

A Guardian of Salt and Flesh
Vanessa Molina... 265

Come Back
Mo Moshaty.. 290

Isla del Encanto Perdido
Richie Narvaez... 315

And Then I Wake Up
Wi-Moto Nyoka 333

Nacho
Daniel A. Olivas 356

The Ache
Monique Quintana 368

In the Black and White Woods:
My Personal Experience with Santa Muerte
A.E. Santana 377

We Cast Our Own Curses
Richard Z. Santos 385

ABOUT THE AUTHORS 402

ABOUT THE EDITOR 412

ACKNOWLEDGEMENTS 413

BEYOND & WITHIN 415

FLAME TREE FICTION 416

Introduction

V. Castro

STORIES HAVE BEEN PART of human history since time immemorial. Our very existence is a story and that is why it is so important to preserve those traditions, ideas, thoughts, and mythology that have been part of the fabric of our culture. And stories would not exist without storytellers. Some were originally crafted as explanations for happenings in the natural world. Some to instill fear to keep the earliest of us safe in an unpredictable environment. People also told stories to entertain, to share with their community in laughter and joy. Stories and storytellers have always existed and always will. They feed our imaginations and souls. Storytellers are a vital part of humanity.

Latin American Shared Stories captures the rich and varied voices across a multitude of heritages. Our experiences are not all the same nor are the beliefs or the ways in which we tell a story.

I believe storytelling comes from the soul, those depths of us we don't completely understand, yet there is stored emotion and knowledge there. Stories can be like ghosts who reside in the walls of a house without letting anyone know they are there until lights flicker or an icy chill runs the length of our neck. They are compelled to make themselves known sooner or later. Many of our ancestors were prevented from telling their tales the way they would have wanted to, or they were simply erased out of existence due to colonialism. Perhaps like cosmic smoke from a snuffed-out life, those remnants come to us to continue those beautiful dreams or nightmares that were lost. We now live in a time when we can do that. This book is one of those opportunities.

In July 2024, I ventured to the Amazon rainforest in Ecuador followed by a trip to Mexico City. The language was the same, I blended in both places with a similar shade of brown skin; however, the experience couldn't be more different. In Baños, Ecuador, a woman roasted guinea pigs on spits on the street and offered fresh juices. In Mexico City, I had roasted elote on a boat also selling pulque to drink. In Mexico City I wandered the remnants of a great civilization replaced by a cathedral. Then I stood over the bones of people who were sacrificed but now on show in a museum, the blades that sliced open sacrifices no longer wet with blood but preserved behind glass. After, I retreated to the W Hotel with a rooftop club. I saw no temples during my time in

Ecuador. It was rushing water, tangles of foliage, thick humidity, lush forest, and I stayed in a village with the Kichwa people. Trails of large ants carried leaves on their backs in the thick mud on the trail I followed to my hut on stilts.

Both experiences enriched me in different ways, but were equally unforgettable and valuable. That is Latin America. There is a shared history of conquest, but each country, culture, and indigenous people has their own beautiful story. Each culture has evolved differently. And those who no longer live in the countries of their ancestors have a whole other book of experiences related to assimilation, identity, language, and existing. You will encounter that in here as well.

There is only one contribution, Dr. R. Andrew Chesnut, who does not have Latin American heritage. I have included his essay because his in-depth scholarly work with Santa Muerte is important and eye opening. Part of sharing our stories is dispelling stereotypes, fear, and hate. Whatever your thoughts are on Santa Muerte, she is a cultural icon. Her veneration is alive and well as I discovered at a local market in Mexico City and my subsequent journey to a shrine dedicated to her. I have also visited a very well kept shrine to her in Los Angeles, California.

The more we know about each other and our experiences, the more unified we can become. Like the goddess Michtecihautl, once the skin is pulled away, we all have the same flesh, blood, cartilage, and bone. Our brains are made from the same stuff; however, we can learn from having different perspectives and experiences because in this one life it is impossible to experience everything. There simply isn't enough time in our relatively short life spans. Stories can take us to those places. Our imaginations can be ignited and inspired by others not like us. Our empathy for each other only can deepen.

I hope you will enjoy submerging yourself in these wonderful and strange tales as exceptional as the storytellers. There are writers you might recognize and others who will be new to you. They vary in culture, gender, education and profession. Their voices are a testament to the beauty of Latin American storytelling.

If you enjoy their work, please check out their other works and connect with them online. And if this book touches you in some way, please leave a rating or review.

Thank you so very much for taking a journey with us.

V. Castro

From Parts Unknown

Hector Acosta

THE CITY SANK underneath Jorge's feet, cobblestone streets dipping and rising like the scales of a giant snake. Abuelas, thinned and gray-haired, pushed past him, lugging giant bags and hurrying to catch the nearby combis. Tourists lumbered in large, sweaty masses, led by guides who pointed at the buildings surrounding El Zócalo and through bits of history from Mexico City's main plaza. In the distance, La Catedral Metropolitana plunged through the sidewalk, a group of workers in hardhats and reflective vests working to staunch the bleeding of stone, concrete, and soil caused by the earthquake from a few months ago.

Jorge hated the city. Hated how no matter where he went, there always seemed to be more people than space available, hated how la contaminación from too many vehicles on the road hung thick in the air, burning your throat and nose the moment you went outside. And most of all, Jorge hated Mexico City because even before the earthquake, the city had been sinking, receding into the soft clay bed it'd originally been built atop of.

The realization came to him as he lay in bed one night, thin bedsheets draped across his body while a fan circulated stale air across his tiny room. Pulled from his dreams by the groans of the building, his bed tilted as his room shook and the building succumbed to its breaking foundation. Fear had gripped his entire body, keeping him unable to move, even as tremors overtook the building and angled his bed to the right. Shouts for help lodged in his throat as Jorge stared at the stains on a tilted ceiling, unable to do much of anything else. As the hours passed, the stains changed, years of water damage shifting into black and red pools, like the cells of some unknown organism. Eyes, dry and red from going without blinking, watched as the ceiling expanded into a wide and everlasting vista. Jorge witnessed the stains colliding among each other, feeding on one another and growing bigger. One, resembling a giant, feathered snake crossed across the vista and sent the others scattering, screeches and sounds like gnashing bone penetrating Jorge's mind. The rest of the night, Jorge waited for the stains to reach out and take him.

They never did.

Dropping his travel bag, Jorge stopped and dug around the red fanny pack tied around his waist. Pulling out a clear medicine bottle, he unscrewed it. Three green pills, the same color as the few U.S. dollars left in his wallet, fell into his hand. After a moment of indecision, he placed one back and crushed the other two between his teeth. His fingers tingled as he stuck the bottle of pills back in his fanny pack and dug out a scrap of yellow paper. His tongue ran up and down the length of his teeth, seeking out any remains of the crushed pills as he read the note one more time.

Ven al Templo. Te pago.

The note had been waiting for him after a show in Corpus Christi. Jorge had been in a sour mood that night, angry about the low turnout and the promoter trying to use that as an excuse to short him out of his pay. He'd been about to head back to his motel room when he found the note and recognized the handwriting as Miguel's.

Another headache rolled through Jorge, carrying with it a low hum which settled on his ears. Jorge looked around the plaza, tension gripping the back of his neck. His eyes landed on a big, bald-headed Mexican watching him over by the fountains. The man stood apart from the various groups of tourists snapping pictures and buying souvenirs. Rather than the shorts and t-shirts everyone else around him wore, the Mexican had on a neatly pressed blue business suit and black dress shoes. Calm professionalism poured out of him.

The tension on Jorge's neck reached down and squeezed his heart as the businessman started walking towards him... Every step the man took sent a tremor across the plaza and caused the buildings to shed tiny chunks of themselves. Only Jorge seemed to notice this, even as a piece of building the size a watermelon came within inches of a mother and her child.

Jorge was about to run when the Mexican turned and waved to the same mother and child. Blinking, Jorge watched the reunion and wondered what happened to the stone he'd seen almost crush them less than a minute ago.

Calmate cabrón, Jorge thought, reaching back into his fanny pack and popping a third pill. Swallowing it dry, he read the last two words of the note again. Te pago.

I'll pay.

Stuffing the note back into his pocket, Jorge picked up his travel bag and started walking again. It had been years since Jorge had set foot in Mexico City, having chosen to ply the trade he learned here across the border and in Japan, where the pay was better but the schedule and style of the matches left his body exhausted and sore. He turned his attention back to the question of how his brother had managed to find him. The last time Miguel reached out to him, it was to tell him of their father's passing. The conversation had lasted only a couple of minutes, the static of the phone line filling the silence between brothers. Jorge attending the funeral was never discussed.

Many of the paths he used to take were closed off to him now, some still in the process of being repaired, others simply gone and replaced with congested streets or blocked-off avenues. This troubled Jorge, who couldn't imagine forgetting Los Callejónes. Miguel and he would run through as boys on the way to El Templo, the sound of their chanclas hitting the cracked pavement of Mexico City yet to wake up.

A spark of pride ignited in Jorge's belly when he reached a familiar looking building. Built in the same style as the countless others Jorge passed by on the way here, El Templo stood apart by the mere fact it remained upright, untouched by the earthquake even as the building next to it sank so low to the ground its wooden door frame was in splinters. The walls of El Templo, which Jorge remembered as being as red as the marks left behind on a chest after a hard chop, had lost their color, revealing the gray bones of the building's original material.

A cracked plaque hung next to the door. Jorge stopped to run his finger across the etched words, just like he'd done countless of times before entering.

Gimnasio.

* * *

Jorge's father greeted him as he stepped into El Templo.

The sight of his father threw him off balance, the ground beneath his feet becoming malleable. Closing his eyes, Jorge took deep, even breaths, el viejo's hard stare burrowing from out of his memory and pressing against Jorge's skull. The smell of leather soaked in sweat and blood stretched Jorge's nostrils as the sound of bodies slamming against the ring mat crashed against his ears. The ground shuddered.

"Jorge."

Using the voice like a ladder, Jorge climbed out of his memories and opened his eyes, the ground becoming solid once more. His father's eyes were still there, but he turned away from them and faced a brother he hadn't seen in years.

The days when no one could tell the two twins apart were long gone, Miguel lacking the dark circles crowding Jorge's eyes and crow's feet signaling his age. The bulbous nose all Reyes men inherited somehow fit the contour of Miguel's clean-shaven face, and the soft, pillowy chin Jorge remembered mocking throughout their years together was shaved away, by a scalpel if Jorge had to guess. Miguel wore a pair of training shorts and a tight tank top revealing a trim body, and most surprising of all, tattoos.

They circled most of Miguel's arms and legs, deep black markings reminding Jorge of the roads of a map which had been cut up and then randomly pieced together again. Some of the designs were only an inch in width, others so large they swallowed any visible flesh around it. They traveled up, down, and around Miguel's limbs, and as far as Jorge could see, reached all the way to his neck and chest.

Jorge pointed to the tattoos. "That's new," he said before pointing to the wall. "Eso también."

His brother nodded and asked, "¿Te gusta?"

Jorge glanced at the wall again.

The painting took up one entire side and featured the red, white, and green backdrop of the Mexican flag. In the center, where the eagle perched atop where a nopal cactus should be, stood their father, El Rey Justiciero in all his masked glory. He had on his most iconic mask, the black one with gold accents around the eyes and mouth and a small crown framed on its center. Behind the mask laid two hard, black pearls, and Jorge imagined the artist who painted the picture dipping into tar to get the right color.

"No," Jorge said.

Miguel laughed, and gripped Jorge's hand in an unasked handshake. "Es bueno verte, Jorge," he said, patting him on his back.

"It's good to see you too," Jorge said and looked around El Templo – the name he and Miguel gave the gym their father ran after his retirement from Las Luchas. It looked much like Jorge last remembered it, with the same dim lighting and workout equipment already outdated when Jorge and Miguel used it. The place was hot, stank of sweat and despite it all, was packed. Men danced around heavy bags and feigned punches, the clang of weights cutting through grunts of exertion. Over by the corner stood a small ring with four young boys inside of it, all of them running through the drills as a gigante of a man stood by a turnbuckle and watched them, arms folded across his chest.

This should be mine.

"I got your note," Jorge said, much too fast.

Miguel smiled, his head tilting to the side. "I wasn't sure you'd come. You've had other invitations, right? Unless I'm wrong, I don't think you've set foot in Mexico in over a decade."

It was true, Jorge refused every offer thrown his way to step back into Mexico. Even being close to the border in towns like Juarez was too much sometimes, his dreams filled with a multitude of swarming beasts with gaping mouths and eyes which never blinked existing in a sunken world.

"How you find me?" Jorge asked.

"I've got some guys who travel back and forth, doing a couple trips a year to towns across the border. Told them to let me know if they ever hear of you wrestling in those areas."

"You got some guys?" Jorge mimicked. "I thought you were just a wrestler, Miguelito."

Another tilt of his head, the smile still plastered on. "You're mad."

Biting the inside of the cheek, Jorge said, "I'm tired." He considered popping another of his green pills, but wasn't sure they were even helping.

"Come on," Miguel motioned, "let's go to my office where we can talk."

It took them almost ten minutes to cross the gym, Miguel greeting every person they passed on the way to the office. He reminded Jorge of a politician on the campaign trail, a smile etched on his face as he gave workout advice, asked how everyone's niños were doing, and made a point to shake everyone's hands. Reaching the ring, Miguel motioned to the trainer.

"Jorge, meet Carlos."

Up close, the guy was still a giant, at least for a Mexican. Deep brown skin and thick, long, black hair marked him as an Indio, though from what region and tribe Jorge couldn't guess. He moved with an unexpected grace, easily sliding between the ropes and jumping down to the ground. "I heard a lot about you," Carlos said, offering his hand.

The grip was strong, but not challenging. Jorge noticed Carlos had the same type of tattoos as Miguel.

"Carlos helps me run things here. You might remember him as El Tormentor," Miguel said.

Jorge knew at least three men who went by that moniker at one time or another, and none were as tall as the one standing in front of him. He said so.

"Your dad trained me." Carlos's words were measured, as if he thought about everything before it came out of his mouth. "He was a great man."

He was an asshole, Jorge thought. "You still wrestle?"

"No," Miguel answered for Carlos. "He suffered an injury a few years back. He's our lead trainer here and does a hell of a job."

"Thank you, Miguel," Carlos said. "Is there anything else you need from me?"

Miguel shook his head, and Carlos turned to Jorge. "It was nice meeting you. We will see each other again I hope."

Jorge watched him climb back up to the gym. There was nothing in the way the man moved hinting at any kind of injury, and Jorge wondered if Miguel was lying to him.

"You've become popular," Jorge said once they were inside Miguel's office and he'd closed the door behind him.

Miguel shrugged in a manner Jorge guessed was supposed to exude humbleness. "People know me here," he said, taking a seat behind his desk. "Siéntate."

Ignoring him, Jorge walked over to the wall lined with photographs of El Rey Justiciero, from his starting days in Guadalajara wrestling for tens of people, to one of him shortly after winning el campeonato mundial in front of a crowd of thousands. Jorge stopped at one taken on the day of the funeral. Their father was laid out in an ornate, gleaming white casket, the same mask as the one on the mural draped over his face. Without it, Jorge would have never recognized him, the cancer having eaten his powerful body and leaving nothing but a thin husk behind. Even the mask no longer fitted him correctly, the eyeholes drooping to sallow cheekbones. The picture captured many of the attendees of the funeral, church pews filled with past and present Mexican luchadores, their somber funeral attire clashing against the colorful and exaggerated masks they hid their features behind.

"You should have attended," Miguel said.

The leather of the chair Jorge sat in was warm and stiff underneath him. "He wouldn't have wanted me there."

Reaching underneath the desk, Miguel opened a drawer and took out a bottle of whiskey, along with two shot glasses. "If it means anything, at the end, he admitted he handled things wrong with you. Kept saying he was going to reach out to you one day and make things right."

Jorge raised his hand. "Stop. I didn't come here to make peace with a dead man."

Filling the two glasses, Miguel slid one Jorge's way. "No, you're here because you owe El Vikingo money."

Shit. The whiskey slid down Jorge's throat in a wave of fire before settling in his chest like a purring cat. "Your guys tell you about that too?"

"You know how it is," Miguel said. "Word gets around. ¿Cuanto les debes?"

Closing his eyes, Jorge hesitated for a second. "A million pesos," he finally answered.

"That's a lot of feria."

Hearing the number aloud twisted his stomach and brought bile up his throat. "I swear they rigged those first few races so that I won. It wasn't till I started betting big that suddenly everything went a la chingada."

"It's why I'm here."

"I can't pay you that much."

Leaning forward, Jorge pressed against his palm against the table. "No chingues, Miguel. Not after giving me a tour of this place." He motioned around them and said, "Looks like shit, but I counted a good dozen people here. They gotta be paying you something, right?"

"They don't pay me anything."

Jorge blinked. "You're joking."

Miguel shook his head. "I don't charge anyone. That'd be like the church charging the people who come to pray."

The headache clawed and trembled behind Jorge's eyes. Shaking fingers brought out his pills and he swallowed two more. "This isn't a church, Miguel. El Templo? We gave it that name as a *joke*."

Miguel refilled Jorge's glass. "It was never a joke. Not to me. Not to Dad."

Snatching the glass, Jorge drank it, the liquid pushing back the headache far better than the pills. "Al diablo contigo. I did everything that man asked me to do right along with you. Every weight he added to the bars, every mile he told me to run. Every bump he asked me to take. And for what? For him to refuse to give up the name to one of us."

"One of us meaning you?"

Jorge shrugged. "Claro. I was always the better of the two of us. Even Dad knew that. The night he told me I wasn't ready for the responsabilidad the mask brought with it, that's when I knew I had to leave."

"Maybe he was right."

"No, he just didn't want to share the spotlight with anyone. Surprised you didn't prop his casket in the ring and have one last match."

"You still didn't have to leave. You could have waited."

"Like you did? I didn't have that sort of patience, hermanito."

Jorge didn't tell Miguel the other part. About the city becoming too much for him, and how it never stopped shaking, and the more Jorge walked among the streets, the surer he was it was getting ready to swallow him whole.

Looking down at his glass, Jorge was surprised to find it empty. "Me debes," he told Miguel. "You owe me. Me leaving was the best thing that could happen to you. But I'm back now, and I could take everything here, starting with the office," Jorge swept his arm, striking a framed photograph on the desk and causing it to almost fall to the floor, "but I won't. I just want a small piece and then I'll be gone, and you can be the sole heir to El Rey's legacy."

"I already told you, no one pays any membership fees."

"There's gotta be money. What about everything our father earned? Dad was always tacaño, he must have saved a fortune by the time he died."

"The cancer took most of it," Miguel said, the simplicity of his words vibrating against Jorge's skull.

"There has to be money." Jorge pushed the chair back and stood. He dug through his pockets and pulled out the crumpled note, throwing it at Miguel. "Why send me this then, huh?"

The note bounced off Miguel and he said, "Because you needed to come back."

The ground shook, Jorge's hand holding on to the chair as the office's floor rocked back and forth. Photographs fell off the wall and shattered behind him, pencils and pens rolling off the table and being swallowed by the pockmarked floor. Everything moved. Except Miguel.

No, that wasn't true. While Miguel never stirred from his chair, he did move. Or at least, his tattoos did. They shifted in his skin, living things that congregated and pulled away from each other, dancing to a drum beat Jorge swore he could also hear. He watched as the ones by Miguel's shoulder pooled together, shaping themselves into fangs and eyes and mouths. Then into beasts too big for the flesh, and too enormous for the eye.

The last thing Jorge saw was Miguel putting away the bottle of tequila, his brother's glass still left untouched.

* * *

The beasts trembled with hunger.

They were numerous and large, existing in a cosmos littered with others like them. Jorge peered at them through cracks in the reality which blinked in and out of existence, taking his sight with them until he managed to stumble across another crack. This never allowed Jorge to see the entirety of the beasts, and knew it was intended. Just like he knew the things on the other side used the cracks too, pushing parts of themselves into Jorge's world, shaking cities and bringing buildings down as they grasped for something to feed.

"You see them now."

Miguel stood against the backdrop of metal lockers, only a few feet away from Jorge, who was seated on a metal chair, hands cuffed behind his back. A sharp pain cut across his shoulders, and he wondered how long he'd been out for. Looking around, Jorge realized they were in a locker room of some sort. From somewhere beyond the room, he could just make out the sounds of a crowd.

"You drugged me."

"Sí," Miguel said. He'd changed out of his workout clothes, and was now wearing black and gold tights and wrestling boots. A bare chest revealed the extent of the tattoos, which covered almost every piece of available flesh. They remained still, which Jorge was thankful for. "Though the way you were throwing down the drinks, I think even regular alcohol would have gotten us here. That and this," Miguel added, tossing Jorge his bottle of pills. Bouncing off his chest, the bottle hit the floor, little green pills scattering among his feet, "probably didn't help you."

Pushing against his restraints, the chair threatened to spill over, taking Jorge with it. "What the hell is going on, Miguel?"

"You should have told us. Dad and me." Miguel took a few steps forward and reached down, plucking one of the green pills off the floor. "We would have shown you not to be afraid. That you didn't need these." He nodded at the pill and flicked it at Jorge.

Jorge stopped rocking his chair and stared at his brother. "Estás loco."

"Do they even help, Jorge? Do the pills keep the world from shaking underneath your feet and block the things at night from reaching for you?"

"Let me go!" Jorge screamed.

Miguel sighed. "They don't do they? What we see once can never be forgotten. Though I will admit you gave me pause when you told me we named El Templo."

"We did!" Jorge grasped this point, because in the wrongness of everything else, it was one thing he knew to be true. "We named it that because we used to say Dad was stricter than el Señor Goméz at church. All his rules and stupid little rituals he made us do before setting foot in the gym. Don't you remember Miguel?"

"I remember the rituals. Mejor que tú."

From the side of the room a door opened and in stepped Carlos. He wasn't dressed to wrestle, wearing the same clothes Jorge first saw him in. In one hand he carried a black lucha mask. In the other, a knife.

Jorge started to rock the chair again. "Is this a joke? Is that it? Alright, very funny. Pero ya no más."

Carlos ignored Jorge altogether. Walking over to Miguel, he presented him with the mask. Miguel nodded and accepted it.

"The rituals aren't exact," Miguel said, fingering the fabric of the mask. "But some things remain the same. Las mascaras," he said, stretching the mask, "to make us more than the men we are. And to make us one, like they are." The mask was one of El Rey's, the same one Jorge had seen his father buried in.

"But there are some consistencies, like la comunión. Father never had a chance to show you, so it falls on me." Taking the blade from Carlos, Miguel held it in both hands and bowed his head. When he raised it, he spoke not to Jorge, but to Carlos. "Know that we do this because we must. Because we need the strength to face them."

Carlos lifted his shirt. Jorge expected to see the same myriad of tattoos like Miguel had, but instead he saw something worse. Scars. Scars all over his abdomen and side. Some were faded, neatly stitched zigzags. Others had been done in a hurry and were still fresh, peeking out from stained bandages.

Miguel lifted a bandage. "Father did this first. Then, when he gave the mask to me, it was done to him. Until the cancer came." He cut as he spoke, Carlos's flesh giving easily to the blade, like a flower opening for the sun. Flecks of blood arced and hit Miguel's mask, more blood flowing down Carlos's side as Miguel took a chunk of the man.

"Stop, stop!" Jorge shouted, bile pushing up his throat. "What the fuck!"

Pinching the sliver of flesh between his fingers, Miguel separated it from Carlos, who never once uttered a gasp of pain. He pressed his palm against the wound afterwards, Miguel muttering a few unintelligible words and putting the bandage over Carlos's side again.

"I reacted the same way the first time I saw it. And Father had prepared me for it. I would have done the same for you, if we had more time." Miguel walked over to Jorge, the piece of flesh dangling from his fingers. "Abre."

It took Jorge a moment to process what Miguel was saying. "Miguel, stop this."

"What must be done," Miguel said, grabbing him by the shoulder. "Carlos."

Wordlessly, the gigante walked over to him. Jorge fought the restraints again, shaking and trying to push away from Miguel. This stopped the moment Carlos's calloused hands landed on him, one on his shoulder and the other on his jaw.

"The earthquake made the tear bigger. Soon they will be upon us. Please, Jorge, open."

Jorge shook his head, a petulant child refusing to open his mouth to be fed vegetables. His eyes pleaded with Miguel, who said, "Carlos, if you will."

Fingers gripped his chin and squeezed. Tears welled in his eyes as he tried to keep his mouth shut, but it became too much, his mouth opening to scream. This was enough for Carlos, who jammed his fingers into Jorge's mouth and kept it open.

"Acceptamos la ofrenda," Miguel muttered and deposited the flesh upon Jorge's tongue.

A surge moved through Jorge, the landscape twisting and shifting as it had countless of times before. Only this time, Jorge blinked and the ground became still, the world aligning back to its true nature. Carlos stood next to him, a bridge formed between them, all the man's memories and experiences passing on to Jorge. He saw his father the way others saw him, as a man tasked with keeping the world from being swallowed up. A man forced to pass on the responsibilities to his sons.

And Jorge remembered. Remembered the teachings of his dad. Remembered El Templo not as the building itself, but as the ground beneath it. A ground in which his ancestors had once stood and sacrificed the willing and unwilling to keep the snake they saw in their dreams from feeding on the world. How when the men from across the other world came, Jorge's ancestors took them and treated them as gods, not because they were, but because if they could be treated as such, they would someday be the ones tasked with ensuring the beasts would never be sated.

Carlos's offering slid down his throat, and when he could talk, Jorge said, "I see it. I see it all."

The fabric of Miguel's mask stirred, and Jorge imagined his brother smiling beneath it. "Then you know what must be done."

Jorge nodded.

* * *

The crowd was small, though not the smallest Jorge ever stood in front of.

He walked down the ramp, eyes focused on the ring.

It's the same as any other match, Miguel had told him when he freed Jorge. "Don't think of it as a fight, because you could never hope to beat one of them. None of us could. But you can dance with them and keep them busy, let their hunger grow to the point they will retreat behind the cracks."

The ground swelled underneath him as chant moved through the crowd. For a moment, he wished for his pills again, or for a drink.

"How long can I do this for?" Jorge had asked as he changed into his wrestling gear.

"I've done it for five years now. Father, well, Father did it for most of his life."

"Until the cancer."

The ring was his anchor, and Jorge found himself focusing on it. The more he did so, the more the ground moved underneath him, and the louder the chants from the crowd got.

El Rey. El Rey.

At least he had the mask. It felt strange and hot on his face. But also reassuring. Another layer to put himself behind. He stepped into the ring by sliding through the first rope. He paced back and forth in the ring and tested the ropes. They felt good.

The crowd became still as a darkness surrounded them. The hairs on his arms rose and a loud hum rubbed against his ears. Across the arena, on the same rampway Jorge walked through, the blackness pooled and started to take shape. The chants grew louder.

The thing was like a sketch drawn by a small child, limbs too large, head too small, too many fingers on one hand, not enough on the other. Jorge stared, even as every part of him shouted at him to look away. Even as his mind felt like shattering. The thing...la cosa took a step forward.

So did El Rey, the ring mat feeling solid under his feet.

Sucker

Alyssa Alessi

THERE WAS NOTHING like a summer night in the city. Music pouring from car windows with the bass thumping long after they've turned the corner. Thighs out, smoke swirling, and heels dangling between my fingers as my feet ached from hours of dancing.

They turned the lights on in the club when it was time to leave, forcing all the nocturnal beings to shield their eyes not only from the obnoxious fluorescents but from the realization that their dance companion looked a lot better in the dark. Fuck, it was too late, I spent the last five songs rubbing my ass on this guy that had eyes set too far apart. I couldn't unfeel his dick through my cheap polyester dress. He begged, "Mami, come home with me." Those creepy spaced-out eyes pleading for more than just cheap feels while I was slow winding. I shook my head no and stumbled away, trying so desperately to get lost in the crowd of other drunk brunettes.

"Give me your number then. C'mon, you can't leave me hanging like that," the voice unfortunately not trailing off like it should.

Leave them hanging? I could and I would. If they had the audacity to follow me or go as far as to reach out and grab me after I had already said no, which happened more times than I'd like, I'd have to pull out my best trick. I could vomit on the spot. My stomach was usually empty, except for the nine or so Long Island Ice Teas I got for free that night. I would go out without eating so my stomach would be as flat as possible, making my ass look its best. With nothing to hold the liquor down, I'd think hard of something futile like fish milkshakes, and out some of the acidic alcohol would come. I'd try to aim for their shoes, careful not to get any on myself and it would send everyone in a six-foot radius in frantic frenzy of "What the fucks!"

Out I'd slip into the humid Boston night to light up my menthol cigarette. And that's exactly what I did. I started my way down the sidewalk, past the lingering cops, through the laughing women clambering into their cars, away from the loud chatter of where to head next and more towards the quiet block of closed businesses and the train station. I stopped to lean against a light pole to slip my black heels back on before I stepped in glass or worse. The closer I got to the station the more the street was littered with trash. A few empty nip bottles here, a single brown discarded sock there, and scattered McDonald's cheeseburger wrappers blowing in the sticky breeze. The stench of urine rising from the concrete as I crossed the parking lot and towards the platform. An echo of glass hitting the pavement sent my eyes scanning the secluded lot. A man was ducking behind the dumpster about thirty feet away, shooting up, jerking off or maybe just minding his business. My phone buzzed with text alerts.

Yo where you at? Across the screen several times. I sucked at responding. I looked up again to see the man peeking his head out from behind the dumpster, then retreat when he realized I was looking at him like some predatorial peek-a-boo. I spent the first part of my night dodging men, yes, but not because I was afraid. I'd never give them the satisfaction of thinking for one second I was afraid. It wasn't in my nature. I took a few steps closer towards the dumpster when tires rolled to a stop behind me.

Vero, my best friend, roommate, wingman, therapist, partner in crime, my everything pulled up hanging her head out of the passenger window of a black BMW.

"We going to the Afties, get in!" she sang.

"Who's we? Who's that driving?" I asked, trying to get a look at the driver.

"Oh that's Nico. You don't know Nico? This my mans from way back...we went to middle school together," she said stroking the back of his neck.

I was going to get in regardless of who was driving. Dumpster man would live to see another night, because I had places to go. And I wasn't about to wait around for that last train anyway. I opened the door to the backseat to find two guys already back there, staring at me with a hungry gaze.

"Hey, wassup?" I nodded in an attempt to sound friendly and not annoyed. I was always coined the "bitch with an attitude," whether I tried or not.

"How you doing?" a dark-skinned man said more like a statement, licking his lips.

"I can't sit in the middle, y'all have to push over." I waved my hand at them urging them closer in the tight space.

"Yeah, iight," the other guy with too much fake jewelry draped around his neck protested.

I took a big inhale off my cigarette, resting my arm on the open car door.

"Listen, I get car sick as fuck and I just threw up like two minutes ago."

"Oh hell no, what the fuck?" They whined like two twin babies.

"Yo Nico, tell your peoples to move over, because I will throw up back here for real."

After several minutes of negotiating with dumb and dumber, I was relaxed in the window seat behind Vero. She reached back to hold my hand as we drove off with the bass vibrating our seats. I rested my head against the door, letting the wind that almost felt cool wash over me in a sobering embrace. I was car sick, I wasn't lying. I was drunk, nauseated, and starving. A deep hunger clawed from within, sending my bones into an aching throb. When

I got this hungry, everything seemed too loud and overstimulating. Even over the music, I could hear the three human hearts thumping a few paces faster than normal. That was the rhythm of a heart on ecstasy. My mouth began to salivate just thinking of the drug's effects and I cupped my face in my hands instinctively to hide the pain of my teeth protruding from my gums. I had to put my focus elsewhere to distract the hunger. The scent of the nameless man-child next to me was comparable to food left over in the fridge. A plate that has certainly exceeded its best-by date, but you haven't eaten for two days and it's all you got. Like it would do the trick but there may be consequences tomorrow. His blood was tainted, he drank too much sugar and not enough water. He ate Jamaican beef patties and the occasional sub shop food. His cologne was from CVS. I told myself silently over and over *he wouldn't taste good*.

The car slowed to a stop and Nico the driver was rolling up a blunt, the scent of the grape cigarillo conjuring the nausea that finally had settled. He parked outside our destination hoping we would all have a smoke session before heading into the party, but my ass was already out of the car.

"Where is shorty going?" one of the guys in the back asked Vero.

She rolled down her window. "Ally, come back, wait for me. We're gonna smoke up real quick and we can go in together." Her pleading mattered but not enough to keep me.

"I'm good," I said lighting another cigarette. I didn't like to smoke with random people. There was something about putting my mouth on the same thing as randos that grossed me out. Inner thoughts were written all over my face as my lip curled upward in disgust. It was enough to settle my teeth like cold water to an erection as they were sucked back up into my jaw. Nestled back into the tiny slits they stayed hidden in.

I walked away, leaving Vero with the car full of losers and heard what I often did as I turned. "Stuck up bitch." I leaned into the role and made sure my ass swayed just a little bit more than usual as I started down the alley.

Maybe cheap cologne guy was right. My standards were sometimes unrealistic, but I had high hopes for that evening. I was headed for The Mansion, and The Mansion had something for everybody, especially on a Saturday night in July.

The Mansion, the Afties, Benny's spot, all acceptable names for the house at the end of the alley. It blended in somehow, even when it should have stuck out like a sore thumb. In a section of the city with mostly brick low-income housing and scattered triple deckers, was this monstrosity of a single-family home. With black-out shades and sound-proofed walls, it was very unsuspecting. When you got to the door, you had to say, "Three for the bean" to get in. Once inside, all you had to do was choose a room. There was a poker room with black walls and a massive round table, usually well-lit and full of geriatric forty somethings. (Yes, that was geriatric when you were forever twenty-two.) There was a full bar that made you feel like you've never left the club with the excited chatter under purple lights. Once you went upstairs, you had the option to dance in any of the themed rooms that called to you. The long dim hallway stretching on forever with green, red and blue lights pouring from the cracks of the doors. There were no signs that stated which room was which, you just threw yourself in and got what you got.

I found myself in the 80s freestyle room first, with TKA's 'Louder Than Love' blasting through the floor speakers. The slow and smooth rhythm of the song already had me swaying my hips as I walked through the small, crowded room. I pulled a joint out from my wallet and lit it while I danced with myself. There was usually an older crowd in that room, same with the 70s disco but sometimes it was what was needed. It was a necessary transition back into dance mode, that time to connect with the music again to feel sensual before feasting and resting.

After only four hits of the joint the song was over, and I was ready to move on to the next scene. My body craved a good dance, one that would leave pools of sweat down my bra and the right guy drooling. Only the dancehall room could give me that and I opened and closed doors until 'Tempted to Touch' greeted me. I loved the dancehall room the most because it reminded me of the earlier days when I was too young for the clubs, back when Vero and I spent our weekends scouting for the best basement parties. The Afties was basically a giant basement party for adults, with no one to tell us to go home.

A beautiful woman with long black hair and a silk maroon halter top danced with her arms up behind her, pulling her girlfriend in closer by the neck. Her veins pulsed with the beat of the song, or the strobe light tricked me into thinking they were. It didn't matter, she looked delicious either way.

A tall guy with braids down his back bent over his dance partner and humped her from behind. My teeth couldn't stay hidden any longer and I didn't try to force them to. I leaned against the wall and danced like I was alone, my hands like a cool cloth moving from my neck down to in between my legs. My brain ignoring the words to the song and only hearing the rhythm that drove my pelvis. Dinner would come to me if I closed my eyes and let my snake-like body siren-call the meal over.

"Excuse me," someone whispered in my ear.

"Can I dance with you?"

I didn't respond with words, I just pulled him closer to dance. He was the best-looking guy I'd seen in a long time. Lashes darker, longer and better than mine. Full lips and just the right amount of dark stubble on his square jaw. He wore black jeans, a black tee shirt, and had tattoos running down his right arm in a full sleeve. He smelled of sancocho on a rainy weekend. He had hints of cinnamon and laughter, and I knew he'd taste of pure joy.

After dancing for a few minutes, I led him out the room so I could hear his voice. I wanted to know if it was as smooth as the way he moved.

"Where are you from?" I asked.

He let out a low laugh and replied, "Providence. Where you from?"

"I'm from right here. I never seen you here before, that's why I asked."

He followed me downstairs to the bar where he paid for two 'Henney straight-ups.'

"You come here a lot?"

"No," I lied. "But I've been here before. I don't party like that."

Except I do party like that and then some.

"Ok, I see," he said nodding his head up and down grinning at me.

An orange cat sauntered across the bar, surprising him but reminding me that someone lived there. The owner was a man in his fifties named Benny that not only couldn't let go of the fast life but was definitely into his own dark shit. He always offered free drugs to the younger guys and would take them to a VIP lounge that I've only heard of, never seen. What happened at the Afties, stayed at the Afties, an unwritten rule that no one questioned.

"You want to go back upstairs?" I asked hoping he'd say yes.

He nodded in agreement before ordering two more drinks.

There was a room upstairs that played 90s slow jams, had about six velvet sofas and was lit by only one red light. It was one of the sexiest places I've ever been in, other than my own bedroom. A crystal chandelier hung from the center of the ceiling where the red glow hit perfectly. Thick black curtains were draped about, dividing the room into separate quarters. The room was hot and smelled of sex and amaretto. There were a few leopard-print throw blankets tossed around on the sofas in case people were feeling modest. The people who found themselves in that room were usually free spirits without a care as to who sees something as dull as skin. If you were there, you were completely overcome by lust with no time to worry about others and what they thought. I loved this room and knew it well.

My favorite sofa was in the back right-hand corner.

"What's your name?" I asked the gorgeous creature as we sat down.

"Angel," he whispered with his lips brushing my ear. "What's yours?"

I drank the rest of the Hennessey in my cup before whispering back, "It's A. Just A."

He almost gave me the look of "No, what's your real name?" but I didn't give him the chance. Over the sound of others letting out light moans, I grabbed his neck with my black acrylics and kissed him hard. He slipped his hand up my dress sending my teeth all the way out of their slits. I moved my mouth away from his, careful not to startle him with sudden sharp fangs. I kissed his neck gently until I reached his collarbone, his scent sending me to straddle him. His trap muscle was calling my name, almost dizzying me. The way my insides screamed in agony, I knew I couldn't bear to wait another minute. My teeth pressed into his skin as my body rocked back and forth on his hand. He kissed my neck as I sucked from his trap muscle. His warm blood was just as pure as I imagined and I tried my best to drink slow and enjoy every second, careful not to drain him. I sucked slow and steady, just enough for him to feel like it was sexual. The liquid was fire, warming what little soul I had left. I could no longer hear the music or the sighs of pleasure, I was deeply fixated on my feeding.

Vero appeared in the red room, knowing exactly where to find me. Her hand pulled my hair back out of my face, like your best friend holding your hair back as you threw up after a long night. With her teeth already out, she began to suck on the other side of Angel, his other hand finding its way up her dress.

His hands began to slow and weaken and that's when we knew we had to stop. I wanted to save him to have another time, but I couldn't stop drinking. Vero, belly full from others she had that night, had to pull me off.

"Damn bitch, that's too much. He's cute as fuck, don't kill this one. He'll come back looking for you if you stop now."

She was right. I released my teeth from his shoulder and licked the blood that dripped down towards his chest and over his Mother of Guadalupe ink. I fixed his shirt and knelt to kiss his lips, as he fell slack on the sofa like he'd partied too hard. He'd lie there in a deep comfortable slumber until late the next day.

I used the leopard throw to wipe my leg and then covered him with the faux fur.

Vero and I stumbled out into the pre-dawn blue glow of the early morning, drunk off the divine meal. Floating, drifting, in an absolute state of euphoria.

"I thought you were going to kill his ass. You need to stop being so fucking picky and just eat a little here and a little there. You don't have to drain all the hot guys in Massachusetts, you know."

"Shut the fuck up," I laughed lighting my Newport. "He's from Rhode Island."

We walked the five blocks home, arm in arm, as fast as we could to beat the sun and just as I opened the heavy door to our building, I looked down to see I was barefoot.

"Fuck, I lost my shoes at the Afties."

"Oh, maybe you left them in the red room and that guy will come back to find you like some hood Cinderella."

We laughed, but I went to bed that morning secretly wishing he would. Maybe the routine was getting old. How many years could I spend running then chasing? Maybe even at twenty-two, I was getting tired. I was hard on the exterior because I had to be but what if I was really just a giant sucker? A sucker for lust, love, blood, simplicity. A sucker—

Southward, Then Upward

Gustavo Bondoni

⌖

"PLEASE SIT DOWN," the secretary who'd walked them into the small meeting room said.

The minister and his lawyer had already arrived and the judge stared at them across the table. Romero swallowed, knowing that he wasn't exactly welcome. In Peru, he was a respected lawyer, but his titles meant nothing in Patagonia. He hadn't revalidated them, and he knew that he was allowed in the room for the decision only because his Argentine partner had asked for special permission from the judge.

"I've come to a decision," the judge said. She pushed a folder across the table and said, "You can read it on your own time." She turned to us. "I've found in favor of the Ministry. Argentine law is quite clear that ownership of the land is only reversible if there is some demonstrable fraud, criminality or adulteration of the public records. I see none of this here."

"But…" Romero began.

She cut him off. "Mr. Romero, I have both heard and read your argument, but there is no way, within the framework of the law, that I can give the land in question to the Tehuelche people."

"It belongs to them."

"Not according to Argentine law. And not according to the treaties they signed when the government offered them historical restitution. They were given the lands they wanted," the judge said.

"But not all the information."

The judge shrugged. "I have no way of knowing if that is true. If such information existed, and it wasn't simply a case of the government guessing right for once, that knowledge went to its grave with the people who signed the documents thirty years ago. And even if it did exist, that would have no bearing on my decision. The treaty is perfectly valid." She pulled off her glasses and rubbed the bridge of her nose. "I know you're trying to bring justice to the world, and we all like you for it, but there's another thing you need to consider. The newly planted lands are the only thing standing between several European nations and starvation. The Ministry has the best farm technicians in Argentina intensifying yields. Even if you take this to The Hague, you are unlikely to do anything but waste other people's money. This is just too important to take a risk on. I'm sorry."

Romero nodded and stood. His partner, a man named García, took the folder with the decision and thanked the judge effusively. He had to continue working in the city of Trelew, after all. Romero grunted his salutations and left.

He drove quickly across the bright green landscape. The expanse that had once belonged to the Tehuelche people from the mountains in the west to the Atlantic in the east were now worked by an alliance of private owners and government employees.

Fifty years ago, this had been desert land, barely good enough to support a few flocks of sheep. But that was before climate change had pushed the soy line south.

About halfway across the country, he had to decide whether to slow down and run on solar energy alone or spend fifteen minutes charging. He sighed and began to look for a pole: in Patagonia, energy from the hydroelectric plants was plentiful, and private cars were few and far between, so charging stations were everywhere, and free.

Even so, Romero ground his teeth. He hated accepting gifts from the enemy, but he still had five hundred kilometers to go.

Nightfall saw him arrive in Aldea Beleiro, a town whose sudden growth had overwhelmed the city planners. Adobe-walled houses with solar panels on the roofs and double-glazed windows gave anyone with the eyes to look a clue as to how this community had come to pass: ecological concerns had been first and foremost... and when the soy boom came, the town, once a remote flyspeck in the middle of nowhere, had grown explosively.

He parked beside the central square and walked to the bar beside the police station. At the door, he took a deep breath and entered.

Silence spread over the ten occupied tables as people realized who had just walked in. Every eye followed his progress.

When he reached the bar, Amilcar took his order.

"How did it go?" the barman said as soon as Romero had his beer.

"As we expected. They said no." He said it loud enough for the entire bar to hear. He didn't have the energy to have the same conversation a dozen times.

To his surprise, no one complained. No one blamed Romero and told him he was incompetent. Instead, everyone present came over to either hug him or shake his hand and express gratitude at the way he'd fought for them.

Until the very last person.

"I want to see the folder," a woman said.

Romero looked up. A dark-haired woman with pale skin and ice-blue eyes, perhaps in her mid-thirties, gazed back at him without flinching. Romero didn't know her. He shook his head. "I'm sorry. Are you part of a legal team? Are you with the Original People's League? I can't let you take these. We're trying to stay away from any political circuses."

"I'm Tehuelche," the woman replied.

Romero shook his head. "I'm glad you feel that way. It does you credit. But this is for the people in the town. Descendants of people who used to live here."

Amilcar arrived. "Romero, this is Juliana." He paused. "Juliana Davies."

It took Romero a moment to understand, then his knees went weak. He'd heard of her. Seen the signatures on the checks. This was the person behind the fight to make Argentina accept that the new situation – the southern movement of the soy line which had turned Patagonia from an arid, cold desert, to one of the richest agricultural areas on Earth – meant that all the old treaties had to be renegotiated. He'd thought she was…

"I am Tehuelche," Juliana said again. "My great grandmother died in Esquel a couple of years before I was born. She never left the mountains, and she was the very last of the native speakers of the language before we revived it in the 2050s. My mother had a video of her speaking, and made me watch it when I was a kid." She looked around. "And now I'm back where I belong." She put her hand on her stomach. "And my child will have a Tehuelche father." She smiled. "I mixed the old blood with the new."

Romero wordlessly handed the woman the folder. She took the stool beside him and leafed through the pages, grunting every once in a while. "This is pretty much what I thought it would be. And we can't take it to The Hague."

"Why not?" Romero felt the righteous anger rising again. In Peru, the descendants of the Incas had taken back their land by the simple expedient of never leaving it and waiting out and marrying the invaders…but in Argentina, things had been different. Most countries in the world were recognizing indigenous rights…but not here.

"Because the defense will simply present the numbers this report shows in the second appendix, and the press will tell the world that, in order to make a land grab, the Tehuelche are willing to put tens, perhaps hundreds of millions of people at risk of starvation."

"We can run the farms!" Romero said.

Juliana shook her head. "No. We can't. If they give us a single acre of land, the Argentine government is going to withdraw every person currently working on the land and put those resources further north. We just don't have the knowledge or the manpower. We had to win here in Argentina."

"But we knew they wouldn't give in. Why fight at all?"

"Because if they ceded something, even a fraction of what we were asking, we could hire people to farm it. But if we win in The Hague, we'll become murderers. I thought we might get a few acres."

Romero shook his head. "They are fighting it to the bitter end. They remember what happened when they gave too much to the Mapuche."

"That was a mistake on the Mapuche's part. They should never have tried to form a separate country with land on both sides of the border. At least the Argentines didn't actually send in the tanks. But this isn't Peru. Argentina doesn't have an indigenous majority."

"But they took the concessions back." Romero sighed. "And now it's affected us. What are we going to do now?"

"Plan B," Juliana said.

* * *

Romero knew he should just go. He knew that his reason for being there was over, and that, sooner or later, the failure in the courts would be laid at his feet. He should get back to Peru before things got out of hand.

But curiosity compelled him to accept Juliana's invitation to drive over to her land and see what plan B was. It was quite a drive. He wound his way up a gravel road through a forest that stood on ever-steeper foothills.

He arrived to find Juliana and her work team facing off with another group of Tehuelches. They looked just about ready to come to blows.

He parked the car – it was a communal car, not his own, and he supposed it technically belonged to Juliana – and rushed to place himself between the factions.

"What's happening here?" he said.

The leader of the group opposing Juliana was a guy from Esquel named Guillermo, who Romero knew well, and who he'd always gotten along with.

"This isn't your fight anymore," Gullermo said. "We all respect what you tried to do for us. We respect that you came all the way here to help us any way you could. But now it's not a legal matter. It's a matter between us, our ecology and our gods."

Romero smiled. "I know I wasn't able to win the case," he said. "But I'm still a good lawyer. And a good lawyer is trained to help navigate conflicts."

"All right," Guillermo said. "Juliana wants to cut down the forest. She says it's on her land, so she can do whatever she wants. If you tell me that the law is on her side, you can't help in this situation. We already know the law is on her side. And we're still going to stop her from doing it."

"Bullshit," Juliana said. "In the first place, I'm not going to cut down the forest. I'm going to remove a few trees to clear space for the soy. In the second, yeah, it absolutely is my land so go away. I tried to do this a different way, but I couldn't, so this is how I choose to continue."

"Your mother and the tribe Elders had an agreement," Guillermo said. "This is the sacred forest. It replaces the one that was stolen from us. That was the way we said it would be. You can only take timber from small plots at a time. If you cut it down in swathes, you're no better than the Argentine government."

"I can't make that work," Juliana replied. "I need large fields. It's already hard enough to irrigate these hills as it is. And I'm not even sure if a lot of the area isn't too steep for soy anyway. We're looking into it."

"It's holy ground. The forest needs to be continuous or the spirits of the few ancestors we've been able to reinter can't make it from one side of the land to the other."

"Things change. This is for the best for the tribe. When we set this forest up, no one imagined the soy line would move this far south. We thought it would stop four hundred kilometers north. Even now that the climate is under control again, the line is stabilized way down in Santa Cruz," Juliana replied.

"And that's the other reason you can't cut down the trees. The forest line running up the spine of the Andes is our best hope against the desert coming back as the climate cools again. You'll be risking desertification in the long term in exchange for a few profits in the short."

"Profits that will be used to consolidate the Tehuelche's position here in Patagonia. Hell, we can use the money to buy back some of the land they took from us in the first place. Including the land they refused to give us during the trial," Juliana retorted.

"Which is going to turn back into desert because you chopped down the windbreak."

"The wind comes from the ocean side, not the mountain side."

"Not all of it."

Romero stepped between them, arms in the air. "Stop it. Just stop it," he shouted. "Can't you see that you're all letting your emotions get away from you?" He turned to Guillermo. "Are you actually against Juli's idea of getting money to buy the land everyone wants?"

"What? Of course not. We just can't destroy the one place where our ancestors' spirits are." He shook his head. "You don't understand. We were gone. Dead. The last Tehuelche speaker," he nodded to Juliana, "her own great grandmother, was the last one. And then we got a second chance. The Argentines gave us land. We chose a good stretch by the mountains to replant our sacred forest. We re-buried all of our dead that we could find. Hell, Juliana's own great-grandmother is buried here. We can't lose it now. Not again. Not for anything."

Romero held up a hand to forestall Juliana's response. He asked her: "Isn't there any other land you can use?"

"Sure," she replied. "It's right there. Check it out." She pointed past the trees to where a tall peak began. The top couldn't be seen because it was lost in the clouds. "And the rest of the land we got is great for ritual stuff, but it's rocky terrain, or river valleys. Or so vertical you couldn't cultivate moss there. We weren't thinking in terms of cultivation back then, only in terms of being considered worthy of recognition. Things changed, and we need to change with them."

"Not at that cost," Guillermo said.

Romero broke in again. "Isn't there any way to clear the ground so that the forest can keep its continuity? If the spirits can cross it from one side to the other they should be happy, right? In fact, they should help keep an eye on the crops."

Guillermo raised an eyebrow. "If you knew how tired we are of outsiders coming here and being condescending to us, pretending to believe in our spirits while secretly laughing at us, you wouldn't dare be a part of this conversation."

Anger welled up from deep in Romero's gut. He took a single calming breath and reminded himself that these people were friends of his, and that they had opened their hearts to him. "And I think you're forgetting where I come from. My entire country, every single mountain – and there are a whole lot of mountains in Peru – is a holy place. I walk among the ghosts of my ancestors every day. I feel the wind from their breath on my skin whenever I'm in the hills. In Peru you don't question whether your great grandparents are watching over you: all you need to do is to walk out into the mountains and you'll never doubt again."

Guillermo shuffled his feet. "I'm sorry. You're right. But you also need to accept that even though you might understand some of what we feel, and some of our customs, our situation isn't the same as yours. This isn't Peru."

Romero looked out at the mountains looming hazily purple and blocking the western horizon.

They reminded him of home.

* * *

Romero slept fitfully that night, trying to decide whether to stay with the Tehuelches to try to help them some other way – even though he'd utterly failed them as their pro bono lawyer – or to return to Peru.

He knew he wouldn't stay long in his home country; after centuries of injustice, Peruvian society had finally achieved peace by the simple expedient of accepting that what had once been a stratified, racialized society had now intermixed to the point where there was little to differentiate Inca and colonizer blood. It had been a joyous realization, and with it, the country had transitioned to a state of peace with the land and with one another. Capitalistic structures had been reworked to be more friendly to the environment and to those who chose other forms of life.

As Guillermo had reminded him, though, most places weren't Peru. It was clear that the world was heading to a new era of harmony with the planet. All the signs were there. Different movements gained momentum in different parts of the world.

But the battle was far from won. A lot of people, powerful people especially, still resisted. And if there was one thing that could help the movement in those places, it was a good lawyer.

Then, when he finally got to sleep, he was visited by one of his ancestors in his dreams. The wrinkled, wizened, white-haired visage of his *abuelita*, his grandmother, came to him and said: "Romerito, you should be ashamed of yourself. If the solution to all your problems was any easier to see, it would affect the planet's orbit." Then she swatted him with her knitted bag, and he woke, flinching from the blow.

Lying awake after the dream, he realized it definitely wasn't a sending from beyond. Though his grandmother certainly had a penchant for expressing her displeasure by physically smacking wayward boys, she had never given any indication that she knew the earth was anything but flat. Orbital mechanics were well beyond her.

Besides, there was another thing that disqualified her as a supernatural vision: the cranky old lady might have been past ninety, but she was most definitely still alive.

Even so, Romero smiled as he lay in a darkened guest room in Aldea Beleiro. His grandmother's non-ghost had liberated the solution from his subconscious. Sometimes you needed the help of your ancestors after all.

* * *

"Impossible," Juliana said when she saw his diagrams.

Guillermo just hunched his shoulders, his posture saying that he had hoped Romero's idea would be better.

"It's not impossible," he said. "I grew up looking at these terraces all my life. They're everywhere." He went to the next slide, which showed a staircase of enormous horizontal shelves extending from the steep sides of a mountain, covered in planted food crops. "My people grew all their food there for hundreds of years. It can be done."

"The terraces in Peru took those hundreds of years to build," Guillermo pointed out.

"They were built by people using hand tools and llamas," Romero retorted.

Juliana held up a hand. "How do you expect us to build agricultural terraces along the sides of the mountains? We don't have the experience or the materials to put something like this together."

"But Peru does. Look." Romero pulled up the next slide, the one he'd been investigating online for the past five days. It was the one that would make or break his proposal. It showed a structure built against the side of a mountain in the same shelf pattern as the Peruvian fields, but built of a latticework of interconnected tubes and pipes.

"Is that a mountain?" Guillermo said.

Romero nodded.

"That thing is huge," Juliana added, tapping the terrace structure in the image with her pen. "What's it made of?"

"Plastic," Romero said.

"Plastic?" Both Guillermo and Juliana said the word at the same time. They seemed horrified.

"Recycled from the Pacific garbage patch. Not only is the process they use carbon neutral, but turning this plastic into new things guarantees that the carbon inside it is kept there. And look. The pieces are perforated to allow them to support vegetation, and designed so that the root systems actually bind the platform to the mountain."

"All right," Juliana said. "I'll grant that the engineering works, and I'll even grant that it isn't an abomination. And

I assume you're going to tell us that it can be built with a couple of screwdrivers and a drill."

Romero smiled. "Not that simple, but you only need to rent basic heavy equipment."

"Granted all that, I don't think we can afford the cost." Juliana smiled. "It's a catch-22. I can't build the terraces without the soy money, and I can't get the soy money without the terraces." She sighed. "We can spend as much of my mother's money as we need to do things for the Tehuelche. That is what she wants it used for. But there's a limit. We just don't have enough to do major infrastructure work. Not this kind of high-tech stuff." She waved at the monitor.

Romero smiled at her. "You haven't asked me how much it costs. I'd hate to have done all the work and not get to give you the whole pitch."

"All right. How much?"

Romero's grin widened. "I just want to admit up front that I'll get a ten-percent commission on the plastic."

"Just tell me, so I can tell you no. How much?"

"Zero dollars and zero cents. Also, free shipping."

"I'm not in the mood for this," Juliana growled.

"And I'm not kidding," Romero replied, thoroughly enjoying himself. "Have you heard of the Collective?"

"You mean those crazies in Africa and California?" Guillermo said.

"And Peru. And Portugal. And Costa Rica, and a dozen other places, with a new city or state or country member added every couple of weeks. Yes, those guys." He breathed out. "Well, one of their communities is New Venice."

"The nutcases floating out in the Pacific?"

"Well, yes. But don't call them nutcases because they've agreed to send you that entire shelf, built from the plastic bottles they harvest out of the sea, to match the topography of whatever mountain you want to start with, completely free of charge. All you have to do is to truck it from the port. I think we can pay for a few trucks."

"And in exchange?" Guillermo asked. "I assume we have to join their collective."

"No. Not unless we want to. That's how it works. Each member community shares what they can, when they can with one another and with anyone else who needs it. Maybe if we have excess soy, we can send it over to someone who is having food troubles."

"Why did they agree to this?" Juliana asked.

"Because I explained that we need this to make our community viable." Romero paused, then decided he could be completely honest. "Also, it appears they've found a new way to strip all traces of paper from plastic without burning it and sending carbon into the atmosphere… so now they have more plastic than they know what to do with."

"Ah. But still."

Romero shrugged. "That's how it works. Peru is already looking into joining as a full country member. The only problem I see is that they can't deliver the structure until six months from now. They said something about a shipment of microchips."

"Six months?" Juliana said. "I don't know if I can get the rest of it organized in six months. Hell, even if we do… does anyone know anything about farming? What kind of yield can we get out of a plot that size? Is our dirt any good? What's the market price for a ton of soybeans?"

Guillermo shrugged. "I'll help you. Everyone will. And I suspect that so will our ancestors."

"But will we be able to do enough with this little plot?" Juliana said.

"We can always make more if the first one works out," Guillermo said.

They started to argue about who should be in charge of what, and completely forgot Romero was present.

That was fine by him. His sense of having failed them in the trial was still strong, but now he realized that maybe he'd been sent there to plant a different kind of seed alongside the soy that was already in the planning stages.

He smiled and let them discuss it. It was nice to have someone else doing the arguing for a change.

Whispering Shards

David Bowles

◇

ATOP A HIGH CRAG, overlooking the fertile valley where the imperial capital of Tollan sprawled majestic, the sacred retreat of Yollichan kept watch over rivers and stars. Built of turquoise and timber by the unparalleled craft of the elven *tsapame*, this mountain monastery had been the home of the divine sage Seyaka, long before he was crowned Emperor of Anawak, that highlands basin ringed by volcanoes and dominated by lakes.

Now ten years had passed since Seyaka – earthly incarnation of Ketsalkowa, Lord of Order – had left Tollan. As the empire crumbled, beset by barbarians without and civil unrest within, the former captain of the imperial guard kept a dutiful vigil within the sturdy walls of the unassailable retreat. Melsinki was his name, a vassal so utterly dedicated to his liege lord that other faithful followers were shocked when the emperor, having abdicated his throne, announced the captain would be remaining in those lands rather than joining the joyful retinue of the god in exile.

The rueful murmuring had stilled when Seyaka had placed in Melsinki's hands the greatest weapon ever crafted in the sea-ringed world: the Ironwood Sword, hewn from the densest wood of the desert by the goddess Itspapalo as she led the Tolteka people to the promised land, the valley which now cradled Tollan.

"Beloved Melsinki," the former emperor had pronounced, "with this weapon guard my favorite place of meditation and all the secrets it contains. Suffer no trespass or theft but keep all agents of chaos and destruction at bay until such time as I or my sister return to claim what is rightfully ours."

"And if I should die before that happy moment?"

Before the former emperor could reply, he was interrupted by Ketsalpet, his older sister and principal counsellor, the morning sun making her silver-rimed hair shimmer.

"Then your sons must take the task upon themselves, Captain."

So it was that a decade later, in the courtyard at the heart of the retreat, Melsinki was putting his two eldest boys through their paces, making them practice the first three *olintin* of the *makwawi*, the complex series of movements intended to prepare swordsmen for basic combat. Upward and downward diagonal slashes. Quarter-spindle side cuts. Forward and reverse saw. Deflecting and countering. Using shield for defense and attack.

Watching from a doorway was the youngest boy in the family, Mapach. He had been a babe in his mother's arms when the family had moved to the monastery, so he knew little else of the world. His mother, Istamik – a former priestess – had often taken him and his sister Eya with her to the small marketplace in the nearby town of Shilotepek, but that meager glimpse of civilization had no lasting impact on him. He was a wild child, immune to even the strictest discipline, who spent most of his time roaming the hills, catching swift hares in snares of his own devising.

Except when his brothers studied the sword beneath their father's grim tutelage. Then did Mapach sit and watch unmoving, like the statues of warriors that adorn the imperial palace in Tollan.

"Lower your weapons," Melsinki commanded. His sons complied. Their practice swords were of the sort used by cadets across Anawak. Smaller and lighter than a true makwawi, these macanas had long leather-wrapped handles that ended in flat wooden blades the length of a man's forearm. Actual battle swords had obsidian razors glued into a groove along the edges of the blade, slicing sharper than any metal forged by the Washteka heathens in their cruel kingdoms north of Anawak.

The exception was the Ironwood Sword. Its puissance was divine, arising from the sacred and inscrutable glyphs carved along its length by the goddess Itspapalo herself.

It needed no obsidian to wreak havoc, only a skilled knight with pureness of purpose, a man among men, admired by the gods themselves.

Melsinki was such a man. And he yearned to shape his sons into worthy heirs.

Mapach, observing his brothers, had his doubts.

"Tapashin," the aging warrior addressed his fourteen-year-old, whose black hair was cropped close to the scalp, "I want you to attack your elder brother as if you were fighting upon muddy ground on a riverbank."

"Using the fourth olin, Father?" asked Tapashin, readying himself.

"Aye," Melsinki replied.

The eldest of the three boys – Ochpan, who had just turned sixteen – lifted his blade and prepared to parry his younger brother's attacks.

Mapach narrowed his eyes as he studied the exchange. Though he had not been trained, he could clearly see the flaws in Tapashin's grip and arc, the weakness of Ochpan's stance. Once they had both bruised each other to the point of cursing, their father halted the match and began to point out the very errors that Mapach had noticed.

Bored, the ten-year-old went back inside the monastery, avoiding the kitchen and other areas where his mother and sister might be working. Wandering through a maze of halls in the north wing, he came to a room he was forbidden to enter: the Chamber of Gifts. Here the former emperor had set aside all the precious items brought to him by foreign dignitaries and lords of tributary towns.

Mapach easily bypassed the traps set to keep intruders out. Many times had he snuck into the chamber to marvel at its riches, his parents none the wiser. Today, however, the feathered tapestries and gilded vases did not dazzle his eyes, nor did the jewel-encrusted drums or statues of stone and coral.

Instead, his roaming and mischievous eyes were drawn as if by an invisible force to a box of cypress wood, forgotten at the bottom of some shelves in a dusty back corner of the room. Retrieving the object, Mapach found that it was sealed not by a lock, but by a series of movable jade tiles set into the lid. After puzzling over the mechanism for a quarter watch, the clever boy saw that the tiles could be arranged into a particular pattern: the uppermost glyph on the Ironwood Sword, an ancient symbol for sacred magic.

Once he had shifted the tiles accordingly, there came a whir and a click, and the lid popped loose. Lifting it, Mapach found an obsidian mirror lying within, nestled on a folded purple cape. The mirror was about the size of the boy's head, surprisingly heavy as he lifted it in both his wiry hands.

In fact, it almost slipped from his grasp, though not due to its weight.

For a while Mapach had no smile upon his face. His reflection grinned back at him.

* * *

In the kitchen, Melsinki and his two eldest sons had just sat on mats around a low table. His wife and daughter placed steaming bowls of maize gruel before them and took their seats as well.

"What of Mapach?" asked Istamik.

"I believed him with you, dear. He watched his brothers train for a time but then disappeared."

"The brat is probably off hunting rabbits again," muttered Eya. "Are you certain he isn't part coyote?"

Her brothers snickered at the jest, but Melsinki, staring at the bits of chili pepper and tomato in the gruel, gave a soft sigh.

"We could do with some meat in our diet. If not Mapach, then his brothers and I should go hunting soon."

Tapashin nodded excitedly. "Perhaps we can bring down another deer, Father!"

Istamik lowered the folded tortilla she had been using to lift food to her mouth. "Better I take a bit of silver to the market to buy fish and venison. It is unwise to leave the monastery unprotected, husband."

Ochpan looked at his father. "But it's been ten years. The warding spells left by Emperor Seyaka have held all this time, keeping us practically invisible. Is there really any danger?"

As if in answer, from all around them came the sound of flapping wings.

Leaping to his feet, Melsinki seized the Ironwood Sword, which he had left leaning in one corner of the room, and rushed out to meet the enemy he feared the most.

Just beyond the main gate of Yollichan they were descending: six black-headed condors the size of people, some gripping weapons in their brutal talons.

As they landed, the birds of prey transformed, revealing themselves to be men with long, tangled hair and black, feathered cloaks over cotton body suits of the same dark hue.

One of the shapeshifters stepped forward. His arms were bare: large, corded muscles bunched and flexed as he hefted a mighty ax.

Melsinki saw that its head was of a dull, coppery metal. Its haft gleamed with the polish of ages, a glow like that of the divine sword in the captain's grip. It might have been hewn from the same tree.

The Bronze Ax, he realized with chagrin.

The only weapon on the sea-ringed world that could challenge the Ironwood Sword.

Melsinki assumed a fighting stance, heart heavy.

"I shan't fight fair," said the ax-wielding priest, his Clear Speech clouded by a Washteka accent. "Lower that weapon. Give it to me. Or watch your family die."

Closing his eyes, Melsinki muttered the requisite incantation.

"From this mortal flesh into undying wood."

The glyphs on the ancient sword began to glow, as orange as the sun.

***

Too late, Mapach understood what he held in his hands.

His mother had told her children the story many times, attempting to prevent their wandering off into the hills and mountains, exposing themselves to the dangerous sorcerers who now roamed Anawak with impunity.

The Vulture Monks.

That order of shapeshifting clerics had been founded by Teskatlipoka, high priest of Tollan. Serving only the Pandemonium of Destruction and Chaos, the brutal brotherhood had done all it could to remove their rival from power, for Emperor Seyaka was dedicated to the Pantheon of Creation and Order. Though the ruler of the Tolteka people had banished the dark monastics from the empire, they had regrouped in Washteka lands and fashioned the instrument of Seyakat's fall.

An obsidian mirror.

When the emperor was tricked into looking upon himself in that gleaming black, all his piety and confidence were eroded. The wrinkles on his face, his greying hair, all the signs of his mortality were amplified mockingly – and it seemed he could see his very soul, tattered and senescent. In answer to his anguished shock, the same disguised priests fashioned a mask for Seyaka, permitting him to hide himself from his people.

"But no matter what garments he wore," Istamik would whisper hoarsely to her children in the still of the night, "no matter how he obscured his face, Seyaka's reflection grew older and more brittle, till the emperor's every waking thought was of the corpse that stared out at him from the mirror. 'I am but a mortal man mere moments from death,' he moaned to his sister. 'How dare I stand before the Tolteka people and seek to lead them along the path to perfection?' Thus did self-doubt snarl in his heart, driving him so far into madness that he at last ordered his sister to seal him up in a tomb."

As the three boys and their sister would huddle together upon their sleeping mats, their mother's voice would go quieter, raspier. "Then did that madness seize the entire city of Tollan. The Vulture Monks roamed the streets, slaying children and then reanimating them like marionettes of cold flesh and bone, sent back by their cruel puppeteers into their homes to wreak unspeakable harm on their families."

It was a horrible story, one that Tapashin and Ochpan remembered as true, though they had been but toddlers when the Vulture Monks had terrorized the capital city. Now the zombie waifs of Tollan seemed to jerk through the darkness of their sleeping chamber as they often did in their nightmares.

Invariably, Mapach – having been safely ensconced in the womb during those ill events – would speak up loudly in the ominous darkness.

"But that was not the end, was it, Mother? Emperor Seyaka had a vision."

"Aye, that he did," Istamik would answer. "He understood his true nature as the incarnation of Ketsalkowa, Lord of Order, born a man to bring hope to Anawak and beyond – yea, unto every region of the sea-ringed world. Emerging from his tomb, he routed the Vulture Monks once more, though he then abdicated his throne to pursue his true mission."

Their mother would then always lean close to their faces, whispering, eyes wide.

"But the shapeshifting priests of chaos yet remain, dearest ones. Wandering. Waiting. Searching for the House of Life, the watchtower that keeps entropy from overwhelming heaven's design.

"This place. Our home. Therefore must you keep to its grounds, or those fiends might find you, slay you, make you an undead doll, and wreak the destruction of everything and everyone you love. Do you understand me?"

A hard lesson from a hard woman.

One that Mapach had never learned.

Until today.

Looking down at the mirror, he saw his reflection mouthing soundless words.

All dead. Except your sister. Make haste. Save her.

* * *

A roiling dark power kept the boy from setting the mirror down. Instead, he rushed back with the glinting obsidian still in his hands, retracing his path along the labyrinthine corridors till he reached the high-ceilinged hall just inside the main gate.

The sight that greeted him burned itself indelibly upon his soul.

His mother lay in one corner, limbs cocked at impossible angles, half her face missing, brains dribbling slowly onto the clay tiles.

Near the arch of the entrance, his brothers sat back-to-back, yet facing each other, their heads twisted like ghoulish owls, bloody tears staining their cheeks.

Closer, between Mapach and the Vulture Monks, his father was sprawled, gutted like a fish, entrails piled beside him with ironic care. His eyes were glazing as he gasped his last, not even recognizing his youngest son before him.

The shapeshifting clerics stood in a semi-circle at the center of the hall, their backs to Mapach. One shifted his weight from one foot to the other, and a gap opened through which Mapach saw his sister, a thin girl of thirteen summers, dragging the Ironwood Sword behind her as she paced frantically back and forth, eyes wide with horror and hate.

"Back! Back, you bastards! One of Melsinki's children yet stands against you!"

Guffaws of cruel mirth echoed through the hall. The leader of the Vulture Monks lifted the Bronze Ax and gestured at the dead boys behind her.

A miasma of purple and black gurgled from the arcane runes on the metal of his weapon, and with a flick of his wrist, the chief cleric flung that shadow magic at the corpses of Tapashin and Ochpan.

"Lik'enesh kamınaqesh!" he snarled in the Old Tongue.

The dead boys twitched and convulsed before surging to their feet and shuffling backwards towards their sister, at whom their black eyes stared from over their knobby spines. Their arms reached back, grasping at her with awkward spasms as she screamed in abject horror.

"Enough!" cried Mapach, stepping over his father's legs, mirror tight against his chest. "Leave her alone, you villains!"

The monks spun, their sneers melting into raucous laughter at the sight of the ten-year-old gripping such a fell object. The leader lowered his head in mocking respect.

"Our eternal thanks, young ally. Long have we searched for Seyaka's hoard. Had you not revealed it to us, we might have spent centuries, oblivious."

"Mapach?" called his sister, her voice trembling with something beyond terror. "Is this true? Did you call them hither?"

"No!" he replied, though doubt gnawed at his guts. "Never!"

Twirling his ax slowly, the leader of the Vulture Monks took several steps towards Mapach, a smile broadening across his bland, flat features.

"Oh, but you did. You removed that device from its keeping place. Do you not understand, boy? Our master put a sliver of his soul into the making of that mirror. Even now, that fragment of Teskatlipoka calls out to us. Can you not hear him? He whispers your name, boy. Mapach, only living son of the quite deceased Captain Melsinki."

Snarling as if angered by the mocking epithet, the zombie brothers of Mapach renewed their attack against Eya, who could not lift the Ironwood Sword, but dragged it in great arcs in front of her to keep the puppets at bay.

Blows to the temple, their mother had once muttered as she retold the story of the undead waifs of Tollan. *Only thus did the horrified families put their menacing children forever to rest.*

Mapach dashed to the right of the Vulture Monks, arcing his way through the hall till he reached his sister's side. Lifting the obsidian mirror, he bashed first Tapashin and then Ochpan in the head, cracking open their skulls and sending them flailing to the ground.

"A novel use of such a puissant tool. Give it to me, Mapach. I shall demonstrate its full power for you."

"You will have nothing," Mapach rasped, "that the Lord of Order has left in our care. Be gone from this holy place, devils. The Pantheon demands it!"

Howls of glee echoed like hollow horror all around him.

"Let us see just how dear they hold you, boy!" shouted the chief cleric. "Brothers, blast him into oblivion!"

The Vulture Monks raised their hands, plumes tearing through their blood-speckled skin as they groaned a single syllable in the Old Tongue.

Shadow magic leapt from curled fingers.

It curdled and burbled as it wended through the air in fits and starts, a haphazard and erratic path that nonetheless had a singular target.

But Mapach had spent most of his childhood trapping hares with nooses of agave fiber. He knew how to wait for that final sideways bolt of the prey.

As the noisome energy erupted at him askance, he jerked the obsidian mirror right into its path.

Shaped itself by shadow magic, the black circle not only deflected the attack, but redoubled it, flinging destruction in a sphere all around Mapach before bursting into pieces in his hands and slamming him into the ground with such force that he lost consciousness at once.

* * *

Awaken, boy.

The voice came not from a man's lips, but from within Mapach. Without hesitation, he knew it to be Teskatlipoka. Or, rather, the sliver of him with which that cruel mage had imbued the obsidian mirror.

Mapach opened his eyes and sat up.

Nothing remained.

More precisely, nothing *organic* remained of what had been Yollichan.

The timbers were gone. The corpses of his parents and brothers, too.

Likewise wiped from existence were the Vulture Monks. And his sister.

The turquoise had been strewn in a circle around the stone foundation. Glinting in the sun as well were bits of gold and silver, jade and sapphire. Stone mortars. Clay cups.

And obsidian. Shards of it in an arc before him. Thrumming with power. With purpose. With personality.

Beside him, as intact as the day it had been carved a thousand years before, lay the Ironwood Sword.

I shall help you to wield it, boy.

Mirrored in the bits of black, like a reflection upon a moving stream, was the visage of a handsome man with a terrible grin.

"You have no such power, trickster. Else you would have taken it from Emperor Seyaka while he rested in his tomb."

Ah, You are cleverer than I had credited. Or my shadow magic has dimmed your innocence. So harken. You have opened a new path, Mapach. What no man could break, you have shattered. Now take these shards. Embed them along the edges of the blade. Meld shadow and light into a truly devastating weapon.

The idea was horrifying. Repellent. And yet—

I have glimpsed a possible future. You could become a tepishki, a wandering swordsman. All Anawak would know your name, Mapach ipil Melsinki. For I should make you great.

His mouth dry with dread and hope, the boy muttered, "Why?"

I hunger. Your deeds would nourish me. Not only on the blood of your enemies should I feed. I should sip on their very souls.

A pause, burgeoning with malevolent mirth.

Or sit here if you prefer. One Vulture Monk survived. The Bronze Ax kept him safe. Even now he flies to Washteka lands to call upon his brethren. You may wait for them and perish in despair. I care not.

The broken image of Teskatlipoka winked.

Your soul will sustain me until another comes along.

The choice was clear. Sighing, Mapach stood and started to search amid the scattered stone and precious metal. Soon he found the copper and stone coffer that contained his father's repair kit.

Extracting a clay jar containing an adhesive mixed from bitumen and turtle dung, he returned to the Ironwood Sword. To the obsidian shards.

One by one, he picked them up.

Smeared them with glue.

Set them in the groove.

* * *

After a long while, the boy spoke.

"Now *you* hear *me,* trickster. I follow Ketsalkowa, Lord of Order, God of Creation and Light. When I wield this sword, it'll be in his service, no matter what the source of my strength is. If you are fed by the work I do, so be it. But I'll never kill because you demand it. No, I'll follow the command given my father. 'Keep all agents of chaos and destruction at bay.' Until my god returns. And I'll go even further. I'll hunt every one of your disciples down. Then I'll find you, Teskatlipoka, and slice your throat with these shards of your soul."

There was silence. A hint of laughter.

Very well, boy. We shall see how long you endure my whispers.

For I am old and patient.

Mapach then stood, gripping the Ironwood Sword by its pommel and lifting it carefully to his shoulder. The weight was heavy, but not unbearable.

"Whereas I," he replied, "am young and hungry for justice. Let's see who wins."

Before he could leave the ruins of Yollichan, however, a scrabbling sound came from just out of view, where the path that led to the valley disappeared around a bend.

It would seem the destruction that you wrought was visible from afar. It has drawn unsavory, vicious men who are driven by greed.

There were three of them, sauntering slyly into view. Knotted, grimy hair. Bodies painted black. Filthy grey loincloths and capes. Highway robbers, once unheard of in Anawak, now a common threat to travelers on the imperial roads.

The men's eyes widened at the sight of all the precious gems and metals.

"Turn around," Mapach called. "These are the treasures of Our Revered Lord Seyaka Ketsalkowa."

The tallest of the men, whose bloodshot eyes glowed lurid in the late-morning sunlight, spat greenish phlegm at the ground.

"What hast thou, ten summers, at best? Mind thy tongue, knave. We thinc uncles have arrived to dispose of these riches as we see fit."

Mapach lifted the Ironwood Sword from his shoulders and held it out before him, his wiry arms trembling with effort.

"You are no uncles of mine nor respected elders of any community hereabouts. Leave or feel the bite of my blade."

At this threat, the other two men guffawed, though the red-eyed thief slowed his steps, taking a moment to appraise their chances against such a dire weapon in the hands of a child.

Then he shrugged and rushed at Mapach, drawing a stone knife from his waist.

Let me – the shards began to say, but the boy's mind was filled of a sudden with his father's voice, calm and confident, calling upon the Pantheon as he always did before wielding their holy weapon.

"From this mortal flesh into undying wood," the boy whispered in echo, lifting the sword and spinning as the head robber reached him.

The obsidian shards sliced across the man's belly, opening his skin with such effortless ease that he took two more stumbling steps. Then his guts spilled from the widening gap, and he pitched headlong into the ruins of Yollichan, squealing in agony.

With angry growls, the other two came dashing towards Mapach.

The glyphs carved into the ancient wood were glowing. But the red-gold solar light of the Pantheon was flecked and speckled by the purple-black of the Pandemonium.

In that paradoxical fusion, the fundamental duality of the cosmos found puissant expression. Creation and Destruction: two faces of a single coin. Two phases of a single force. Two facets of a single source.

The boy's body shuddered with epiphany.

Tears streaming down his face, Mapach smiled.

And swung.

Two heads went tumbling onto the rocky soil.

* * *

Mapach patted the dirt where he'd buried the bulk of Seyaka's treasure under an outcropping. He set a stone atop the site as a marker and then felled a few pine saplings to drag back and forth over the foundation of the former retreat, obliterating traces of his steps back and forth.

As for the highwaymen, it had taken the better part of two watches, but the obsidian shards had finally absorbed their souls and rendered their mortal flesh into dust that was lifted by the wind and swirled away over the precipice.

For a time, the fragment of the Lord of Chaos had nothing to say beyond groans of delight and contented sighs.

Yet his fiendish nature reasserted itself at last.

These morsels are but the beginning, boy. Many more men shall you slay to slake my eternal thirst.

"I'll kill whom I must and no more, prattle as you might. Accustom yourself to the truth: in binding your shards to this weapon, I have bound you to *me*. Do you not ken? *I* wield the Ironwood Sword, so *I* am your master."

This time the silence was thick with ire. But it broke into soft laughter.

Aye. I concede you this small victory. Yet in binding me to yourself, you have exposed your heart. I see guilt blossoming there. I shall nurture it until you beg me for release, "Master." For my power is addictive and my voice untiring.

Mapach sighed and gave no reply. Slinging across his back a pack heavy with gems, the boy took up the Ironwood Sword and set off along the winding path that led down the forested mountain, into the green valley with its glistening rivers, towards the white ziggurats that rose like a divine promise at the heart of Tollan.

He whistled an aimless tune as he went.

The melody muffled the whispers.

Listen to This

Arasibo Campeche & Carra Flowers

"WANT TO GET a closer look at her?" Kobbo asked from the door to the doll's room. "After all, she's the real star."

Héctor shook with excitement. This was his first time visiting her room. He savored the moment and walked in. Her muumuu dress, coiffed hair, and large breasts that seemed so caricaturesque on TV were much more lifelike; instead of the foam it was made of, her skin resembled flesh. Her high heels were not just props, but expensive designer shoes. The lipstick looked freshly applied. His hand trembled as he approached her.

"¡No la toques! It's a bitch to clean the felt," Kobbo said, then smiled like a man with a secret, which made sense. He was the Gossip King of Puerto Rican TV. Bending the truth, telling half lies, while sprinkling in edgy comments here and there to spice things up had made him one of the wealthiest men in Puerto Rico. People loved to see and hear about the mishaps of others, especially if they were funny!

La Comay, as the doll was called, was even more of an icon than Kobbo. When people walked down the streets, they'd say, "Did you hear what La Comay said about fulanito? Or what about that politician whose wife turned out to be a lesbian – I guess he's so bad at sex that she gave up on men entirely."

If Kobbo was king, she was a goddess.

Héctor fussed with his mustache. What did that make him as a co-host of their show? He'd only been working with her a week, after all. He smiled, as he looked into La Comay's black silver-dollar sized button eyes. Whatever role he played, he'd do so swimming in money.

"That's enough staring. Let's go get ready for today's show," Kobbo said.

"Should we bring her with us?" Héctor asked, ready to carry the doll like a newlywed would carry his wife.

"We don't need to worry about her," he said, still smiling.

They exited the dimly lit room into a white hall illuminated by fluorescent lights. Héctor was distracted by his thoughts. Why were there cosmetics on the table in La Comay's room? Perhaps it was part of the mystique, or the room had several occupants. But it didn't seem like she'd enjoy sharing. Héctor caught himself thinking of the foam doll as if she were alive and chuckled.

He continued following Kobbo, taking in the multitude of picture frames that hung from the walls: TV personalities, news anchors, and shows. Some took nearly half the height of the wall, while others were smaller – some were oval and some rectangular.

Since there were only three local TV channels in Puerto Rico, he'd watched most of the people and shows on the wall as a kid. His heart raced with excitement, imagining his own picture on the wall. It was so clear in his mind – him on a stool next to La Comay, wearing his signature Panama Jack hat, beaming at the camera.

Héctor bumped into Kobbo. Despite being a bony, skinny old man, Kobbo didn't budge. They'd stopped by a door with HÉCTOR painted in the middle.

"We finally got your super exclusive room ready," Kobbo said with a laugh and slapped Héctor on the shoulder. "Loosen up, we have plenty of time. Have a few before we start."

Héctor watched him turn down the hall and disappear, then realized he had no idea how he'd gotten here. Was La Comay's room to the left, or right? He shrugged, figuring everyone got turned around their first few days, and entered his room.

His room was lit by warm yellow lights. It was furnished with a couch, one chair, and a desk with a mirror. The setup was the same as La Comay's. He had gifts from Kobbo here. A sealed bottle of Don Q rum, a small foam cooler full of ice, cans of Coke, and a pack of plastic cups sat on the desk's corner. Héctor fixed himself a stiff drink and sniffed it.

The sweet smell of Caribbean rum loosened the tension in his shoulders and relaxed him. After a drink, he laughed out loud – a big belly laugh – practicing for the show, then a knock at the door.

He followed the assistant with the iPad until they reached the stage. Héctor still swooned from how much more impressive it was than on TV. A deep red carpet, the color of oxygenated blood, spanned the length of the room. Shiny bundles of multicolored balloons decorated the walls, as if you were at a kid's birthday party. The SXC that stood for the show's name, *SuperXclusivo*, hung in the back in big red letters. Everything looked loud. In the middle of it all sat the mother of gossip herself, La Comay, on her throne. Kobbo leaned in behind her to puppeteer her mouth with his right hand and her left arm with his own.

Héctor sat on the stool reserved for him next to La Comay, feeling privileged. Only a handful of men had ever sat on this chair.

"Hello, Héctor," Kobbo – no, La Comay said.

"Hola, Comay," Héctor answered.

After a quick sound check, the theme song started— Near staccato beeping of teletype machines, a recording of a woman singing, "Suuu Suu Super Exclusivooo. Es la hora del bochinche ¡La Comay!"

Indeed, Héctor thought, exhilarated, full of electric ecstasy. *It's the hour of gossip!*

Lights flashed as if attempting to trigger seizures. Laugh track and blaring horns echoed throughout. The show's flair and bombastic feel was incomparable to simply watching it on TV – Héctor saw the air vibrating with the noise.

For the first few segments of the hour, La Comay ran videos of artists and famous people caught doing embarrassing things, with commentary that went to the tune of: "Did you see who this or that salsa singer is dating now?" Or "This baseball player said that the woman with him at dinner was just a friend, but apparently and allegedly he showed her the bat and let her catch the balls in her mitt." Or "The mayor of Humacao was getting a shoeshine the other day and look, his socks have holes. I know that town is not a big city, but they should have enough of a budget to buy their leader new socks. That poor shoeshine boy is gonna pass out from the smell!"

Héctor always cackled right on cue. The laughter was better than when he'd practiced.

The more he laughed the more he felt like laughing, a positive feedback loop. Why was gossip so tantalizing and funny?

"Hey, Héctor," La Comay whispered after a commercial break.

"Yes, Comay," he said, hairs on end. Something really good was coming.

"¡Cierren! ¡Cierren!" *Shut the doors!* She yelled, lifting her legs in between each word.

The sound of doors slamming came from giant speakers.

"Do you remember our friend, Padre Rrrrrrroberto?" La Comay asked. Exaggeratedly rolling her R's and stretching out syllables was a staple of hers.

"Yes. Yes. The Catholic priest. Very wholesome person." Héctor nodded and smirked, "I heard he wakes up very early to give mass."

"He's up early giving something," she said. Laugh track and the sound of a braying donkey flooded the studio. Héctor laughed and shook his head, as if indicating, *Uh oh, the good father stepped in it now*.

"Do you like the beach, Héctor?" La Comay asked.

"Oh yes. Very much. Sometimes I go swimming for my health." He patted his stomach.

"Ah. Do you like digging?" La Comay asked.

The doll's face turned to him. He tried to imagine Kobbo's hand inside, manipulating the foam head but only saw La Comay, only felt her, as if she were an independent being with a unique soul.

"Well, when I was a child, I loved digging in the sand. I was fond of building sandcastles. Is Father Roberto taking the kids from his parish to the beach?" he asked, knowing this wasn't the case but that the segment required him to play along. He'd been in comedy his whole career, after all – coy naivete was a natural fertilizer for jokes.

"Did you ever find a nice conch when digging around?" Laugh track and the gurgling of bubbles. A clip of a news anchor saying, "Ay yay yay Comay, qué problema," played for a few seconds.

"What?" Héctor said, hesitation taking hold for a split second, then he cackled as he realized it was a sex joke. La Comay cackled too, her legs swinging back and forth

– high heels strapped tightly to her feet, hand against her forehead as she laughed.

She stared up at the ceiling, made a fist, and yelled, "¡Qué Bochinche!" or *What a gossip!*

"Producer, roll the clip," she said.

In the video, a man and a woman sat beside each other on a beach. The man is Padre Roberto. The pair is unaware they're being recorded. They stand and the man gently slaps the woman's ass, presumably to clean off the sand, then in one swift motion slides his hand in and out of her bikini, nearly exposing her butt.

Laugh track. Cackling. Alarm sounds. A short clip of an aged priest reciting the Lord's Prayer runs for a few seconds.

"Stop the video, producer. Stop the video." The video paused when Padre Roberto's hand was in the bikini. "Héctor, is that or is that not Father Roberto?"

"Sure is, Comay. He's being really helpful."

More laugh track.

La Comay stares straight at the camera "Padre Roberto, I hope you wash your hands before blessing the Eucharist."

The braying donkey is back.

"God doesn't live there, Father. He doesn't like to hide in caves."

Héctor can't remember ever laughing this much.

"¡Seriedad! ¡Seriedad," La Comay yells. *Get serious! Get serious!*

Spotlights swing around and focus on the doll's throne. "Father. This is a serious matter for the Church. Call me. I don't want you to lose your job. Or just come down to the studio and talk it out with my manager, Kobbo."

"There's more to talk about, Comay?" Héctor asked.

"Well, Héctor, apparently and allegedly two people have become three!"

"Three? How?"

"Based on the information given to me by one of my secret agents, *not by immaculate conception*!" La Comay cackled. A woman yelling Hallelujah thundered throughout the studio; a video of the Pope crossing himself; a baby giggling.

Before he knew it, Héctor's first week on the show was done, and he was exhausted.

* * *

Héctor exited the studio and headed back towards his dressing room. His gaze darted up and down. He was wired, thinking of the show. The back and forth between him and La Comay, his off-script remarks, the cameras capturing it all. The chemistry was undeniable.

He ran his hand over the wall, considering the best height for his future pictures. Layers of paint had smoothed the rough concrete surface, allowing his hand to glide with ease. His hand slid off the wall then bumped a door with a hollow thud. Was this door here before? The door creaked open until the inside doorknob knocked against the wall.

"Sorry, I didn't mean to bother you," he said.

There was no reply. The door sported no name. He reached for the door handle to close it but stopped. A 7-day candle sat on top of a table. The glass stamped with a picture of Jesus, palm held forward, shooting a beam of light. A flame danced on the freshly lit wick. It cast soft light on a stack of newspapers. He entered and picked the top one. The headline read "Disgraced Mayor Steps Down." He caught a glance of the magazine cutout beneath it, "Company Executives Under Investigation for Fraud." He thumbed through the rest of the stack, skimming various papers listing bankruptcies, infidelities, scams and other scandals. The last showed a black and white picture of La Comay, captioned with, "No Secret Left Untold." He skimmed a few sentences. The author was comparing Comay gossip to news reporting. Where was the line between gossip and news? How did La Comay find out all the stuff she did?

Her sources had been a topic of debate for as long as the show existed. Some people even said that Kobbo spoke with spirits. The truth was probably more mundane. Héctor's own opinion was that La Comay's secret agents, as they were called, potentially included everybody. She had mounds of dirt on politicians and artists because people came in droves, begging her to use their findings. They'd remain anonymous of course – who wanted to be called out as a *bochinchero*, a busybody? – but they could gloat to close family and friends. Everyone liked to show off that they knew something you didn't.

The power went out. This was a normal occurrence since Hurricane María in 2017. The power grid was shit. The candle had been a strange sight at first but maybe someone knew the power was going to go out right before it did. It wasn't unreasonable that La Comay had an agent in the power company. Someone would turn on the generator soon enough. Héctor threw the newspaper back onto the stack and chuckled. She really was nearly all powerful, he thought.

He exited, candle in hand, heading in the direction where he thought his room was, the weak flame guiding him as he'd left his phone in his room during the show. He licked his lips. Sweat beaded on his nose. Héctor needed a quick drink before heading home. The dim candle glow only illuminated a small sphere in front of him. He trekked slowly down the hall, staring at the wall on his left, watching for any portraits or adornments to help him recollect the path out of here.

The hall was…off. The ground started inclining downward, yet he knew the whole building was level, and there was no basement. The perimeter illuminated by the candle twisted. Not by much, but by enough that he knew he was not just heading down, but also winding around.

He followed the slight bend. The candle went out. In the darkness, just barely out of sight, he thought he saw an afterimage of a figure…no, it couldn't be.

Fear stopped him from calling out to the figure, even though he knew there was no one there. The air turned sour. *Coño*, if he could only get to his room. This was probably stress from a long week and exhaustion taking its toll.

A couple of swigs of that bottle and he would be laughing out loud again. He continued navigating in the dark as best he could, until he found the door to the stage. How had he ended up here again?

He stepped into the set of *SuperXclusivo* for the second time today. An orange emergency light flickered at the back of the room. The door latched behind him with a sharp click. He turned and tried the door. Locked.

"¡Carajos! What's happening here?"

There had to be another exit. As the orange light flashed his eyes were drawn to the chair on the middle of the set. La Comay sat on her throne, in the same position he'd seen her last. Her legs were crossed. Was that a scratching sound from behind her chair?

"Kobbo, are you here?"

There was no reply. He squinted at the chair. The orange light was starting to give him a headache. Floaters appeared in his vision.

The puppet's chair appeared to hover above the dark red pool beneath. He moved forward, blind between flashes of light, until his feet hit on a chair leg. It was on the floor – obviously it was on the floor. Chairs didn't levitate just because.

He smiled now, realizing he was alone with her. If only he had his phone for taking pictures and videos.

"This is a demon!" Padre Roberto stepped into view from behind her throne. In his hand was a glass bottle – presumably full of holy water – and a cross weaved from palm tree leaves. He looked like the Boricua Van Helsing.

"Help me destroy her. She's not natural," Padre Roberto said.

Help, Héctorsito. He wants to kill me. And Héctor looked at La Comay. She remained still. Padre Roberto started unscrewing the bottle. Héctor didn't hesitate. He paced towards Padre Roberto and slapped the bottle to the floor where it shattered. The priest, startled, grabbed Héctor, managing to seize him in a headlock. Héctor felt the pressure around his neck and struggled to get free. His hands were useless, but he searched with his feet and slammed with all his weight onto Roberto's left shoe. The priest groaned, then slipped on the broken glass, bringing Héctor down with him. The emergency lights broke up the action in Héctor's vision. The father landed on his back, releasing his captive. Héctor took a hit to his shoulder, rolled away from the priest, towards La Comay and got up, winded. The father took a while to stand. When he did, blood trickled down his head. He mumbled something unintelligible at Héctor and staggered away into the dark. Héctor was still dizzy and couldn't follow him, but he doubted the Padre had any fight left after suffering that head injury. At least not for a while.

He stood, catching his breath. This was his chance. He grazed La Comay's hand with his finger. He squeezed her hand, and said, "You're welcome."

It felt real, like it would squeeze back. He imagined leaning in and putting his ear in front of her mouth. Would she tell him secrets? Another urge rose. He could strip the doll from the chair and then sit in her throne. He laughed as hard as he could. His voice echoed throughout the room. He leaned in to her face. If he took off her dress, he'd probably be the only man alive who'd seen La Comay naked. Did the doll have nipples? Pubic hair? What a treat to feel so powerful. For an hour a day this doll had nearly the entire country in the palm of her hand, and now he had her. Didn't he deserve an intimate look after saving her life?

Her mouth seemed to move. Did he have a concussion? Was that even how concussions worked? He traced his finger over her lips.

Her mouth fell open.

Inside was a real tongue, a morsel of pink flesh stitched to the back of her throat. Had this always been here? Can't be. Wouldn't have anyone noticed? A viewer? One of her secret agents, or whoever was devoted enough to light a candle in their room and go over Comay news. The tongue looked smooth, as if the taste buds had been scraped off with an apple peeler, like the tongue of a cartoon.

A hissing sound. The smacking of lips from behind him.

La Comay's mouth remained still. Was the sound real or pareidolia?

"Dime un chismesito." *Give me a little gossip*. Her finger tapped his hand ever so gently.

Héctor bolted up straight. White lights kicked back on.

He paced – almost ran – to the door, which was now unlocked. It took a while, but he found his way back to his room. He texted Kobbo about the incident. After three drinks that were mostly rum with splashes of Coca-Cola, he calmed down. Kobbo texted back that he'd called the police and that the priest wouldn't be a problem in the future. That no one got away with touching her. Héctor read that message once more. Kobbo seemed obsessed with ensuring the doll remained pristine. It had been Héctor who'd touched her, not the priest. Héctor kept this detail to himself.

He spent some time scrolling through social media to see if news of Padre Roberto had been posted, but didn't find anything. Then he went to the show's Instagram page to read what people thought of his performance. Today had been his best show yet. The comments showed people loved him.

His mind kept going back to what he'd seen. A tongue. Going over it now in his mind, he realized how silly it was. There was no tongue, no voice, no moving hands or fingers. Just a tired old man too out of shape to fend off a priest and not lose his breath. The best thing to do would be to take his shoes off, lie on his couch, and nap for a couple of hours.

* * *

His bladder woke him. He checked his phone. It was midnight. The bright light from the hall filtered in through the gap between the door and floor. Héctor wasn't sure he was ready to waltz around the halls again, wandering with no sense of direction, but his bladder was ready to burst worse than the Hindenburg when it was aflame. He turned on the light in his room and spotted the plastic cups. A minute or two later, he bent down and placed the last filled cup on the corner.

The sound of sobbing came from the hall. Was the priest back?

Héctor opened the door and stuck his head out. The noise came from the left. He started walking to the noise. Someone could've gotten hurt in the blackout. He started to dial 911 but the line was busy. He'd seen on the news that this was a common occurrence after a blackout, or had he heard that from La Comay?

The sound was close now. The next sob coincided with a clapping sound. Was this a freaky thing instead of an emergency? He thought of calling out, but maybe he'd miss something good and slowed to a skulk.

He reached the room that contained the sobbing and slapping sounds. The door was closed. He put his ear close.

A whisper, "Dime un chismesito."

He froze, hand stretched out towards the doorknob, and waited, feeling the wet heat growing in his armpits. Could it really be that voice again?

He slowed his breathing to a crawl. *Clap, then a muffled oomph.* Héctor gripped the door handle tight and ever so slowly twisted the knob. He pressed his face to the door, so he could get a good peek without opening it the whole way. The hinges didn't squeak. His jaw dropped when he saw an old man with his back to him, kneeling on the floor, wearing only underwear. The man was surrounded by 7-day candles that had the Jesus face blotched out with black ink. The old man's back was bright red. A multi-tailed leather whip swung over the old man's shoulder and clapped his back. He slightly turned his head to one side; it was Kobbo!

"Forgive me," Kobbo said. "I love you. I'll find you something good. I'm sorry he touched you. No one will touch you ever again. He'll get his soon enough."

It wasn't clear what was happening. Who was *he*? He leaned in a bit more.

La Comay was sitting in a chair in the corner of the room.

Héctor grabbed his phone out of instinct. Taking a picture was more important than his fear or understanding the situation. He'd caught Kobbo *in flagrante*!

Kobbo brought his face down to La Comay's feet, kissed her high heels, and said, "One word from you will heal me."

The phone slipped from his hand and clattered on the floor. Héctor cursed. Kobbo turned. "You're dead, cabrón. She doesn't love you. Only me. No one else can touch her."

The doll's dress shifted, like a big rat was scurrying underneath. Héctor turned and ran down the hall, his heart thumping in his ears. Bile that tasted like sour rum climbed up his throat. He ran faster.

The click-clack of high heels like a shoe model racing down the runway followed him. He didn't dare look back. Salty tears reached his lips.

From behind him, "¡Qué *Bochiiiincheeee!*"

Mestiza Death: How the Spanish Grim Reapress Morphed into Mexican Santa Muerte

Dr. R. Andrew Chesnut

※

Meet Lady Death

SOME OF YOU may have encountered the Bone Mother during visits to Mexico or through popular TV series like *Penny Dreadful* and *Breaking Bad*, or perhaps noticed her image on votive candles in supermarkets across Los Angeles, Houston, New York, and other cities home to large Mexican and Central American communities. For others, this may be your first introduction to the Godmother (*la Madrina*), another common moniker for her. For those already acquainted, please be patient as I briefly introduce her to newcomers who have yet to meet Holy Death.

Santa Muerte, as her Spanish name suggests, is a Mexican folk saint personifying death. Whether depicted as a resin statue, votive candle, gold medallion, or prayer card, she often appears as a Grim Reapress, complete with a scythe and donned in a tunic akin to her European male equivalent. Unlike official saints canonized by the Catholic Church, folk saints like Santa Muerte are venerated as spirits of the deceased, revered for their miraculous powers. In Mexico and across Latin America, folk saints like Jesús Malverde, Maximón, and Rey Pascual (Santa Muerte's Guatemalan cousin) enjoy a fervent following, often surpassing the devotion afforded to Catholic saints.

Folk saints typically have deep roots in Latin America, embodying the essence of the regions and social classes they hail from. For instance, Niño Fidencio was a folk healer in early 20th-century Mexico, while Pedro Batista led a religious community in Brazil's hinterlands during the same era. These vernacular saints resonate with their followers on a personal level; as a Mexico City street vendor put it, Santa Muerte "understands us because she is as tough [*cabrona*] as us" – a stark contrast to the reverent tones used for the Virgin of Guadalupe. Unlike other folk saints, including Argentina's San La Muerte and Guatemala's Rey Pascual, Santa Muerte is not just another death saint but the very embodiment of death itself.

Her name, Santa Muerte, is pregnant with meaning. In Spanish, *la muerte* (death) is a feminine noun, which has led some to mistakenly attribute her gender to this grammatical detail. However, since male death saints exist in Guatemala and Argentina, the reason for her femininity must lie elsewhere. Notably, she and San La Muerte are the only saints in the Americas with "death" in their names, underscoring their unique positions. The term "*Santa*," meaning "saint" or "holy," further accentuates her role as a folk saint. While "Holy Death" can be used in English, "Saint Death" seems a more fitting translation, reflecting her status among the devout. The alternative "*Santísima Muerte*" translates as "Most Holy Death," emphasizing her supreme sanctity. This name variation and others highlight her as a revered female folk saint who as a psychopomp guides souls to the afterlife. Those familiar with Spanish will recognize that "San" in San La Muerte denotes a male saint, contrasting with Santa Muerte's distinctly female identity.

Gendered Death

Any introduction to Saint Death must necessarily consider her distinct gender identity. Across the Americas, many folk saints exist, and other supernatural skeletal figures perform miracles in countries like Guatemala and Argentina. However, Santa Muerte is unique as the only female saint of death spanning from Chile to Canada. Her skeletal form is androgynous, devoid of any gendered features. It is instead her clothing and hairstyle that signify her femininity. Devotees and creators of her mass-produced effigies typically depict her in the garments of a nun, the Virgin Mary, a bride, or a queen, with her outfits ranging from red and black baroque tunics to white bridal gowns and brightly colored satin robes, which leave only her skeletal hands, feet, and face visible.

Historically, like her male counterparts San La Muerte and Rey Pascual, the Godmother was depicted with a bald skull. Yet, in the last fifteen years or so, inspired by devotional leader Enriqueta Romero (Doña Queta), most followers now enhance their figures with wigs – commonly in shades of brown or black, though occasionally in blond, red, or even pastel hues. This has given rise to a flourishing industry in Mexico, where Santa Muertistas establish businesses to dress and style these figures as the Pretty Girl (la Niña Bonita). But Santa Muerte transcends mere aesthetics; she is primarily revered as the Powerful Lady (la Dama Poderosa), whose miraculous abilities make her a formidable presence in both folk and Catholic realms in Mexico, competing even with Guadalupe, the national patroness.

Aztec Death

To most Americans and Western Europeans, Santa Muerte might appear akin to a female Grim Reaper, a figure rooted in medieval Catholicism. Spaniards, familiar with their own feminine death figure, La Parca, need no gender-based adaptations. In contrast, many

Mexicans view her as a modern manifestation of an indigenous death goddess, typically from Aztec or Mayan cosmology. Despite seeming strange to outsiders, this view aligns with local historical narratives and national myths, placing the White Sister within the context of pre-Columbian Mexico.

The prevailing narrative of her indigenous roots suggests she evolved from Mictecacihuatl, the Aztec goddess of death who, with her consort Mictlantecuhtli, governed the underworld, Mictlan. The couple, like the Bony Lady, were often depicted as skeletal figures. The Aztecs believed that those dying naturally would enter Mictlan and also sought the gods' intervention for earthly matters. Following the Spanish conquest, which suppressed native religions, these beliefs morphed into a syncretic form with Catholicism. It is believed by some devotees that Mictecacihuatl re-emerged publicly in the figure of Santa Muerte at Doña Queta's shrine in 2001, donning Spanish-style tunics and the traditional European symbols of death – the scythe and scales of justice – masking her true Aztec origins.

Spanish Death

Leading Mexican and American academics trace Santa Muerte's origins to medieval Western Europe. Mexican anthropologist Katia Perdigón Castañeda asserts that "the history of the present concept of death and its iconography, reflected in the contemporary Santa Muerte, are more related to Judeo-Christian religion (Catholicism in this particular case) than the forgotten and unknown voices of the vanquished, in other words, the pre-Hispanic peoples." Others specifically connect her to the Grim Reaper of medieval European Catholicism. During the Black Death in the fourteenth century, which claimed at least one-third of Europe's population, death became a constant presence, personified as the skeletal figure we recognize today. Artists, clerics, and performers employed this imagery, and Catholic clerics even staged performances in cemeteries featuring actors in skeleton costumes. These "dances of death" symbolized the inevitability of mortality as dancers moved one last time before being escorted to the afterlife by the Grim Reaper.

In the Americas, Spanish clergy introduced the Grim Reapress, La Parca, to indigenous populations, using it as a catechetical tool. Some indigenous groups, such as the highland Maya of Chiapas and Guatemala and the Guarani in Argentina and Paraguay, integrated this figure into their own cultural traditions, often blending it with re-emerged beliefs about sacred ancestral bones. A clear example is found in Guatemala and Chiapas, where the Franciscan saint Pascual Bailón was syncretized with Mayan religion to become Rey Pascual, a skeleton crowned as a king. Although never canonized, Rey Pascual remains a prominent figure in folk traditions.

Heretical Death

References to Santa Muerte herself first appear in Spanish colonial records from the late 18th century, over a century after Rey Pascual's emergence. In 1797, a document titled *Concerning the Superstitions of Various Indians from the Town of San Luis de la Paz* mentions Santa Muerte for the first time. This inquisition record describes Chichimecas in present-day Guanajuato gathering in a chapel at night, consuming peyote, lighting inverted black candles, and performing rituals involving paper dolls, Holy Crosses, and a figure of death they called Santa Muerte. The effigy, bound with a wet rope and threatened with whipping or burning, was demanded to perform a miracle related to local political control. The Church responded by destroying the chapel where the effigy was kept, echoing recent demolitions of Santa Muerte shrines along the Mexican border.

Other Inquisition records from the same period describe a similar case of "Indian idolatry" in central New Spain. In 1793, in present-day Querétaro, a Franciscan friar reported that during Mass, a group of "Indians" placed an idol on the altar: a skeleton named the Just Judge, depicted as a complete human skeleton standing on a red base, crowned, and holding a bow and arrow. This suggests a fusion of the Grim Reaper with the figure of Christ as the Just Judge. Similar syncretism is also seen in Argentina, highlighting the complex interplay between indigenous traditions and Catholic iconography in the Americas.

Rocky Mountain Death

Facing persecution by the Church, devotees of the Skinny Lady made their worship even more secretive, leading to her disappearance from the Mexican historical record for over 150 years. During this time, Mexico declared independence from Spain, suffered defeat in a war with the United States, and endured the turmoil of the first great revolution of the twentieth century. Although the Powerful Lady undoubtedly remained with her followers through these events, no record of her in Mexico re-emerged until the 1940s. For the next half-century, Santa Muerte appeared almost exclusively as the Lady of Love, symbolized by her red votive candle.

The Spanish did not only bring La Parca to Mexico. Wherever they conquered and colonized, the Grim Reapress traveled with them across oceans and into new territories. One of the more surprising discoveries in 16 years of research is that Santa Muerte also has historical roots in the United States. As part of the Viceroyalty of New Spain, the modern-day states of New Mexico and Colorado formed the northern frontier of Spanish rule in North America for nearly three centuries. Santa Fe, the oldest state capital in the U.S., served as the cultural and administrative hub of this frontier, which was otherwise dominated by indigenous populations.

As the Christian cross followed the Spanish sword, the Church sought to replicate Iberian Catholic traditions, rituals, and organizations throughout its empire. Holy Week, the most sacred time on the Christian calendar, was celebrated with grand processions and pageantry in Spain, and these traditions were recreated wherever possible in New Spain and beyond, including the Philippines. In the towns of New Mexico and southern Colorado, brotherhoods of Penitentes, originating in Spain, organized Holy Week activities. These Catholic lay groups became known for their public acts of penance, which included processions featuring death carts carrying life-sized wooden effigies of a skeletal figure, Doña Sebastiana or Comadre Sebastiana.

Godmother Death

The term "Comadre," which lacks an exact English equivalent, is a term for the godmother of one's child. Sebastiana, however, takes her name from Saint Sebastian, the Roman martyr. During Holy Week, the Penitentes used these death carts and their skeletal effigies to symbolize both the suffering and death of Jesus Christ and the importance of a Holy Death (Santa Muerte). Doña Sebastiana was not only a menacing reminder of mortality but also venerated as a supernatural personification of death. She was often referred to interchangeably as Santa Muerte or Comadre Sebastiana, marking her as a uniquely Mexican-American iteration of the Grim Reapress, blending both Spanish and Mexican traditions.

Doña Sebastiana was typically depicted as a skeleton with snow-white hair, seated or standing in a rustic wooden cart, wielding a bow and arrow or a hatchet to signify the inevitability of death. This imagery has clear roots in La Parca, the Grim Reapress of medieval Spain. Yet, Sebastiana's name and her depiction holding a bow and arrow suggest another layer of syncretism: the merging of Saint Sebastian with La Parca. Saint Sebastian, a third-century Roman martyr who survived being shot with arrows, became associated with a Holy Death and the Black Plague in medieval Europe. Europeans, who likened the randomness of plague outbreaks to an indiscriminate rain of arrows, turned to Saint Sebastian as a guardian saint during the pandemic. It was during this same era that the figure of the Grim Reaper emerged in European iconography.

This syncretism continues today, with Saint Sebastian maintaining a unique resonance among LGBTQ+ devotees, often linked to his historical depictions, which are imbued with homoerotic overtones. Remarkably, the fusion of Sebastian, La Parca, and Santa Muerte reflects a centuries-long evolution of the personification of death, from medieval Europe to the Penitentes of the American Southwest.

Sebastiana, like other Catholic saints transformed into Skeleton Saints, was not merely a personification of death akin to the Grim Reapress; she was venerated as a supernatural death saint by the Penitentes, who regarded her as Santa Muerte. Based on my 16 years of research on Santa Muerte and my focus on vernacular religion in the Americas, I had long suspected that for members of the Brotherhood of the Holy Blood of Christ (*Hermandad de la Santa Sangre de Cristo*), Sebastiana held far more significance than being an artistic representation of death. If Filipino Catholics venerate Santa Muerte as part of Holy Week processions symbolizing Christ's victory over death, it is reasonable to imagine the Penitentes of remote mountain villages in New Mexico doing the same. In 1933, local eyewitness Ely Leyba wrote in *New Mexico Magazine* that the Brothers believed "if any person would pray to the image of Sebastiana, their lives would be prolonged." Leyba also described how Penitentes in Trampas, New Mexico, prayed the rosary while pulling the skeletal godmother in her cart during Holy Week.

A remarkable hymn, or *alabado*, further demonstrates that these rosaries were prayed specifically for Sebastiana, portraying her as part of the celestial family of saints. Composed in northern New Mexico during the late 19th century, the hymn *Ayudad almas queridas* ("Help us dear souls") imbues Sebastiana – referred to interchangeably as Comadre Sebastiana, Santa Muerte (Holy Death), and Physical Death – with extraordinary supernatural powers. In the following stanzas, Sebastiana's divine agency is unmistakable:

Now Holy Death (Santa Muerte) comes
dressed as a woman lawyer
to defend this cause of the Lord turned
into a sacrament.
My Godmother Sebastiana, crucified,
lays out that pathway to God
She has traveled on her knees.
Holy Death has set out, riding in her cart;
with God's orders she represents the souls.
Now Holy Death sets out to visit a sick man;
commending his soul to God so that he might
be freed from hell.
For forty days she was prostrate on Calvary
accompanying Jesus,
my Godmother Sebastiana.
Now they pray a rosary for her prostrate on Calvary;
my Godmother Sebastiana gives her blessing.

Sebastiana is depicted as God's Angel of Death, representing mortal souls, commending them to God, and even bestowing blessings. What makes this practice particularly unusual – and heretical from a Catholic theological perspective – is that the Penitentes prayed the rosary for Sebastiana, Lady Death herself. In Christian theology, death is not a divinity and should neither be prayed to nor for. While contemporary Santa Muerte devotees praying the rosary to the Skeleton Saint might be controversial, it is even more striking that members of a Catholic brotherhood did so historically.

In a modern twist linking Comadre Sebastiana and Santa Muerte, a parish priest in Chimayo, New Mexico – a native of Barcelona – commissioned a wooden sculpture of Sebastiana in her death cart. Installed in 2010 in an exhibit room attached to the Shrine of the Black Christ of Esquipulas, one of the most visited Catholic sites in the U.S., this addition highlights the enduring legacy of Sebastiana in a town renowned for its grand Holy Week processions.

Jealous Death

Returning to Mexico, four anthropologists – one Mexican and three American – documented Santa Muerte's role as a love sorceress in their research from the 1940s and 1950s. Frances Toor and Oscar Lewis, both discussed earlier, highlighted her presence in Mexico City, while Gonzalo Aguirre Beltrán, writing in the late 1940s, described love-related prayers to Santa Muerte among a predominantly Afro-Mexican community in Guerrero, a coastal state along the Pacific. Isabel Kelly's and Lewis's mentions of her role in love magic, along with Aguirre Beltrán's observations, demonstrate that by the late 1950s, the Pretty Girl's influence extended widely, if not yet nationally. While Toor and Lewis encountered her in Mexico City, Aguirre found her along the Pacific coast, and Kelly noted her love-related invocations in north-central Mexico.

Research in the 1960s and 1970s expanded knowledge of her reach, uncovering devotion to Santa Muerte in remote areas like the mountainous region of Veracruz near Catemaco, a hub of witchcraft and sorcery, and even as far south as Chiapas, where Rey Pascual is venerated. In her 1970s book *Mitos y magos mexicanos* (*Mexican Myths and Magicians*), María de la Luz Bernal became one of the first scholars to document organized devotion to the Bald Lady (*la Pelona*). Based on fieldwork during the decade, she described groups of women dressed in black kneeling before altars dedicated to the Skeleton Saint. These women, clutching lit candles, chanted prayers in unison, imploring Santa Muerte to grant them power over the men in their lives. Their pleas included cries of "Most Holy Death, torture him, mortify him," as they sought the aid of the Powerful Lady to dominate unfaithful or disobedient husbands and boyfriends.

Big Screen Death

Santa Muerte's rising popularity is reflected in her transition from small-town lore to a national cinematic debut in the 1976 film *El miedo no anda en burro* (*Fear Doesn't Ride a Donkey*). This campy, comedic horror film stars La India María, one of the most beloved characters in Mexican cinema, portrayed by the prolific actress

María Elena Velasco. The movie features a surreal and macabre scene involving the Bony Lady. As an old man in a wheelchair plays a haunting dirge on an organ, La India María, fixated on the image of Santa Muerte above the keyboard, sings a darkly humorous song about the Grim Reapress's role in claiming the dead and guiding them to their final resting place.

Trying to frighten the organist, she sings, "Death takes you when you least expect her... Death, super ugly and bald, grabs you. Pulling them this way and that, carrying them here and there, that's the way she takes the dead with her." This moment stands out as one of the rare depictions of Santa Muerte during this era that does not cast her as a love doctor. Instead, she takes on her traditional role as the chilling Grim Reapress, aiding La India María in spooking the old man with visions of his own impending demise.

Public Death

From her first mention in historical records in 1797 until 2002, Santa Muerte was venerated in secrecy. Devotees kept altars hidden in their homes, and medallions or scapulars bearing the image of the Skeleton Saint were worn discreetly beneath clothing. This contrasts sharply with today, when many followers openly display their devotion through T-shirts, tattoos, and even cowboy boots adorned with her image. The history of persecution by the Church and the unorthodox – or even satanic – connotations of worshipping a personification of death compelled adherents of the White Girl to keep their practices private, often confined to close family or small circles of friends.

For over two centuries, devotion to Saint Death remained an occult practice, both in its focus on a semi-secret supernatural figure and in its concealment from the wider public. This prolonged period of clandestine veneration came to an end in late 2001 when an unassuming quesadilla vendor in Mexico City made the bold decision to publicly display her Skeleton Saint, bringing her faith out of the shadows and into one of the city's most infamous neighborhoods.

Belinda Matos & The Bronx River Wishing Stone

Angel Luis Colón

◆

IT CAUGHT BELINDA'S EYE as she passed the intersection of 229th and Bronx Boulevard. A sudden glimmer breaking the grey haze of the January morning. She tried to ignore it, but once that shine hit her periphery, it was too late.

She had to see what it was.

Maybe it was a ring? Something valuable lost the night before. An argument between a couple after too many drinks. Someone dropping part of the haul from a robbery as they ran away from the police. A person in grief that simply lost track of something once precious.

Belinda turned and stepped down towards the bushes framing the area near the overpass and nearly stumbled towards a storm drain caked with wet leaves and trash. The smell nearly held her in midair before she regained her footing, but she saved herself. The object wasn't hard to find. It caught light at almost any angle and Belinda wondered if she had simply stumbled onto a flashlight, but she soon found it half buried in the leaves: a rock the size of her thumb. It felt warm to the touch and almost seemed to glow. There was a comfort to it, something familiar, something soothing.

"What are you?" she asked breathlessly. "So pretty."

As she turned it in her hand, Belinda watched the rock's coloring shift like mother-of-pearl. One moment it was streaked with blue and the next, it had hints of gold and silver flecks. She turned it again and it matched the color of her eyes. Her reflection stared back at her, warped by the curves of the rock and the way the light reflected it off its surface. It made her think of staring at the back of a spoon, the way one part of her face warped as she turned the stone around.

"Wow," she said like a child examining a new toy.

Belinda clutched the rock then, the world returning into focus. Car horns blaring. The soft murmur of people walking. Far off, she heard loud salsa music. The quick chirp of a police siren. She was home. Stray thoughts flittered out of her head. She'd felt as if she was miles away for that small moment. Now, she was back to the cold, grey reality of the Bronx.

And she was going to miss her bus.

Hurrying back to the sidewalk, Belinda nearly tripped over the little concrete divider, but found her footing. She jogged towards her stop, turning her head over her shoulder to see her bus coming, its marquee confirming it was the express – the last one she could catch that morning. It would be nice to make it to classes on time, she thought. She still had the rock clutched in her hand. She moved it around, enjoying the warmth and weight of it in her palm.

Belinda was greeted by her friend Grace as she got to the stop. Grace was her bus buddy. An ever-smiling woman in her fifties who served as a bright spot to Belinda's darker days – if she caught her bus on time. She always wore vintage clothes and wore her hair differently almost every day. Belinda always asked where she found the time to look her best and Grace would simply smile, saying that one day Belinda would learn how to *find* the time.

"Buen dia, mi amor," Grace said as the bus slowed to a stop a few feet away.

"Good morning," Belinda said in a sing-song voice. "Can you believe I made it on time? Que milagro, right?"

There were seats on the bus – another miracle – and they were able to sit next to each other. Belinda liked days like this. The bus ride was a little over a half an hour and having someone to talk with was so much better than shutting the world out with her music. Grace was also pretty fun to be around. She reminded Belinda of her *bisabuela*; a woman who was kind and loved to talk.

And Grace was *just* like that. A partner in *chismé*. Someone Belinda felt like would take her secrets to the grave. She really didn't have that at home.

"¿Y cómo estas tu mama?" Grace asked.

Belinda smiled weakly. "Ella está bien. Siempre quejándose." Belinda's Spanish was weak, but she practiced with Grace. Her parents and siblings only spoke English, so it was a treat to speak this way.

They spoke about their plans for the day. Belinda had classes and a shift at the Lehman College library until closing. Grace talked about taking care of her grandchildren – twins – who were getting too big and fast for her, but she wouldn't dare admit that to her son. They both laughed as Grace related stories about the toddlers' messes and her son's overreactions. As Grace spoke, Belinda felt off. As if something wasn't quite right.

It was a feeling she was familiar with, of being watched. She slowly turned her head and caught sight of that feeling's source. An older woman scowling at them from her seat. Makeup caked the corners of her narrowed eyes and the edges of her flared nose. She sneered as she watched them, sucking her teeth and setting her jaw. There was cruelty in those eyes.

But this was the Bronx and Belinda was a Puerto Rican woman. She was taught that kind of look received a response, so she turned her body to better face the woman.

"Can I help you?" Belinda's tone matched the woman's stare.

The woman muttered something but didn't turn away at the challenge. Instead, she set her jaw and kept scowling. Not an annoyed scowl either, but the kind of scowl Belinda knew all too well – that white lady scowl. She got it on the Upper West Side or in the more affluent areas of the Bronx. This look of disdain reserved for 'invaders', those who were a shade darker than beige and had the nerve to exist outside while these women occupied space they felt entitled to.

"Ignórala, mija. Háblame de tu clase de historia," Grace pleaded. She loved hearing about Belinda's classes.

The woman shook her head then and leaned over, pointing a withered finger at them like a crone in a fairytale. "Why don't you speak English?"

This wasn't the first time Grace or Belinda had heard this sentence. Separate or together. There'd always been someone completely at a loss that two Latinas would have the nerve to speak Spanish in public. Belinda felt the heat rush to her cheeks, but Grace quickly slipped her hand over and held onto Belinda's forearm.

"Con calma, niña," she whispered.

Belinda nodded, but she was pissed off. The morning was going so well and along came this decrepit woman casting a shadow over everything. Misery loved company, her mother always said, and there was misery seated in a bus – gray and violent. Belinda couldn't understand why people acted that way. She gripped the stone she'd found tighter, the heat of it intensifying, but bringing a strange comfort. As if it was trying to console her like Grace was. Somehow, she took more solace in that warmth than she did in her friend's words.

"Está bien," Belinda said, "I'm fine. I just…" Belinda looked at the woman. Her hand was burning, but she maintained her grip on the stone, something inside her terrified to let it go. She wanted to say something to this woman. She wanted to get through to her and show her what she'd done was wrong. "You know what?" Belinda waved her words away. "No, I'm *not* fine." She curled her lip and turned back to the old woman.

"I'm so sick of people like you always having to say something to show how ugly you are inside." She wanted to curse, to say the ugliest things she could think of to send that misery back to the woman. Most of all, though, she wanted the woman to shut up. She wanted her to never talk that way to anyone again. To never spread misery out of that hole in her face. She wanted the woman to choke on her words.

The woman, though, was clearly not done. She pointed again and opened her mouth to spew more nonsense, but instead gasped, as if she was trying to swallow while talking. Her eyes widened and she went to speak again, but the same thing happened. The woman brought her hands to her lips and blinked. She tucked a finger into her mouth, as if to pry something out, but nothing was happening. Her lips began to darken, and her eyes darted back and forth in panic.

"Miss, are you okay?" Belinda asked, a wave of shame washing over her. She was mad, but hadn't intended to provoke this kind of response.

The woman's eyes widened further, the veins beginning to show as tears welled up. She opened her mouth again, and this time her tongue flopped out, comically large; the blue veins beneath pink muscle throbbing and threatening to burst. She pawed at the swollen thing with both hands, her mouth opening wider and wider. Something snapped as the woman groaned in pain.

Belinda slapped the stop signal of the bus. "Oh my god, help! Something's wrong. Driver, driver, please stop the bus. This lady needs help." A few men rushed to try to calm the woman down as she was clawing at her tongue, blood pouring from it as it continued to swell. The bus stopped as more people panicked and screamed. The woman fell to the ground then, trembling as a louder snap sounded, her jaw distending and the bone breaking. The skin of her mouth cracked, and blood flowed freely from her tongue, mouth, and nose. Her body violently contorted as her hands moved from her mouth to her throat, and then slowly drifted down; her hands balling into tight fists, the skin around her knuckles blanching.

Grace made the sign of the cross then and said an 'Our Father' while Belinda could only watch as the woman convulsed one last time, her body going still, and silence set in on the bus. The old woman's eyes went dim, and her hands opened, small cut marks lining her palms where her nails had pierced flesh during her final moments.

Blinking through tears, Belinda brought a hand up to wipe her eyes. She blinked as a knuckle grazed her eyelid.

Her hand was still balled up into a fist. She opened it and the stone was still there, warm against her palm, the sun catching it just right to cast a beautiful amber glow on the bus ceiling right over her head.

* * *

Belinda walked the rest of the way to school, leaving her too late to go to her first class, so she decided to try and process what she'd just seen at the campus library. She'd separated from Grace, who called her son for a ride after the paramedics and police ensured everyone was okay after the event on their bus. Belinda promised to text her but wasn't quite in the headspace to deal with anyone.

At the library, Belinda found a free reading room and sat silently while she stared at the stone in her hand. Her palm was red and raw around where it rested. She wanted to see if the rawness was worse beneath the stone, but she couldn't let it go. It was too precious. She had to hold onto it.

Belinda thought about the bus, about that old woman's face splitting open as her tongue, as fat as her head, flopped around. She laughed softly, nearly giddy at the memory. It was quite a sight, wasn't it? To see her pay that way. To watch her eyes as she realized there was no way back, no means of saving her.

"I did that, didn't I?" she asked softly.

The stone pulsed in her hand, its colors muddled and swirling. It felt like it was staring right back at her.

"*We* did that..." she whispered.

The stone thrummed in her palm, the heat picking up again. It agreed with her. It brought her comfort in its weight and heat. It was on her side; she was sure of it. Look at how it defended her. It was fate to have picked it up, to have seen it shining in the sun, a beacon to something better. That woman had died, though, hadn't she? Was that something deserved? But what else should have happened, Belinda thought, should people get away with being like that? No. She'd dealt with that nonsense her whole life.

Maybe finding this stone was the start of something new for her. A change of life for her. No more feeling helpless or angry. No more taking it on the chin the way her parents taught her – to suffer in grace like a good Catholic. Like a good victim. The stone, this random nothing, a scrap of earth nobody would have recognized any value in...

Like her. They had value. Together they were better than they were alone. It was silly, but it felt as if her thoughts and the stone were one.

There was a knock at the door then. Belinda snapped out of her thoughts and looked around. Outside, the sun had gone down. What time was it? She checked her phone: 6 p.m. No. That wasn't right. She'd come in before noon. Had she really sat there the whole time staring at the stone? Clenching her fist, she rolled the stone around her palm. Her skin tingled, like pins and needles.

More knocking.

"Um…" It felt like she'd forgotten how to speak. "Yes?"

The door opened. A young man. Maybe her age. "Sorry, I was just checking if you were done. I've got the room for a study group in a few minutes."

Belinda took a moment to register all that.

The guy looked a little confused. "So, like…" He motioned out of the room. "I sort of need the space *now*?"

Belinda nodded but remained in her seat. "Could you give me a minute?"

"Listen, they said you've been in here all day and like, I get if you've been sleeping or whatever, but we're only supposed to use these rooms for an hour or two."

"I understand that. I just need some time to get my things together." Belinda slowly stood. Her legs felt stiff. Arms felt heavy. She stretched. It felt like she hadn't slept in days. Was the stone doing that to her? No. It was what happened that morning. The shock of it must have hit her worse than she realized. If anything, the stone was helping her. It was keeping her safe. The interruption, though, that was frustrating. More than frustrating. There had to be another room available. There were always rooms available.

The guy walked in, exasperated and darting around. Shifting the chairs and working to move the desk over. He was acting as if Belinda didn't understand what he said and now resorted to passive aggressive nonsense.

Belinda watched him as he moved around the room, doing his best to steer clear of her, but eyeing her with anger. Why was he being so rude, she wondered. She felt that heat in her hand again. This time it stung the way hot ash did if it landed on exposed skin.

"Miss, seriously…"

It didn't feel like Belinda screamed. It didn't feel like she did anything, really. The burning in her hand intensified and she heard her own voice, as if standing beside herself. Eight words: "Can you just give me a fucking minute?"

And he was gone, but not without a trace. The walls of the room held evidence of his existence. Thick chunks of matter, varied hues of red and grey. The carpet was soaked. Dark liquid pooled beneath the soles of Belinda's shoes, staining their white colorway. The smell of it was what struck Belinda the most. It reminded her of visits to the *viveria* with her *bisabuela* when she was a child. Wet earth, blood, and shit. Belinda leaned forward and dry heaved. Her hand was on fire, and she finally felt the need to release her grip from the stone, but when she willed it, nothing happened.

Belinda looked at her hand and saw it was gnarled and locked in place. The skin around her knuckles frayed and blackened like burnt paper. It was as if the stone had taken root and was beginning to grow through her – making them one.

No. She'd made a mistake. This thing wasn't here to protect her. She'd found something evil, something *wrong*.

Belinda ran out of the room and towards the front desk. Others in the library, having heard the commotion, investigated the reading room and the screams began. Phones were held up, lights turning on to capture the event. Others tried calling for help or just ran out of the building. Belinda, though, had her eyes on one thing: the paper cutter next to the librarian's printer. She made her way to it and lifted the guillotine blade, placing her arm beneath it at the wrist. She had to rid herself of this thing.

No…por favor, no me dejes…

Belinda froze before she could lower the blade down and sever the connection between her and the stone. She wasn't in control of herself anymore, it had her and the voice she heard was one she knew.

"Bisabuela Belén?" It couldn't have been her. It was a trick of the stone, a way to keep her from acting out and saving herself from its presence. No, she had to do it. She had to stop this before she did something even worse than what happened in the reading room. What if she hurt everyone on campus?

Belinda closed her eyes and took hold of the handle on the guillotine as tight as she could. Pull down, she thought, pull down as hard as you can and don't look. She found the strength, the voice in her head barely a whisper. She didn't second guess, didn't hesitate. She brought down the blade with her full weight, the blade piercing the skin of her wrist and then…

Belinda opened her eyes and stared down at the blade embedded in her arm at the wrist, a trickle of blood coming from the skin she cut through, but it wasn't enough. It didn't even hurt. There was something else beneath her skin. Something familiar, the way it shined. It was just like the stone. The colors, the glow.

What had she done?

* * *

Belinda rushed into the house, her mother walking towards her to tell her something, but Belinda raised her arm to stop her, desperate to protect her from this curse, only for her mother's face to split open like a blossoming flower. Her father followed, rushing to his wife's collapsing body, but never making it, instead he was sent flying through the far wall of the living room as Belinda screamed.

Why did she come home? *How* did she come home? She couldn't remember. She couldn't pinpoint what had happened from when she tried to remove her hand and when she arrived home, and the chaos continued. It wasn't going to end, was it? It was going to continue, and she couldn't do anything to stop it. Belinda turned to leave the house, but stopped as she realized there were more people out there. It would be better to stay back and avoid others.

She turned in place, a whirlwind of fear, worry, and grief churning within. Where did she go? Was that screaming she heard outside? Oh God, she thought, what happened on her way back home?

Belinda rushed to her room, and she collapsed on her bed. She held her withered hand up, the stone's influence now fully up her forearm and beginning to stiffen her elbow. The weight of the stone was gone, replaced with a nagging pull at her shoulder. It was spreading and would continue to spread, but she couldn't understand why. All she did was pick up a pretty rock. All she'd done was live her life. She didn't want to hurt anyone.

No, that last part, it wasn't true. She *did* want to hurt that woman. She wanted that guy at the library to go away. The stone knew that. Was that why it kept hurting others? Was it acting out something awful and dark inside of her she had ignored?

Belinda sat on her bed, realizing the questions didn't matter. There were sirens outside. Close. Those were for her. They would come for her, and she would hurt more people and even though she knew they probably would hurt her just as fast, she didn't want it to happen again. She clenched her eyes closed and wept. At first, controlled gasps for air and then finally a wailing that carried through the house as heavy fists pounded at her front door.

"I shouldn't have come home," she said, "I shouldn't have done any of this. I shouldn't have…"

The stone began to heat up again, responding to her desire. It knew what she wanted, and it wanted to deliver it to her. But what would the price be for that?

Did it even matter? She knew there was no place she could run.

"I shouldn't have picked you up. I wish I would have just walked past."

* * *

Belinda was cold.

She sat on the ground, the space around her empty, an amber light bathing her head to toe. She stood and sniffed, wiping her eyes dry. This wasn't her bedroom. This wasn't her home. She brought her other hand up to wipe her nose with the back of her arm and realized it wasn't heavy anymore. There was no stone. No wounds.

Belinda hastily inspected her body and clothes, looking for the bloodstains – any sign that what happened did in fact happen – and found no evidence.

Instead, she found silence and this strangely lit space. Impossibly vast but seemingly enclosed. There were no doors or windows. No signs of anyone or anything but herself.

"Hello?" she called out and her voice echoed back in layers, as if she was answering her own call. "Is anyone there?"

This time there wasn't an echo.

"¿Hay alguien ahí?"

"Who's there?"

"Who the hell was that?"

The questions came in a rush, all phrased differently, some in other languages, but there was a common factor among them: the voice.

They were all Belinda's voice.

Belinda turned in place, staring at the light above her. She made out familiar shapes in the distance. Blurs of color and movement. Sometimes a familiar pattern would come into focus. Strange geometrical sights would disappear to give way to something feathery and then that amber light again, growing in strength and fading as it shifted from amber to gold to yellow.

"Where am I?"

The other Belindas joined in.

"What is this?"

"Am I dead?"

"Ma, where are you, Ma?"

It took longer for the quiet to return and as the voices faded, another voice boomed, "What are you? So pretty."

The ground shook. Belinda nearly stumbled over and landed on her hands. Exasperated, she began to weep again, rolling over on to her back and staring at the murk above her as another image began to take focus: her face. Her smiling face, staring down at her, the light shifting in color and intensity as the larger Belinda stared down at the smaller.

"Wow," the voice boomed.

Belinda thought she sounded like a child.

Maternal Instinct

Rios de la Luz

ALMA FAVELA was six months pregnant when she first heard scratching behind the walls of the small house she had inherited from her dead husband. The house was a quaint rectangular home built in the 1930s. A simple layout with two tiny rooms and one bathroom. Their front door was painted dandelion yellow and a garden of wildflowers bloomed full and tall in the front yard. Alma's husband was gentle, inquisitive, and never believed in an afterlife. His name was Rodrigo. He had great hair, nice teeth, and he made Alma cackle until she could barely breathe. He was adventurous and careful with his words. Even when he was annoying, Alma loved him. Alma missed the spoons smeared with leftover peanut butter, slimy and shining. It used to drive her into madness, touching the oily peanut butter, leaving behind residue for her to scrub and clean. She missed his piles of laundry behind the bathroom door. She kept a secret stash of his dirty laundry. When she missed him, she snuck into her small bedroom closet and sat in the dark, inhaling the scent from his clothes. She missed his hands, how he cracked his knuckles when he was nervous, how his hands always looked familiar to her, as though she held them in a lifetime before. But he was gone. Death was simple. He was there and then he wasn't.

Her in-laws went no-contact as soon as Rodrigo died. It was a swift look into their true colors. They forbade Alma from attending the funeral as they claimed the baby could be anyone's. Alma swore to hold spite in her chest just for them. She hoped one day they would regret their decision to cut the baby out of their lives. She hoped it poisoned them. Alma's friends were far as she preferred an introverted existence. Alma was an expert at being a hermit. She sent the sporadic text to her friend with occasional spiritual psychosis and she called the only uncle in her family that wasn't judgemental. She kept to herself and binged books. She painted abstract ethereal portraits of her garden, the sunrise, the houses on her block. She wondered which houses were haunted. What secrets hid behind their walls? Which houses nurtured the energetic traces of tenants who lived there prior? She wrote short stories. About wolves and glitches in time. She wrote about turkey vultures and religious oppression. She wrote poems to the birds in the neighborhood. The grackles. The mourning doves. The ruby-throated hummingbirds. She kept a journal of dreams. Dreamscapes of lush geography and magical forests. Buildings that were only familiar in these subconscious cities. She wanted to know herself deeply. She wanted to erase the parts of her past that scarred into her bones. She was determined to be the lineal factor that stopped generational trauma.

Her mother was wicked to the point of being cartoonish. The quintessential evil parent. It was unbelievable in a lot of ways, but Alma lived through it. She survived her mother. Sometimes, Alma laughed to herself as she thought about how absurd it was that she was punished for simply existing. Alma was born during a sun shower. Her family had a passed down superstition from her great-great grandmother, Hortensia. She convinced the family that being born under a sun shower was a sign of a witch becoming betrothed to a helpless spellbound man. This could only mean Alma's path to becoming a witch was imminent. Alma's mother, Esperanza, had her baptized immediately. Nuns flocked around Esperanza like obedient ravens and they prayed. Perhaps Alma was destined to be born of madness. Perhaps this was where her craving to be an artist came from. A thirst to make sense of the world and a way to express her curiosity about rot and collapse. When the nuns dispersed from the hospital room, Esperanza whispered into Alma's ear. *Birth splits you open and then when we die, we're just little seeds, waiting to wriggle out, we wait and we wait, and it always ends in death.* As newborn Alma tried to find Esperanza's breast, Esperanza amused herself by covering baby Alma's mouth. *Good girls wait, Almita.*

We wait.

Alma was under the assumption that her mother haunted her house. When a whiff of rose and patchouli lingered in the warmth of the air, Alma quickly turned to see what was in the corner of her eye. She saw plenty of shadows with concentrated opacity to them, darker than the night, a depth of a long existence. She heard the scratching behind the walls travel above her head night after night. Something was on the roof. Alma assumed this was her mother's doing. It annoyed her more than it scared her because it made terrible sense that her mother had followed her into this house. Because of death, this was Alma's nest, her own place without constant evil eye supervision penetrating into the back of her neck. When Esperanza was alive, she ached for loneliness but she never got it because of Alma and because of poverty. As a child, Alma lived in a small apartment with six of her cousins. Even with family crawling all over the place, no one batted an eye at her mother's corporal punishment. Alma remembers all of her cousins as having dark beady little eyes that darted away from her when she came out of their shared bedroom bleeding and swollen. No attempts at an "Are you okay?" or pity-driven pats on the back. It was as though Alma was the problem. A curse in the shape of a girl.

The maternal haunting started with the kitchen cabinets and drawers. They were left open with silverware in disarray. Doors closed on their own. Lights flickered randomly. Tapping on the windows faded in and out at three in the morning. Jewelry went missing for weeks at a time. Candy disappeared. The TV turned off and on into channels of static. On Sundays, the TV blared public access sermons from decaying looking pastors. Alma thought it was possible that there were multiple ghosts. Maybe Esperanza led them there. These hauntings were reminders to Alma. She was more afraid of being like her mother than anything else in the world. She was also the most exhausted she had ever felt in the entirety of her life. Newborns are hauntings of their own. Alma often asked herself, *what if my baby doesn't live past childhood, what if my baby disappears into a void, what if my baby grows to loathe me?*

Esperanza was excessive in aggression and disdain. With mess came punishment. Isolation. Ridicule. Comparison to a made-up perfect child. Psychological games created to interrogate Alma. *Who do you think you are? Why did I get punished for bringing you into this world? When will you learn?* Spilled milk was an ordeal. Esperanza slapped Alma in the face every time she accidentally dropped crumbs of food on the floor. Specks of mud on her shoes or on the back of her heel meant she had to scrub the floors with a toothbrush. Evidence of play was scoffed at and came with an excessive chore. So Alma tried to stay as still as she could. Barely a word spoken to prevent a potential fleck of spit from catapulting out of her mouth. Barely a cough or a grunt or an inhale of loose mucus. Alma was hyper aware of the body that Esperanza told her sloppily kept her together. Alma's relationship to her own body was malformed and complicated.

Then Alma became pregnant. Her body became a home for someone else. Her personal hauntings interweaved into her DNA swirled in her womb water and yet her baby still thrived. Heart. Lungs. Brain. Bones. Ether. All components of this baby were perfect. A healthy baby with no father, but healthy meant Alma was off to a good start. Healthy meant her body listened to her prayers. She prayed every night to any saint who cared to listen. *Please let my baby survive me. Please let my baby survive. Please let me meet my baby. Please.* She was eternally grateful Esperanza could never meet her grandchild. Alejandro Alba Favela. He was born on the first day of spring. Alma panicked as he cooed on her chest. The tremendous responsibility of keeping a creature alive settled into her. She felt an overwhelming warmth. A rush of monarchs twirling in her belly. She could only feel love and this was undeniable proof that she would never be like her dead mother.

The fever dream that is watching over a brand new baby is a blur and a bending of time. Half of the time, there's a sense of dread. The other half is relief. Relief when the baby sleeps. Relief when the baby latches. Relief when a baby in the house feels familiar, as though there could be no other timeline, no other way to exist. This helpless creature needed to exist for Alma to feel like there was some form of fairness on the planet. She could not and did not want to remember life before Alejandro.

The relentlessness of watching over a new baby meant falling behind on simple tasks. Alma was alone and awakened every three hours throughout the night. Then there was the continuous scratching behind the walls. Her house was a mess. Piles of laundry sat in hills at the foot of her bed. The dishes in the kitchen were stacked and caked over with remnants of forgotten food. At night, the dishes tumbled onto the floor. Her bathroom was wrecked with bloody toilet paper and oblong pads strewn everywhere. She could not remember the last time she showered. The faucets turned on and off in the middle of the night. Dust settled on cabinets and dressers. Alma thought this was how she would die, in a tiny haunted house under piles of her own filth. Mess made her feel shame, ashamed her mother may have had a point about her, ashamed that grief had finally clawed into her chest. She missed Rodrigo deeply. It hurt to think about him never meeting Alejandro. Her chest ached when she thought about him. It made her dizzy. She wanted to scream until her throat went raw. There was nothing she wanted more than to have Rodrigo meet his son.

Then there was her Alejandro. He was perfect and quiet, until he wasn't. At two months old, it was as though something took over him. Alma was stuck in the middle of it. A postpartum body with no sense of connection to anyone. No sense of connection to itself. Just her and the baby. The baby who would need her until the day she died. Just her and the baby. Just her. Alone. Just her. Afraid. Only Alma to look after little Alejandro. Who cried and cried and sometimes made sounds that could be suffocation or gas or death or a simple dream. Every night, in between his feedings, Alma woke up hour after hour to watch him breathing. *Make sure he's breathing. Make sure he doesn't lie too still.* Her ear to his tiny mouth and nose to make sure his lungs were doing their job. Every night, the scratching behind the walls scraped into Alma's dreamscapes. The clawing screeched into her ears every night, making her dream about a hysterical urge to keep her body spinning in circles and then abruptly catapulting into the dark sky where red-tailed hawks pecked at her eyes and her palms. Every night, Alma panicked, fed him when he was hungry and watched over him as though tragedy was inevitable in her life.

Then she saw the creature. It was early in the morning. Crows cawed outside. Alma woke up groggy and drenched in sweat. In her sweaty pajamas and glistening face, she checked in on Alejandro. A short naked duende creature with long yellow nails was trying to breastfeed Alejandro. The creature's breasts leaked a milky substance onto Alejandro's face. Alma froze in disbelief. She slapped herself. The creature tried to leap out of the crib, but Alma got a hold of it and her first instinct was to strangle it. Alejandro's wailing filled the room. The creature was the size of a toddler with wrinkly moss-green skin. Alma felt sick. The creature was warm and very much alive and as Alma looked into the big yellow eyes of this being, the creature was obviously scared, but more so, the creature had the depth of grief in her eyes. Alma let go of the creature's neck and started to sob. The creature whimpered and held her belly. A red ooze poured out from between her legs. It looked slimy and smelled like wet dirt. Alma stuck her face into a pile of laundry and screamed. She swore she could hear the ocean, but it was Alejandro's crying. She got up to clean his face and held him to her chest. He stopped crying and let out a hiccup.

"Look, I don't know if you're even real. I don't know what you are, but I'm not going to hurt you. Get out of here. If you come back, I will kill you."

Alma opened the front door and pointed. Her sinuses were wrecked from crying and her hands trembled at the sight of this thing. The creature looked down with awe at a glittering red button and snatched it up. She put the button in her mouth and walked outside through the wildflowers. Alma took in three deep breaths and tried to ground herself. What did her feet feel? The hardwood floor. What could she smell? Her son's sweet barely-there hair. What could her body feel? A cold layer of drying sweat from her pajamas. Alma took in one last breath and kissed Alejandro on the top of his soft head. She settled him down and gave him a gentle bath. She checked his face for any allergic reaction to the creature's liquid and sobbed while washing his hair. She felt faint, but held herself together. She wasn't sure what to do about the creature. That gnome? Duende? Small demon? Did she need to kill it? Did she need to report it somewhere? Was this creature responsible for all the missing keys and candy that Alma kept in ceramic bowls by the front door? Was the creature real? She kissed Alejandro on his forehead, relieved he was okay. Alma considered her mother being behind this as an elaborate plan from the afterlife, but Esperanza would never approve of that creature. If something looked "dirty" her mother wouldn't give it the time of day.

Alma decided the creature had to be a duende. A duende explained the missing keys, candy, toys, and the clattering at night throughout the kitchen and bathroom. Alma settled Alejandro into his crib. The red body fluid from the duende was a blob on the outer space rug, as though it were a newly formed planet orbiting our sun. Alma got on all fours and examined the ooze. She hovered her hand over the fluid and then stuck her right hand into it. The consistency was like mucus, it felt sticky, and smelled sour. Alma felt the burn of bile rise in her throat and ran to the bathroom. She finally took a shower. As the steam of the shower built up inside, she smelled herself and shame overcame her. Her mother would have murdered her if she ever got this dirty as a kid. This made Alma belly laugh. She covered her mouth so as not to wake the baby and hopped into the shower.

At two months postpartum, her body felt like a distant entity that she had to figure out how to retrieve. How did she do it before? Would she ever love her body? How deeply did her mother's gaze demoralize her? The hot water felt like salvation. Alma thought about Rodrigo sleeping beside her in bed. Peace for a moment. Then the wailing started again.

As fast as she could, Alma wrapped herself in a robe and opened the door to the baby's room. The sad little duende was in his room again. Alma wanted to throw up. The duende pulled at Alejandro's feet, trying to drag him. Alma understood that motherhood meant sacrifice and making decisions that would be difficult and maybe bizarre, maybe life-altering. She felt no choice but to kill this thing. Alma was never a fight-or-flight survivor, she froze in times of panic, but this wasn't about her, it was about her son. The duende grabbed Alejandro's arms and then tugged him up by his underarms.

"Get the fuck away from him."

The duende lifted Alejandro up towards the edge of the crib. Alejandro's face was red from screaming.

"Put. Him. Down."

Alma bolted towards Alejandro, but the duende didn't budge. Alejandro's cries turned into screeching. The duende bit Alma's arm and drew blood, but Alma wasn't frightened, she was enraged. Why was this happening to her? Why was this a part of her motherhood journey? She bit the creature back. She latched onto the duende's shoulder with her teeth, took a chunk from the tough skin, and spit it onto the floor. The blood was bitter and metallic. Blood poured out of the duende's shoulder and into the crib. It let go of Alejandro, who was unscathed, but still wailing. The duende moaned in pain. Alma's chin and neck were covered in blood. She felt pity for the creature and she wasn't sure why.

"Why are you here? I told you I would have to kill you if you came back. Why are you back? Why would you come back?"

The duende pointed out the back door. They walked outside and it pointed to the neighbor's house. Alejandro continued to cry. Alma took him to her breast until he latched. The duende pointed to the next door neighbor's house. Alma's yard was outlined by a chain-link fence and the neighbor's house was guarded by a wooden privacy fence. She had seen her neighbors once or twice. A middle-aged man named Raul and an older woman, whose name she forgot and who she assumed was his mother. He worked during the day, some kind of office job, based on his outfits, and stayed in at night. They waved to each other if they both happened to check their mail at the same time, but they never spoke to one another. Alma assumed they knew Rodrigo was dead, but because he was the extrovert in their relationship, they minded their business. Alma heard Raul's mother singing to herself some mornings when she left the windows open, but otherwise, she didn't know much about them.

The duende scratched at the wooden fence with her yellow nails. She clawed harder and harder, her nails high-pitched against the wooden boards, blood continuing to spew from her shoulder. The creature continued scratching. Alma ran inside to the kitchen and grabbed a hammer from the junk drawer. Alejandro continued nursing. Alma felt a sense of warmth when she looked down at him. She held the hammer firmly in her right hand.

She thought about bashing the duende's head in, but couldn't find the heart to do it. Maybe it was her newly found mother's intuition or the idiocy of postpartum fog, but Alma slammed the hammer as best as she could into the wooden board. Over and over. She banged against the fence until it finally gave way. She switched Alejandro to her other breast and kept the hammer in her hand just in case. He drank happily. It dawned on her to simply walk over and let herself into their backyard. She walked through the house, out the dandelion yellow door, over to the house next door, unlatched the neighbor's fence and watched as the duende made its way through the makeshift hole they had just made together.

The duende pointed to the storm cellar in the neighbor's yard. Alma struggled, but managed to open the cellar. The waft of decay overtook all of her senses. The duende ran down the steps and yelped as she pulled at something small in the corner of the cellar. It was gaunt and clearly dead. The duende held it in her arms as she stepped out of the cellar. She put her breast towards the tiny thing, but the small creature was lifeless in her arms. It was her baby. The duende hummed to her baby. She held it to her chest and rocked side to side as though she were trying to lull it to sleep.

"How did it happen?"

The duende placed the baby gently on the ground and covered its face with her hands. Someone suffocated the baby. Alma felt sick.

"Who did this?"

The duende pointed to the neighbor's house. Alma felt faint and ran back to her own home. She wanted to throw up. She took Alejandro into her room, and placed him in his bassinet while she changed into fresh clothes. She chose a black floral sundress with tiny sunflowers patterned throughout the fabric, white gym socks, and her comfy red slides. Finally, she washed the blood off her face and looked into the mirror and wondered if she was dreaming. Was she in some kind of postpartum delirium? The duende returned to her backyard. Alma stepped outside with a hand shovel, a baby blanket, and a wooden crate. She dug at the earth beside the maple tree that held memories of Rodrigo. Taking selfies together. Making out without a care of who could potentially see them. Having hours of conversations and revelations by this tree. The duende watched and whimpered as Alma dug into the earth. Alma placed the baby blanket into the wooden crate and the duende placed her baby inside.

Then the duende helped with the digging until there was enough space for the crate. Alma grabbed the crate and placed it gently into the mini grave. They buried the baby together and then gathered wildflowers from the front yard to place atop the new resting place.

The duende fell asleep next to her baby's grave. Alma went inside to check on Alejandro who was sound asleep. She grabbed her cleaning supplies and scrubbed at the ooze on the rug. She wiped the blood off of the crib and changed the fitted sheet. She went through the kitchen, bathroom, and bedroom. She tidied each space because these were the menial tasks that could clear her head. She checked the backyard and the duende was gone.

After the burial, the hauntings stopped. It would be years later before Alma suspected the duende had returned to her old neighborhood. Raul and his mother were found murdered in their beds. Someone broke into their home, tore out their tongues then tore into their bellies. Viscera and maggots took over the house. Evidence of small footprints were photographed but never deciphered. No suspects were ever found. Alma had her suspicions but never spoke a word of it.

By that point, Alma had sold the little rectangular house and moved away with Alejandro to the small desert town where Rodrigo was buried. They visited Rodrigo often and Alma looked forward to confrontations with his parents. The town was full of ghosts and gossip, but most people were kind and welcoming. Alma felt a sense of peace living close to her husband's corpse. She talked to him at every visit as she cleaned his headstone and she let Alejandro run around the cemetery as though it were a playground. She let Alejandro explore and get dirt under his fingernails and on his knees. She let him be a kid and it gave her a sense of warmth and justice. Alejandro grew and grew and grew until he finally left the nest and Alma had no choice but to live for herself.

☼

Taíno: An Untold Story

Ivette N. Diaz

YIRABEL AWOKE WITH A JUMP, her heart racing from the nightmare. She placed a hand on her chest to calm its thudding. Their *bohio* was bereft of her parents' slumbering breaths in the dark, humid morning. All was quiet except for the nighttime ballad of the coquís. It had been three nights since her parents had disappeared.

The chief and nobles insisted that there was nothing wrong and that her parents were only on a long hunt, but she knew better. With the state of things, her parents would never leave her, or her brother Luco, alone for more than one night. One, if not both, would have returned by now.

With sleep now out of her grasp, she arose in silence, attempting not to wake up Luco, who slept in fits beside her on their mat. He had been struggling with feverish nightmares since their parents' absence. Even the mashed-up herbs she used on him didn't work. The heady herbal smell still lingered in the air as she tied her long, dark-brown hair back and crept to the kitchen only a few feet away. She stared at her parents' empty mat as she made herself breakfast.

A sinking feeling formed in the pit of her stomach. While she wanted to go back to the chief and nobles, she knew that neither she nor her brother were welcome back. She exhaled a frustrated breath. Being ostracized because Papi was from Spain angered her. He came with the other Spanish visitors that had landed on their island, Borîken, in their large *canoa*. Yirabel thought it was romantic that while his people had moved on to find gold, Papi had instead fallen in love with Bibi and the Taíno community.

Bibi told her that from the beginning, the chief and nobles frowned upon their union, which is why Papi and Bibi had been banished to the outskirts of the village. She was proud that Papi worked hard to learn the Taíno's language and ways, eventually earning the respect of many in the village. She loved her blended mix of Taíno and Spanish culture, speech, and beliefs. Yet the stubbornness of the chief and nobles kept them as outsiders because the chief believed the *zemi* didn't accept them. She knew he was wrong because despite the chief's boastful claim that the *zemi* had granted him spiritual powers she knew he didn't actually possess them – she and Luco did.

The coquís had quieted their singing by the time Yirabel finished her breakfast. The sun's rays still had not stretched over the horizon, and the sugarcane stalks that her Papi taught Bibi to grow were slick with dew, which would evaporate once the sun rose into the sky. Yirabel inhaled the sweet and earthy scent, hoping that the ominous feeling in her bones would not indicate the pace of the day. She got to work clearing a few stalks and pulling casava and yuca to prepare for the day. By the time Luco woke up, she had his breakfast ready.

"Where's Bibi and Papi?" Luco sipped on his water.

"*No sé*, but I'm sure they're fine. If we hurry and finish our chores, we can go look for them. *Waiba*," she ordered kindly. She didn't want to alarm Luco, but she wanted to enact her plan to find her parents today. She felt a stirring in her stomach and sent a silent prayer to the Almighty *Zemi* to protect her parents and guide her on their mission.

It was a little after the high sun when they finished their chores. The cicadas were buzzing as Yirabel gave Luco a quick lunch and packed an empty sack with provisions for their journey. Before dismissing her, the chief told her that her parents were hunting in Yuké and may have gotten lost. While Papi might get lost, Yirabel knew Bibi could never get lost.

"Where are we going?" Luco asked Yirabel as he handed her his empty plate.

"To Yuké, to find Papi and Bibi."

"How will we know where to go? El Yuké is huge." Luco tried to rummage through the sack. She swatted him away. He stuck out his tongue in response.

It was a good question. Yirabel paused and listened to the nature around her murmuring her prayer. Footprints with a faint glow appeared in the dirt heading away from the Rio Grande east towards Yuké. She pointed at them. "Look Luco. The Almighty Zemi will guide us to them."

A stir in the wind captured Yirabel's attention. She felt the air shift and saw a dark shadow move through the sugarcane stalks. A hollow face emerged, smiling malignantly. Her breath caught in her chest at the sight of Guacar. What was he doing here? They wouldn't be able to venture into El Yuké without protection. She needed something to ward him off. An idea formed. Shielding Luco, she pulled him back toward the hut. Guacar's words followed her inside. "You will never save them." An anxious knot formed in her stomach.

Luco grunted as he fought to put on the dark green *máscara*. "I hate wearing this. Why do we have to?" Yirabel pulled on her mask, then knelt and helped him place his *máscara* safely over his face. She touched the *máscaras* as she murmured a prayer. They glowed a bright green, then faded, a protection ward placed over them. Then she handed him a *vejiga*, the dried cow bladder smooth in her hand. It rattled from the dried seeds inside as he pulled it close.

"I know, but remember? Papi and Bibi explained that these *máscaras* will help keep the evil spirits away."

"Like Guacar?" Luco's hazel eyes, which matched hers, widened as he tilted his head to search behind her. Yirabel could have kicked herself. She could still feel Guacar looming about. Panic filled her. What if he was right? What if they couldn't find their parents, or worse, found them too late? The Almighty Zemi's presence filled her, and she slowed her breaths.

"Yes, but it will also help us blend in with the forest so predators can't find us." *And other enemies*, she thought to herself, but she didn't dare say it out loud and scare Luco more.

Luco started whining within a couple miles of their trek. The trees created a canopy from the sun, yet they did nothing to stop the sweat dripping down their bodies and pooling behind their *máscaras*. At the first pool of water she came across, they stopped to swim for a few moments. Yirabel enjoyed the cool water until her skin prickled. She felt another presence around them.

Guacar lurked in the shadows of the nearby tree line, approaching them slowly. The heat melted away as the air turned ice cold. The *máscaras* glowed. They would keep him at bay. She quickly gathered their things and pulled Luco out, forcing the *máscaras* back on. Guacar hissed and backed away.

The forest whispered to her, guiding her further into its depths. Light filtered through the moss-covered trees and danced on their arms, yet she hardly noticed as the sun sank lower in the sky. As she was about to concede defeat, she heard voices.

"They're speaking Papi's language." Luco's joyful voice echoed in the clearing. "Maybe they know where he is. Let's ask them."

Yirabel grabbed Luco by the arm before he could run off. They knelt on the ground as she peered through the thick underbrush. Luco stared at her curiously through the holes in the *máscara*. She calmed herself before she spoke in a low voice. "Do you remember what Bibi and Papi said? We can't trust anyone until we observe them first. We will stay quiet and hidden." Yirabel bowed her head and whispered her prayer to the Almighty Zemi.

"Bibi and Papi said not to use our powers away from home unless ab-o-so-loot-ly necessary!"

Yirabel tried not to laugh at Luco's attempted impression of their parents. "I know *mijo*, but this is absolutely necessary." She closed her eyes and whispered her prayer. The earth stirred beneath her. The ferns murmured, the orchids shivered, and the air hummed with warning. "Luco, these are not good men. We must not make a sound!"

Luco nodded solemnly. "I heard the forest's warning." Yirabel smiled at the gift to connect and talk to nature they shared from the Almighty Zemi. She cupped his chin in her hand, then placed a finger on her lips and motioned for him to follow her.

They swayed with the ferns and trees, mimicking the earth's noises and movements as they slithered through the tall grass. The insects scattered and the reptiles bobbed their heads before slinking away. The ferns in front of them parted a few inches as they approached, revealing an opening to a rocky area. A skinny waterfall poured into a pool of water that thinned out and became a river.

Yirabel peered through the ferns, a glint of metal catching her eye. Three men were talking to her right. A fire crackled on a rock not far away from them. Sacks, tools, gear, and weapons were scattered around. She had never seen conquistadors this close up before. They were arguing in Spanish, with a few words drifting through the air for her ears to catch. Her breath caught. Guacar floated around the men, who were so entrenched in their discussion, they did not feel his presence. She scanned the area for more. It was empty.

A moss-filled vine stretched out and tapped her on the shoulder. It pointed to her left. Tucked in the corner, on the rocks near the forest line, were two more people bound and gagged.

"Bibi! Papi!" Luco said. Yirabel clamped a hand over his mouth and pulled him away.

"*Qué es eso?*" one conquistador asked, breaking the conversation. Guns clicked and footsteps approached their hiding place.

She pulled Luco further into the brush, ducking as Guacar appeared, grinning and pointing in their direction. The conquistadors' loud stomping allowed her to avoid them until she found a dense area of trees with low hanging moss. Once safely behind them, she pushed Luco down into the dirt. His hazel eyes flickered with fear. She leaned her face into the tree and whispered into its smooth bark.

The tree shivered, followed by the one next to it, and so on, until the trees opposite their hiding place shook violently, catching the men's attention. They shouted and jumped over the thick grass in that direction. Guacar glared at her, growled, then chased after them.

Once the men disappeared, they crouched low and crept back towards the clearing. "Stay here," she commanded Luco.

"But I want to see Bibi and Papi," Luco whined.

"I know *mijo,* but you need to lie low and stay safe. I promise once I help them, I will bring them to you right away."

Luco huffed and folded his arms, but he obeyed and sat cross-legged on the ground, scooting under a large fern. Once he was hidden from sight, she checked the clearing before she exited. Her parents' eyes widened upon seeing her when she removed her *máscara*.

"*Mija*, what are you doing? The men will kill you!" Papi protested when she removed his cloth gag. Once he was free, they helped Bibi.

"Where's Luco?" Bibi asked the moment they pulled the gag from her mouth.

"He's hiding in the trees. The conquistadors are being led away by the forest."

Her mother's dark eyes squinted. "You used your powers?"

Yirabel nodded. "I needed help finding you and Guacar is following us." Bibi gasped, clutching her warded necklace.

"Those men are bad news. They will bring more soldiers and burn down El Yunque if they see there are more of us." Papi's tan features frowned.

"The only reason they haven't killed us is because of Papi. Once they found out he was one of them, they spared us, but we weren't sure for how much longer. They asked me many questions about our people and if there was any gold here. I pretended like I couldn't understand them, but they would have figured it out. We must warn the tribes. Luco!"

Yirabel's brother burst out from the bushes and leapt into Bibi's outstretched arms. She hugged him and kissed his forehead.

Luco pushed off his *máscara* and turned to Papi. "Yirabel used her powers." Yirabel rolled her eyes.

Papi's laughter rumbled out. "Don't worry, Luco. She told us it was to protect you." He ruffled Luco's long black hair.

"I don't need protecting." Luco pouted. Yirabel playfully pinched his arms while he tried to squirm away.

"You will all need protecting now that we have found you! That was a nice trick you pulled." The conquistadors stepped from behind the trees they had disappeared through earlier. Guacar smiled wickedly from between the men. The one who spoke had a long peppered beard and held up a gun.

Papi stepped forward, his hand held out. "*Por favor*, I beg you. They are just children. Let them go."

Another man with a black curled mustache sneered at them. Guacar mouthed words into his ear that he repeated. "They are an abomination. How could you muddy our line with that?" He jutted his chin towards Bibi. Yirabel felt a fire grow within her belly that turned ice cold in her veins. "None of you will be going anywhere. This disgusting display ends here." The conquistadors lifted their guns.

"Run!" Bibi yelled, pushing them towards the trees. Gunshots rang in the air. The family ducked and pushed into the forest. Bullets whistled past them, cutting through the foliage.

Their route was hampered by the dense forest and Luco, whose short legs kept tripping on roots. They entered a clearing and stopped, panting. Papi scooped Luco up and handed him to Bibi. He placed a hand on her cheek. "Go. I will distract them."

Bibi grabbed his hand, yanking him back. "No! I won't leave you. I will stay while you take the children."

Yirabel felt a heaviness in her chest. She didn't want to lose any of her family. "No. I will stay. You go."

"No, Yirabel. We must protect you. Go home with your brother," Papi ordered, yet his light eyes were soft with emotion.

"I didn't come all this way to leave you behind. We either all go together or stay and fight. They will come for us either way." Yirabel set her shoulders back. The rumors of the conquistadors in their ugly metal armor, barbaric words, and actions were infecting their island. Their home. She would not let them hurt her family or her people. Not today.

Papi's brow furrowed. He opened his mouth to speak, but a deafening noise cut him off. He yelped in surprise, then fell to the ground, grabbing his arm. Guacar appeared in their midst, cackling. Bibi rushed to Papi's side, huddling down with Luco. Yirabel swiveled around. The conquistador, with the long peppered beard, stood behind them, gun held high, still smoking and propped on his shoulder. She tried to push her family to the right, but Black Mustache appeared from behind the trees, his gun aimed at them. The last man popped out from her left, panting. They were surrounded. Bibi helped Papi stand. With his uninjured arm, Papi pulled Yirabel close, attempting to shield his family.

"I told you that you wouldn't save them," Guacar taunted. Tears stung Yirabel's eyes.

"This was fun, but we are sick of this haunted place. It's time to end this and send you to the hell awaiting you." Peppered Beard's gravelly voice lilted over the clearing to them, along with Guacar's laughter.

Yirabel glared at Guacar, then closed her eyes. "Almighty Zemi, Guacar is influencing these men who do not love like You have taught us. They are only filled with hate. Please fill me with Your power so I can take them down once and for all to protect my family and my people. Your people."

The wind picked up. A tingling mixed with warmth started at her feet and worked its way up throughout her body. The trees whispered, the ferns shook, the coquís song filled the sky, and the wind roared in her ears. Time slowed down and she could feel every blade of grass move. She opened her eyes. Guacar leered at her, hovering over the clearing.

"You have desecrated this land and dishonored your God. Our Zemi. We will not be wiped from this land. You will."

"Oh, the abomination knows how to speak our language," scoffed Black Mustache.

"And it will be the last voice you hear," Yirabel called out. She walked forward, then knelt down and dug her hands into the damp soil, inhaling its moldy scent. Ferns lashed out and wrapped their long tendrils around the arms of Black Mustache, pulling his gun from his grasp. He struggled, yelling for help, but the vines from the trees wrapped around his mouth and neck cutting off his voice. His eyes bulged as the ferns pulled him down. The ground shook, opening to reveal a small cavern where insects of all kinds churned within its depths. Black Mustache fell inside and was enveloped in the ground. His muffled cries were cut off as he disappeared.

"What witchcraft is this?" the conquistador to her left yelled as he charged. Yirabel stood, yelling a command in Taíno to the trees. The nearest one bent low, capturing the man in its branches. He battled against the onslaught, but more trees wrapped their branches tight around his body. The gun fell.

Birds of prey pelted the sky and circled the area, awaiting their next meal. The trees swayed back and forth with intense motion until they leaned back, scraped the ground, and then launched forward. They released the conquistador into the air, his screams echoing into the distance until they were snuffed out with a thud. The only sound left was the screech of the birds of prey as they swooped in the distance. Guacar snarled. He stepped into the last conquistador's body.

"*Demonio!*" Peppered Beard shouted as he shot off a round, the smoke curling in the air. Bibi screamed. Yirabel stood her ground, her hands reaching forward. A rush of wind blew from behind her, gusting so strongly she struggled to keep upright. The bullet slowed, a breath away from her nose when it was pushed back, flying out of sight.

Peppered Beard dropped his gun in shock, then turned and fled. Yirabel undulated her tongue. The water from the waterfall rushed over the trees from her left, pursuing its prey, and disappeared into the trees. A moment later, a ball of water sprang from the tree line with Peppered Beard trapped inside, upside down. He gurgled, his face turning purple. The ball of water stopped in front of Yirabel. She parted her hands, creating a pocket that allowed Peppered Beard's face out. He gasped for breath. Guacar forced himself out of the man's body and splashed through the bubble onto the ground, panting. She stepped forward and leaned down to be eye level with them. Peppered Beard's eyes were wild, shifting back and forth, as he tried to understand what was happening.

"I wanted to correct you. We are not demons." She glanced at Guacar, whose face was a mask of rage. "We are people who serve the same Almighty Zemi." She faced the conquistador again. "You just chose to see Him as a Zemi of hate. We know He is a Zemi of love. You will not see us in hell, but you will see your brethren there – those who lie and kill our people in the name of Zemi, who wants you to know that He does not agree with what you are doing. Now your punishment awaits." Peppered Beard shook his head as the water covered his face again. With a toss of her hand, the water bubble sailed into the air, taking Peppered Beard to sit at the bottom of the ocean where no one would find him.

Guacar roared and leapt at Yirabel. She stumbled backward. Suddenly, a bright light filled the sky. Guacar cowered back, then slunk into the shadows of the trees. As the light faded, a figure smiled at her as He disappeared. The Almighty Zemi! Warmth spread through her. Once He was gone, the air stilled, the trees rustled back into place. The coquís quieted their song, and the ferns tickled Yirabel's arms as they calmed. Something rattled behind her. She jumped and turned to see Luco shaking his *vejiga*.

"That's right! Go away and leave us alone," he shouted, his voice muffled behind his *máscara*. A fern next to him shook to the rhythm of the rattle until Luco stopped.

Yirabel laughed, ruffled his hair, then pulled him into a hug. She knelt down and pushed up the *máscara* from his face. "You did a great job. You're so brave!"

"I know! I'm just like you, Papi, and Bibi!" Luco grinned from ear to ear. Yirabel pulled him into another fierce hug until he scrambled away.

Bibi was on the ground gathering herbs from the surrounding brush that offered themselves to her. She created a salve and placed it on Papi's arm. "Thank the Almighty Zemi that the bullet only grazed you! You have a gash, but nothing too serious. This will help with the pain and cleanse the wound to prevent it from getting infected." Using a vine that had dropped down from above, she tied Papi's arm to his body and roped it loosely around his neck to keep it from moving.

Papi stood and kissed her on the top of her dark head. He pulled them all close, tears glistening in his eyes. "I am so grateful that you are all safe. Let's praise the Almighty Zemi for His help and protection." They held hands and murmured their thanks.

Bibi picked up their hunting gear. She handed a spear and arrows to Yirabel to carry, allowing Papi to protect his arm. "I'm ready to go home," she said as she kissed Yirabel on the cheek.

"Me too," Papi chimed in.

"Me three! I'm hungry!" Luco complained.

They exchanged smiles. Yirabel reached into her sack, pulling out a mango that she handed to Luco, who hummed as he munched on it. She gave mangos to her parents and took one out for herself. They ate in silence until she felt the need to speak. "I think we need to speak with the *cacique* and *nitaínos*. They would have left you both to die because of their dislike for Papi. We cannot have them become like those conquistadors."

Bibi rubbed Yirabel's shoulders. "You are absolutely right, *mija*. We will speak with them together. As for tonight, I just want to go home with my family and be thankful that we have another night together."

"Ab-o-so-loot-ly!" Luco mimicked.

Their laughter rose into the darkening sky. The stars twinkled above them. Yirabel stared up at the moon that smiled down at her. Peace filled her as she heard the Almighty Zemi speak into her soul, "Well done, my good and faithful servant." She smiled back, silently thanking Him again for His protection, their gift, and His love.

The Mother of Canals in Dade County

Laura Diaz de Arce

THE HEAT of the straightening iron bit into the side of Mary's scalp. It was a comfortable pain, the welcoming of an old friend that struggled to tame her hair that yearned to curl in the humidity. Each clamp of the tongs had an uneven rhythm she could focus on. The click as it subdued her hair to a more acceptable texture.

She would have to finish her hair straightening, complete the rest of her makeup to be at church well before the 7 a.m. sermon. George had been wanting to get there earlier and earlier and give her less time to prepare herself, though he demanded the same level of attention to her presentation.

"My love, you look like a vision," he said while she worked. His hand clutched at her shoulder, inevitably running over a bruise she'd been ignoring. He'd said women like her were insatiable, and his duty, as her

The Mother of Canals in Dade County

husband, would be to tame her in their bedroom. He read her hesitation as coyness. Her easing away as an invitation. The nervous flicker of her eyebrow as seduction. There were little markers of his affection across the planes of her body. Reminders of the nights before where the wounding of her was his foreplay.

He leaned over her and kissed her cheek, and Mary was treated to the sour smell of his breath. He smelled of discounted Folgers, overpriced cologne, and sweat. A haunting combination that stained him and her.

"Get a move on, Mary. The Lord does not like to wait."

She burned through the last strands before tucking them back behind her bangs. She doused herself in hair spray and pink polyester before tucking herself into the front passenger seat. George put on the radio and otherwise they were silent on their short car ride to New Bethlehem Evangelical Church. This was fine by Mary – she'd become less inclined to talk these days. Her tongue felt thinned in her mouth, unwilling or unfit to broker argument. It was not that George was violent all of the time, more that he won his battles by attrition. He'd nag, argue, and scold for longer than necessary, until any thought against his drew an overwhelming sensation of exhaustion that it was just easier to do what he said, think what he wanted, be what he wished.

His violence did not always need a fist, he'd won the fight before it started.

One of the church's a/c units was broken. It let out a low, pitchy noise that reverberated in the rafters. Mary had a suspicion that perhaps her hearing was more acute than others, because the congregants appeared not to notice it. She had an hour of sermons to witness beneath the hard white ceiling reflecting that pitchy buzz. A buzz so sharp she could feel the vibration of it on her tongue.

This was a far cry from the church she'd grown up in. People could be a little more relaxed, and they could come for community. But George had been clear about his beliefs before they got married. Her community forsaken, and she gifted herself to his congregation.

On a hot August Sunday, Mary fought the urge to close her eyes. She folded her features into that masked face of prayer. But her thoughts were not on Christ. She dreamt of cool, muddy water on grassy embankments.

Sometimes when her husband wasn't home, Mary would sneak out to the backyard and take a dip into the man-made canal. It was dangerous to do it. Every body of water stood the risk of having a gator or a water moccasin no matter the location. Those beasts had never paid Mary any mind. She'd gotten up close next to a few and if anything, they had always bowed out of her way.

If she closed her eyes, pretending to pray, she could be there. She could feel the slithering wetness climb from her toes up to her calves. She could smell the heat-dried dirt that kicked up in the man-made wilderness. Low plants curled around and cut her toes.

Meteorologists are still tracking Tropical Storm Andrew to get a better grasp of its path. As of yet, the storm may dissipate before reaching the Caribbean.

Some days Mary was allowed to volunteer at the retirement home sponsored by the church. It wasn't particularly enjoyable, but it got her out of the house. Spending the day helping clear bedpans, wash dishes, change sheets and fold clothing was somehow more bearable to do when it wasn't being done in the walls of her own home. She'd gladly trade the brand-new tile countertops for the peeling beige Formica at the facility.

There she could move around the maze-like layout of the facility in silence. Too many of the residents were far gone into dementia. They might be propped up outside their rooms or in the common area by their aides. Their reactions were molasses, and they were little more than urine-soaked, wheezing statues.

The isolation of her tasks suited her. And she had no necessity for friends.

Except one.

La Señora Carmel was a senile woman who, though late in her eighties, had been spry enough to run her way around the retirement home. She thought every aide and volunteer was her daughter, including Mary. She would grasp Mary's hand and rub her thinned, bony fingers that were worn soft through time over Mary's. While Mary was not typically taken with people, La Señora Carmel reminded her a little of the women who had raised her in the orphanage.

"Mi hija, que tan linda estas," she would say and press a paper kiss on Mary's hand. She smelled like foot cream, baby powder, and violetas. "Tienes piel tan suavecito, como un rio."

She died last night. According to the charge nurse, her last words had been about how loud the rain was, although there was none.

Mary stood in her empty room. La Señora Carmel's body had been carted away to the funeral home that morning. They'd already boxed her belongings. Little photos and trinkets, her figurines and her perfumes were in a box on the dresser, ready to be claimed by her real daughter. If Mary stuck out her tongue, just a hint, she could still taste the scent of that foot cream and powder. The shape of the old woman's figure sitting up against the bed, a stack of cards, also in that box, their shadow lingering on her nightstand.

Mary was not given to ghosts, but what a pleasure to be haunted in that little room with one of the few people she had come to care for.

"Well, Mariquita, si me ayudas a ponor las sábanas en la canasta—" Another volunteer, Maya, walked in, carrying a laundry basket in one arm and a spray bottle balanced on her elbow.

"Mary," she corrected. No one had called her Mariquita since she was a child. She never went by the name. George had a hard time pronouncing it. Her name gave her nightmares. She heard her mother calling it on her deathbed. *Mariquita de mi tierra. Traje mi tierra conmigo.* An imagined thing, it must have been, since Mary's mother died shortly after giving birth to her. There was no way she would remember, but the women at the church orphanage had said it. And she had heard them whisper about her mother. *La pobre loca. Escapó solamente para morir.*

She had no father on her birth certificate. Her mother said it was Cuba and no one else was her parent. And then she hemorrhaged. She, the daughter of a dead, madwoman immigrant she'd never met could still hear the sound of her mother's voice in her dreams.

"Mary," Maya said, a little whisper to herself. "We'll strip the bed to get it ready for the new resident."

"I'm sad I didn't get to say goodbye to her," said Mary while helping Maya on the opposite side of the hospital bed.

Maya let out a sing-song humm. "Her suffering is gone."

Maya leaned over the bed to untuck the stubborn corner. A chain slipped loose off her shirt collar, and hanging in bright gold was a cross. Dangling next to the cross was a matching golden owl pendant dotted by little black stones for eyes. Mary took another long look at the woman. She had a white feather tucked into the base of her hair and she wore an evil eye necklace. On her ankle there was a small tattoo, some symbols in black slashes.

"I thought you were with the church," said Mary.

"I am," said Maya.

"A parishioner?"

"Yes." Maya's face was turned away from Mary's focused on the task of unfolding a new fitted sheet.

Mary stuck her tongue partly out of her mouth. There was a sour scent in the air, like an overripe orange. Maya's scent was that of watery leaves, bark, and the night sky. But when Mary mentioned the church, that sour smell made it taste astringent.

"But you don't want to be," said Mary.

Maya's eyes were overlarge, and dominated her face beneath a strong set of brows. From across the bed, Mary could see that her irises were rimmed in a bright yellow. The type of yellow of a yield sign. Mary did not want to yield. There was a challenge in that golden gaze. It resulted in a curl in Mary's belly.

"I have accepted Christ," said Maya, turning her head but keeping her eyes on Mary. "But that does not mean I have left everything I was."

They were interrupted by Mr. Walter, walking into the room, searching for his bed pan or jello, it was difficult as his words slurred.

"Aye, Mr. Walter. Look at you, let's find your nurse," said Maya. She smiled at the old man and put a hand on his elbow and shoulder. "And look at that," she tapped his upper back, "you've put your shirt on backwards." Maya escorted the old man from the room.

At home that afternoon, there were men in her backyard with vests and hard hats, looking at the canal.

"I'll go see what that's about. Stay," George said to Mary.

She watched from the window as the men gestured to the canal length. One held up a set of papers at George and pointed down the water's length. Mary couldn't hear what they were saying, and their faces were turned away. Her nails scratched at the windowsill. A possessiveness tingled her toes at their intrusion.

George turned back towards the house. Mary ducked away from the windowsill.

"What was that about?" asked Mary, when George shut the screen door.

"Those guys are with the county. Seems they were lowering the canals because of the storm season. They're trying to figure out why they aren't able to pump water out of our canals."

"Well if the storm isn't coming, do they still need to drain them?" Mary asked.

"It's none of your business," said George.

Mary snuck glances at the men walking up and down the canal while she made dinner. She could almost feel their agitating steps as they trudged on the embankments.

The men left when it started to get dark. She only half listened to the news and George's commentary on it as he settled in for the evening. It kept her agitated through her already unnerving nights.

Nights were the worst. It was the two of them in their pastel-toned home. Their townhouse was in the latest suburban beachy style, compliments of a catalog. Peaches, faded pinks, and light blues splayed on wicker furniture. There were seashells everywhere. Patterns on the sinks, seashells in bowls. Seashell pillows and prints of the beach on their walls.

Never mind that Mary hated the beach and that to her, the ocean smelt of death.

At night, that palette glowed a sickly beige, the color of a rat's tail, by the light of the TV. George would stretch out on the couch, half asleep. If she were lucky, he'd be tired enough to leave her alone. If she wasn't, he'd get up from his place on the couch. His shadow, a growing presence in the artificial light would be her only warning as it lingered over her to her place at the kitchen table.

There was a time, early on in their relationship, where she actually somewhat enjoyed sitting together. He was good about it then, before their marriage. He didn't begin pressing or demanding until after their wedding day, when it became her duty to provide marital covenant.

He demanded that regularly.

She'd hide at the table, or linger at the sink, even when the dishes were done. She'd sometimes let the water wash over her fingertips. The soothing coolness lifted away the trapped feeling for stolen moments. The water keeping her from the kitchen that held sterile promises in the night.

That worked less than half the time. His figure would darken the doorway. His presence took up the space in the hall, and he would come forth and envelop her, swallow her form in an imitation of seduction. Succumbing with unwillingness.

When he fell asleep, she was unable to keep away from her own temptation. Those men had stomped her embankments she needed to reclaim its safety. Mary slithered from their bed and crawled out of their home through the back sliding door. Not wanting the neighbors to see her still nude, she army crawled, dragging her belly through the grass and dirt to the edge of the canal.

It was a compulsion to dip her fingers in. The night outside was her solace and the water called her as a siren song just as she called to it.

With a beastly stillness she tilted her head forward. She stuck out her tongue and let the tip dip into the canal's surface. There she tasted the heady combination of flora and fauna. The earthy sediment that turned the canal its tea-color. The water vegetation that lent herbaceous and sulfuric notes to its taste. Mary extended her tongue further, and there the slick algae that stuck to turtle shells, fish scales and alligator tails coated her taste buds. Then there were those lingering chemical notes. Fertilizer, run-off and trash that made her tuck her tongue back.

When she stretched further, she could see her reflection on the surface. Her neighbor's patio lights gave her a sickly, yellow hue. The color of rotting lemon. She'd never been a good judge of beauty or looks. She found her body and the bodies of those around her to be inelegant. Her desire lay in sleekness. She kept her black hair long as it reminded her of water, and that hair cascaded its way into the canal. She closed her eyes to the sensation and wriggled deeper into the earth.

As she opened them, she could see a serpent, some sort of water snake gliding beneath. It was close enough to grab, and her fingers scratched at the edge, wanting desperately to touch it. Then the canal swallowed her wrist, her forearm, up to her shoulder. Hand outstretched, she could not touch the snake as it bobbed in the still water. Beckoning.

A dog barked down the street and it woke her from her revelry. She swiped her arm out of the water and shimmied her way back to the house, leaving traces of dirt beneath her fingertips to comfort her.

According to meteorologists Tropical Storm Andrew will probably reform as it hits the hot waters off the Caribbean. It's going to be a wet weekend.

There was one staff bathroom that the volunteers at the retirement home were permitted to use. It was set in the back with three small stalls and a backdoor to a side street. With halogen lights and peeling paint, its neglectful state was a contrast to the shining bathrooms in the guest lobby. But volunteers and staff weren't permitted to use that one.

The bathroom had an open drain in the floor that smelled of mildew. Every once in a while, something would creep from the drain, and Mary would sense its little legs scraping on the concrete edges. The small scraping movement of a centipede or cockroach tickled her.

On Thursday, she found herself more restless than before. An itchiness that settled over her. She scratched at the places where skin folded. The most vulnerable and weakened areas on her joints where the flesh was loosest, open to tearing. The base knuckles of her fingers were red and screaming with this picking. She let the cool sink water wash over her hands.

To her left, she heard a toilet flush and Maya exited the stall. Their conversation from the day before was haunting Mary. While she was typically loathe to talk to anyone, seeing Maya let all the words come unbidden.

"What do you mean not everything you are?" asked Mary, shutting off the water and peering behind her as Maya left her stall.

"¿Que que?" Maya opened the faucet and began to wash her hands.

"Yesterday, you said that accepting Christ didn't mean you had to give up everything you were."

Maya ripped away a paper towel and leaned back away from the sink as she dried. "I mean we have a history, you know, before the Christians came."

"We?"

"Us," Maya said. She turned, and in the mirror reflection was a gigantic owl, its lemon-colored gaze trained on Mary. Brown and white feathers peeked in annoyance.

Mary blinked and the owl was gone.

"I mean," continued Maya, "that we have older traditions, beliefs, and spirits of our own. We can share the gospel and our own songs." Maya placed a hand on Mary's cheek.

"*Us*," said Mary, the word dripping from her lips as if in a trance. Her eyes closed and she could hear the shadow of a song. The sound of her dying mother's voice calling to her. *Mi tierra, muero pero traje mi tierra.*

She licked her lips and she could taste the night sky and wet leaves. If she listened carefully, she could hear the wind of an oncoming storm. Miles away her body was a different instrument to those rhythms. Her innards swaying with the force of the gusts. "What traditions?"

"I don't know yours," said Maya. "Mine were given to me by my mothers, who got it from their mothers. Yours are different."

"How do you know they are different?" asked Mary, not noticing that she had again put her hand under the faucet, her fingers on one hand violently rubbing against the loose tissue between each digit.

"I'm not sure. But you feel it. We both feel it. And something is coming. ¿Sientes? It is making my kind fluff our feathers."

"Then what is yours? Why can't you just say it?"

"Mine are the earth and air and everything in between. Yours are, well, yours are something else." She gestured with her chin to the faucet. "You are of the waters—"

"¿Algen puede ayudarme con el Señor Pilar? Necesita una nueva pamper," one of the other volunteers said, coming into the bathroom.

"Ok, al pronto," said Maya, smiling at Mary and winking as she left.

"¿Y de que estaban hablandon?" asked the other volunteer.

"Mierda," replied Maya.

Mary didn't remember to shut off the water when she left.

Defying earlier projections, Tropical Storm Andrew has formed into a category 2 hurricane, with expected landfall on Jupiter Beach. Those in evacuation zones along the coast are urged to seek shelter.

Saturday services were canceled. It was just as well, she'd lain in bed all day with a migraine. George was too busy to argue the point as he tried (and failed) to hire someone to board up the house. He called multiple members of the church and his job to see if any of them may have sons or nephews who could work quickly. None were found. Many were unwilling since the hurricane didn't look as if it would hit them.

"It's going to West Palm. To the country clubs there, and they are paying good," said one of the contractors he called. "Why don't you do it yourself?"

"Well it's just me and the wife, and my back has been acting up, but where do I even get lumber?" George replied, after the seventh rejection.

"There's some in South Homestead, last I heard. Worse comes to worse, you can try duct tape on your windows."

George set off to hunt for wood to board up their home. Mary lay in bed, nursing the pain in her skull. Light was painful, and she covered her face beneath coral-colored sheets in that pastel prison she was in. When her fingers glided across her scalp, there were two tender, pointed bumps above her eyes. When she stuck out her tongue, she tasted rain, even though it was dry and sunny as the distant hurricane sucked away the humidity.

What had been only a tropical storm less than three days before had turned into a hurricane. She had known it. Deep in her bones she had tasted the wind. The anger in those winds and the storm. It tasted like sea water. It tasted like death.

When George arrived home, cursing from the lack of available supplies, he had Mary help him prepare their

The Mother of Canals in Dade County

home by commanding her around whatever menial tasks that he felt would be good for storm preparation. A skillset he had little experience in. She'd been born and raised in Florida weather and knew the preparations by heart. But every time a hurricane was to come, she'd get ill. The heady winds roared in her own skull, but at least she understood the need to bring in lawn furniture.

She could feel the difference of the storm in the way it reminded her of how trapped she was. There was a rising nausea that settled in her belly. When she went to the bathroom, while sitting on the toilet, she noticed a peeling between her toes. The edges of her feet had a blackened sheen to them and itched. She put her hands to the little bumps at her head, and noticed with distress that they were ever-so-slightly taller and more pointed.

Hurricane Andrew has adjusted its track south and is now a category 5 hurricane, with 165 mile per hour winds. We now expect it to land in Dade County.

George had taped the windows, but also paid an exorbitant amount to buy plywood. They spent the morning boarding up the windows.

Then they were together in darkness.

Mary wrapped her fingertips in band aids to hide the fact that her nails had fallen off. They'd begun loosening the night before, and as she washed her face, the nail of her ring finger caught on her hairline. When she pulled it had broken free and hung limply on a strand. When she examined her other fingers, she slipped off her nails one by one, leaving a mucus-like sheen on the nailbed.

George didn't notice the band aids, thankfully. He was too wrapped up in the news and in making sure their home would be under control. Mary sat on the couch next to him, breaking to make lunch and dinner, in the glow of the TV until that too went out.

Then there was nothing but George's demands on her body. He needed to relieve stress, he said. That nausea grew.

When the first bands of the hurricane hit, it sounded like an oncoming train. Mary could feel it more than hear it. The sound woke her, but the feeling of it made her restless. She tiptoed from their bedroom and took a peek out of the edge of the kitchen window.

Across the lawn, the canal's water was a turbulent series of waves. They beckoned her. They begged for her to go outside. There was Maya's voice in her ear. *Us*, she had said. *Like us*. She watched in horror as the water of the canal was pulled along in great gusts to the lawns. Mary needed to touch it. She needed to make sure it was alright. *Us*.

Barefoot, in her pajamas, she wrenched open the door. A gust knocked her on her ass as the door was torn from it's hinges, but she crawled on her belly, closer and closer to the water. From a tree in a neighbor's yard, yellow owl eyes blinked at her from in between the branches. She stood, because the storm was a new song. Rain, rocks, sticks, trash pelted her as she marched against it to the water's edge.

Behind her she heard George calling. She turned in time for him to run out after her, only to witness a broken pole lance him through the foot. He screamed. Mary smiled.

The wind whipped around her, pulling and tearing at her skin and hair as she was lifted into the hurricane's embrace. She could feel her body flake away. Layers stripped like a peeled orange. But this was not death for her.

Human skin, muscle, sinew, and flesh tore. As it was carried away by the wind and rain, something new emerged. Beneath the flesh were scales, silken and smooth. Coffee-colored patterns dotted her form. Beneath her hair unfurled two horns. Their mighty points thrashed at the wind, calling down the rain in a language only nature knew. She'd been the pretender and in its place was the remnant made whole.

The hurricane dropped her and she slithered on the grass, heading back towards the canal.

Eaten Alive

J.F. Gonzalez

AVERAGING IN SIZE as large as a dinner plate, the South American Goliath Bird-Eating Spider is the largest spider in the world.

Cindy Jacobs had seventeen specimens in her collection.

They were among one hundred arachnids she kept in various cages in the spare bedroom of the large Tudor-style home she shared with her husband Scott.

Spiders had always been her obsession. Her collection started with a single red-knee tarantula. Thanks to breeding and careful selection from various rare animal dealers, she was able to amass quite a menagerie.

Feeding them was always a problem, though.

The smaller spiders were easy. All she did was pour a bag of crickets into various cages and let nature take its course. For the larger tarantulas, small vertebrates were a necessity and her neighborhood pet store kept a steady supply of pinkie and fuzzy mice on hand.

Feeding the Goliaths was like feeding a small python. She had to kill the mice and small rats she bought for them to avoid damage to her pets.

She didn't mind though. It was all part of the research she was doing.

She stood in the basement of the house watching the Goliaths as they fed. She had taken them downstairs individually in shoeboxes for this experiment, which she'd been working on the past few months. She wanted to prove her own theory that they'd feed on anything.

According to current scientific data, Goliaths fed on insects and small vertebrates such as frogs, salamanders, lizards, snakes, rodents and birds. This was their natural diet in their native habitat, the jungles of South America. In captivity, hobbyists generally offered them small mice. By instinct, the spider would sink its fangs into its victim, injecting it with venom that would render them paralyzed and would immediately begin digestion of the flesh. The spider then sucked all the fluids out of its meal, leaving an empty shell of skin.

The venom of a Goliath Bird-Eating Spider is no more toxic than that of a red-knee tarantula. What made their bite so painful and potentially dangerous was the length of their fangs. At one inch in length, they could inject their venom deep into your muscles, causing severe pain, partial temporary paralysis, and in severe cases partial necrosis of tissue.

Scott had become verbally and physically abusive with her the morning he found that her research with the Goliaths had cost the life of their house cat, Betty. Cindy had been excited when, after starving her two female Goliaths for over two months, they'd lunged at the cat after Cindy lowered her carefully into the bathtub with a set of tongs. She'd released one of the tarantulas into the bathtub moments before and waited till that first one was occupied with sinking its fangs into Betty before releasing the second one, which made a quick lunge for the cat's hindquarters at the first scent of prey. Cindy had hated the cat anyway. Breaking its neck had been relatively easy.

That phase of her experiment proved to be a milestone. Only Scott hadn't been so happy. She'd born the scars from his beating for over a month.

It had taken all her effort and vigilance to keep him out of the room she kept her spiders in. She'd had a locksmith install a special lock on the door months ago. Day jobs kept them away from each other during daylight hours. His philandering and drinking kept him from the house at night, leaving her to continue her research and plan the current phase of her experiment.

It had been hard to starve all seventeen of her Goliaths, but it was the only method she knew of to create a sense of ravenousness in them. All of the experts in arachnids unanimously agreed that spiders – especially tarantulas – would not eat prey that was larger than themselves, even if they were starving. Cindy had proven that theory wrong with Betty.

She was proving it now with Scott, who lay paralyzed on the basement floor. She'd taken him down with one well-placed taekwondo kick that snapped his neck, severing his spinal cord, and she'd waited till he regained consciousness before she started bringing the Goliaths down one by one.

The pain and horror in his eyes was evident as the first one crawled tentatively onto his stomach and then stabbed its fangs into his flesh.

The rest had followed suit as she released them.

She stood watching, wondering how many feedings it would take for Scott to be completely desiccated.

El Puente

L.P. Hernandez

EMBERS POP FREE from their charred mesquite prison as if to take their place among the constellations. New shapes to replace the old. New stories sparkling over a new world. And beneath them, a man whose blood makes a trail to his fallen body wonders why it is taking so long to die.

One by one, the embers fail to reach the heavens, winking out of existence like so much he has known. So much before him he can never know. He wears one ragged boot. The other is likely in a buzzard's belly. Its leather was cracked and flaked, the porous sole inviting detritus rather than keeping it away. He left it behind. With the wound above and to the left of his heart, he didn't think it mattered much.

He has enough knowledge and will to coax a fire from nothing but wood and grass. Better to die to that familiar sound than listen to his own final breath. But the fire is waning. With his remaining boot, he nudges the nearest chunk of wood. It does not invigorate the fire but crumbles with a puff of smoke. He taps another and it achieves the desired effect. Flames bloom with tatters of sunlight. His skin stiffens and he shivers. It is not the cold of the world around him. It is the cold within, and no fire will touch it.

His death will come soon, he thinks. He has been drinking from puddles as he found them, has eaten only grasshoppers. There is nothing to forage, only mustang grapes out of season. He has no bow, and no animal would wait for him to throw his knife at it.

There are warriors in his blood, but it is still, pooled in his veins as his heart counts down the minutes. He was born of violence, and so there are conquerors in his blood. Two enemies on a sinking ship.

"It would have been better to die in battle," he tells the wind. Wood pops and a frenzy of sparks rush the sky but do not reach it. That is not their destiny.

"How would you know?"

The voice might have come from the earth. Might have been a memory. He twists, seething, and lifts his head. Blood returns to his fingertips like shards of glass.

"Who said that?"

The canyon walls rise to either side of him. This place had a different name once, but it is an empty space in his mind. A held breath neither coming nor going. His voice returns to him, and he does not recognize it.

The deer steps free of the shadows kept at bay by the fire's glow. Its hooves are as quiet as the beating of butterfly wings.

"Have you lost your words?"

The man sits upright. The muck in his veins stirs. He feels the strain of it. The clot in his chest bulges with the pressure. The deer did not speak, could not have. But there is not a soul within fifteen miles. The man who shot him, running away, wouldn't waste the effort to pursue him. There is only grass grown wild around the yellowing bones of bison felled from a rifle aimed out the window of a passing train. The thunder of rolling iron replacing the thunder of the herds in Comancheria.

"My words?"

He looks beyond the deer. Maybe it's domesticated and its master near.

"Your language."

Still squinting, he says, "I never had them. They lashed us until our tongues moved like theirs."

The deer is old, or perhaps diseased. One eye is onyx. One eye is a ghost, grayed beneath a film the color of a cloud-hidden moon. A buck with one broken antler. The other is hardly a two-knuckle growth but still looks too heavy for its thin neck. Its tongue lolls from its mouth. The deer nibbles at a bit of scruff, the shallow roots breaking free of the earth with the slightest tug.

"Is this how you want to die?"

It's such a surprising question the man laughs then clenches his teeth at the fresh pulse of pain.

"A warrior's death, if I had a choice."

"But you ran away."

"He had a gun."

"Seems like that was your wish. To die fighting."

"Wouldn't have been a fight. He would've put four bullets in me before I was close enough to touch him."

"Many warriors die far from the battlefield."

The man spits, lays his head across his arm again. "Yeah, well, doesn't matter now. Least I get to die hating him. Him and his kind."

The deer folds its legs beneath its body. "What would you do to them? If you could do anything?"

* * *

He blinks and opens his eyes to unfamiliar colors and an unfamiliar perspective of them. He is running, but grass tickles his face. He is chasing a coyote, its tail dusting his nose. Shoulder still aches but the pain is different. A dream, must be.

Just over there.

A series of yaps, but he understands.

Where are we going?

He is not chasing the coyote. They are running together.

To the beginning.

The coyote runs faster. His legs become a blur attempting to match pace. His paws become a blur. *Paws.*

The beginning of what?

The coyote, his companion, sprints as if fleeing a prairie fire, but it's not smoke he smells. The meadow parts and they stand together. What he sees, through his new eyes, he understands in principle. He knows the word for it, but it is disconnected from any memory.

Oceano.

Ships on the water and rowboats on the shore. Men in armor on the sand. Men in hides on the border between the prairie and the beach. Not *his* people. These are fishermen, not warriors.

This is the beginning. Those men on the beach are the forebears of the men who will cut the tongues from your mouth and replace them with their own. They will burn your gods for theirs. They will build churches over your burial grounds. This is the beginning. Two worlds. Nothing in common but the air they share.

An elder steps forward. He holds something against his belly. A hare, maybe. A man in armor meets him, flanked by men with shields. The hare passes from the elder to the conqueror. In place of words there are gestures. A bow and sweep of the arm. The man in armor points to the ships. His hands spread to indicate the distance they traveled.

We can end it here. We can poison the water on the ships. They will become a curious addition to the horizon. Until time and the weather have their way.

The coyote retreats to the safety of the tall grass and rests its head on its paws.

They would not return? Spain would not send more ships?

The coyote licks its paws, hesitates.

This has not happened, and so it is not known. Spain might send more ships. An armada. They might blame the coastal tribes for what they find floating on the water.

The stink of sweat and fish wafts from the armored men. He smells sickness too.

It might be worse?

Might, but you would not know. This would change everything, including your birth.

My birth?

How could it not? The coyote yawns and stretches.

This is only a dream. This isn't real. This would have been hundreds of years ago.

It is your dream, brother.

Not this. Something else. Does my father still live? The man who...

In your time he does not.

My time?

You are dreaming. Are you not? Dreaming and dying alone in a canyon.

How did he die?

Alone. Shitting his guts out. Father and son. At least you will die with your pants on.

He is not—

He is. Or does your mother have green eyes?

On the beach, the men have separated. The hare's paws graze the sand. An afterthought.

Did he know the pain he caused? The suffering?

He did know it, but not in life.

Where is he now?

The coyote who was once a deer stands and shakes the sand from its fur. The coyote who was once a man does the same.

*Where they all go. Where **we** all go. After, and before.*

After and before?

The coyote winks its milky eye.

It is not your fault you lost your words, brother. In the old tongue, there are words for it.

Ships on the horizon. Men with an apocalypse in their blood. Some of which found its way to him.

Somewhere else, please. Not this.

* * *

The woman is made old from the life she led, not the years behind. Another woman, gray braids like shed snake skins on her back, sits beside her. Their hands are a loose pile of fire-kissed flesh.

Hello? he calls.

The woman seated on the bed shudders as if poked with a cold finger.

I am with you, brother. She cannot see you. Your aunt. Your mother is passing between worlds, so she may.

What are we?

You do not have a word for it.

He remembers his mother's skin in the sun, darker than his. In a generation, all she knew of the world had turned on its head. The old gods did not intervene. Those that fought were killed. Many that did not fight died anyway, blood on their lips and sweat shimmering on their foreheads as they whispered about the cold. The rest assimilated. The Spanish god was their god now. The man on the cross who was not one god but three.

Best not to fight. Best to smile. She had a nice smile.

"I prayed you would be born with his eyes. I prayed to their god and ours," she says.

Mama? You can see me?

Her eyes are closed, lips barely moving.

"He would know you were his, and he would not harm you. Us. I hoped."

He hated his eyes. His too-short nose.

"We could not stop what happened to us. It is like fighting the river with only your fingers."

He hovers inches from her face. *Are you not angry? Why did this happen to us? Our people lived in peace for thousands of years.*

Eyes closed, she smiles. It is not a beautiful smile now. She is missing teeth.

"My son, you had your whole life to find another path. Why am I not angry? I do not know what happens next."

* * *

The fire smolders past his feet. The knot of pain in his shoulder is cold now, the pain like a memory. The deer's head is draped across his torso.

"That was a lovely dream."

He holds the scent of his mother in his lungs. Not how she smelled at the end but from the past. Ash and salt and something sweet. The scent told the story of her life.

"Who are you?" the man asks.

The deer snorts, almost like a dry chuckle.

"The name would not make sense to you. Too much has changed since it was given to me. There is a story among your people. Those native to the lands south and west of here. They tell of emerging from darkness, from a time before the sun. A deer, they said, and maybe some still do, led them into the light."

The man strokes the soft hair of the buck's ears.

"It was you?"

Another snort. The embers flare for a moment.

"It was a beautiful story. Does not matter if it is true. Your time in the sun is over. I am here to guide you back to darkness, to the long sleep."

The air around them is silent, only the wind rattling the bones of skeleton branches. There was a time before his people, and there would be a time after. He sits up, cradling the deer's head between his hands.

"I feel better. I feel like I can walk again," the man says.

The deer stands, shakes the dirt from its fur.

"Good. Follow me."

The man stands, stretches. His fingertips scrape the heavens but do not mark it. With his remaining boot, he kicks dust over the dying fire until the only light is from the stars. The deer trots ahead and the man follows.

"I feel better. Stronger," he says.

"Good. Do not look back."

The man stops but the deer keeps going.

"What is behind?"

The deer stops, pivots its body.

"A dead man, but that is not all he is. Some get lost on this path. They wander back to what feels familiar. It isn't, brother. It is only recent. Do not grow roots in this place."

The man closes his eyes. He touches the area above and to the left of his heart. No pain. No blood. He cannot will it to hurt. The flesh is unblemished.

"It's me?"

"It is an echo. It will fade as echoes do."

It would not be a bad place to grow roots. Much feels familiar here. But he walks and does not look back. There is tension with every step, the connection between the past and himself like a rope pulled taut. He stops again.

"What's the meaning? Huh? What's meaning? All I did was suffer. All I did was hurt."

The deer speaks without stopping, and the man shuffles faster to catch its words.

"What is the meaning of a life? Is that what you would know? Of your life? My brother, there are many who suffer. What did you learn from it? There are many who hurt. What did it teach you?"

The man scoffs, "Learn from it? Teach me? I had no power. All it did was make me hate."

The deer's trot is now a run, and the man dodges bushes and exposed roots to close the distance. The white flash of its tail is like a far-off lantern.

"Wait! You're too fast!"

The deer darts left as if fleeing a mountain lion and disappears.

The man stops. It still feels like his body, like his legs. He is still bound by their limits.

"Hello?" he calls, his voice swallowed by a crack in the canyon wall.

"Brother?" he says, not knowing a better name.

The crack is just wide enough for him to enter. He twists his body and sidesteps, his cheek scraping the earth. *My cheek? How do I even have a body?*

"Some lives are not meant to be whole. Complete. Some lives are meant to offer only a sliver, a glimpse of the experience available. Life is not a story. You may not reach the end of it with a full understanding of its purpose. You are meant to live it. That is enough."

There is no light, no breeze. The world has stopped around him. His hands probe the darkness. His fingertips feel nothing.

"Are you here, brother?" he says, fear adding a tremor to his voice.

"I am with you."

"I cannot see," he says. He would leave but there is no light behind to guide him.

"You see enough. When you are ready, walk forward."

* * *

The man sits. There is earth below him. It is the only thing he is sure of.

"I do not understand, brother. Why am I here? I was shot. I understand that much. But why was I born? To be hated?"

"Were you only hated?"

The voice is in front of him and behind, to the left and right.

"No. My mother...I had a sister, too."

"So, what is your question, brother?"

He drags his fingertips over the surface of the world. He remembers a time when hatred was in the background of his life, whip cracks and screams beyond the wall of his understanding. He remembers his sister on his mother's back, the man with the green eyes who sometimes watched him from the balcony. He remembers the smell of rain on the wind before the first rumble of thunder. He remembers his mother pointing to a deer beyond the range of Spanish rifles. She whispers in his ear a story he will soon forget.

"What was my purpose in this life? I bore no heirs. I have never loved a woman. I fought no battles. I ran from shadow to shadow with a jackrabbit's heart in my chest."

A tiny light ahead. Not like a star but like a hole in the fabric of the universe. Then another, and another. One pursues the other. Ten, then one hundred. Swirling. There is a figure before him, a deer no longer.

"Your life was meant to be lived, and what you gathered from it you will return to all that is."

"I do not understand."

"You are not meant to. You are only meant to gather. Some men die as heroes. Some men die shitting their guts out. Neither is a complete story, just a moment in time."

The man steps forward. No legs now. No dirt beneath his fingernails. He feels like a breath on the wind.

"Some lives are bridges between what was and what is to come. They hold that space. They connect two worlds. In the stories of your people, there was once only darkness. A time before memory. A deer led them out of the darkness and into the light. It is a beautiful story, brother, and not far from the truth."

They hover over the precipice. To the spirit that was once a man, the lights swirling over infinity feel like home.

"You could have been the man in armor on the shore. You could have been the man who offered the hare. Maybe you were. In this life, you chose a different path. A lonelier path. You took hate into your heart and harbored it there. You kept it hidden. You could have spread it. Like a wildfire. You protected those embers, walked them into the canyon and waited for them to cool. You are a bridge, my brother. You are the thief and his victim. And the burden is no longer yours. Step forward. With your story. When you are ready."

Night of the Nagual

Pedro Iniguez

THE SUN BEGAN TO SET as Memo ambled down a rural road on the outskirts of Tochtepec. The dirt path wound through a fertile valley where farmers grew chili peppers, beans, and squash. The only schools were in the city and like many other children in the state of Puebla, he'd had to trek back home alone to his house in the country.

A breeze swept across the road, grasping his arms like long, cold fingers. For a moment he thought someone had called his name but he realized it had been the moaning wind and the creaking trees. He wasn't scared, though, and it hadn't bothered him that none of his classmates chose to walk with him. Memo preferred being alone. At an early age he'd learned how cruel other children could be. He glanced down at the raspberry-colored scrapes on his knees. The pain had finally subsided. He sighed. Kids his age delighted in tormenting outsiders or those different from them, and Memo was very different. More than anybody could ever know.

Navigating the cruelties of schoolyard bullies had become a daily exercise in survival. Sometimes his classmates would whisper obscenities about him and giggle. Other times, during lunch break, they'd shove him into the mud and relish in his anguish. Though he'd tried not to let their abuses bother him, deep inside they always had, and every act of callousness stung more than it should have.

There was a weight tugging at his heart. Memo wished he could get away, but being in school was like being a caged bird. He wanted nothing more than to soar and be free.

But when the sun went down, it was a different story. He reveled in the nights when he could be himself, the dark of the world a cloak keeping him hidden, safe. Just him, his family, the cool, sweet evening air, and the sounds of the crickets in the distance.

Memo glanced at the reddening sun as it sank below the green, low-lying hills. Almost home. He could almost taste his mother's warm pozole and the freshly made tortillas.

While he trekked his way up an incline in the road, Memo felt his backpack straps starting to dig into his shoulders just as his feet were beginning to ache. He paused to rest against a fencepost. That's when he saw the old woman sitting in front of the farmhouse on the rocking chair. Her hands trembled as she sprinkled chickenfeed on the ground. Her hens pecked around her sandaled feet in a frenzy of flying feathers.

The house behind the old woman was decrepit as evident by the peeling paint and rotting clapboards. Even the chain-link fences around the chicken coops had rusted to the color of ground coffee.

The farm belonged to Marco and Isabela Ochoa, though the old man had passed long before Memo was born. The last time Memo had seen Doña Ochoa was in passing when he was three years old and his father had taken him to the doctor in the city.

Memo had waved to her then, as she swept the floors of the porch, which hadn't been as dilapidated.

Memo's father had warned him not to pay heed to the old woman if he were ever to come across her on the road. She was a strange person to be avoided. But today was the first time he'd ever encountered her on his way home.

"Mijo!" Doña Ochoa said. She waved a wrinkled hand, beckoning Memo over.

He nodded and trotted towards the house. Doña Ochoa wore a colorful Poblana dress with a shawl draped around her shoulders, her twin grey braids falling over her chest like strands of rope. She reminded Memo very much of his own grandmother.

"Hola, Doña Ochoa," Memo said.

"Mijito," she said, reaching out and clasping her cold hands softly over his. "You should hurry home before nightfall."

"Why is that, Doña Ochoa?"

Her eyes narrowed as she squeezed his hands. They were cold but soft. "You mean you don't know about the naguals?"

Memo shook his head. "No, Señora."

"Ay, mijito! The naguals are powerful witches and shamans with the power to shapeshift at night. They roam the roads in search of prey to eat."

Memo scratched his head. "Witches? I've never heard this from my parents."

Doña Ochoa pursed her lips and nodded. "Si, mijo. There are many unusual things people won't discuss in public. The world is a strange and magical place. You see, sometimes nature imbues people with unique gifts. Naguals, for example, can become animals by night and feast on prey like lone wanderers as their bestial urges cannot be denied, no matter how hard they may try."

Memo rubbed his chin. "How do I spot a nagual?"

"It is near impossible to tell who may be a nagual. Sometimes they may be people who wander the roads at night. Or strangers that offer gifts at dusk. You should always check to see if you are being followed."

The hairs on the back of his neck turned prickly and Memo offered a glance at his back. "How do you know all this, Doña Ochoa?"

She grinned. "Más sabe el diablo por viejo que por diablo," she said, laughing. "The devil knows more because he is old than because he is the devil."

"I still don't understand," Memo said, gazing upon the darkening fields. "I've never encountered one along the road. What should I do if I come across one?"

"Sit," she said, pointing to an empty rocking chair beside her. "I'm going to tell you a story. Stories hold wisdom, and I hope I may impart some on you, child."

Memo took off his backpack and sat beside her.

The gleaming crown of the sun had nearly vanished behind the horizon, turning the world dark blue. The faintest stars began to dot the sky like pinwheels spinning on black fabric.

"I'm going to tell you a cuento my abuela used to tell me when I was your age. This story took place a long time ago. It is the tale of the little girl and the nagual."

* * *

A long time ago, at the height of the Mexica Empire, little Meztli was heading home at night after a long day of selling medicinal remedies on the mainland. She lived with her curandera mother and her father who tended the chinampas, the floating gardens on Lake Texcoco in the old capital of Tenochtitlan.

It was Meztli's job to gather the herbs her father had harvested and sell them to locals outside of town. She was a smart, well-behaved girl and her parents trusted her with traveling alone.

As Meztli skirted along the edge of Lake Texcoco, little did she know that a nagual had been stalking her. When Meztli was far enough from the nearest village and well out of sight from public, the nagual transformed into a coyote and chased after her.

Fortunately, Meztli heard the nagual's steps crunching over the twigs behind her, and before her pursuer could snatch his jaws around her little neck, she climbed the nearest willow tree to safety.

The coyote, angered by Meztli's shrewdness, yipped at her, chomping, and snapping at the air around her dangling feet as she sat perched on a large branch. Though she was safe for the time being, Meztli began to cry, helpless and all alone on that tree.

The coyote sat on his haunches and eyed the girl in the tree, plump and full of life. After some time, he began to drool and lick his lips as he circled the willow tree, trying to think of how to reach his prey.

Far from home, and no one to help, Meztli remembered her parents teaching her that a nagual could only remain in their animal form by night. Yet their human personalities were still intact inside the beasts. So quick-thinking Meztli concocted a plan.

"Coyote, wait," she said. "You don't want to eat me."

The coyote tilted his head in confusion. "Hm? And why not?"

"Because I am malnourished and riddled with disease," Meztli said. She stuck out her arm. "See?"

The coyote eyed her up and down and said, "You look perfectly fine to me."

Meztli shook her head. "No, no. I am very sick. In fact, I must take my medicine." She reached into a leather pouch and pulled out a handful of dried mushrooms she'd bought from the local priests and healers. "These teōnanācatl are the mushrooms of the gods, Coyote. They imbue those who eat it with powerful properties and cure all manner of disease such as the one that riddles me. I will gladly let you have them in exchange for my safe release."

"You must think me a fool," the coyote said. "How do I know they'll do what you say? Throw me a sample and I shall judge for myself."

Meztli threw down a few dried stems and caps and the coyote gobbled them up. Before long, the coyote rolled over on his back and stared at the night sky. "My, the stars are zipping madly along the sky," the coyote said. "It looks so wonderful."

"Indeed," Meztli said staring at the stars, sitting motionless above. "The stars are very lovely tonight."

"The crickets are chirping a wonderful melody," the coyote said now, his ears perking up. "Can you hear it?"

"Yes," Meztli said, "their song has a lovely cadence."

"Why," the coyote said, "I think I hear Quetzalcoatl speaking. Can you hear? He is divulging the secrets of life."

Meztli nodded her head. "Yes, Coyote. He is indeed very wise."

The conversation went on until the sun rose and the spell of the nagual was broken. The coyote reverted to his human form, and embarrassed, the man stood and stumbled home.

As for Meztli, she returned home, secure in the warm, loving embrace of her family.

* * *

When Doña Ochoa finished her story, the sky had grown black. She turned towards the full moon and smiled, its pallid light catching on her soft, wrinkled face. She seemed to bask in its glow like an iguana basking in the sun.

"Did you enjoy the story, mijo?" she said turning back to Memo. He saw the moon reflected in her eyes; two blue orbs hovering in an ocean of night.

"I enjoyed it very much, Doña Ochoa. I loved how the little girl tricked the coyote and bought herself precious time."

"I'm glad you liked my abuela's tale, mijo." Doña Ochoa placed two trembling hands on her armrests and pushed herself up. The hens at her feet squawked and scurried inside their coops. "I hope you learned a valuable lesson about deceit."

Doña Ochoa fell on her knees and clutched the ground, her nails digging into the earth. A long tail sprouted from the end of her spine as her arms and legs transformed into four muscular back-bending limbs, the ends of which brandished sharp, curved claws. Her torso morphed into a furry, spotted trunk and her head elongated into a feline face, fangs bared like spears.

"Doña Ochoa, you're a jaguar!"

The jaguar turned her thick neck towards Memo and licked her lips. The beast's muscular legs, glimmering in the moonlight, coiled as she prepared to pounce.

Memo shuffled backward towards the road, his shoes dragging on dirt. He kept his eyes trained on the jaguar and her sharp teeth. "Doña Ochoa," he said, "learning not to trust people is something that has gotten me through every day of school. Here's a lesson for you: Never judge someone before you've gotten to know them."

Memo suddenly shrank a quarter his size into an oblong shape. His eyes grew wide and round and his face sprouted a small, curved beak. Long, brown feathers protruded from his body as his arms curved and turned into wings. He puffed out his broad chest and screeched out a defiant hoot.

For a moment that seemingly stretched into perpetuity, the jaguar stared down the owl and hissed. And as the jaguar sprang forward, Memo flapped his wings and darted into the sky until he was just a speck against the full moon.

La Diablada

Ruth Joffre

⌖

ON THE NIGHT the devil was vanquished Qori was sitting in the stands, smoking a cigarette. Around her, tourists were cheering as a performer dressed as the Archangel Michael slew Lucifer with a giant sword constructed from cardboard and aluminum foil (to give it that added shine that the faithful liked). In previous years, when costumes were damaged, the sword was replaced with whatever was on hand that day. A cardboard tube that could be retrofitted into a spear or a pickaxe borrowed from one of the miners of Oruro, who would gladly offer their tools in the fight against El Tío, the Lord of the Underworld, who lived inside the mountain and was only called "Lucifer" above ground, where the Church was watching. Qori always preferred when the actor playing the archangel used a pickaxe to kill El Tío. It felt more honest – truer to the experience of the miners who descended into His underworld each day to mine tin, silver, copper, zinc, and other precious metals for the smart devices she wouldn't buy even if she could afford them – but then again, the Carnaval de Oruro wasn't really for the miners. Not anymore. Not since the Spanish invaded and introduced their own icons. Once, Oruro had been a center of religious pilgrimage – the festival a series of rituals and ceremonies conducted by her indigenous ancestors – but now it was mostly a dance showcase, and that was fine. It made for good entertainment, anyway. She only wished the tourists in the stands wouldn't gawk at her.

A young woman had been staring at her for the better part of half an hour. Qori could feel the stranger's gaze burning a hole in her outfit, as if demanding to know why she hadn't bothered changing out of her muddy overalls and work boots, if she realized she was still wearing her hard hat inside a football stadium, and what it meant that she had on a man's canvas jacket. She didn't feel any need to explain herself, so she finished her cigarette and gathered her empty beer bottles, heading for the exit. At the bottom of the stands, she hazarded a single glance up and realized the young woman was following her (and being not at all subtle about it, either). Qori thought maybe she could shake her tail, disappear inside a sea of tourists leaving the stadium for a drink, but she mistimed it, leaving the crowd behind her as she passed through the tunnel into the cool night air. No sooner had Qori stopped to pay her respects to the mountains, whose dark silhouettes loomed over the city like sleeping giants, than a voice shouted, "Señor! Excuse me, Señor!"

It had been a long time since anyone had called Qori that, and it stopped her in her tracks. Estafania had used that term in private, sometimes to tease but more often to seduce, as when she wanted Qori to untie her dress or keep her warm on a cold winter's night – but that was a lifetime ago, back in Potosí, and nothing good would come of dredging up those memories, she knew. By the time the young woman caught up with her in the parking lot, she had buried them under what was left of her heart and fixed her face into a scowl. "Do I look like a señor to you?"

Momentarily taken aback, the young woman said, "Yes," with the certainty of somebody who thought they had figured out the secret password to a club only to be stopped by the bouncer demanding proof they belonged. She tried to square her shoulders and muster up her courage, but her voice was laced with desperation when she asked, "Do I?"

And Qori had to admit she could see it in the boxy cut of her button up, how she tucked it into the front of her slacks, which covered the tops of her boots. Her hair was a bit long, perhaps, but pulled back into a ponytail and clasped at the nape of her neck it looked androgynous, though the overall look was ruined by her bright purple knapsack. "You're a bit young, though."

"I'm seventeen," the young woman said, as if that were ancient.

"Like I said. Young. You've got to be at least twenty-five to earn a señor."

When Qori started walking, the young woman followed. "And who made that rule?"

"No one, but it feels right, doesn't it?" At that, the young upstart had no response, and for a time they walked together in silence, careful not to disturb the stillness that had descended onto the city, where taxi cabs sat idle at street corners and restaurant owners loitered on the sidewalks, letting their cigarettes turn to columns of ash, as if waiting for the festival to end and life to begin again. In this quiet, in which all they had was each other, Qori relented and lowered a little of her guard. "What's your name, kid?"

"Umberta, but my friends call me Bert."

"A strong name," Qori said, nodding her approval. "The kind that ages well."

"You really think so?" The young woman brightened, as if that were the only compliment she had ever wanted to receive. It opened a floodgate of questions about Qori's experiences: how did she choose her name (she hadn't), how long had she been wearing men's clothing (as long as she could remember), did she identify as a man or a butch lesbian (she didn't bother with labels), had anyone given her shit for how she looked (more times than she could count), and had anyone ever threatened her or said he would show her "what a real man is."

Something in her sneer at the word "real" made Qori pause. "Are you in trouble?"

"I left that behind in Santa Cruz," Bert said, with a shrug too forced to be nonchalant.

Now Qori understood: Bert was on the run. "And what brings you to our fair city?"

"This is just where the bus stopped. I didn't even know Oruro had a carnaval."

"So, you just arrived today," Qori reasoned aloud, a hint of trepidation in her voice as she eyed Bert's knapsack and realized everything the young woman owned must be inside there. "Do you have a place to stay yet?"

"I'll manage," Bert insisted, bristling at the unspoken suggestion that she needed help.

Qori's chuckle was rueful and full of worry. "You'll sleep in the street, you mean."

"Who says I'm staying? I could hop on a bus at any time. Sleep anywhere."

"You could," Qori allowed, stopping at her front door, their conversation having wound a path through the streets of Oruro, into the foothills of Cerro San Pedro, where the mountain stood watch over the sand dunes and scrub grass of a large, arid park. She could point Bert back towards the bus station, wish her well on her journey to wherever, and hope that somehow, someway, she picked up the skills needed to survive this hardscrabble life ahead of her. "But we both know you won't," Qori said, before unlocking her front door and stepping inside.

For a long moment, Bert stood frozen on the doorstep, her expression a mix of frustration and exhaustion, gratitude and the kind of self-destructive pride born of fear, though of course she would never admit that out loud. *Look at her*, Estafania would have said. *She's just like you were at her age. Too stubborn to know what's good for you.* Too intent on wearing an outfit like armor to realize that everyone could already see she was wounded. It took meeting Estafania for Qori to understand that being herself didn't have to mean being alone. She could let someone in now and then. She waved at the floorboards in the corner. "You can sleep there."

Her place was tiny (little more than a one-room shack with stone walls and a tin roof), but it had a window looking out over the city and a washtub where she could rinse off the day's dust, and that had always been enough for her. Only after Bert stepped inside did Qori realize how low the ceiling was and how much taller the young woman must be: a good fifteen centimeters, if not more. She had to bend her knees to get a nice angle out the window. She spent a few minutes just walking around, looking at the stones collected on the windowsill, the wooden figurines standing on the shelves, their faces ancient and unfamiliar. "How long have you been living here?"

"About thirty years now. I've lost count."

Something tender passed over Bert's face then, as if it only just occurred to her that aging sometimes meant outliving everyone you ever loved. She tried to hide this expression by bending down to scrub her face in the washtub, but Qori saw it: how unprepared she was to face down the realities of life. Before Bert even finished washing up, Qori had already decided they would head over to her manager's office in the morning and get the young woman a job working in the mine. Water sputtered out of Bert's mouth when she said, "You work in a mine?"

Qori pointed at her muddy clothes. "Where did you think I worked – city hall?"

"I thought that was just, you know, your aesthetic," she admitted, self-conscious now and reassessing all her assumptions about the older woman: the deep wrinkles in her cheeks, the folds of flesh under her chin, the slight stoop in her back, reminiscent of Bert's grandfather. All of that led Bert to wonder, "Is it safe for someone your age to work in a mine?"

Qori's eyes narrowed into a challenge. "How old do you think I am?"

Suddenly uncertain, Bert opened her mouth, then closed it. She dared not guess.

Something mischievous played in the grooves of Qori's face, then faded as she explained, "It's not safe for anyone to work in the mine. But it's a job." She slapped Bert's left shoulder and was surprised to find it so soft and rounded. It looked sharper in the button-down shirt. "Besides, it'll help you build some muscle while you figure out what you want out of life."

"Good point," Bert said, with a chuckle that betrayed real panic. She had never known what to do with herself or where she fit in the world. Her mother had grown purple potatoes for a local market, and her father raised llamas for their wool, and she liked both jobs well enough, but neither of them had seemed like the key to her future, she said, as she settled down to sleep in the corner, removing the firm objects from her knapsack so she could use it as a pillow. "I've always been good with knives. Perhaps I should be a butcher," she mused, but Qori was already snoring, the staccato rhythm like that of a chisel chipping away at a stone, revealing a vein of precious ore underneath the surface.

Every morning for three months, Qori and Bert descended into their own deaths. "A mine is like a tomb," Qori explained. Sunless, airless. Its narrow tunnels seemed to squeeze your lungs inside your chest and fill them, gradually, with dirt, all the hazardous particulates hanging around the air, which was flooded with noxious gasses. A modern mine might install some semblance of ventilation to protect workers, but that one had been operating off and on since the 1500s, supplying silver, tin, antimony, and zinc first to the Incas, then the Spaniards, and now the state, and no one had bothered retrofitting the mineshafts. Miners wore bandanas over their mouths, but this would do nothing to protect them from the cave-ins and cancers, the little flecks of silica that embedded in their lungs, making it difficult to breathe. For this, they turned to El Tío. Someone had built an effigy deep in the mine, piling rocks and mud together to form the bust of a horned man, his eyes a pair of plastic red jewels glittering devilishly in the light of their headlamps. "Here you go, Tío. My last cigarette," Bert said, fitting it delicately between the statue's crude lips.

"And I offer you this alternate death," Qori said, placing a bird's skull atop a pile of daily offerings, which included rocks, bones, candy wrappers, chewing gum, bits of wire and cloth and old boots worn through at the soles, and even a few coca leaves, which the miners still chewed to help ease the pain of hard labor. "May you accept this creature's death in place of my own."

Both women bowed their heads. Bert said, "Do you think he's really listening?"

"Of course he is. El Tío hears everything underground. It's why he hates us."

"We must be disturbing his beauty sleep," Bert said, suppressing a snicker.

Qori pinched the young woman's arm but smiled all the same.

Behind them, a man grumbled, "You ladies done yet?"

In a flash, Qori whipped around and shone her headlamp at his face. Momentarily blinded by the light, he stumbled back, raising a hand to shield his eyes against the sudden glare. Once he could see again, she hocked up a wad of phlegm the size of her big toe onto his filthy boots, then smiled at him. "Yeah, we're done."

He started towards her, as if to throw a punch, but the man behind him grabbed his arm.

"Don't. That woman's an agent of El Tío. You don't want to get on her bad side."

"Her? Come on. She's just an old woman pretending to be a man."

"No, I'm telling you. She's made a deal with El Tío. She's older than she looks."

Another man said, "Yeah, I heard she's been working here since my father was a boy."

While the men debated the divine possibility that El Tío could grant a person immortality (and wondered why He would bother giving a woman such a gift when, technically, girls weren't even allowed to work in mines in Bolivia – Qori and Bert just got special privileges because they were twice as productive as the men, which was another sign that she was in league with El Tío), Qori shook her head and waved off their nonsense. With Bert, she descended to the deepest parts of the mine, where after centuries miners had at last uncovered the curved edge of the tin deposit. Once alone, Bert asked, "Who were those guys? I've never seen them before."

"Just some little boys throwing a tantrum because I don't work topside with the cholitas." Indigenous women (many of them wives of miners) who worked the mountain of discards by the entrance of the mine, picking through this rubble for impure ores with low percentages that could be traded in for a fraction of the value. "You know how some men get when you show them they aren't the strongest in the room."

Bert did know. How many times had one of them offered to hold on to her pickaxe so she could take a break only for them to grow belligerent when she politely informed them she wasn't tired? If her presence made them that sore, then Qori's must drive them to distraction. Still, a part of her did wonder how a woman of Qori's advanced age could move like she was in her twenties and breathe this toxic air so easily when even Bert had started coughing. She debated asking this: "Is it true what they said? Did you make a deal with El Tío?"

Qori continued swinging her pickaxe. "What do you think?"

"I think thirty years in this mine would kill anyone, including me."

Qori shrugged, heaving up another swing. "I guess I'm just used to it," she said, but when the tip of the axe struck rock this time, it broke clean through, unleashing a pocket of compressed air powerful enough to break through the tunnel wall and knock Qori clean off her feet. Her head slammed into the rock, knocking her unconscious, as the tunnel collapsed around them.

When next she opened her eyes, the tunnel was pitch black. She knocked at her headlamp a few times until the light sputtered to life. She lay crumpled at the end of the mineshaft, covered in dust. Before her stood a mound of rubble tall enough to block passage through the tunnel. Qori would have to dig her way out. She screamed for Bert, thinking (praying) she had been caught on the other side of the rockfall, able to bring others to their aid; but there was no response. She was alone again.

Without the help of her pickaxe, she started chipping away at the mound, flinging smaller rocks behind her with both hands. When all the little ones were picked off, she began heaving the bowling ball-sized ones, careful not to overexert herself or hyperventilate in a panic. Oxygen was limited, she knew, and she needed to work quickly and methodically. She couldn't afford another cave-in now. She climbed up onto the heap, trying to pry a small boulder free, and that was when she heard it: a groan.

"Bert! Can you hear me? I'm going to dig you out."

A weak voice to her left said, "Qori. Qori, I can't feel my leg."

"That's just because you're pinned. Once I get you out, you'll be fine."

But it took half an hour to reach Bert, and by then she had lost consciousness. Blood loss, Qori guessed, judging by the boulder that had pinned Bert's leg. She tried to pick it up, but it was wider and thicker than Qori's chest, and she couldn't get a good grip on it, nor could she position herself behind it with enough leverage to push it free, though she tried. She must have worked on that boulder for ten minutes before she heard someone behind her say, "It won't work."

She knew who it was. She recognized the voice: El Tío.

He was leaning against the wall, smoking a cigarette – the same one Bert had offered him just that morning. His horns were longer than Qori remembered, swirled into three tight curlicues instead of two, but his skin was still ashen, his black tunic still speckled with dust. "What a pity," he said, before taking a drag. "She's so young."

"You could save her. You could get us both out."

He flicked the spent ash onto his own tongue. "In exchange for what?"

"That cigarette, for one. She's given you an offering every day for three months."

"You want me to spare her life for this? It's garbage. Hardly worth anything." He sneered as he tossed that half-smoked cigarette into the shadows. "I don't know why you people insist on giving me this shit. What am I supposed to do with a bottlecap? Or a flower? You think anything actually grows down here?"

With narrow eyes, Qori said, "I think there's more life in the underworld than you care to admit, Tío." She pointed his name at him like a knife, digging the letters through the air as if they would actually hurt him, though she knew better. "I've worked these mines long enough to know there are creatures down here most people couldn't imagine." For decades, she had been working the deepest point of the mine – the place beyond which all life moves without shadow, its motion detectable only through vibrations: the tremor of rock beneath her feet, the waft of breath against her cheek, the rustle of wings and clicking of claws as life found its way into the holes she dug in the heart of the mountain. Here, in this hollow place best known for swallowing people alive, she had met death. Held its hand, walked with it to the end of the tunnel. And then, at the last second, turned back and ran. She had been running for so long.

"Yes," El Tío said, as if he could read her thoughts. "How many years has it been?"

"One hundred and fifty-six." That had been the deal: immortality, but under the condition that she descend every day into El Tío's realm and work the mines under his watch. For a time, it had seemed like a fair trade, because Qori could go on working indefinitely, providing for herself and Estafania long past when her mortal colleagues would fall victim to pain and illness. As long as they moved every twenty years or so, nobody would know how old she really was. Who cared about some old woman, after all? Most people ignored her anyway, allowing her to work alone at the end of the tunnel, never close enough to them to engage in miserable chitchat, but never quite so far that her colleagues wouldn't know where to look in the event of a collapse. She could hear them now, working on the other side of the rubble, but it would take them hours to break through and Bert didn't have that kind of time. She needed help now.

El Tío shot her a rueful smile. "Are you prepared to make a deal on her behalf?"

She considered Bert where she lay, her breathing shallow, her features ashen. "I am."

"Wonderful. Except: I never make the same deal twice. We will need new terms for this."

I should have known, Qori thought, both crestfallen and hopeful. "What do you propose?"

From the way he grinned at her then, with his mouth too wide and teeth far too numerous, Qori knew she had made a mistake by letting him open the negotiations. He swept forward, tunic kicking up dust as he brushed past her to kneel over Bert, looking not like a doctor checking on a patient but like a thief intent on discovering what was most precious to her, what would be worth ripping from her when she was most vulnerable. He tilted his head maliciously, considering Bert, the way Qori anguished over her. At last, he said, "I think you two should be separated now. You will continue to fulfill the terms of your agreement with me, but Bert will never be allowed to set foot in my realm again or her life will be forfeit. Do we have a deal?"

Outwardly, Qori pretended to be heartbroken, as if she could not bear to live without Bert at her side at every moment, but inwardly she elated at the excuse to force Bert out of the miner's tomb and back into the realm of the living. To sell this lie, she asked, "But what will she do?"

"It doesn't matter. It won't involve you, anyway." That was the point: to isolate her again and reduce her life to the hardships of the mine, the endless toil of immortality. She decided then, as he extended a hand to her, that she would put an end to her deal with him, that one day instead of descending into the mountain at dawn she would watch the sun rise and set over Oruro and die peacefully in bed, as Estafania had eighty-four years ago. It had been too long, Qori decided. She had lived enough. He said, "Now: do we have a deal?"

After some forced hesitation, she reached for his clawed hand.

"One more thing," he added, withdrawing his hand. "I want you to dance."

"Dance? No, I can't. I wouldn't even know how. Estafania was always the dancer."

"And yet those are my terms. Dance the Diablada or your friend dies because of you."

The Diablada, she thought. *Of course*. It was the dance people did at the Carnaval, before the archangel slew the devil. Over the years, she had seen hundreds of variations of the moves. A 360° twist, a series of kicks, a sideways shuffle performed in unison with hundreds of dancers all dressed as devils. She had no space, no costume, no faith in the battle between good and evil, but none of that mattered. Her goal wasn't to vanquish a demon. It was to make El Tío laugh. And so she moved her feet, bobbed her head, clapped her hands to a beat only she could hear, and when, in the throes of movement, her headlamp cast its light on his face, she saw his head flung back in laughter, and she knew: she had won. He extended his hand again, and she took it.

For years afterwards, there were stories of the cave-in, of that ancient woman who climbed up out of the rubble with a girl on her back and not a scratch on her. Some said she was an amaru made flesh, a dragon dispatched from the spirit world in human form because it wasn't the young woman's time to die yet. Some said she was the spirit of the mountain itself, bitter and inflexible, ruined by human greed and the desire for profit. But the miners knew: it was Qori. She had made another deal with El Tío. Why he bothered with them and no one else, the men never understood. It baffled them as much as Bert's sudden departure from Oruro and Qori's unexplained death one summer day when she didn't show up to work and everyone realized: they had no idea where she lived. They didn't even know her last name. All day, they told each other stories about her. There was that time she hauled a minecart's worth of ore on her back. Or that blisteringly hot afternoon when an orphan delivered an unmarked letter to her and she rewarded him for his discretion with two centavos and a stone carving of a llama. Or that week she ran off with a woman half her age, only to slink back one night with a broken heart and a hat with a fresh bullet hole in it – but most of those stories were just rumors, salves made of words and spit, offerings to El Tío.

The Stained Walls

S. Alessandro Martinez

✑

ROSARIO WAS CLOSE to finding her sister. She knew it. She felt it in her soul.

The picture filled her phone's screen as she tapped on the thumbnail. Her sister, Elena, stood in the middle of a quiet intersection, flashing a peace sign and displaying the blue butterfly tattooed on her wrist. The brilliant sunshine glinted off sunglasses framed by curtains of dark auburn hair. Behind her, in the shade of a banana tree, a dented sign identified the street's name as "Cuchumaquic".

A quick swipe of Rosario's thumb brought up the next photo. This one had been taken farther down that same street, she now knew. It depicted a rectangular four-story apartment building, so old that the painted white stone façade had turned mostly gray. Streaks of accumulated black gunk dripped down the sides from its flat roof, where antennas, satellite dishes, and jumbles of power lines congregated in a mass of chaos. Windows reflected

The Stained Walls

the bright Yucatecan sun, making it impossible to see through them. Below, all manner of palms and other tropical vegetation grew wild in the vast green yard that encircled the building.

Putting the phone away, Rosario looked up. That same building loomed over her now, looking even more ancient in the darkness of night. The clouded black sky, the eerie quiet of the neighborhood, and the fact that the apartment building sat alone in a cul-de-sac did nothing to help her uneasiness. All the trees she'd seen in the picture were now barely discernible silhouettes of jumbled, jagged shapes where anything could be hiding, waiting.

A thick dread settled upon her, digging sharp nails in between every vertebra of her spine. This building that she'd been searching for for so long…this…black hole that took her sister. A part of Rosario hadn't fully believed this place was real until this very moment, as it towered before her, daring her to take just one more step forward so that she would be within its concrete grasp.

Enter my halls of vanishing.

"Screw you," Rosario muttered. She had come this far. There was no turning back now. That wasn't an option.

Cancún wasn't all clear skies, white beaches, and parties. Like every other city in the world, there was a darkness that lurked beneath even the friendliest of avenues and boulevards.

"Where are you, El?" she whispered, hoping the wind might carry her words to whatever unnamed corner of this building held her sister.

If it held her sister. Rosario couldn't be one hundred percent certain that Elena still remained on these premises. She could have been moved. It had been months after all. But this was the first place Elena had gone to the day she arrived in Cancún for spring break. The same day all communication had ceased.

What had happened?

Breath filled her chest, stretching Rosario's lungs as she gathered her courage. Who knew what she would find in there? Nothing good. Of that she was certain.

Up one, two, three steps onto the stoop with her suitcase. Rosario raised a trembling fist to knock before spotting the intercom next to the door. There were eight buttons, all unlabeled, though the button for apartment one was marked with a star. She pressed it, eliciting a harsh buzz through the speaker. Her finger left behind a sweaty print.

After a minute, a staticky voice said, "¿Sí?"

Rosario leaned in, anxiety threatening to steal her voice. She managed to depress the button again. "Hi, I'm Rosario González. I, um, want to rent a room here."

"Un momento."

Rosario waited, her sweat and the heavy, humid air causing her t-shirt to stick to her skin, a sensation she'd always hated. From inside came the sound of a door opening and closing. Behind the frosted glass of the front door, an indistinct figure took shape, growing larger as it approached. Finally, with the sound of a lock turning, the door swung inward.

Standing just over the threshold stood a stocky woman in a colorful huipil dress. If Rosario had to guess, the woman looked to be in her late seventies, although her short, wavy hair possessed much more black than gray. Her tanned, lined face broke into soft smile that deepened her severe wrinkles even more.

The woman reminded Rosario so much of her own grandmother that she was momentarily taken aback and had to push out the words stuck in her throat.

"Uh, hi. I'm looking to rent one of the apartments for a week? Sorry it's so late. My flight got delayed and—"

"Is no trouble! Come in, come in," the old woman said in English with a heavy Mexican accent, ushering Rosario inside with grandmotherly encouragement.

The building's foyer – hotter and more humid than the air outside for some reason – consisted of nothing but a small open space separating the doors of apartments one and two, with the foot of the stairs starting at the back wall.

"I am Señora Carmen Ruiz, the landlord." She took Rosario's hand, clasped in both of hers, and gave it a warm squeeze. "We are happy to have you. Is just you? No friends? Family? Boyfriend?"

"Just me," Rosario replied with a chuckle. She couldn't help the smile on her face. An image of this Carmen

Ruiz popped into her head – bustling about in a kitchen, spoiling grandchildren, and going shopping with her little old lady friends.

Elena was probably fooled too. The thought exploded so quickly into Rosario's head that the smile vanished from her lips in an instant, her face losing all emotion. It was like her brain had been reset to its default factory settings.

"All okay?" Carmen asked.

Okay, maybe she shouldn't judge this woman just yet. Not until she had more concrete information. Still, something had happened to Elena immediately after entering this building, and the person managing it couldn't be trusted. Rosario had to keep her guard up at all times.

"Yes, I'm okay." The smile refused to show itself again, her facial muscles rebelling against her. Instead, Rosario rubbed at her eyes. "It was a long day of flying. I'm just a little tired." It wasn't a lie.

"No problem. We get you upstairs."

Rosario pretended to not be out of breath by the time she and her suitcase reached the fourth-floor landing, though she was sure her face was flushed with exertion. Carmen had not even broken a sweat in this heat. The old lady had probably climbed these stairs an uncountable number of times.

"Long climb," Carmen commented in Spanish, then laughed.

"Yeah, I'm not used to so many stairs," Rosario answered in Spanish as well. She hoped her accent wasn't too terrible. The day she had moved out of her parents' house was when she had stopped speaking Spanish. She'd wanted to get back to using it regularly, so she'd been trying to teach her boyfriend Ethan so she could have a conversation partner.

Well...ex-boyfriend.

When finding Elena had become the only concern in Rosario's life to the exclusion and detriment of everything else, Ethan had left. Rosario didn't blame him anymore. Being almost completely ignored for months would break anyone. At least Ethan had said he wished her the best of luck and hoped Elena would be found safely.

The landlady cleared her throat, reclaiming Rosario's attention. "You are alone on fourth floor here. Nobody in number seven at moment. Much privacy."

Taking a set of keys out of her pocket, Carmen unlocked the apartment's door. As they walked in, she flipped on the lights. Small black dots scurried away from the sudden illumination to hide underneath wicker furniture and framed prints of the beach on the walls. Rosario's skin prickled at the sight, though she tried not to let the disgust show on her face. Her family was originally from this same part of Mexico, and years of visits here had taught Rosario that it was impossible to keep bugs outside where they belonged.

The apartment itself was small, but not cramped. The main space was a living room-slash-dining room with worn chairs, a sofa, and a dining table. A low wall separated the tiny kitchen where an old refrigerator rattled and hummed. Two doorways, one at the back of the living room and one to the left of it, presumably led to bedrooms. The whole place smelled like stale mothballs.

"Looks cozy." If this were any other building, that would have been Rosario's true reaction. But knowing that Elena had been here, possibly in this very apartment, before vanishing tainted everything from the tiled floor to the popcorn ceiling.

"How you hear about this building?" Carmen asked.

An electric shock zapped Rosario's brain, releasing a flood of adrenalized panic.

Crap.

"Oh, my cousin lives here in Cancún, and she knew I was visiting, but that I didn't want to stay in an expensive hotel. She talked to someone. I don't remember his name—" She broke off as if trying to recall.

"She talk to Rodrigo?"

"Yes! Rodrigo, that was it." Rosario bit the inside of her cheek to prevent herself from screaming with relief.

Carmen nodded, seemingly satisfied. "Okay, I am down on bottom floor. There is sign on my door. Come knock if you need anything." She placed the keys in Rosario's hand. "Get some sleep, mija. We can settle payment tomorrow. Is 850 a night."

And with that, the landlady exited the apartment, saying goodnight as she made her way down the stairs. Rosario stood there, reeling over the price, until she realized the amount must've been in pesos, not dollars. Duh.

When the landlady was out of sight, Rosario closed the door. She then turned to face the apartment once more. Here she was. Alone in the last place she knew her sister to have been.

Last April, Elena had traveled to Cancún for spring break with a group of friends. Their parents had asked Rosario to go as well, saying they would even pay for it. But Rosario was up for a potential promotion at the office and decided that she couldn't afford to let the opportunity pass. It was a decision that had been eroding her mind like a rampant cancer ever since Elena had failed to come back home.

The two photos Rosario had on her phone, the photos she stared at every day, were the last ones Elena had texted her before communication had stopped altogether. The U.S. Embassy and Consulate seemed to be doing nothing more than twiddling their official thumbs, as were the local authorities here.

When weeks passed with no progress, Rosario hadn't been able to stand it any longer. Pushing aside her job, her friends, Ethan, and every other distraction, she took the investigation into her own hands. According to every internet search she conducted, every map she could get her hands on, and every city official's office she spoke to, the street called "Cuchumaquic" did not exist anywhere in Cancún. Searching Google Maps and Street View for hours every day produced nothing as well, save for frustration and headaches.

It had actually been Ethan – before he left – who suggested Rosario's family hire a private investigator here in Cancún. She couldn't believe she hadn't thought of that herself. Money was no concern, of course. Rosario and her parents would gladly give up every last penny they possessed to have Elena returned safely home.

It had been the right call.

After the P.I. received the two photos, the man had scoured the city street by street, until one day, months later, the quest bore fruit. He had found the apartment building.

That day had been yesterday. Without hesitation, Rosario had booked the earliest flight she could get. Now she was here. No ideas. No plans. Only determination.

Determination that was faltering. What the hell was she doing? She hadn't even told her parents that she'd left the country. What if Elena had been kidnapped by human traffickers? Did she really think she was going to go up against a ring of hardened criminals, save her sister, and get back home in one piece?

Stupid.

Stupid.

Stupid.

Rosario crumpled onto the overly warm tiles of the floor and let the tears flow. Sobs from deep within her

The Stained Walls

core burst to the surface, as if they'd been drowning and desperate for air. She should have come with Elena. How could she have put a job above her own sister?

Curled up, hands covering her face, horrible thoughts scurried through Rosario's mind as if the bugs in the apartment had burrowed into her brain. If she couldn't find Elena, she would never see her sister's goofy smile again. They would never go to their favorite sushi restaurant. She would never hear Elena laugh at their dad's lame jokes. They would never spend an evening together talking late into the night. And Elena would never—

Stop it. Get up.

Crying and fearing what-ifs wasn't getting her anywhere. Rosario had come all this way for a reason. There was no more time to waste. No point in unpacking. She wasn't here to vacation. She was here to find Elena and get her sister home.

Where to start?

Standing up, Rosario wiped the tears from her face and surveyed the apartment. She hadn't noticed before, but now that she took a good look, she saw that everything was coated in a thin blanket of dust. With a step over to the dining room table, she traced a finger along its surface. A dark trail was left in the layer of gray that covered it.

Strange. Rosario assumed someone would keep these apartments clean for renters. But not that foreboding.

Carmen was elderly. If she was the one who did all the cleaning, then she probably couldn't get around to dusting the empty apartments all that often.

Knock, knock, knock.

The sound caused Rosario to start, nearly tripping over her own feet as she spun around.

Was that Carmen at the door?

Who else would be coming to see her, especially at this hour?

With a tentative step over to the door, she peeked through the peephole. There was nobody standing outside, at least not that she could see. Maybe she'd been hearing things. Against her better judgement, Rosario flung open the door, only to find there really was no one. Making sure the keys were in her pocket, she stepped out onto the landing and closed the door behind her.

"Hello?" she said. Or meant to say. The word had come out as a whisper. She had no desire in that moment to repeat herself in a louder voice.

The door to apartment seven across from her sat resolutely shut. Carmen had said no one was currently renting that one. She headed towards the stairs and was about to descend when she realized it was probably too late to go around knocking on doors. Rosario could go around tomorrow, see if any of the other apartments were occupied, and ask if they'd seen her sister.

Wait. What if they're all in on it? The paranoid thought struck her like a blow to the chest, knocking the air from her lungs. Why had she rushed here alone and with no plan?

Taking out her phone, Rosario composed an email to Ethan. He'd freak out less than her parents would. Maybe. In the email she told him where she was, what she was doing, and all the information the private investigator had sent her on how to get to the apartment building. Ethan wouldn't be checking his email at this time of night, but he'd see it in the morning.

After hitting send on the email, Rosario stared down the staircase. She had all night to think of ways to gather the information she was after without arousing people's suspicions. Far easier said than done. But she couldn't just go around busting down doors.

Knock, knock, knock.

As if her body knew something she didn't, a chill shot up from the base of her spine all the way to her scalp. All her muscles tensed, causing every single hair to stand up on her body like a cat that knows it's about to use up that ninth life.

Terrified, she peeked over her shoulder before the rest of her body turned as well. No one stood behind her, although her body remained on guard and refused to unclench.

Knock.

It was coming from apartment seven.

Knock.

The door trembled with the rapping from the other side.

Knock.

Without thinking, she ran over and made to grab the doorknob, but froze. Her hand hovered around the tarnished metal. Obviously Carmen had lied. There was someone in apartment seven. A cocktail of emotions rocketed its way through Rosario's mind. What was her strategy here? Even if the door was unlocked, she'd fling it open, and then what? If she saw something she wasn't meant to see, what would she do then? Again, the fact that she had no plan, that she was being so incredibly reckless—

"Help..."

Rosario's muscles didn't so much as tense this time as constrict so tightly over her bones, she thought they would shatter at any moment.

"Is someone out there?" the muffled voice – so small and despondent – whispered through the door. "Please help."

An electric current got her muscles moving once more. Rosario's hand clamped down so hard on the doorknob, she was surprised it didn't crumple in her vice grip. She couldn't tell for certain, but the voice had sounded enough like Elena's that she was going to get into this apartment, right here, right now, even if she had to claw through the walls.

With a twist of her wrist, the knob turned and the door opened without fuss, surprising her. A blast of heat nearly pushed her backward. Darkness met Rosario's eyes, a darkness so dense it seemed to be an actual wall. The faintest smell tickled her nose. It reminded her of animals, of a farm.

"Hey," she whisper-shouted.

No answer.

"Are you okay?" A long pause. "Elena?"

Still nothing.

She sent a probing hand over the threshold, feeling along the wall to her right until her fingers found a switch. They flicked it on. Bare bulbs flickered to life with a buzzing hum, illuminating the space beyond the door. It wasn't an apartment.

It was a staircase.

At first, Rosario thought maybe it led to the roof. But no, what she saw made no sense. The stairs went up and up and up. There were no turns at all, at least from what she could see. This had to be some sort of illusion. If this were real, it would have to be sticking out of the top of the apartment building. More bare bulbs hung from the upward-slanting ceiling at irregular intervals, illuminating walls made of gray, unfinished wood.

Her throat simultaneously gulped and constricted, getting the ball of saliva stuck in the back of her mouth. Rosario couldn't comprehend what she was seeing. The concern for her sister pushed her forward, however. She was now convinced it had been Elena's voice that had spoken through the door. In that moment, the illogicality of this staircase didn't matter. Saving Elena and getting the hell out of here in one piece was all Rosario needed to focus on.

Despite all her bodily systems sending urgent signals not to do it, Rosario stepped into apartment seven. What she had at first thought was brown carpeting that covered the stairs, she now saw was dirt.

What the hell was going on in this place?

She closed the door behind her, in case Carmen or someone decided to come up to the fourth floor, and began climbing the stairs. The space was much narrower than a usual staircase, and the ceiling so low, she had to avoid bumping her head on the hanging lights by dodging around them. Rosario had never been claustrophobic before, but being enclosed in this impossible place ate away at her nerves. Instead of creaking like normal stairs would, the moist dirt crunched underneath her shoes with every step she took upwards.

For some reason, it had been weirdly hotter and more humid inside the apartment building than it had been outside. Here on this staircase, the temperature had more than doubled. Rivers of sweat flowed down her back, and the thick air settled in her lungs like she had inhaled a swamp.

She stopped counting after reaching sixty stairs. There seemed to be no end to them. No end to this cramped shaft that led ever upwards. More climbing. Her legs burned, the muscles filling with lactic acid. Up, up, up. Had she just passed sixty more stairs? Sweat drenched her entire body like she had gone swimming fully clothed. But she couldn't give up. Elena could be at the end of this impossible staircase. Just a little more.

Every so often, she would call out as loud as she dared for the source of the voice that had asked for help, but an answer never came. Still, Rosario climbed, fueled by hope that she would find Elena here. And fueled by fear that she would find Elena here.

Her body screamed for a respite. Rosario ignored its demands for as long as she could, but eventually collapsed onto her hands and knees. She could feel things wriggling around in the warm dirt beneath her palms, but she didn't care. How long had she been going up this damn staircase? She'd lost all sense of time.

What now? Did she continue on after a short rest? Her throat was parched, her sandpaper tongue trying to lick any moisture from the roof of her mouth. Or did she make her way back down, losing all the progress she'd already made? Tears prickled her eyes. The thought of leaving Elena made her sick.

Turning around to see if she could make out the bottom of the staircase where she had started, Rosario was met with a startling sight that threatened to unravel her brain.

She was at the foot of the stairs. The door of apartment seven sat right in front of her.

"No…"

She'd been climbing for so long. So long! Laughter or wailing (or maybe both, she couldn't tell) burst from her mouth. Either this was a dream or she'd gone crazy. Those were the only two possibilities, and Rosario refused to entertain any other explanations.

Joints popped as she hauled herself up from those dirt-covered stairs and brushed herself off. As she stared, dull with exhaustion at the door, the patterns in the wood formed faces. Faces that sneered and mocked her stupidity.

"Shut up!" she hissed and kicked at it, wishing those faces would step out of the door so she could throttle them. Maybe they were the ones who had called out and lured her in here. Those bastards.

Instead, she spun away from them. She would rather climb more stairs than look at those imagined faces. But just as the stairs she'd climbed had disappeared behind her, the endless stairs leading upwards had vanished as well. In their place there now stood a wall covered by two deep red curtains of some thick material, hanging from a rusted rod near the low ceiling. A coy sliver of light peeked out between them.

Curtains covered windows, of course. Rosario knew she had to see what would be on the other side of that glass. She had to know where her endless climbing had gotten her. She moved towards it, a ship at sea guided by a beacon.

The Stained Walls

Light fingers graced the edge of one curtain before clutching it and ripping it aside, the metal hoops at the top clanging against the curtain rod. She pressed her face against the uncovered window, trying to comprehend what was revealed.

A wide-open sky greeted her. Everything, absolutely everything, was colored sickly shades of green. The sky, the sun, even the wispy clouds that hung in the air like corpses floating in tainted water.

It was all so...unnatural.

She had never been a violent person, but Rosario's fist punched through the glass, as if some deep part of her mind wanted to instinctively destroy something that shouldn't be. Cuts opened up on her knuckles as sharp edges caressed her skin with their razor kisses. She paid no mind to the pain, however. Her thoughts were compelling her to make sure the window itself wasn't tinted. That this wasn't another illusion like the staircase, because that was a trick, right? Everything in this madhouse apartment was trickery?

No, the world outside really was green.

Peeking her head out of the aperture she had just created in the glass, Rosario looked downward. The building went down forever. She couldn't even begin to count how many stories were below her. She couldn't make out the foundation, but she didn't have to. There was nothing else to see around them but ocean. The apartment building rose out of a vast, jade ocean.

Rosario wanted to vomit. But before her stomach could complete that initial heave, from out of the corner of her eye, she saw a dark shape fly at her. She had no time to identify what it was other than something writhing and rubbery, before it raked talons across her cheek.

With a scream of agony and panic, Rosario withdrew back inside and flung the curtain closed. She knew that wouldn't stop anything from getting in, but whatever had attacked her didn't follow.

Chest heaving, she stood statue-still, her body scrunched like a coiled spring, ready to let loose should something come after her again. Blood dripped from her cut knuckles, over her fingers, and onto the ground. And though her body remained rigid, her mind raced. Had Elena gone through all this too? Had they tortured her sister like they were torturing her now? For what purpose? Anger began to replace the fright at the thought of Elena alone and afraid. Her sister had never caused trouble in her life; had never caused harm to anyone. She was a good person. Someone who deserved only the best.

How dare these people? How dare they—

Knock, knock, knock.

Rosario spun to face the door to apartment seven where the knocks came from.

"Oh screw you!" she screeched. Her jaw clenched in such fury she thought her molars might crack. "Give me my sister!"

"Rosario?" That soft voice from before. Only this time, there was no denying who it sounded like.

"Elena!" The exultation that blossomed in Rosario's chest pushed aside everything else as it took root. She rushed the door and burst through like a SWAT team, her own body the battering ram. She would save her sister and get her out of this hellhole, fighting tooth and nail if she had to. No one would stand in her way. No matter how big or well-armed, she'd rip through everyone who opposed her. She would even tear out little old Carmen's throat with her teeth if that bitch tried to prevent them from leaving.

Then everything inside her withered in an instant on the other side of that door. There was no Elena, only a room. The space looked to be larger than any apartment in the building could be, yet there were no decorations, furniture, windows or even any kind of partitions to demarcate different rooms. It was all one big space, all evenly lit by some unseen light source. The unpainted walls were covered in myriad black stains from floor to ceiling. Rosario couldn't tell whether the dirty patterns were grime, mold, or both.

What caught her eye and held it was the shapeless pile of crumpled clothes in the middle of the room. She hastened over, trying to stifle her ever-growing fear. It was immediately apparent that these were not Elena's, not only because Rosario was well aware how her sister liked to dress, but also because someone still wore the clothes that lay before her.

Well, what used to be someone.

A scream swelled in Rosario's lungs before getting stuck behind the knot that had formed in her throat. She staggered backwards like a drunk, her injured hand clasped over her mouth, not caring about the blood now on her lips. Of all the things she'd experienced tonight, this was the worst. Never in her life had she ever seen a dead body. A dead, decayed, desiccated body.

The corpse lying curled up at her feet was what she imagined a mummy would look like after thousands of years. Its papery skin was the color of old leather, and its clothing hung loosely from its frame, revealing the emaciated form underneath. And while the receded lips pulled back into a rictus grin, and the sunken eyes were only two black pits, there was something familiar about that face. It definitely wasn't Elena, but the feeling that she might know this person disturbed Rosario even more.

She had to find out.

Fighting the urge to retch, she knelt down and reached for the back pockets of the corpse's pants. Despite the immense heat – had it gotten even hotter? – a chill flooded her every vein. Using two shaking fingers, she reached in and pulled out a worn leather wallet. Once it was free, she moved away, falling onto her butt and scooting backwards across the grimy floor. The body didn't smell, but she still held her breath until there were several feet between them. The thought of even a single particle of dead flesh getting into her nose sickened her to the greatest degree.

Rosario opened the wallet and sucked in a breath so big, she got lightheaded. The driver's license confirmed she indeed knew this person. In fact, he had contacted her only just yesterday. The corpse she shared the room with was the private investigator she and her family hired to find this apartment building.

The poor man had found much more than he had bargained for. A stone of festering guilt dropped into Rosario's trembling belly. She had sent this man to his death.

But how could this be? A body couldn't look like this in only a day, could it? What would cause a person to look so ravaged and drained of life?

The husk of a man that lay before her let out a weak cough before writhing on the floor in short, pained movements.

That scream that had gotten stuck in Rosario's throat now escaped, filling the entire room with its piercing trill. A piece of her soul shriveled at the sight of this ruined body, still alive somehow. She couldn't fathom the agony the man must be in, which is why she kept screaming. A thought struck her like a blow to the back of the skull. Were they going to do this to her? And had they done this to Elena?

"No, no, no!" Rosario hit the sides of her head with clenched fists, trying to wake herself from this nightmare.

A whispering floated into her ears. Through a blur of tears, she saw the lipless mouth of the living corpse moving. A strained, wispy voice attempted to form words, but was unable to do so.

"W-What?" Rosario asked. She didn't want to even look at the poor soul's horrifying form.

At a snail's pace, the investigator moved his twig-like arm across the floor until one of his skeletal fingers was pointing at a spot on one of the filthy walls.

"What is it?" Rosario asked.

He kept trying to speak, but the endeavor was futile. Rosario rose shakily to her feet and stared at the living dead man on the floor, before turning to follow his pointing finger. With tiny steps, her shoes dragging along the floor, Rosario shuffled towards the indicated spot on the wall. A feeling of dread washed over her, a feeling that whatever she was meant to find would break her completely. But inch by reluctant inch, she closed the distance between her and that stained wall.

Rosario didn't think her psyche could take any more traumatic shocks. She didn't think her throat could constrict any harder than it already had, or that her stomach could twist itself into an even tighter knot.

These weren't just random stains.

They were faces. Faces, hundreds of faces – like someone had fingerpainted them using filth or mold or whatever it was – decorated the walls. They all stared at her with dull eyes, passive and unblinking. When she took a step to the right, every moldy eye would follow her movement. When she would step to the left, they all observed, watching, yet bored. And there, near the floor, where the mummified corpse of the private investigator had pointed, was the face of Elena, staring at her with a look of indifference, as if gazing upon a stranger.

Rosario fell to her knees, all breath, heart, and soul vanishing from her body. She reached out trembling hands, wanting to cup her sister's face, but her fingers only made contact with the warm plaster of the discolored wall, smearing her own blood onto one of Elena's cheeks. The black stains that made up Elena's eyes looked at Rosario with intelligence, but no semblance of recognition.

"Elena?" Rosario sobbed, still trying to find a way to reach into the wall to pull her sister out. "Elena!"

"No have to yell. She hear you."

Rosario's head snapped in the direction of the voice. There, standing at the open door Rosario herself had just come through, stood Carmen. The little old lady looked just as warm, kind, and grandmotherly as when they'd first met. However, now Rosario knew the truth. This woman was evil. Whatever the hell was going on in this damn lunatic building was her doing. It had to be.

"What did you do to her?!" Rosario shrieked. She jumped to her feet, primal instinct wanting her to pounce upon the landlady like some wild beast, savaging her with fist and nail.

"I did nothing," Carmen said. She gestured around with a limp hand. "Was the building."

The nonchalant manner in which she delivered these words fueled the rage churning inside Rosario's core.

"Get my sister out of there!" She jabbed a finger in the direction of Elena's outlined face. As soon as Elena was free of the wall, Rosario was going to make this lady swallow her own teeth.

Carmen shook her head, her expression weary. "Not possible. But don't worry. You be with each other soon. Closer than ever before. And mija, soon you learn this building…is not just a building."

And with that, before Rosario realized what was happening, the landlady left, closing the door behind her.

"No!"

Rosario dashed for the door. But before she could reach it the entire thing faded out of being, like the memory of a dream. In its place was simply more wall with more stained faces, all watching her.

Scratching, punching, and kicking the wall did nothing. The faces didn't care and Carmen didn't return. At the top of her voice, Rosario screeched to be let out until her vocal cords were raw and she tasted blood. She eventually collapsed, exhausted, as the room continued to grow hotter and hotter. Sweat ran from every pore, all the moisture leaving her body to evaporate in this hell.

Without warning, the entire room shuddered, followed by a monumental creaking, as if the building – not a building? – was about to collapse. And in that moment, whatever illuminated the room – not a room? – was extinguished, plunging Rosario into darkness.

Something grabbed her wrist.

* * *

Rosario understood now.

She understood how perfect everything was.

She and Elena together. Always together from now on, forever. There was nothing to worry about any longer. No problems to deal with. No hardships to endure. She and her sister were at peace.

Just as Elena had been, Rosario now was too.

This building – oh, so much more than a building – had an intelligence and a purpose far greater than her own.

She was one more nail in Its structure. One more blood cell in Its body. One more step towards Its goal. She was one more stone in Its bridge.

Yes, a bridge. A bridge spanning two worlds that would be complete in due time. Then…then It could bring the rest of Itself through.

Building, bridge, body. Yes, It was all and one.

And now she and Elena were one with It.

* * *

After retrieving his luggage from the trunk, he thanked the driver. The man behind the wheel gave him a nod before speeding off into the humid Cancún morning. Damn, it was like walking around in a sauna here. He pulled up the photos on his phone to check them one more time. He glanced at the nearby street sign.

"Cuchumaquic"

Yes, this was the right place.

Before he knew it, he was at the end of the cul-de-sac, the old, worn apartment building looming over him. Was she in there? Only one way to find out.

Up the front steps he went. An intercom was set into the wall by the door. He pressed the button marked with a star.

A crackly voice answered. "¿Sí?"

He bent towards the speaker. "Hi, do you speak English? My name is Ethan. I'm looking for someone."

※

The Snake God's Wake

Juliana Spink Mills

THE MUSEUM on the Avenida Europa gleams in the rain, damp concrete reflecting the silvers and reds of rush hour traffic. She ducks inside, breathless, fifteen minutes before closing time, waving away the offer of a printed guide.

The minute hand of the battered pocket watch spins one last time and settles. She rubs a thumb across the worn casing, willing her skittering heart to settle, too. The hands haven't twitched in nearly a hundred years. But they moved today, and she's the last of her family left in São Paulo to heed the call.

Upstairs in the exhibition room, lights strobe. Walls flicker with old movie reels, no sound but the whir of projectors. The installation in the next room is the opposite: sound but no image, and the entire showcase forms a confusing cacophony of disjointed sensation. It's now ten to closing and the place should be deserted. Yet, in the shifting half-light, she finds what she came for.

He tears his eyes from a Silver Screen diva and bows his head, acknowledging her presence. "Keeper."

She doesn't call him by his name, although she knows it from a thousand childhood stories. Brown skin, red hat perched jauntily on dark curls, uneven gait. They make a pair, the two of them: the Keeper of Ways, and Saci, self-appointed jester to the chaotic patchwork court of myths that form Brazil's cultural and spiritual core.

"A god is dying," he tells her. One hand is fisted at his side. "A god will die tonight."

"Which god?"

"A snake god. Older than this land, older than time. It has been called many things in many places, but here we know it as—"

"Boitatá," she chimes in. She knows the tale of the giant fire snake, one of nature's protectors. She's heard all the stories. Once, it had been her great-grandfather's job to know this. "Why am I summoned?"

"To witness. But also, to learn. This god, for thousands of years it has wheeled, circling, burning, mouth in tail and tail in mouth. But all things end, and its fire is almost out." He eyes the darkening screen. The show is over, the museum is closing. "We should dance. Will you dance with me?"

"Here?"

"No, not here." He opens his fist, presses the contents into her hand. "Tonight, you will meet three prophets. One is lost, one is false, and one is true."

She stares at the objects lying in her palm. There's a white cowrie shell, for vision. A fresh green sprig of rue, for protection. A scarlet Pau Brasil seed, for knowledge. There's a blue saint ribbon, too, and he wraps it around her wrist and knots it three times. It's a binding, to keep her safe on her journey.

Outside, the rain has thinned to a drizzle. They weave around umbrellas, pink and orange, or solid utilitarian black. Everyone is in a hurry, but as they move up the Faria Lima, through the Largo da Batata, and into Vila Madalena, things change, and now the scuttling humanity on the sidewalk bears the giddy semblance of a Friday night crowd.

He tells her stories as they walk, and time skips like pebbles on water. She laughs. Nothing feels real. Somewhere, someplace, the snake god coils and recoils, dipping in and out of layers of reality. Serpent venom drips into her ears and down her throat, and she swallows bitterness and touches the rue in her pocket, willing the taste away.

On and on they go, round and round. Circles in the wind, circles on the ground, carved into the dirt and the urban trash, glimpsed in the scuff marks on lumbering buses. The circle of ribbon on her wrist, dark blue for the orixá Ogum, courage and strength. The circle of moon, bright behind the clouds. Everything is both far away and all too close, broad and slender, high and low, circles and spirals and layers upon layers.

Maybe this is as it should be, and she's just never noticed it before.

Or maybe she's drunk on the dark, and the night, and the curve of his lips when he smiles.

In the heart of Vila Madalena, a whole block of the neighborhood has been cordoned off for revelry. People spill out of bars and onto the street, and a dozen different beats and rhythms mingle and blend under the urban skyscape of neon signs and streetlights. In line for the toilet, she meets the first prophet. The bulb illuminating the narrow hallway is as blue as the ribbon she wears, the haze of cigarette smoke so thick you could seize it like clay and mold it.

"No one smokes inside anymore," she says. "This is a memory."

The prophet grins, delighted. They lean forward, their long black hair a liquid flood. Waves of sound and scent cascade, dragging her under, drowning her. Suddenly she remembers being young and brash, needing nothing but the pulse of music under her skin to keep her sated. She is lost in sensation, and it takes very little to set her nerves alight, taking her to the brink.

The vision fades along with the smoke. The prophet holds out a hand for payment. "Remember that feeling," they say, taking the cowrie shell. "Keep hold of it. It may lie in the past, but it was as true as anything in this world." She reaches out, not yet steady on her feet, but the water spirit Iara is already gone.

On the way out, dancers surge around her like the ones in her vision. But as they twist, faster and faster, she realizes this is not the half-remembered joy of flying, but something darker. Her heartbeat quickens. She seeks an exit, but she is surrounded. Hands reach out, touch her hip, her arms, her mouth. She backs away and collides with a firm body, solid ground in this shifting madness. It's him, and he pulls her away and out into the night.

She's shaking as he holds her tight. They sway in the rain mist to a beat of their own until she calms. The terror seeps away. Instead, the moment gentles, turns melancholy. A precious interlude. She wets her dry mouth and tastes again the bitterness of venom. He twirls her once, then reluctantly sets her free. He touches her wrist, a fleeting fingertip against the dark blue ribbon. "You've lost one." It's true; the knot was stolen by the dancers and she never even noticed. Now, only two knots remain. In her mind, the snake god laughs.

They wander the empty streets, at one with the unhoused, the sex workers, the late-shift laborers slouching home, exhausted. "The snake god, Boitatá. What does it want from me?" she dares to ask.

He frowns, disappointed. "You should know this. Why else did you come out tonight?"

She came because she was called. She came because of the whirling hands of the old pocket watch. She came because she was drawn, moth to flame, to the stark, modern museum. She hazards a guess. "My ancestors made a covenant. And now it has come due."

He tilts his hand, so-so. "Do you know what was promised?"

A lifetime, many lifetimes, of prosperity. Paid and paid and paid. But in exchange? She licks her lips, tastes the venom, shakes her head. This, she was never told. From the corner of her eye, she spots a gleaming coil, the scales moon-bright under a wash of neon. When she turns to look, there is nothing there.

Saci tugs her around to face him, her hands held captive in his own. "The snake god is weary and it longs to rest. But the world has old, old patterns that must be followed. Renewed. Circles upon circles upon circles. If you take this burden, you will gain power and knowledge beyond all you can imagine. You will be ageless. You will be one of ours. But you will also be bound to the turning of time. It is a blessing. And a curse."

He lets her go. She shivers. The wind picks up in a rattling hiss, scattering crumpled fast-food bags. A soda can rolls off the sidewalk and onto the road, where it will no doubt be crushed by tomorrow's traffic. She wraps her arms around herself and wishes for comfort, but that's not what he's here for.

He's watching, sorrowful, as if he can read her mind. "I am here only to guide," he tells her. "I cannot interfere. I have done too much already."

Their steps carry them along the Rua Groenlândia with its elegant buildings, ghost of a past that was ruthlessly trampled by the city's breathless rush into the twenty-first century. He is silent, but she knows where they're heading, can feel the tug of it under her sternum. This way leads back to the museum and the dying god.

The night darkens, tightening around her like the smooth coils of a gigantic beast. On a street corner, bathed in poisonous traffic-light green, she finds the second prophet. They lean against cold metal, all teasing bare midriff and tiny white shorts, wearing their trademark Panama hat at a jaunty angle. The prophet winks, sly and knowing. "You here for a good time, nenê?"

She shakes her head and holds out the sprig of rue. Somehow, she knows it's the right token. The prophet reels her in by the hand and kisses her deeply, all teeth and tongue. They taste of burnt sugar caramel and river water, of midnight trysts and the thrill of a secret rendezvous. She floats, expecting another vision of flesh and pleasure.

Instead, she's four years old, safe on her mother's hip as the New Year's countdown begins. Everyone is dressed in white, but beyond the sand, the sea is black and restless against the glare of bonfires and candles. Her parents share a smile, slow and sweet. The countdown swells, soars, comes to a screaming crescendo. Fireworks erupt, the sky splashed bright with color.

She comes back to herself to find the prophet holding her chin, their mouth so close they share her breath. An arm circles her waist, trapping her beribboned wrist tight against the small of her back. The prophet's eyes are heavy-lidded. "Ah," they say, satisfied. "That was good."

"But was it worth the price?" She feels untethered without the rue. Exposed. Caramel fades, leaving a sharp bitterness behind.

"A strong memory like that, warm as mid-morning sunshine? Better than rue, trust me. Remember it!" The prophet kisses her again, on the lips and on the forehead. Releasing her, they tuck the sprig into the brim of their hat and melt into the shadows. She hears the faintest echo of water, of a departing splash. Uauiará the river dolphin is gone. It isn't until after she follows Saci across the street that she realizes they took a second knot as well.

"A trickster, that one," says Saci when she shows him. But he sounds like he approves, so she swallows her hurt and fear but steps away a little, widening the gap between them. He's here to guide her, but she's not sure she can trust him. After all, he's a trickster, too.

The sidewalk shudders, and this time she knows she's not imagining scales instead of concrete, or the fire that rises to lick at her ankles and calves. The taste of venom swells, and she gags upon the bitterness.

They turn a corner and find themselves back at the museum. It should be an empty shell this late at night. Instead, it's a house for the dead. The snake god Boitatá is a vast creature. Sinuous coils pour from windows and balconies, lavishly multicolored, a sharp contrast to the modernist building it has chosen as its tomb. Its tail streams out the door and all the way down the path to greet them. The hissing is fainter now, the heartbeat a slowing drum, pulsing softer and softer as life seeps from its body.

In contrast, there are actual drums pounding out a wild rhythm that intensifies each passing moment, without words, without reason. Bodies writhe and spin, backlit by the glowing embers of the dying god. She recognizes the dancers from the bar, the lost prophet at a window, the false one draped lasciviously against the door frame. And more – the grounds are heaving.

She spies indigenous gods of the Guarani, Tikuna, Makuxi, Kaiowá; the orixás that followed the slave ships across the ocean from Africa; the saints and myths of European colonizers; even a kitsune or two, thanks to distant waves of Japanese immigration. Curupira dances with Saint Anthony, Exú grins at the moon goddess Jaci. It's a riot, a rave, a wild and reckless celebration. It's a wake, for sure. A send-off worthy of the old spirits and new, a rift between times, between space, between eras and centuries.

She doesn't want to go inside. She doesn't want to be here. Her mouth is sour and pinched from the bitter, bitter venom. In her pocket, her great-grandfather's watch ticks out a warning. She plucks at the ribbon, the blue of it a dark stain in the bright artificial glare of the entryway. It seems a scant protection against all that awaits inside. But her guide offers his arm, and her feet betray her. As he sweeps her along, the prophets flank them: the false one on the left, the lost one to the right. They shed their human guise, and she dares to finally name them out loud.

"Iara." The water spirit, the lost one, the drowned one, trapped in an endless cycle of enticement and death. "Uauiará." The false one, Boto the seducer, who sheds his dolphin form to walk upon the land and ravish the willing. "Saci-Pererê." Trickster, guide, protector. Friend. She takes courage in their presence and holds her head up high as they wade into the throng.

Upstairs, Boitatá is waiting. Flames dance upon the air currents, caressing her bare arms as she is escorted forward. All at once, she knows her part in this, clear as the crystalline rivers her prophets were born to. She kneels, bows her head. The drums fall silent. The very building holds its breath.

She closes her eyes. Centuries of familial devotion have all led to this moment. The Keeper must become the Kept. Visions arise, not of the future but of the past. Iara's dance floor frenzy. The Boto's stolen childhood dream. But something plucks at her mind. Where is the third prophet, the true one? On her wrist, one knot remains. In her pocket, the crimson Pau Brasil seed promises knowledge. The visions are tempting – pleasure and warmth, lovers and family – but that is all they are. Enticements. Temptations.

What is real in all of this? What is truly inevitable, and what is entirely her own choice? She opens her eyes and *sees*, for the first time ever.

The snake god is dying, but the circles live on. The cycles will continue, with or without Boitatá. The saints and godlings, the orixás and the forest divinities, they would see her take on this mantle, and she would no longer be anything but *theirs*, to shape and to hold.

She does not want to be shaped. She does not want to be held.

She stands, unpicks the last knot, and drops the ribbon at her feet.

The silence breaks. A wail of sound presses down upon her. Still, she stands tall. Boitatá opens one vast, burning eye. She holds its gaze even though her own eyes water at the heat. She coughs, chokes, spews out a torrent of golden venom, but she stands her ground regardless. She takes the memories the prophets gave her, and weaves them into a cloak, wrapping them around herself. It should be her shroud. Instead, it is her shield.

She pushes her way through the crowd, all the way down the stairs, all the way to the street. Each step is a battle. Each breath hurts, tears, burns. But she makes it out, and when she does, the noise just. Stops. She turns around and the museum is dark and empty.

Saci is waiting at the curb. "Impressive," he says. "I didn't think you'd be that strong."

"I'm not strong," she counters.

"Then what?"

"Stubborn, I guess."

He laughs, shaking his head, and then rests a hand, briefly, over her still-galloping heart. "Truth is strength. And you are nothing but true." He steps back, taps two fingers to his forehead in a lazy salute. "It was an honor." He turns to go.

"Will I see you again?" she can't help asking.

He shrugs. "You're no longer Keeper." His smile curves, grows, spreads. "But maybe."

The kiss, when it comes, is light as a butterfly's touch, sweet as honeysuckle nectar. It washes away the last, lingering bitterness of Boitatá's venom. She opens her eyes, and he's gone.

There are no more buses. It's too far to walk, and she is so, so tired. She flags down a taxi, gives the driver her address. The Avenida Santo Amaro is quiet, the night at the tipping point between rest and rise. Soon, the early commute will fill the city of São Paulo once more with movement. But right now, these streets are hers alone.

She digs in her pocket and brings out the battered watch and the Pau Brasil seed. The watch is still, the hands are dead. She doesn't know if it will ever stir again. The seed is cracked, right down the middle. "Oh," she says, a little heartbroken. She could do with knowledge, she thinks.

"Don't worry," says the taxi driver. "It was never more than a symbol."

Their eyes meet in the rearview mirror. She blinks and, for a second, dark eyes and dark hair become a brilliant white, a star in the liquid depths of the galaxy. Cool water soothes the snake god's burns, and she takes a deep and shuddering breath. "Naiá."

She knows the cautionary tale. The fair maiden Naiá fell in love with the moon. When she drowned, chasing Jaci's reflection in the water, she was transformed. The water lily nods in the mirror. "Once, yes."

"You're the true prophet," she realizes. "Where were you, tonight?"

"I was waiting. Truth and knowledge; you had to find those inside you. Once you did, you were able to make your own choice."

"I *chose* to remain myself. Is that so bad?"

"You were offered power. You picked freedom." The water lily's joy is blinding. "It is very good indeed. And now your path is yours to forge."

She pinches the cracked seed, rolls it between her fingers. Rough and smooth, reality and promise. The first step of a journey, a shining path that unfurls before her. "Thank you."

The lily's smile turns sorrowful. "Truth is a difficult path. I learnt that the hard way. But it is worth the effort."

The taxi drops her off at her front door, just as the first light of dawn touches the sky. She walks through the silent house, out the kitchen door and into the tiny garden. She takes a clay pot, adds pebbles for drainage, fresh soil. Presses in the Pau Brasil seed, and waters it with care.

She sets the flowerpot in a sunbeam and tips her face to the sky. The snake god's venom has been washed away, and nothing remains but the faint memory of honeysuckle.

A Guardian of Salt and Flesh

Vanessa Molina

THE SECOND I open my eyes; I am temporarily blinded by the ray of light that slices through the darkness. I inhale sharply, taste iron and salt and something else, something I can't place. It's earthy, like grass. There is pounding in my head and when I try to push myself up, my arms tremble. A cold chills my bones, traveling through my limbs as I realize I'm soaking wet. I don't know where I am.

"Oh, good, you're awake."

Suddenly I'm gasping, trying to sit up as I claw for air, the sudden fear of being pressed between waves causing shivers to rack up and down my body. It feels like my insides are on fire, like I'm drowning on dry land, yet when I try to grab hold of something, all I meet is empty air. My hand slaps against the ground I'm sitting on, and I feel the dirt underneath, tiny pebbles digging into my palms.

"Go slow," the voice says. It is not an unkind voice, but one that echoes loudly in my head. It's not until my heartbeat slows down that I realize the voice isn't coming from my head but echoing in the darkness. I try to adjust my eyesight.

"Where am I?" I ask as I take in the cave walls, the tiny strip of land I am sitting on, and the hole above my head that only lets enough sunlight in to make out the vague outline of someone in the dark.

"You're in a cenote."

"But why am I here?" I ask as I raise my hand to shield my eyes from the sun, hoping I can peer into the darkness a little better. "Did I fall?" I ask.

The person veiled in darkness shifts. "In a sense." Their voice is as deep as a man's and soft as mother's.

"I fell?" I don't have any recollection of falling, but my body shivers at its own memory, like it knows what it's like to fall into the darkness while my mind can't recall it.

"What do you remember?" they ask.

I shake my head, and it hurts. Something rattles inside my skull and pain blooms across my temple as I rub my head.

"Ah," they say in understanding. "What you're feeling right now is the pieces of your shattered skull. It broke in the fall."

"It broke? I don't understand. If it's broken, shouldn't I be in a hospital? Can you help me?"

"I've already helped you enough. Now it's time for you to help me."

"I don't understand," I say, and tears begin to prick into the corner of my eyes. They sting from the salt clinging to my body.

"You were pushed down a cliff," they say. "You fell into the water and split open your head."

I lower my hand from my head and see a little bit of rusted blood on them.

"I fished you out. Unfortunately, you died."

"Is this the underworld—" I start, thinking about ancient traditions and stories, about how the Mayans believed that cenotes were the entrances to the underworld, but they cut me off.

"This is not the underworld, but rather a place in between. I've denied your entry. That does not mean you're alive, just leaning closer to the dead than the living."

"Who are you?" I finally ask.

They finally step forward. He's still cloaked in shadows but close enough to the light that I can see a vague outline and I gasp.

They stand before me, skull face peering into me. They're half skeleton, their bones gleaming in the light, and half bloated corpse, their stomach gaping like a dark abyss. They are a grotesque figure, more decaying skeleton with rotting flesh than anything else. I recoil.

"I am Ah Puch, the god of death," they say before retreating back into the shadows.

My mind spins and it takes me a few minutes to recover, to steady my breathing enough to continue the conversation. "Why have you denied me entry to the afterlife?" I ask.

"Because I'm giving you an opportunity to avenge your death."

I squint.

"You were pushed," they repeat.

"But—"

"There is a man, foreign man," they say, losing patience with me. "He sends men to dig and destroy sacred areas, careless and disrespectful to the land and the living. I want you to stop him."

"But why me?"

"Because he is the one who pushed you."

And then my memories start to bleed into the spaces between my shattered skull and I remember. I remember protesting the American company building their new resort on sacred land. I remember the broken artifacts discarded as the bulldozers dug through the area. I remember sneaking into the property at night, hoping to sabotage the machinery, hoping to rescue the few artifacts that remained intact before they could be sold off to foreign countries. And I remember being caught, being chased, the confrontation with the owner and being pushed. And falling. Falling, falling, falling.

"What do I have to do?" I ask.

* * *

My head is spinning by the time I make it out of the cave. I walk home, padding on bare feet, leaving a trail of water in my wake like breadcrumbs. By the time I make it home, it's already dark.

I hesitate at the door. I don't know what I look like and I can't imagine, covered in blood and dirt and sweat, salt and sand clinging to every crevice of my body. I had hoped everyone would be asleep so that I could sneak in, take a shower, make myself presentable, but the lights are on. My mother, my grandmother, my aunt, and my older sister will be home. I brace myself and open the door.

The living room is empty, the couch devoid of any member of my family lounging on it, but the sheet that my grandmother keeps over the couch to keep it from getting dirty lies askew, like someone had been sitting on it recently.

"¿Mamá?" I call into the empty house.

Something clatters in the kitchen, and I make my way there.

I see my mother by the dishwasher. Her head hangs heavy, and her shoulders shake like she's trying not to cry. And then her head lifts, catches my distorted reflection on the window above the sink and she yells before she spins around.

"¿Mamá?" I say again as her hand flies to her mouth to stifle a scream.

"Mami," I start to walk forward but she scrambles away.

"Get back," she says, suddenly reaching for the old pan she was washing. Water and suds fly everywhere as she waves it towards me.

"Mami," I whine as I hold my hands up in surrender. "It's me. Put that down."

A Guardian of Salt and Flesh

"I heard yelling," my older sister Olga calls out from the other room. She walks in, carrying a plate. I think they just had dinner. "What's going on—?" She stops at the second doorway that leads to the dining room, her eyes flying from me to our mother and back to me. The plate falls and clatters on the floor, shattering in a way that I imagine my skull shattered when I fell. "Santa Maria," she says as she makes the sign of the cross. "Mami, get away from her," she says as she inches closer to our mother and away from me.

"It's just me," I say. "I got into an accident, but I'm back."

Olga starts shaking her head as she reaches our mother and wraps her arms protectively around her.

"No, no, no. You're dead. We saw your body. We buried you!" she yells, then leans closer. "We had a novenario for you," she hisses, talking about the traditional nine days of prayer that follows a funeral. "La vecina chismosa complained that our arroz con leche was too sweet."

My head begins to throb again. "How long have I been gone?" I ask.

"Gone? GONE?" My sister is hysterical now while our mother remains silent, trembling in her arms. "YOU DIED TWO WEEKS AGO!"

"Oh," I say, wondering what my body is now. I remember what Ah Puch said. I am not alive but closer to dead.

Then I feel someone's gentle touch on my arm and turn to see my grandmother's weary face. I expect her to wear fear like my mother and sister, but her weathered face remains impassive.

"Abuela," Olga hisses. "Get away from her. We don't know what that is. It could be a ghost or a demon wearing Xochil's face. Don't touch it."

"I'm not contagious." I roll my eyes.

"Yeah, well, we don't know that. You could have rabies."

I open my mouth to argue but then my grandmother steps forward. "That's enough," she says. "Can't you see our Xochil has returned to us?"

Olga begins to argue but my grandmother says, "Did you break one of our good plates?"

Olga's eyes fly to the broken plate on the floor and a new fear flashes across her face. "It was an accident," she says as our grandmother picks up a ratty old dish towel so old the edges are frayed. She raises her hand. "Si no lo limpias ahorita mismo," she warns as she swats Olga with the towel. "Vas a ver," she swats her again.

"It was an accident," she whines as she dives for the broom and dustpan. "And it's Xochil's fault."

"Don't blame your sister," she says before looking back at me. "And you, you're sopping wet. You better get yourself cleaned up." I start to move but then she swats me as well. It stings against my arm, and I wince. "You better clean up that puddle of water you're standing in first. In the meanwhile, I'll tend to my daughter."

My mother is still standing still, pale and scared as she stares at me.

My grandmother starts to lead her away in a slow shuffle. "And clean the muddy footprints you left when you walked in here. If the floor is still dirty by the time I come back here, vas a ver."

* * *

Showering proves to be a struggle. When I look down at my body, there are countless bruises. I rinse the dry blood away until the water turns clear. When I finish my shower and try to untangle my hair, my brush falls on the ground and when I bend to pick it up, something rattles in my head.

I find my family sitting in the living room, silent and waiting for me. I clear my throat, waiting to see how they'll react. I'm afraid my mother will turn away from me but when her eyes finally land on me, I see the tears welling in her eyes.

"Mami," I half sob half desperately plead as she stands. Her arms aren't fully lifted before I'm barreling into her waiting arms.

She wraps her arms around me and I almost start sobbing when I catch a glimpse of my sister's face. Her nose scrunches and I hope it gives her wrinkles.

"¿Qué?"

"You look disgusting," she sighs.

"I showered," I say as I point at my still wet hair.

"Mami." Olga leans forward. "She might have rabies."

Not this again. "I don't have rabies." At least I don't think I do.

"You might."

"Maybe I should bite you and find out."

She makes her fingers into a sign of a cross.

"That's enough," my grandmother says. "Even after death the two of you bicker like crazy. Olga, go make your mother some te de Manzanilla."

"Why is it always me?"

"Your sister died."

Olga flinches and I see hurt and pain around her eyes, the eye bags I hadn't noticed are prominent. I almost reach out for her but then she's flying towards the kitchen.

The front door creaks open and my Aunt Claudia comes home. "You won't believe what the vecina chismosa said," she says as she starts taking her shoes off. "She said she saw Xochil's ghost walking through the neighborhood—" She cuts off when her eyes connect with mine. Her mouth opens, trembles, and closes before her eyes roll back and she falls backwards, her body painfully thudding against the floor.

"I think you killed her," Olga says from the kitchen doorway.

"Don't be ridiculous," my *abuela* gets up, her joints snapping.

"Erendira," my grandmother says addressing my mom. "Ayúdame."

Between my mother, Olga, and I, we lift my Aunt Claudia's body and lay her on the couch. The white sheet falls askew over my aunt, and I go around the couch to tug it back into place while Olga is blowing wind on her face with a magazine she found lying around. After a few minutes, Aunt Claudia's eyes flutter open. Olga leans over her.

"What's wrong, tia, you look like you've seen a ghost."

"Olga," my mother scolds and her voice is stronger now.

"But I did," she says. "I thought I saw Xochil."

"About that," I say, and Aunt Claudia's eyes go to me. "Please don't faint again," I say.

Aunt Claudia stares and stares and stares.

"Are you real?" she asks and I shrug. "What's going on?"

"That's what Xochil was about to tell us when you came in," my grandmother says.

Everyone looks at me expectantly. I tell them everything.

***

"So this god," Olga starts saying but my grandmother interrupts.

"Ah Puch," she corrects.

"Right," Olga says. "Ah Puch. He wants you to kill for him? You?" she says before she burst out laughing. "Por favor, you can't even kill a roach."

"I can too," I say. "I just feel bad."

"But you think you won't feel bad if you kill this man?"

"HE KILLED ME!" I say and the living room falls silent.

"What happens if you fail?" my mother asks.

"I will be denied passage," I say.

"Then we mustn't fail," my grandmother adds.

"¿Están locas?" Aunt Claudia interrupts and my mother reaches for my hand and gives me a squeeze.

"This man killed Xochil! We should go to the police!"

"And say what? That my dead daughter was brought back from the dead by a Mayan god to avenge her death?" my mother scoffs.

"What we need," Olga interrupts, "is a plan. Everything else can wait."

"And how will I kill him?" I ask, swallowing hard.

"We'll cross that bridge when the time comes," my grandmother says. "Right now, we're just glad our Xochil has returned to us." Tears prick the corner of her eyes, and I try not to imagine what they all went through.

"Let us rest for now and be thankful for the extra time we've been given. The gods know that's not something everyone gets."

My aunt tries to rise but she looks like she's going to faint again. Olga leans closer to me.

"Maybe you can scare that white man to death. Un susto, you know?"

I look at her as she looks at Aunt Claudia. She might be on to something.

* * *

A Guardian of Salt and Flesh

That night, I lie awake, staring up at our ceiling.

"Go to sleep," I hear Olga whine from her bed next to mine.

"How'd you know I was awake?" I ask.

"I can hear you thinking all the way from here. If you don't stop, I'll go sleep in the living room."

I think of how Aunt Claudia's snoring can be heard loud and clear from the living room.

"What about Aunt Claudia's snoring?" I ask.

I hear Olga's sheets shift as a shudder runs through her body and smile in the darkness.

"What are you going to do?" she asks.

"I don't know." I sigh into the darkness and pull my sheets higher.

I hear more shuffling followed by Olga's padded feet and then my bed dips seconds before Olga tucks herself next to me.

"I thought you were scared of me," I whisper.

Olga remains quiet. "I am, but no more than an older sister can fear their younger one. You're still you. You walk the same, talk the same. And you don't smell like a corpse anymore."

"Did I really smell that bad?" I ask.

"I didn't want to say anything considering you were dead."

I playfully shove her.

We stay like that for a few minutes until I feel Olga trembling. "Are you crying?"

She sniffs. "I'm angry. Do you have any idea what it was like? When you didn't come home, we looked all over for you. Mamá was terrified, stayed up all night praying. Even the neighbors went looking for you."

"And when they found my body?" I ask.

Olga doesn't say anything for a few seconds. Then, "Please don't ask me that. I don't want to relive that."

"Okay," I whisper.

"But now, I'm angry. I'm angry at you because you snuck out. I'm angry because you didn't take me with you. I'm angry because that man killed you. I'm angry because you can't find peace, and I'm angry at that God for making you do something you might not be able to do."

"What do you mean?"

"You've always been kind, even with roaches and spiders." She shudders again. "You can't do this."

"I have to," I say.

"Then you're not doing this alone this time," she says and wraps her arms around me. "We're going to come up with a plan tomorrow," she says. "We will take revenge for what he did."

* * *

In the morning, we're all sitting around our round, wooden dining table. Mami made chilaquiles and everyone eats quietly except me. My stomach turns even as my mouth waters at the smell.

"Aren't you hungry?" Olga asks. "I mean, you've been dead for like two weeks."

"Olga," my mother scolds.

"Do dead people even eat?"

"Is that a serious question?" I ask her.

"Well, I've never met someone dead come back to life before."

"Can we not talk about the dead during breakfast?" Aunt Claudia says.

"But we need to come up with a plan," Olga says.

"She's right," I agree and Olga gasps.

"It only took you dying for you to finally agree with me."

I ignore that.

"Ah Puch," my grandmother says as she walks into our small dining room and pulls a chair to sit. "Said that you need to avenge your death. Is that exactly what he said?"

I try to remember everything, but it feels like it's already fading away.

"Ah Puch said they were giving me a chance to avenge my death and correct the wrong done to the land."

"So basically, stop your killer from destroying more land," Olga says.

"I've been thinking about what you said last night, about scaring him."

"¿Un susto?" Olga asks. "That might not work."

"No, but maybe he'll confess to killing me," I say out loud, a plan starting to form.

"And how are we going to do that?"

"I can confront him," I say. "The ghost of a girl he killed. I can be my justice."

My mother recoils, a lecture already on the top of her tongue. "It's going to be fine, Mom," I say.

"She's right," Olga agrees. "What's he going to do? She's already dead."

My mother bites her lips.

"We're going to need more help," Olga continues.

"What do you have in mind?"

Olga's grin is her only answer.

* * *

I peek through the curtains to get a glimpse of Olga and my mother talking to our *vecina chismosa*. I can't tell what they're saying, but our neighbor gasps as she lays a hand on her chest.

"Get away from there," my grandmother calls from the couch.

"You heard her," I tell my Aunt Claudia who is pressed against the glass, trying to listen in as well.

"She was talking to you. What do you think will happen if she sees you?"

"I meant the both of you," my grandmother calls. She's sitting on her couch, trying to concentrate on some telenovela.

My Aunt Claudia and I share a look before we both

walk over to the couch and wait. A few minutes later, my mother and Olga come in.

"Well?" I ask. "How'd it go?"

"She's going to spread the story to the whole neighborhood," my mother says.

"Everyone will know within minutes with the way her gossip travels. All you have to do is hide until the time is right."

* * *

The plan is simple. We will corner him the way he cornered me. We will make him confess to killing me in front of the whole neighborhood. In another life, that is a form of justice, to have him arrested, to have him rot in jail for the murder of an innocent life. But the law bends and folds for white men, even in foreign countries. What Olga does not know is the anger that travels underneath my flesh like an electrical current, humming for revenge. What she doesn't know is that I have plans of my own. What she doesn't know won't put her in danger. So, for now, I'll follow the plan like we discussed.

We get to the construction site just after sundown. The *albañiles* have already left, but from the light on one of the bungalows, we know that my killer is still in there working. That was my mistake the night I died. I had assumed everyone, him included, had already left. Instead, he caught me. But tonight, this works in our favor.

"Let's go over the plan again," Olga says as she fishes her phone out of her pocket. "I confront him. You reveal yourself enough that he can see you but still staying out of sight of any of our hidden neighbors. He'll think you're out for revenge—"

"I am."

"He'll confess with not only multiple witnesses, but Aunt Claudia will also record on her phone."

"But what if he tries to do something to you?"

"Then one of our neighbors will step in. And we'll record the transgressions."

"How did you get all the neighbors to come out?" I ask as we make our way to our positions. The site looks empty. I don't see anyone hidden.

"It wasn't hard. *La vecina chismosa* already thought she had seen your ghost. We just told her that your ghost visited us, told us you were killed. She was angry as well."

"She wasn't scared?"

"She used to babysit us when we were toddlers. I don't think she's scared of us in any form."

We duck underneath one of the bungalow windows. "Remember, stay hidden. You're the beating heart of guilt, his telltale heart. Now go."

I slink off and crouch behind a bush as Olga straightens. She takes a few steps back and reaches into a sack she'd slung over her shoulder. She pulls out two eggs and begins to toss them at the bungalow. The first slam of the egg echoes loudly as it thuds against the glass. The next one hits the door. By the fourth egg, all provided by chickens from our neighborhood, gladly donated as an act of vengeance, the manager of the site swings out the door, narrowly getting hit by an egg that slams against the threshold.

"What is the meaning of this," he hollers, and I recognize the anger marring his face. It's the same anger he wore when he pulled me by the wrist when he caught me digging through the artifacts.

"What do you think you're doing!"

"Do you not recognize my face? See the similarities?" Olga yells.

"What?" the man asks as he takes a step back. My sister mirrors it, aware of what he's capable of.

"I have her eyes and her lips."

The man squints for a second, confused until my sister says, "You killed her. My little sister!"

The man looks around at the empty lot. I duck lower as my sister begins to walk to where I am hiding. She's positioning herself so that he'll see me emerge from the darkness but none of our witnesses will see me.

The man says nothing, so my sister reaches for another egg. "Admit it," she yells, more so that her voice can be recorded than for his benefit.

"This is private property," he yells. "And you're trespassing. This is against the law. You need to leave."

My sister tosses another egg. It arcs over him and slams against the bungalow. She takes another step back, closer to me.

"I will call the police on you," he says, and I can see my sister is losing her patience. We knew it wouldn't be easy, that he wouldn't just confess to a murder because someone showed up seeking justice.

"I know it was you!" she calls out. "How do you even sleep at night, knowing what you did! I hope when you close your eyes, you see her."

The man laughs. "You're crazy. I don't know who you are or what you're talking about."

Olga pitches another egg and this time it slams against his chest. His nostrils flare and when he takes another step forward, I rise from my hiding spot.

The movement catches his attention, and his eyes widen at the sight of me. When he takes a step back, I know what he's seeing. He sees the anger seeping out of my bloated, pale face. This, I try to say telepathically, is what you did to me.

"You killed her!" my sister says without looking back. I know that she knows I'm standing behind her. "And you know what, she's not going to rest until you admit it. She'll follow you to the ends of the world."

He takes another step back.

"She will haunt you until you admit it."

"It-it was an accident," I barely hear him say, too low for whoever is recording to hear him.

"What?" Olga snarls. "I can't hear you."

"It wasn't supposed to happen," he says louder. "She tripped and fell backwards."

This is not the confession we need. It is not the pressure of his fingers on my arm as he pushed me off the cliff, nor the calm facade he wore as he watched me fall. I start to walk forward. For every step I take, he backs up.

"We both know that's not true," my sister says.

"She fell," he insists.

"You pushed her!" Olga yells.

Now the man looks angry, his eyes jumping from me to my sister. Still, she doesn't look back at me. He has to believe I am his guilt manifesting. "And she will take her revenge."

"I didn't mean to push her!" he finally says. "She ran towards the cliff. She was close to the edge. I grabbed her by the arm to haul her away but then, but then—"

"But then what?" Olga presses.

He looks straight at me when he snarls, "She threatened me." He begins to laugh as he stares at me as if he really does think I'm a hallucination. "Can you believe that, threatening me. She was hysterical, out of her mind. She said she was going to report me for illegally selling artifacts. It didn't take much for her to slip and fall. It was barely even a push. I just nudged her."

"You killed her," my sister says out loud. "And now everyone will know."

I take that as my sign to fade into the darkness before someone catches me on tape.

"No one will believe you," the man says as his eyes jump from the shadows, perhaps searching for me.

"That's where you're wrong," my sister says.

The glint of a phone screen catches his attention as our neighbors start coming out of their hiding places.

His face drains of any color. I watch as some of our neighbors come forward. I'm still hiding in the shadows as one of our neighbors confronts him, before something glimmers in the low light seconds before the man runs towards Olga. She doesn't get a chance to react before he materializes a blade from nowhere and presses it against her throat.

I'm rising from my spot before I can even think, but I don't get to reach them before the man is hauling Olga away from the crowd and into the surrounding forest.

* * *

I run after them, not bothering to spare a glance at the crowd of neighbors. I hear a few gasps as I run after Olga but try not to think about what I may look like, a dead girl who came back to life. A dead girl chasing her killer before he can harm anyone else.

I burst through the trees, leaves and vines slipping against my face, the feeling reminiscent of that night. I don't even have to think of where he's taking her because I already know. My feet carry me to the place I died.

I burst through a small clearing until I find Olga struggling against the man. They're still far enough from the edge but if I do nothing, my fate will also be Olga's.

Olga thrashes in his grip, words flying from her mouth as his left arm wraps tighter around her delicate neck, the other hand holding the blade. I'm afraid Olga will thrash hard enough that she'll accidentally embed herself to the blade.

"You're done for," Olga screams. "They heard you. The police will be here soon."

"You stupid—" His yell cuts off as Olga's teeth sink into his arm.

She slips from his grip but before she can get away, he grabs her by her hair and yanks her in the same way he yanked my arm. I know what will come next.

I run towards them. Olga catches sight of me as the man tries to slash her. She tries to run around him just as the blade arches in her direction. I reach her just seconds before the blade makes contact, pulling her behind me as the blade sinks into my side.

I don't feel it, the sink of the blade into my flesh. There's no pain at all.

The man's eyes widen as he stares into my undead eyes, and I know what he sees. He sees me seconds before he pitched me over. He sees the corpse of a girl he killed. He sees my revenge materialized like a telltale heart. And before he has a chance to react, I hear Ah Puch's words. *Avenge your death.* And I do.

With all the strength in me, I pull his arm towards me and when he tries to pull away, I use his momentum to push him back, our legs tangling, my hands pushing, until we're both pitching into the dark.

My hair slaps against my face as we fall. There's a second of weightlessness, of pressure and wind roaring in my ears.

I hear Olga scream my name, but it sounds distant. All I see are the man's widened eyes, fear clawing them open until they're more white than anything. And then nothing at all.

* * *

I once again wake up in a cenote, alone and wet, but not cold. This time I feel the warmth of the sun spilling into the cave from the hole above.

"Finally awake," the ominous voice says just as I'm sitting up.

My entire body aches once again. There are more parts of me that rattle underneath my skin. I ask, "What happened just now?"

The shadows glide through the darkness, never once getting too close to the sunlight.

"You've completed what you sought out to do," they say. "You avenged your death and stopped the destruction of both the forest and the sacred land. The gates of Xibalba open for you. Come, my child, it is time to leave this plane."

My eyes travel to the tunnel that I know leads to the exit. "My sister," I start.

"She is fine."

"And the foreigner?"

"He met an unfortunate end."

"What about the construction?" I ask. I'm buying more time before I have to go.

"Has ended," is all they say. I assume two deaths is bad enough publicity to stop the building of a resort.

"So, what happens now?" I ask.

Ah Puch's shadows retreat into the darkness. "As promised, you may now pass onto Xibalba."

I didn't get to say goodbye to my family, not the first time, and not the second time. But I'm grateful to have been able to have had more time with them.

Tears spring into my eyes. Ah Puch offers, "People are leaving offerings in places where more construction is ongoing."

"What do you mean?" I asked.

"It started with offerings by your family and neighbors at the edge of the forest near here, followed by some near the now-closed construction site."

"For me?"

"They saw a glimpse of you running after your sister. So now they leave you offerings for your protection, your interference, your help."

"My help," I echo.

"They believe that you can punish those who cause destruction to forest, that you will punish those who come to take what belongs to the land. Some seek your permission to work in certain areas by offering you food, flowers, and candles. There is life after death even when we cannot often see it," Ah Puch continues. "I can see that you do not want to go. Know that I do not offer this lightly, but I can give you another task, one where you get to choose, this time."

"What is it?"

"You may move on to the afterlife, or if you'd like, become a caretaker of this region, a guardian of salt and flesh that looks over its people. The choice is yours."

This time, with much more certainty than the last time I was here, I hear myself say, "What do I have to do?"

Come Back

Mo Moshaty

A JEWEL-BOX apartment hummed with the low pulse of television chatter and SMEG appliances. Once vivid, it was now steeped in sombre greys and blues, lit only by the sun and streetlights. Dead flowers, takeout boxes, and the faint echo of joy that once filled the air. At the heart of the apartment, Marisol McGee sat, cocooned in a wide-weave pink blanket, her gaze fixed on the glowing screen. On the dark wood floating shelves above her lay remnants of a happier time: children's books stacked in uneven rows displaying her author name, toy replicas of beloved characters standing guard. A bright orange book titled *Ixmucane and the Gift* caught a stray ray of sun, but it looked dull against the Newberry Medal that hung beside it. A tattered yarn-doll with worn wooden hands leaned precariously forward; its gaze almost seemed to pierce the back of Marisol's head. Accolades gleamed faintly, dimmed and gathering dust. Slowly, as though lifted by marionette strings, Marisol rose, the blanket slipping silently to the floor. Outside the sun bled into the horizon, surrendering the day to shadows. She sat at a small table on her balcony, legs crossed against her chest, scribbling through a well-worn Moleskine book.

The first day's passage read like a heart ripped clean in two with the resonance of understanding and acceptance.

At the end of my street there's a train station. A train that will take me to places I've never been with you; it will take me to people I've yet to meet. People who will someday fill the hole you've left in my heart. I used to think of you as a dragon, a king, a unicorn. I now think of you as a monster. A monster that hides under my bed keeping me awake. I pray for the daylight, so the monster goes away.

And as grief always carries us away to somewhere either decadent or demolished, Marisol's journalized thoughts began to travel backwards...

Abuela used to say that if you whispered your sorrow into a muñeca quitapena, it would take the pain from your heart away. I never knew if she meant it as a comfort or warning. I don't write to heal. I write because the ache needs a place to live. But what if the muñeca never lets it go? What if it carries the pain forever, and it becomes something else? Something that changes you.

And forwards, dripping in future-faking and raw-skinned eyelids...

I miss his voice, even now. It's sick, isn't it? To long for someone who did this to me, someone who took pieces of me every day until I was hollow. And yet, some part of me, the softest, sickest part, still needs him, like he was something holy, and I wasn't. In therapy we talk about how I'm "processing", that I'm building boundaries. But all I can see are labyrinth walls where he's just on the other side and I'm turned all around chasing passage after passage, lost over and over. I write, and I write, but nothing fills the space that he left.

Like I said, sick.

I've started folding paper into little shapes, like the worry dolls we used to make in school, the ones with pipe cleaners and scraps of cloth. I don't know why. Now, I can't stop. My night stand is full of them. And all they do is stare back at me. And they never speak. I'm beginning to wonder if Abuela was right.

To the simple shredding of her mind. Slow. Deliberate. Inevitable.

I woke up and found a doll in my hand. Not the paper ones I make. Much different. Tiny. Handstitched and beautiful. Maybe something I'd found while sleep-walking. I think it whispered my name. Every time I hold it, it's already warm. Sometimes it looks like it's breathing. I've hidden under the mattress at least four times. Today, she's back.

That night, Marisol dreamed in colour, not the soft pastels of children's books or old sketch pads, but sharp, jagged reds. Thick, pulsing blues. Gold of marigolds too bright to be real. She stood barefoot in a cornfield under a night sky that pulsed like breath. The wind was warm, and it whispered to her, low and endless.

Marisol, Marisol, Marisol.

The stalks parted with a soft rustle, revealing a woman, ancient, proud, wrapped in a woven shawl. Her face, painted like a doll, had lips stitched tight with black thread, cheeks hollowed in faded pink. Eyes, dark and endless, pierced through Marisol as if she were nothing. Jagged pink thread spiralled from her temples to her throat, crossing like a twisted binding.

In her hands, she held the warm doll, small, delicate, woven from cloth and corn husks, its hair made of human strands. "This one's full," the woman's voice cracked, raw and dry. "You've given it too much sorrow. It can't carry it for you anymore."

Marisol tried to scurry back, to run, but her legs were rooted in the earth. Roots crept up from the soil, wrapping tight around her thighs, anchoring her to the ground. Her arms stiffened, bound at the wrists with red thread. She pulled her mouth open to scream, but her lips were sealed with stitches, the thread pulling painfully, tearing at her mouth and unravelling in the breeze. The doll-woman's laugh, soft and cruel, carried on the wind.

The same dream would haunt her for many weeks to come. Sometimes with Greg standing somewhere within the field, watching her, sometimes it was his hands pulling her into the ground. Sometimes, he laughed along with the ancient woman.

Four months later, one solitary passage, written 1,387 times, gleamed from the worn Moleskine pages.

I'm writing it down. If I disappear, if I start to forget who I am I want this to be here.

I'm not broken. I'm not crazy.

Her new "unbroken" life consisted of black coffee, chain-smoked cigarettes, and the constant blue stains beneath her left pinkie, battle scars from her left-handed scribbling. She tried to distract herself with hand-sewing or solitaire but always came back to the book, the one thing that seemed to fill the hollow. Over and over the words poured and the scribbles soon gave way to rips in the page.

She slammed it closed heavily. She took a long drag quickly, letting the nicotine make her dizzy, she let it twirl within her mind, smiling giddily, enjoying the buzz, eyes closed. Her eyes were pulled gently open by a gentle beep and the smell of coffee which brought her back. She allowed a smile to touch her lips briefly at the tin roof tinkling of her spoon in the cup. Greg always did that so loudly. Everything about him was loud. Loud, dismissive, disconnected. The clink of the spoon was all it took to bring her back.

"You know it wasn't the actual phrase; it was just something in your voice told me we were going to go through this again." Greg tinged his spoon on the edge of the mug, purse-lipped. He pointed at her palm side up.

"So, what gives? What now? I didn't call at ten on the dot?"

Marisol sat opposite with her arms crossed, she knew where it was heading, where it always headed. Camp Projection's 4 Step Program. In all the rollercoasting years they were together, Greg had only pseudo-apologized or taken blame a handful of times. It wasn't his style. He didn't look good in accountability, made him soft.

"You're such a smug son of a bitch sometimes. You make me feel like a needy child," she said.

"I just, I don't know what to do anymore. I've got my own jobs and my own stresses, and I want to be there, but I can't be there for everything." Greg sipped his coffee, never taking his eyes off her.

"You're not there for anything." Marisol uncrossed her arms and leaned in. Greg instinctively leaned back. *Step 1: The I Beg Your Pardon?*

"Are you ever not disappointed?" he said, "You're a children's author for fuck's sake, can't you at least feign happiness and joy?"

"Do you ever miss me?" Her voice barely made it past her lips, a crack in the surface of her control.

Greg's eyes flickered, but his expression was too guarded to give anything away.

"Like how?" His voice was flat, almost dismissive. *Step 2: Explain Why You Feel Hurt By My Terrible Actions.*

"Honestly?" Marisol rolled her round mahogany eyes. She bit down on the inside of her cheek. She wanted to say more; to scream out everything he had done to her, to herself, but the words wouldn't come. Instead, she rolled her eyes, the motion too practised, too sharp.

"Yes, of course I do when we've been apart for a few weeks. But we're never apart for a few weeks much anymore."

"So, I'm supposed to just understand, subliminally, that you would like your space, Greg?"

"Marisol, you cling." He sighed into the air above her head.

"Since when is wanting someone to spend more time with you than a twenty-minute phone call a week clingy?"

"We're not doing this, Mare."

"No, *you're* not doing this. You never want to be made out as the one who's not trying. If you're going to insist on pretending you weren't after a deep meaningful relationship when you spilled your guts out about your doomed past relationships and your shitty childhood and your SSRI addiction, please let's not continue the charade."

It was Greg's turn now to cross arms. *Step 3: How Dare You Hold Me Responsible For My Actions.*

"I wondered how long it would take you." His voice was heavy with mockery, but the words didn't land with her anymore.

She shook her head, the weight of her own exhaustion settling in her bones. *This*. This had been the last straw.

"Do not." Marisol waved her finger at him, her voice breaking. "You never see your behaviour as wrong. I trust you with a lot. I thought you trusted me. I thought we..." she made an air quote gesture, "transcended just your basic relationship. A place where only we stood. Where is that man who said those things?"

Her hand trembled slightly as she reached for her napkin, dabbing at the water that threatened to spill from her eyes. She had learned to wear waterproof mascara for this very reason. *Never let him see you cry.*

Greg stands putting his napkin into his coffee cup, marking the end of the small talk over coffee. He leads gently into *Step 4: This Conversation Is Over.*

"I'm going for a smoke." Greg's phone beeps, he checks it and smiles, he begins to text. Greg heads outside.

Marisol doesn't move. She stays still, her gaze dropping to the coffee cup in front of her. Her pulse ticks in her throat, and she feels her words still hanging in the air, unsaid, unresolved.

For a moment, time seems to slow, and all she can hear is the rhythm of her own breath, shallow and uneven. She wants to say something, anything, but the weight of his silence presses down on her. The longer she sits, the harder it is to breathe.

And then, as if snapped from a trance, the tears come; quiet, hot against her cheeks.

Her hand reaches for the napkin, but it feels too heavy to lift, too fragile to be useful.

Her hand moves, almost mechanically, as she grabs the crumpled napkin and shoves it into Greg's mug, the action sharp, deliberate. She wonders if he'll notice. He never does. She says the words, but they feel like they're coming from somewhere far away, disconnected from the raw ache in her chest.

"If only you'd respond to me with that vigour," she mutters under her breath, her voice barely above a whisper.

Marisol stands slowly, as if moving through water, the weight of every step a reminder of how much of herself she's lost in this relationship. She pulls on her coat, the fabric stiff against her skin, and walks out of the coffee shop. The cold air hits her face like a slap, but she doesn't flinch. She walks past Greg, his voice rising in a cheery conversation with someone else, and she wonders how he can sound so light when everything inside her feels so heavy.

The waiter calls after her, waving the check, but Marisol doesn't stop. She doesn't even glance back. Greg calls her name, but his voice is lost on her, swallowed by the noise of her own thoughts and the sounds of the city. She doesn't look back as Greg begrudgingly follows the waiter inside, and for the first time in a long while, Marisol doesn't care.

The cigarette had burned down to Marisol's fingers, pulling her out of her daydream. She exhaled a final puff and lit another, the smoke swirling around her head, thick and stifling. She pulled her notebook close to her chest, the paper edges crinkling under her grip. The weight of it felt like a relic from another life. She walked back into her apartment, the stale air settling around her as if nothing had changed. More jazz. More red wine. More walks down memory lane with old black and white photos of her and Greg.

"No one develops film anymore!" Greg once exclaimed, his voice laced with that sarcastic joy he wore so well. He wound his Ricoh Auto 35 Enterprise, the camera clicking as he aimed it at her.

"Then let's start." She grinned, playful, but Greg's gaze from behind the lens was not playful at all. It was hungry. Lustful.

"Yes, ma'am."

Her chest tightened, a dull ache she'd learned to ignore, and then it was gone. She drifted off, a glass of wine slipped from her fingers as she sank into a stupor, the faint hum of Johnny Carson's voice faded into oblivion.

Snap.

The television shut off. The sweet harmonious buzz of appliances ceased, the world around her became dull, the speckles of dust ceased to swirl about the room. The room's blue and grey hues were swallowed up by a sickly amber light. Marisol's body rolled off the couch, landing on the floor with a sick thud.

* * *

Marisol's face pressed into a cold pane of glass. Her breath fogged and cleared in desperate, ragged circles. In. Out. Her lids fluttered open sluggishly, only to snap wide at the pressure building against her. There was a moment of disorientation before she realized what she was seeing, or what she wasn't.

Her hands were gone. No fingers to press against the glass, no nails to scratch at the surface. Just blood-soaked toy stuffing, seeping from where her wrists should have been.

A gasp tore from her chest as she shot upright, her heart racing. Another nightmare. Another useless, helpless fight.

She rubbed her face, trying to steady herself. Her gaze fixing on a single sunray, that peaked though the soft vertical blinds. She sighed heavily, and wept at the use of her lithe, tan fingers. She stiffened as she took in her surroundings and grimaced at the clock. She was running late for excavation time.

Marisol fumbled with the loose bubble of lint on the orange armchair. The office around her was pure Golden Age: soft lighting, gilded frames and velvet distractions, all curated by the anal-retentive Marla Exhipo, LPCC. Marisol and her third therapist had a love/hate relationship.

Marla loved digging, Marisol hated divulging.

"How long has it been over, Marisol?"

"About four months." Her voice came out too quickly, too flat. She couldn't remember the last time she had said it with conviction.

Marla's gaze didn't waver from her journal. It was almost as if Marla didn't even *need* to look at her. "Let me rephrase that. How long has it been over for him, do you believe?"

Marisol blinked, the question dragging her back into her thoughts, each one more suffocating than the last. "Oh God, probably way before that. He'd changed."

"How so?" Marla's voice rose slightly, but there was an edge of indifference that Marisol could hear beneath the feigned interest. The woman didn't care. Marisol figured she was probably too busy sketching the squirrel in a baseball cap again. Winky.

Marisol felt a wave of frustration pulse through her, but she let it pass and brushed her fingers lightly over the small hole she'd created in the armchair's fabric. A pathetic attempt to regain control.

"In a lot of ways," she said, and swallowed the knot in her throat. "I met the most wonderful man a few years ago. Tender, warm, hilarious. And he adored me. We were... there. In it. Passionate and comforting. It was all there." Her voice caught on the last words; the reality of it had finally hit her. "And then as time went on... I just suppose I had worn out my welcome." She laughed, the sound feeling foreign. "My mom says 'He's got a lot of dolls, *mijita*. Let them have him.' She thinks she's helping, but..." She trailed off, unable to finish.

Marla didn't respond immediately, but Marisol could feel the weight of her gaze on her, the scrutinizing, professional stare. And then came the question that always made her skin crawl.

"How have you been handling things?"

Marisol stared blankly at the floor, her mind far away. The weight of every cigarette she'd smoked, every glass of wine she'd emptied, the hours spent sifting through old texts and emails, hoping for some sign that she had missed the moment everything had turned.

She wasn't sure what she'd been doing. "Not much really. Dealing," she muttered, her voice flat.

"Hmm," Marla responded. She began to sketch again. Winky's askew eyebrows now sure to be complete.

Marisol felt her chest tighten as she watched Marla's pen movement, each stroke reminding her that she had been stuck in the same place for months. A place where nothing changed. Nothing healed. Not really. Just the constant, aching reminder that she had loved someone who could never love her the way she needed to be loved.

Marisol's phone vibrated with a sunlight chime: 8:24 AM.

Today, she resolved it would all be different. A new routine. A small act of self-care – no more espresso, Earl Grey instead. She closed her eyes, pulling herself forward into a new day but the tears threatened to pool at the edges, dragging her back into the abyss. All of this by 8:40 AM.

The kettle's shrill whistle added no relief. Her head pounded and a mass of lights threatened to shower her whole line of vision in rainbow. She swooned and steadied herself. Reaching for the teapot handle, her fingers refused to unclench, locked in a painfully rigid fist. Marisol looked down; eyes wide. Her fingers were wooden, polished smooth with splintering at the joints. Unbendable, unmovable. Her breath caught in her throat then broke free into a scream. Thrashing wildly, she knocked at the kettle sending scalding water spilling across her arms. With pain burning through her skin, she spun and stumbled disoriented to the bathroom. She pawed at the sink handle, engaging the tap; shoved her arms under the icy stream of the water, gasping as her hands seemed to soften into fleshy tan skin. Human again.

Wiggling what returned to fingers, Marisol shakingly clawed through the medicine cabinet. Jars and bottles clattering into the sink. Then she saw it: a flicker of grey flannel, a swash of salt and pepper beard.

"You really are such a mess, you know."

Greg's voice slithered out from the mirror. Marisol shook. Slowly, she turned to see an empty tub behind her and let out a relieved sigh. Turning back to the mirror, there he was. Smug as ever, seated on the tub with his fingers steepled under his chin, a signature pose signifying he'd thought he'd won.

"A hopeless, pathetic mess," he sneered. "You know what hooked me first? Your beauty. That 'I don't give a fuck' attitude. That wild little spark. You were fiery, different. No English Rose here. But now look at you. A wilted husk, clinging to the twenty nice things I've said to you for dear life.'

Marisol slammed the mirror shut with jagged breath. She leaned over the sink of band-aids, Q-tips and cracked cosmetic samples. Her scalded hands throbbed, and the walls began to close in.

A jagged scream broke through the air. "You came after me! You said you liked my author photo!" She pointed at the mirror. "You said I was strong, stable…"

"Sexy?" Greg interjected; his voice rich with mockery. "I did. You were my perfect little doll, pretty, easy to pose… right where I left you. You didn't even know you'd been picked, did you? A pretty keepsake for myself. Exotic."

Her body stiffened as her reflection glitched. Her cheeks began to take on an unnatural ruddiness. She brushed her hand against her left cheek, feeling its textured embroidery under her fingertips. Behind her, a feverish, too-solid shape perched on the toilet tank, his shadow stretching long on the floor.

"It was real!" she shouted, tears flowing freely as her blistering hands gripped the sink harder, pulling the skin taut, ripping at the already bubbling seams. "I know it was! You cared for me!"

Greg's face twisted into a cruel smile, widening to make room for a boisterous laugh.

"You wore out your welcome so long ago, querida. But hey, why throw away a good lay you can keep around for a rainy day? So useful. Your little messages, the desperate mile-long emails. Ah. I really had to laugh, you really thought this was precious."

She stiffened as he hopped silently off the toilet tank, leaning closer, his breath hot in her ear. "Precious to *me*? Darling, I collect a few 'precious' things a year. And yes, before you start, even all through those four exhausting years."

Her knees buckled, her head shook violently, trying to rattle away his words. "You're not real. You're not real. It's a bad dream. Just a bad dream," she whispered.

"Oh, I'm real enough," Greg whispered, his voice thickly sweet. "More real than that little fairytale of yours. What was it Ixma?"

Marisol sniffed. "Ixmucane and the Gift."

"Ah yes." Greg paced the bathroom. "Let me see if I have this drivel right. Troubled little girl, worried about the world is given the gift of extreme empathy and magic and can rid the world of all its worries. But she must become a worry doll herself. Ugh, so selfless, so sacrificial...so pathetic. Sound like anyone we know? An autobiography of sorts?" His eyes gleamed with malice. "It was, wasn't it! Ha! Oh, you little worry doll, soaking up every man's problems while you break yourself apart. And look at you now. You're going tits up, Mar. Almost there."

"Shut up!" Marisol screamed, spinning around, half expecting him to be gone. But there he was, in the very real flesh, his shadow engulfing the bathroom.

"Almost there, almost perfect. So easy to play with." His voice now a hiss. "One day, you'll be perfect, perfect enough for me to come crawling back for more. More sympathy, more sacrifice. You should see the other ones." He groaned softly. "So easily trained."

She stared deeply within the mirror. Her burnt hand ached, the pain pulsing with each breath. She raised it high and with a primal scream, smashed the mirror. The glass shattered, sending Greg's mocking laughter echoing into silence.

She crumbled to the floor. Her stomach twisted violently as she vomited on the floor. Propped up on her elbows, Marisol sobbed heavily, her breath catching between screams. The new start would have to wait. Amongst the blood, vomit and tears, the old Marisol had come apart at the seams. Her usual soft black curls now stuck out from her forehead stiffly, simple yarn curls stared back at her in the gleaming shards of the mirror.

She lay gently on top, letting her eyes gently close.

Marisol's head throbbed, her skull under unbearable pressure, as a pain bloomed behind her now-heavy lids. A sharp twitch seized her body, and her nose wriggled at the scent of something thick, musty and synthetic in the air, an acrid sweetness that made her stomach churn. She blinked rapidly, trying to clear her vision, only to find her face pressed against a cold, smooth surface.

Glass.

The suffocating feeling wrapped around her, her lungs barely able to expand with the tightness of the air, her body twisted as if it was splitting at the seams. Her legs hung unnaturally off what felt like a stiff bench. In her desperation, she reached up, her hands searching as she groped for something, anything to hold onto. What met her touch wasn't man-made, it was rough, almost tender in its decay.

Something stung her fingertips as she tugged at it, and then, suddenly, a body came tumbling down from above, landing with a muted thump.

"What the fuck?" Marisol's voice was choked and distorted in her throat. She sucked in a breath and pressed her face against the glass.

"Help! Help me!" She banged her fists against the glass, but her strikes were weak, as if her arms were made of something other than flesh. Her knuckles cracked, the sound like dry leaves being crushed underfoot. From the other side, there was only silence, followed by the distant sound of shuffling, then a voice, faint but clear.

"Knock it off. He'll hear you," the voice echoed from below, distant and muffled. Another voice hissed from the shadows, snide and dismissive.

"Stupid bitch."

Marisol's heart skipped a beat. She turned her head with eyes wide and scanned the suffocating darkness around her. The room outside the glass was little more than a void, save for the opulent red velvet curtains, a single chair.

Through a tear-strangled voice, "What the fuck is this? Why am I here?"

Out of the darkness, a first responder answered, a blonde plastic doll climbing back into its place. "You're here because he put you here, just like the rest of us."

Marisol spun from the glass to face the terror behind her. On the floor lay dozens of dolls of every shape, size and material imaginable. Some of porcelain, plastic, yarn, stuffing filled. Each one froze and stared back at her.

"Who? Who put me here?" Marisol's voice grew with rising terror. Shadows played tricks on her, dancing just out of sight. Her reflection warped in the glass, her body, her hands, now seemed...wrong. The joints were too stiff. The skin, too tight, too smooth, stretched like a drum head.

A raven-haired porcelain doll moved from the shadows; her synthetic skin gleamed faintly in the dim light. The doll's chest looked to have burst forward from the inside. A gaping, red hole stared back at Marisol. "She's really got no idea. Idiot."

The blonde plastic doll straightened her stiff cotton dress, undeterred. "The Master. He put you here."

Marisol's body ached. She looked down, her breath faltered. Her hands no longer moved with the fluidity they once did. They were stiff, bound by spiralling threads of yard and wood, anchored tightly around her wrists. Her nails had become brittle, their edges splintering with each movement. Her heart pounded in her chest as the realization slowly settled in.

Her skin was no longer flesh, but a patchwork of woven fibre, yarn stitching through her old muscles and corn husks where bones belonged.

And the capper, human hair. Strands tangled within her, the roots now pressed into her scalp. Transformation complete.

"The Master?" Marisol whispered hoarsely, the words barely forming in what was left of a working mouth. "What... What is this?"

A red-headed doll with features that resembled more a fox than a lady, sidled up to her. "The Master has collected us," she purred, almost gleeful. "He can pick anyone he wants, anytime he wants, anytime he needs a little.... attention. But I have a feeling me and him are going to take it to the next level."

The raven-haired doll sneered, and her stiff body jerked with anger. She shoved past Marisol to the redhead. "Fuck you, you're just like the rest of us."

Marisol's stomach churned. "Why?" she gasped.

"Who the fuck is the Master?!"

"He doesn't take everyone, you know," the blonde-haired doll said defiantly. "But you? You're filled with it, aren't you?"

"With what?" Marisol shouted through tears.

The raven-haired doll scoffed loudly. "This is getting tedious." Her small porcelain feet clicked on the glass shelf as she sauntered over to Marisol.

"Where should I start? Worry. Fear. Zero self-esteem. Clinginess? You're made for him."

Marisol recoiled, but the movement was sluggish, her body no longer obeying her will. She could feel it, her humanity creeping away from her. They were all women once. Once they had lived, had thoughts, dreams, mothers, fathers, sisters, jobs. Now, they were just empty shells, filled with worry, anxiety, fear and anticipation.

"You're made for him," the blonde doll chimed in, her voice mocking.

Marisol gasped, her mind struggled to grasp what was happening to her. Her breath coming in short, shallow gasps. The room grew smaller.

"No, no, no," she muttered under her breath, her body convulsing, her joints seizing as though something inside her had locked. Her mouth went dry, her throat constricted.

Another laughed, seemed to hum with dark amusement, and echoed from the shadows. "You are becoming one of us. The Master knows the worth of worry. The worth of "Is he ever gonna call me again?" The worth of "It was real," the voice cooed almost lovingly.

Marisol's eyes widened in horror. The worry dolls of folklore, *Ixmucane*, she had written about them, studied them for years. And now, she was becoming one of them. A vessel for worry, a puppet of anxiety and fear. A hollow thing. A pretty, pliable, posable thing.

Was this the manifestation of it all? These poor, pliable dollies? Now just hollow and moulded into forms that could only exist as conduits for their own fear, their own anxieties, their own psychosis, and their own desperate want for Greg to want them as well. The walls pressed down as she desperately tried to push the transformation from her mind.

She looked down at her legs, and the sight struck her like a blow to the chest. Her ankles and knees, once smooth and pliable, now twisted unnaturally. They buckled in ways they shouldn't, the joints no longer working, no longer bending with the fluidity of human flesh. Instead of the softness of skin and muscle, her limbs had become stiff and crooked, a grotesque parody of themselves.

The weight of Greg's abandonment, the quiet suffocation of his neglect, it had driven her to this. This was the cost. The *curse* she had always written about in her books, the one she had once warned others of, had claimed her. Her humanity slipping away, woven into the fibres of something twisted and wrong.

"I don't want this," she whispered, her voice breaking as tears welled up, blurring her vision. "Please... no."

Her voice, once so full of life, now sounded fragile, distant. The words came out as a strangled plea, empty against the reality of this transformation.

The red-haired doll, with eyes now glinting with some unspoken understanding, leaned forward. "I think it's a bit late for that, babe." A burst of laughter filled the cabinet.

It echoed and bounced off the glass. Marisol's voice screamed in despair, the sound of it so raw, so broken that it felt as though it could tear her apart. The horror of it weighed on her, blurring the line between who she was and what she had become. She couldn't tell if any shred of the woman she used to be still remained.

Every part of her screamed to hold on, to fight back, but her body wouldn't obey, her hands felt foreign, her limbs heavy and stiff. The yarn tangled in her chest, in her throat. The hair. It burned her scalp, the strands whispering dark, terrible things she couldn't ignore.

With a final, hopeless glance towards the red-haired doll, Marisol's heart gave in. There was no escape.

For them.

But she wasn't *dead* yet. She wasn't a doll.

With unsteady hands, she slammed against the glass again, her hands cracking, pulling at the fibres wrapped around her new limbs. The pain was unbearable. She couldn't let it consume her. She had to fight.

"No," she whispered through gritted teeth. "I will not become this."

Her joints creaked and groaned as she twisted her body, the husks and yarn digging and pulling against her, something inside fought back. Her palm slammed against the glass and then...

CRACK.

A gaggle of dolls screamed and rushed at her, and Marisol turned from the glass quickly to avoid being struck.

Her heart raced when she saw it. A small hole at the back of the cabinet.

Marisol's heart pounded, the coarse threads of yarn and brittle corn husks bit into her skin, but she pressed on. The hole in the back of the cabinet was small, too small, but it was her only escape. With every strained movement, the weight of her transformation tightened around her, her body a stiff, unnatural thing.

She reached the hole, her paddle of a hand tried desperately to grip the edge. Pain seared through her as she squeezed, her body a grotesque blend of flesh and doll. Inch by inch, she crawled, the husks crunching beneath her, a symphony of anguish in the silence. A final heave, and she fell to the cold floor, gasping. As she rose and trenched forward, her gaze drifted back to the front of the cabinet, the glass now a barrier between her and them. The dolls lumped together, pressed against the glass; faces twisted in silent horror. Lost in their own torment and wait.

But not her. Not yet. Not ever.

There was no need for words. The rebellion in her eyes spoke louder than any declaration. On unsteady and crackling limbs, she walked away from the suffocating dark, her every step a fragile promise to keep moving.

Forward. Forward. Forward.

Marisol's fleshy and blistered fingers grasped the bathroom doorknob and pushed. A single ray of sunshine shot through the blinds, warming her cheek. She ran her fingers against its smoothness and let her lips curl into a smile. She looked down at her hands. Blistered, battered, and still yarned at the wrists.

She smiled.

"Everything in its own time."

Isla del Encanto Perdido

Richie Narvaez

1. The Colossus of Rot

THE JAGGED SILHOUETTES of skyscrapers clawed at the burning, azure sky. Like monstrous glass sentinels, they loomed side by side by side by side, an unyielding fortress encircling the entire coastline of the island, forming a barrier kilometers deep that defied both nature and sanity. Within this colossal wall, mountains had been rent asunder, their peaks shorn and reduced to dust, and the rich soil beneath subjugated, crushed, paved over, leaving only a vast, sterile, flat valley.

Within this stifling canyon, untouched by even the faintest insinuation of a breeze, a bent old man, whose name was Pedro, rode atop a gargantuan green dumpster that dwarfed him a hundredfold. He whistled a song whose words he had long forgotten. Occasionally, he would smile and nod absently, as if to unseen specters lurking in the shadows.

Isla del Encanto Perdido

The many-wheeled dumpster, a grotesque leviathan, crept along on thin tracks laden with an unspeakable amalgam of human detritus – discarded clothes, rancid food, plastic containers, shattered bottles, obsolete laptops, fractured phones, enormous television sets, and stationary bicycles, all enmeshed in a putrid morass of decaying refuse and excrement. The fetid stench emanated from the heap in repellent waves, a miasma of rot.

The sound of bird calls, artificial and hollow, echoed throughout the airless, lightless valley – emanating from speakers hidden in building crevices and atop a maze of spiny communication towers.

After some time, the old man and his giant machine arrived at their destination, squeezing into a slender, shadowed defile between two immense skyscrapers, a minuscule and solitary opening to the endless sea beyond. There, he cautiously descended to a narrow, jagged, rocky path, each step vibrating through his diseased bones. With trembling fingers, he pressed a worn display button – and unleashed an ear-splitting mechanical wail that echoed across the dank canyon. The dumpster convulsed and tilted, casting its grotesque load into the waters.

Pedro stood upon the treacherous rocks, his eyes straining against the horizon. He gazed into the unforgiving ocean, its blackened surface roiling as if concealing some vast, unknowable force that gazed back mercilessly at him. He wanted to spit at it but found his mouth too dry.

Once the loathsome dumpster had dispensed its burden, the man beheld with weary eyes stubborn remnants clinging to the bottom of the dumpster. There was no reprieve for him. The weight of unseen eyes bore down upon him, a reminder of the constant scrutiny of his masters. Should they detect even the slightest pause in his labor, the consequences would be swift and severe. With resignation, he climbed into the tilted maw of the metal beast, shovel in hand, and set about prying loose detritus that had refused to dislodge.

The heat trapped within the metallic walls was excruciating. Sweat mingled with the rancid excretions that coated Pedro's body, an unholy anointing. His every breath came labored, his every motion gave him pain.

At last, when the vile container had been scraped clean of its odious contents, the man pressed the accursed display again to initiate its return to equilibrium. Yet instead of the expected mechanical whine, there was only a sudden, harrowing stillness. The dumpster jerked, halted in place, and then emitted an ear-splitting grinding – a discord so terrible it seemed the island itself trembled at the sound. Amidst the clamor came another sound, barely audible yet unmistakably present – a desperate, agonized whisper – *rising from the water.*

"Ayúdame, por favor."

The old man dismissed the faint voice and struck the cold, unyielding surface of the dumpster, his stubborn will demanding that it work.

But then, again, that voice – quieter now but unmistakable, crept into his awareness like a parasitic whisper. "Tengo hambre. Ayúdame."

His mouth gaped. The voice – it sounded like Spanish, though that in itself was impossible. No one had spoken Spanish on this forsaken isle for decades – certainly not him. The language had long since been buried beneath layers of pavement and glass. It must be an illusion, a tortured echo of a memory.

"Go! Leave me alone," he muttered, covering his ears.

"Por favor."

This time, it was louder. It was no wind nor phantom conjured by his fevered thoughts. He could not deny its origin, for it came from outside the fractured confines of his psyche, a voice anchored in the real and the present.

"You who speak…who are you?" His voice trembled as he edged closer to the source, each step hesitant, burdened by an unnamed fear that gnawed at his very soul.

"Ayúdame, señor."

He saw her then – crouched among the uneven rocks, frail and pitiful, dripping wet, grotesquely thin in a long dress of yellow-orange. Her skin was as jarringly pale as her hair was jarringly black. She pushed herself up, took a step towards him, then fell against the dumpster wheels.

His mind raced. The masters were no doubt watching – what would they do if they saw this aberration?

She crawled towards him, agonizingly slow, her eyes hollow and desperate.

"Dammit," he cursed under his breath and rushed to her, grabbing her frail body and dragging her into the foul maw of the dumpster.

At that moment, the grinding ceased, replaced by the mechanical whine that signaled the dumpster's compliance. The gears shifted, the great steel monstrosity stirring back to life as though it had been appeased by this dark offering.

Pedro climbed up, his breath shallow, his hands trembling. His eyes darted around the horizon, praying that somehow the masters had not seen.

Later, in Pedro's subterranean room, the woman finally stirred upon his tattered couch, her eyes flickering open to the dim, fluorescent light. The walls of the single room itself were covered with fading tourist posters – "Live Boricua!", "Explore San Juan!", "Honeymoon on Vieques!", "Culebra – it's yours!" – and tattered political ephemera, featuring candidates who all looked alike.

In the feeble light, the woman and Pedro regarded one another. Pedro, his darkened skin weathered by years beneath the oppressive noonday sun, bore thinning, curly white hair, combed tightly across his scalp in a futile attempt to maintain order. His thick glasses reflected the flickering light as he stared at her.

The woman, however, was a creature apart – her hair, darker than a starless sky, her skin, even after what should have been a restorative rest, retained an unnatural pallor. Her hazel eyes – ringed by deep shadows which were further emphasized by her prominent cheekbones – seemed not to gaze at Pedro, but pierce through him.

"Awake," Pedro said, breaking the silence with his gruff voice. "About time." He placed before her a plate of steaming, unidentifiable food. "Here. It's Turk-Filay."

She sniffed it and winced – but said, "Gracias."

Pedro frowned, his lips twisting in irritation. "You better 'gracias.' That's good food. That's the last I've got."

Tentatively, she took a bite and chewed slowly, her expression shifting. "¿Guajolote?!"

Pedro's face darkened with confusion. "I don't know what that is. It's, uh, p-pavo – turkey! Turkey, I mean! Turkey-flavored, at least. Just eat it. That's all I have."

"Bueno, Pavo," she murmured, her tone laced with an odd gravity.

Pedro's patience wore thin. "It's turkey! Just say 'turkey'!"

"¿Por qué no hablas tu idioma, Pedro?" she asked.

His gaze faltered, unease crossed his features. "How do you know my name?"

She raised a languid eyebrow, her lips pointing towards the name stitched into the fabric of his worn uniform.

"Right. My 'idioma'! There's no one left to talk to in my 'idioma.' It feels dry, it feels dirty in my mouth."

"El idioma está en tu sangre. Está en la sangre de tu gente," she replied, her voice carrying an unsettling weight, as if speaking not just to him but to something deeper within.

"'Mi gente'? Those people are gone. Long gone."

"¿Estás diciendo que eres el único que queda? Pero hay mucha gente aquí. ¿Ninguno de ellos habla tu idioma?"

"Can't you talk English? I can see you understand me."

But she ignored him, her eyes narrowing as she leaned closer. "Dime – porque hace muchos años que no me llaman aquí, a la Isla del Encanto – dime: ¿dónde están los pájaros? ¿Y dónde está el coquí? Su dulce canción solía llenar la noche y me encantaba."

The mention of the birds and the coquí – the little frogs whose calls once filled the night air – made Pedro chuckle grimly. "The birds and the little frogs – hah."

She nodded slowly, her expression unyielding.

"I don't know what you mean. They're not gone. I can still hear them. I hear them all the time. I hear them now."

Her eyes flashed with a strange intensity. "Pero esas son máquinas que reproducen los sonidos de criaturas que murieron hace mucho tiempo."

Pedro shrugged. "Why bother explaining it? I have to get to work. I can't let you make me late."

He moved to the refrigerator and placed a heavy lock on its door. He cast a final glance towards the pallid creature who had intruded upon his solitary existence – before turning and disappearing into the searing hot world outside.

2. The Sisyphean Labor

When he left for work, night still clung to the island, dark and fetid, as the eerie, synthetic song of coquís drifted from unseen speakers. Pedro trudged towards the depot, and by the time he arrived, the bleak sun had clawed its way over the edge of the towers around him. With that, the coquí song was abruptly replaced by recordings of birds.

In the northeastern sector, Pedro approached the compact waste that was regularly excreted into a dock at the back of each building. He dragged, shoveled, pulled, and pushed the filth into the immense dumpster, the stench of rot curling into his nostrils.

Suddenly, the birdsong ceased, and in its place came the booming voices – voices that seemed to reverberate from every direction.

"WHERE HAVE YOU BEEN? THE GARBAGE IN SECTOR B IS OVERFLOWING."

The words thundered in his ears, disembodied yet omnipresent.

"I'm sorry! Sorry!" Pedro's heart pounded in his chest as he looked up warily at the empty air. "I will get to that right now. Right now!"

But the filth was always overflowing because, even as gigantic as the dumpster was, he could never fit all the refuse in it. He could only take a small portion each day, and so there would always be too much.

Pedro mounted the titanic dumpster as quick as his old body was able and, just as he was about to coax the giant machine forward, he saw her, the mysterious woman, standing in front of him on the tracks.

"Hello! What are you doing there?" he said. "I have work to do and you are in the way. If I press this button, you will be crushed. Move or don't move. It doesn't matter to me."

He was more worried that the owners would see her, and then they would question him, and punish him. She did not move, but instead, in a sturdy voice that belied her frail form, said, "What are these towers?"

"Buildings! For the owners. They live and work and eat and play in there. On some days, in certain parts of this valley, you can hear them laughing in their pools on the roofs. Now, please, will you move or get away or go away? Please."

"He estado ausente demasiado tiempo," said the strange woman to herself. "¿Y quiénes son estas personas?"

"The residents. The owners. Mostly from the States, but many from Europe, and even farther away. They bought up the land and apartments and property and now they can enjoy the beautiful tropical sun and beautiful tropical weather."

"¿Y tú limpias sus mierda? ¿Qué hiciste para merecer este castigo?"

"Punishment? This is my job, lady. I earned it. I—"

But suddenly she was gone, as if she had never been standing there. He thought – he hoped that she would lose herself among the garbage and he would never see her again.

To Pedro's great dismay, when he returned that night, the woman was on his couch, as if she had not moved all day. Her pallor had worsened, so much so that her flesh seemed almost translucent in the dim, artificial light, like a phantom on the verge of dissolving.

"Still here," he muttered, a tremor of unease creeping into his voice. The sight of her, frail and otherworldly, unnerved him in ways he could not fully comprehend.

She looked up at him, her voice a rasp that seemed to carry the weight of ancient winds. "No esperabas que estuviera aquí. ¿Pensabas que había tomado un taxi hasta el casino?"

"Why not?" he replied, "The casinos are always open. Were you looking for a job there?"

She shook her head.

"That's good," he said. "It's all machines now – computers, robots. They mix the drinks, deal the cards, service the owners. If you know what I mean." He chuckled to himself, a hollow laugh in a parched throat.

He moved to the corner of the room, unlocking his tiny refrigerator. From within, he produced a shrink-wrapped pack of Insta McRonald's. He pressed a panel on the pack and it began to heat.

"So how did you get here anyway? You are not a resident who jumped from a balcony. That is obvious. Ah – did you fall off one of those cruise ships? I know they are as big as cities now. It happens sometimes, but usually I just find the bodies."

The food beeped. He opened the pack and spooned a tenth of it into a dirty cup. "We'll have to share this," he muttered, his eyes avoiding hers. "But I will take the larger portion, for this is my home."

She took the food and after swallowing the first bit of the synthetic food, she smiled and said, "Me encantaría un poco de arroz y frijoles con esto."

Pedro looked from his now-empty plate. "'Frijoles'?! You mean 'habicheulas.'"

"Aha!" she said, "¡Te acuerdas!"

"Bah!" he said.

He picked at the viscous crumbs remaining in the pack then tossed it into his trash. He looked at her, eating the rest of his food.

He noticed then that she was staring at the small plastic bucket in the corner of the room, a container filled with dry, gray soil. In the midst of it, a single, pitiful green sprout quivered.

"¿Qué es eso?" she asked. "¿Estás intentando cultivar vegetales? ¿Has recordado cómo es la agricultura?"

He stiffened, his face hardening. "That is none of your business," he growled.

"Quiero hablar de tu gente," she pressed, her voice a strange mixture of curiosity and sorrow.

"If you're not going to speak English," he snapped, "I don't want to talk to you."

For the rest of the night, they sat in the room in heavy silence. Only the hum of machinery everywhere filled the space.

When he went to his cot, he felt he was starving because he had been cheated out of a full meal. He looked at the woman one last time. She was staring at the trembling tiny green sprout then abruptly looked at him.

He snapped off the light.

3. The Awful Plan

The next day, Pedro found himself once more amid the refuse of Sector C, the stench of decay thick in the heavy, stagnant air. Here, he sometimes uncovered scraps of sustenance – morsels abandoned, yet still edible. Once, he had stumbled upon a long, sinewy strip of meat, half-chewed, its surface mottled green. Using a blowtorch, he was able to make a decent meal of it.

Today, however, there was nothing. The heaps of waste, usually teeming with the cast-off remnants of the owners' excess, were barren, stripped of anything resembling food. It was as if the inhabitants of the towering spires of glass had begun hoarding every last morsel for themselves. How selfish they were, he thought. What did they have to fear, perched so high in their air-conditioned sanctuaries, secure and insulated from the world below? Why could they not let him have just a little?

As he mulled over the injustice of it all – his meager existence, the burdensome woman in his home, the indignities he suffered daily – a venomous rage bubbled up from deep within him.

Why should he be subjected to this torment? Why was he cursed to scrape through filth while those in the sky, untouched by toil or hunger, lived in luxury?

As if in answer to his fevered thoughts, the voices erupted once more:

"THERE YOU ARE! YOU MAY NOT HAVE NOTICED, BUT THE RATS ARE GETTING OUT OF HAND. SOMETHING HAS TO BE DONE."

Pedro trembled, his heart pounding in his chest. "Yes! Right away! Yes!" Pedro cried, his voice trembling as he answered the empty sky. "I will get to that right now. Right now!"

His hands shook as he fumbled with the tools of his grim task, and yet, despite the overwhelming pressure from his unseen overseers, a glimmer of relief stirred in his mind.

They had said nothing of the woman. Perhaps – just perhaps – she had managed to slip past their all-seeing eyes. But how had they not – how could they have not seen her?

Still, he knew, he could not keep her. She was a disruption, an anomaly. He barely had enough food for himself. To shelter her, to provide for her, was not a thing he could afford.

As he began to distribute the noxious poison, a large and grotesquely bloated rat scurried forth from the nest, eyes gleaming with fear and hunger.

If there was no spare food for him, what had the rats been eating to get so large? The answer came to him in an instant: each other.

With a reflex born of years spent among filth and vermin, Pedro seized the heavy container of poison and hurled it at the creature. The container struck the rat with a dull thud, but the abomination seemed unperturbed, its corpulent form rippling as it darted away. Snarling in frustration, Pedro drew a tarnished knife from his belt, its blade dulled from years of grimy use. Precision mattered little, for the rat was a hulking beast – slow and ungainly, easy prey for his worn hands.

With a sickening squelch, the knife sank into the rat's bloated flesh, the creature releasing a pitiful squeal before collapsing in a twitching heap. Pedro's face twisted into a grimace as he observed the foul thing – such an enormous rat, thick and swollen with some unknowable filth. It was a creature born of this tainted place, a product of the island's degradation, much like himself. With a resigned sigh, he reached for a plastic bag – those ubiquitous remnants of human waste scattered everywhere – and deposited the carcass inside. The idea of sharing such a filling meal gnawed at him.

As he scattered the foul-smelling powder around the nests of vermin, a desperate, horrible idea crept into his mind. The rat was lovely, big, so very big. But what if… what if it could be more than sustenance?

When he returned to his room, the woman stood before an old, faded campaign poster.

"¿Éste eres tú, no es así?" she asked, her voice strong yet distant, as though it echoed from some unfathomable depth.

Pedro's eyes lingered on the poster, where a younger version of himself smiled with ambition, his face radiant with visions of the future. He laughed. "Hah, yes, a long time ago. When I was young and very handsome. But come, sit down. I have food. Freshly prepared."

Her eyes, cold and unblinking, bore into him. "¿Qué le hiciste a tu isla, gobernador?"

He waved his hand dismissively, though there was a tremor in his voice. "What did I do? Can't you see? I brought the island into the future! Look at the buildings, the towering structures of glass and steel. Look at the technology! It's all modern, all up to date. Puerto Rico of the future, not of the past. Do not speak to me of nostalgia or sentiment. The economy has never been better!"

"Pero aquí no hay puertorriqueños para disfrutarlo. Excepto para ti."

"I did what was necessary," Pedro snapped, his voice rising in defensive fervor. "The island had to prosper. We became the model for the Caribbean. The same has been done in Haiti, the Dominican Republic, Cuba – all of the Bahamas!"

"Les hiciste demasiado difícil quedarse. Dejaste que les quitaran sus hogares. Los apretaste, empujaste, hasta que ya no había espacio para ellos. Hiciste que abandonaran el hogar que amaban."

Her words cut through him like some deathly chill. She shook her head, and her face, once human, seemed to shift – her skin translucent, her eyes glowing with some strange and unearthly light.

"Es una lástima," she said softly, "porque iba a perdonarte la vida. La planta...me demostró que todavía te importaba algo de la cultura, algún vestigio de lo que alguna vez fue."

"I don't know what you're talking about," Pedro growled, fear creeping into his voice. "It's time to eat. C'mon! Buen provecho!"

He held the cooked and prepared rat meat towards her, but with a swift, fluid motion, she knocked it aside, sending it clattering to the floor.

"That's food!" Pedro cried in desperation.

Her face shimmered, the contours of her skull pressing against her skin, as if the very flesh that bound her was threatening to dissolve. Her voice, when she spoke again, was otherworldly, a guttural rasp that seemed to reverberate through the room.

"Deseas envenenarme," she hissed.

"No!" Pedro lunged at her in a frenzy, his mind overcome with panic. In their struggle, they collided with the small, trembling plant he had so carefully tended, sending it toppling to the ground. His eyes widened in horror.

"No!" he screamed, his voice cracking. "I was going to sell that! I would've made a fortune!"

"Deberías morir, pero se supone que yo debo ser misericordioso." She stepped forward and suddenly her frail appearance vanished. She stood in flowing robes, garlanded by yellow and orange flowers. Her face became a bright white skull atop a vivid, living face, her eyes, though outlined in black, shined with fierce life. For the first time he realized – he remembered – who she really was.

"Santa Muerte!" Pedro whimpered, his voice small and broken. "Please, have mercy. I can't die…not yet."

"Vives una vida como esclavo de tus opresores," she intoned, her voice cold and final, "y aún así suplicas seguir viviendo."

Her form seemed to grow larger, darker, as if shadows poured forth from her very being, filling the room with a suffocating presence.

"Podríamos hacer un plebiscito. Qué irónico sería eso. No, creo que en lugar de eso llamaré a un viejo amiga."

Pedro awoke some time later and found that he was strapped to one of the spiny communication towers, his feet bound to the steel post below him, and his hands bound on either side to antennae.

East of the forsaken island, in the depths of the impenetrable sea, the zemi goddess Guabancex stirred from her too-long slumber. Slowly, relentlessly, a vast eye began to manifest above churning waters. It swirled and grew, swirled and grew, until it became a massive cone of white and gray. The monstrous vortex spiraled and churned and swelled, sweeping westward with voracious fury, until it hit landfall on the southeastern coast of the island. Ravenous, the hurricane roared ashore, shredding glass, ripping cheaply constructed buildings asunder, grinding designer furniture and top-of-the-line appliances to dust. It stripped the land naked and bore the waste out into the sea, leaving only bare earth behind.

In days the sun cleansed the soil, the wind carried in seeds.

Some time later, not long at all, as the sun set on the renewed island, a coquí rose out of a stream and sang.

☼

And Then I Wake Up

Wi-Moto Nyoka

"DO YOU KNOW El Coco?" Maritza asks suddenly while picking at her uninspiring salad. She looks forlornly at my French fries.

"The shapeshifter from that show on HBO? I thought it was El Cuco."

"Sort of. It's like a boogeyman. It's what your parents say when they don't want you to do something or go somewhere. They tell you El Coco will get you. My family always said Coco."

"Why is it always fearmongering," I sighed.

"Because it works," Maritza replied flatly before throwing away her salad.

"We just had the regular monsters-under-the-bed," I explain while moving my French fries center to share. "Why?"

"It's my 'sleep obstacle'."

"Your Coco boogeyman?"

"My recurring nightmare," she corrects.

She takes one bite of my French fries, flinches, and places the uneaten half on her napkin.

"What's wrong?"

Maritza doesn't seem to hear my question and continues with a distant expression on her face. "It's this weird, amorphous thing that slides down my bedroom wall—"

"—huh?"

"—and then hovers over my body to like, I don't know, put something down my throat—"

"Ewww!"

"—and kind of smothers me gently? It makes me feel horrible."

"I just sleepwalk. I never dream."

"You never dream? *That's* weird."

She smiles and I smile back then let my eyes drift around the cafeteria.

"I wonder what their 'sleep obstacles' are," Maritza says wistfully, as if reading my mind.

"I wonder if theirs are going away," I respond dryly.

I wait for the witty comeback but Maritza's face falls into a more somber expression.

"It feels so real, ya know?"

"Doesn't it always? Here at the Sleep Therapy Institute!"

My game show host impersonation doesn't lighten the mood and she hits me with, "I haven't had this nightmare since I was a kid. What about you? You been sleepwalking all your life?"

The truth is my sleepwalking came back only recently and I purse my lips together from embarrassment. I know I'm too old to be spending my Saturdays doing this New Age therapy crap but I'm also desperate. I just couldn't take waking up in the middle of the street in my underwear again. My stomach drops at the thought and I lean back from lunch.

"Maybe it's just anxiety," she offers.

"Sure."

***

"Do you remember El Coco? The one I told you about last week?" Maritza asks meekly. She has only a cup of tea this time and there are dark circles under her eyes.

"Yea. I looked it up. The mythical ghost-monster, like a Latino boogeyman. Or, well, not that the monster has an ethnicity. But it's, like, only in Latin American cultures."

Maritza takes a sip of her tea and grimaces before pushing it aside. "Something's happening to me."

"What do you mean?"

"I feel different."

"From the medication?"

Maritza takes a small inhale before admitting, "I'm not taking it."

I can feel my eyebrows come together like magnets.

"Level with me, you don't think any of this is...off? Not even her?" She nods her chin in the direction of a striking woman speaking to a staff member.

"What's her name? What does she do here? When are we gonna have a session with her? So many questions."

"We're not gonna have a session with her," I respond quickly and it's Maritza's turn to move her eyebrows.

"How do you know?"

I don't answer and pull my eyes away from the mysterious woman. Her dark suits, sleek shoes, and severe hair bun, coupled with the expensive smell of her perfume, tell me that she's in charge. But there's more to it than that. She has an icy demeanor that makes goosebumps bloom all over my arms.

"Hello?" Maritza presses.

"The therapy is voluntary. If it's not working for you, screw it, right? There's other things."

"Not for me," Maritza sighs the words out as she reaches for her tea again and tries to take another sip.

"What do you mean?" I ask, keeping my voice calm but feeling a creeping anxiety rise in my stomach.

"I've tried everything. If this doesn't work..."

Her shoulders slump and that seems to punctuate her sentence. Looking at Maritza I begin to notice the new creases in her skin, how thin she seems, and her uncustomarily messy hairdo. I want to tell her that this is the last stop for me as well. That everything they've given me for my sleepwalking has only resulted in nights full of darkness. I don't walk anymore. I don't dream. Nothing happens and I can't even begin to describe how terrifying it is. It's like going into a coma every night and each morning is coated in a dull anxiety that I can't seem to shake.

I think about saying all of this but instead I come back with, "Let's go out for a drink."

She nods.

* * *

My one-time drink offer turned into a weekly post-therapy tradition. Usually, we'd just let off some steam and crack jokes but this time was different.

"And when the doc was done counting backwards it was like I was there in the dream, the nightmare, but I could hear her soft voice letting me know it wasn't real." She shivered.

"It was like lucid dreaming?" I asked.

"She said hypnosis is just relaxing enough so you can really concentrate. That's why we didn't do it at first. I needed to be comfortable, you know? Feel safe."

I snorted a laugh and Maritza looked momentarily hurt.

"What? You don't feel safe. You were talking about stopping treatment."

"I didn't say that, you said that," she corrects.

My lips hover over my glass of wine as I watch her gulp down hers.

"It was…a shadow. It slid up my body and put something down my throat. I had my eyes open and it sounded like I was trying to scream. I couldn't fight back."

I didn't know what to say so I just reached for her hand.

"I didn't see anything else in the room or anyone else. There were no clues."

"Clues? What do you mean?"

"Well, I thought maybe it's a memory in disguise, you know? It's really about something else and I just have to be strong enough to face it."

"A repressed memory or something," I agreed.

I reflected on my sleepwalking and was about to share an anecdote when Maritza dropped a bomb.

"That's what I thought, anyways, until last night. For the first time in ages I didn't have the nightmare but when I woke up to shower I found this."

She pulls up her shirt, carefully, to reveal oval-shaped bruises on either side of her stomach. I couldn't stop myself from inhaling sharply and Maritza did her best to bite back tears.

"Do they hurt?"

She shakes her head.

"Have you gone to a doctor about them?"

She nods. Then she starts to cry.

"I'm pregnant."

I froze and for a long while we just sat there until our waiter broke the silence to ask if we wanted another round. I say nothing but Maritza orders shots.

"Are you seeing someone?"

"No," she whimpers.

"Have you gone out recently? Been around..."

"Rapists?" she chokes.

I feel my chest sink into my stomach as panic takes over. I have no idea how to help my friend or what any of this could mean. The waiter brings the shots and she tosses back two in a row. With each one I look at her stomach.

"Were you...?"

"They can't tell. But if I was, I hope I miscarry."

"We don't have to wait for that. You have choices. I could...go with you? If that's what you decide."

"This is gonna sound weird but do you mind staying over? It's okay if—"

"Of course. And it's not weird."

* * *

The lamp in the corner of Maritza's bedroom gave off a soft glow, more like candlelight than a light bulb, casting shadows on her face that hid her eyes. I couldn't see the tears but I knew she was crying though she did a good job of keeping her voice steady.

"I've always had nightmares, you know? My whole life actually. I used to draw them but then that got me into trouble."

She turned her head into the pillow to dab her face before continuing.

"Kid drawing creepy pics. Monsters, blahblahblah."

She sighed before tucking her hands under her cheek and falling completely silent. I lay on my side, facing her, listening to her steady breathing and then my own. My face is warm from the alcohol, I think, or maybe it's just the blanket draped over us.

"I've been sleepwalking since I was a kid. It started after my little sister disappeared."

I can feel her eyes open and I know she's staring at me.

"What do you see when you sleepwalk?" she whispers intensely.

People never ask me that. They always wanna know about the disappearance. Who took her? How old was I? Or they ask really morbid things about my family and having a funeral without a body. They wanna know my innermost feelings and I can always feel them looking for stitches to pull so they can get close to the tragedy. Like trauma is something you can vacation in as long as it's not yours.

"I see shadows. Everything is fuzzy, heavy, and I know I'm not alone. I sneak around and it feels like I'm getting away with something."

"What kind of shadows do you see?"

Her question makes the hair on the back of my neck stand up but maybe it's just because I'm a little drunk. I'm scared to tell her the truth but I'm also dying to finally tell someone that isn't a doctor.

"It's like a forest but it's alive. And there's something big with them. It wants to get close to me. I'd always wake up with scratches or bloody knuckles like I'd been fighting."

Maritza visibly shivers.

"I'm sorry. I didn't mean to freak you out."

"That's what my thing is like too. When I watched myself it looked like I was in my room but, at the same time, I wasn't. I knew that it had been wanting to get close to me and it was glad to be…with me."

She starts to cry and I wrap my arms around her without thinking.

"I'm scared."

"Me too."

* * *

I slid out from under the covers and tiptoe to the bathroom. The apartment looked so different in the morning sun. There's yellows next to purples, art on the walls, throw pillows with beads, flowers, and clothes tossed lazily on to the furniture. The person who lives here takes up the whole space and I realize that if it weren't for the situation we were in, we'd never have become friends. I'm not the kind that makes much of an impression.

I make my way to the bathroom and frown at the sight of my lopsided afro in the mirror. I have no way to fix it and for some reason this feels symbolic. I smirk at the thought but it fades instantly.

What if something truly awful is happening?

My thoughts are interrupted with a scream and I bolt back to the bedroom to find Maritza, sitting up in bed, staring in horror at her body.

"What the fuck, what the fuck?" she screeches as she tumbles out trying to run away from herself.

I step slowly towards her, unable to believe what I'm seeing. I slowly reach out my hand and put it on Maritza's now very pregnant belly. Something kicks from inside and we both scream.

"I'm calling 911."

Maritza responds with weeping and begins to panic. I gasp as her belly moves and wiggles from the inside.

"Help!" she wails before falling over. Pain seems to strike her like lightning and for a moment all she does is hold her mouth open, soundlessly. The scream tumbles out after and the delay brings tears to my eyes.

"Make it stop," she begs as I scramble to my phone and call the ambulance.

A dark purple substance begins to ooze down the inside of her thighs. She puts her hands on her legs and shrieks when she feels the ooze. She quickly holds her hand up and screams when she sees it's purple. I crawl across the bed and try to hold her down as she kicks in pain.

"Make it stop!"

Her flesh wriggles upwards this time and I punch her belly as hard as I can without thinking.

"Kill it!" she gasps.

I punch down again with all the strength in my body and her belly goes still. We wait in a terrible silence that seems to last an eternity and we both start to tremble.

"What's happening to me?" she croaks.

"I called the ambulance. They'll be here soon just—"

My consoling is interrupted by her violent shaking. Her eyes roll back into her head as a seizure takes over.

"Maritza!"

The purple ooze begins to leak from her ears, her nose, her mouth and finally, her eyes. I cover my mouth in terror and helplessness grips all the muscles in my body as the skin on her belly splits. I scramble off the bed and stumble to the center of the room. Another split freezes me in my spot and I look on, motionless, as her skin is pulled back to reveal branches of shadows blossoming from her middle.

A creature rises from her flesh as the room starts to fade and blur. I can feel all the blood in my body rush up towards my head and that familiar feeling of weighted air wraps around my shoulders like a jacket. The creature slithers down her legs as the room shifts.

All I do is watch.

Maritza is consumed by an army of spiders that bubble up from beneath her. I smell something rotten and can feel a presence approaching from behind me.

I know you.

I begin to slowly turn my head...

The shadows recede like fog and sunlight floods my vision as my eyes reset. Someone puts an oxygen mask on my face and I can only assume the paramedics found us. I look towards the bed for Maritza but there's no sign of the creature or her.

"What is that smell?" says one of the paramedics as they wheel me out of her apartment.

"We can't leave her," I hear myself whimper before everything disappears and I slip into unconsciousness.

* * *

"What does she remember?" asks a throaty woman's voice.

"We don't know yet," replies a second, more timid, voice.

"Why is that?" the throaty voice demands. "Need I remind you she's the only sleepwalker we've got."

"She has to heal. I can't—"

"We can finally start to attack. No more failed attempts at capture, no more evading, no more running. Begin the work as soon as she's up."

I hear high-heeled shoes click away from me and a wave of expensive perfume trails them. I try to see who was speaking but my eyelids are as heavy as rocks. My muscles tense in an effort to move and electric currents of pain roll over me. I try to cry out but only manage a dry heave through my oxygen mask.

"Shh. Rest now. Rest," says the timid voice.

I slip away again.

* * *

When I come to, I find myself in a sparse hospital room. A woman comes in wearing burgundy scrubs.

"Glad to see you up," she says and I recognize her timid voice.

"Where am I?"

"Can you tell me what you remember?" she asks gently.

"You didn't answer my question."

"You're safe. You're at the institute."

"The institute!" I croak while trying to sit up.

Maritza was right and I can feel my heart begin an aggressive rhythm against my ribs as I move to get out of the bed.

"Wait, please—"

"You can't keep me!"

"Wait, please calm down," says the nurse in a surprisingly even tone.

"Screw you. The therapy was voluntary and I don't wanna volunteer anymore, understand? Now, where are my clothes?"

To my surprise Ms. Nice Voice doesn't give much resistance. Her shoulders slump in disappointment and the corners of her mouth seem to settle into a sad shape.

"We're not going to hurt you. We're on your side." Her tone is so earnest that for a moment I feel my cheeks grow hot with embarrassment.

"My side of what?"

"You're the only sleepwalker we've got. No one's been able to get as close as you have."

I feel all the hairs on my body stiffen and stand with terror.

"It's okay, it's okay. I'll explain everything," she continues in her even, soft tone. She then pulls out a small pen light and says, "Let me at least check you first. Can you follow the light with your eyes?"

She swings the pen light to one side and then the other.

"Can you follow the light?"

Her voice feels like sunlight on my face. I follow the light as she continues, "What happened to Maritza?"

I feel my breath slow and my limbs settle onto the hospital bed sheets.

"She had bruises all over her stomach. She's pregnant," I hear myself say.

"What happened to Maritza?"

"She wants to leave. It wasn't working so she fell asleep and woke up scared." My words float in the room with my thoughts. I see them dancing in the air like bubbles.

"What happened to Maritza?"

A warm sensation moves from in between my eyebrows down to my crotch and my voice follows it. I feel a throaty response slide out of my mouth, "The creature tore through her and left her body to its world. It brought the shadows with it before it slithered away."

"What else did it bring?"

"The other. The old one."

"What did the old one do?"

"Reach for me."

"Why?"

Grief dances up from my toes as I watch the light swing, pushing my thought bubbles through the air like dust in a sunbeam. I'm crying and I can't stop and my voice... my voice...

"It reaches because I remember."

A lightning bolt of pain travels down my spine and the room is swallowed by shadows. The air falls on my shoulders like hail and I know immediately where I am. My nostrils flare from the rancid wet smell as a presence rises up behind me and looms over me from a great height. I sprint and am already out in the street when daylight claws its way back into my vision.

Ms. Nice Voice puts her hand up to the cursing man behind the car horn. She wraps a blanket around my shoulders and guides me to the sidewalk as I look up and recognize the outside of the Sleep Therapy Institute.

"Boy, you move fast in that state," she says through haggard breaths.

My hand feels wet and I look down to find blood on my knuckles.

"I'm going home."

***

I've been up for 72 hours and things are getting fuzzy. My appetite swings from non-existent to ravenous and a dull tone of anxiety fills my days along with panic attacks that take over my body whenever I try to sleep. I won't survive like this.

My phone rings for the zillionth time and I don't bother to look. I know who is on the other end. Ms. Nice Voice is leaving another message begging me to come back but explaining nothing. The phone rings again but this time I pick up.

"Tell me everything or I'll change my number," I threaten.

"And then what? Never sleep again?" replies a throaty voice.

I inhale sharply in surprise. *Ms. Husky Voice in Heels.*

"I'm not coming back. You people are nuts. I don't know what you did—"

"I know you don't think we did this to you," she cuts me off with the kind of ease that comes with knowing you're charge. "You're not a stupid woman, Ms. Loretta Ives."

The use of my name catches me off guard and for a moment...

...I'm speechless. She seizes the silence to continue with, "You've escaped it twice now. Three if you count the initial encounter shortly after your sister's funeral."

I feel tears sting the side of my eyes.

"I'm sending you a package, it should be arriving shortly. I think you'll find it useful in ensuring your success. Call me when it's finished."

"When what's finished?" I demand.

There's a brief silence and I swear I can *hear* her smirk. She hangs up and anger grips my throat only to be interrupted by a knock at my door. I creep towards it and pause with my hand on the doorknob. I consider never opening my door again before giving in to my curiosity.

On my humble welcome mat there's a thick, solitary manila envelope. I bring it in to spill its contents over the kitchen table of my sparse studio apartment. The envelope contains what looks like transcripts and sketches, all of them describing encounters with the creature. I find a USB in all the paper and plug it into my laptop.

The next five hours is like falling down a rabbit hole in a hell dimension, as I sift through missing person's case files with witnesses claiming the victims suffered from vivid nightmares followed by an abnormal pregnancy. I read historical texts describing a shadow beast that chooses women from the time they're children as its 'host'.

"More like baby mama," I say aloud to no one and finish a jar of peanut butter.

My cursor hovers over the last unopened folder. *Call me when it's finished,* she had said. I take a deep breath and click on the title "Death and Destruction."

* * *

Standing over the lit candle, the sole source of light in my studio, I watch my breath make smoke puffs in the frigid air. I've turned off the heat just as the file said to do and clench my fingers around the antidote in my pocket. I keep my stance wide and my breathing steady.

Eventually, I hear the heavy breathing that's accompanying mine and the smell follows soon after. The wet rancid scent fills my nostrils as I feel a presence slide down a nearby wall and edge its way closer to me.

"I want to see Maritza."

A breeze washes over me though all the windows are closed, and the flame goes out. The apartment becomes an abyss and I can feel myself being pulled into it. I feel a pressure against my body and keep my hands clenched in my pockets. I keep my breath steady as the temperature continues to drop.

The smell gets stronger and I sense the tendrils before they make their way to my face. They touch my cheeks and forehead as if studying my expression but I know it's just looking for an opening. It's gentle, soft even, and I do my best to stay calm even though I know what's coming next. Wet, squishy, sentient tubes glide up my nostrils towards my eyes and my mouth opens reflexively for air.

I wait.

It stretches up towards my lips as I close my eyes and try not to cry. I have the protection markings on my chest (I drew them on with a pen. DIY brujeria!) and I've taken the poison as per the recipe listed. Ten minutes before I have to take the antidote.

Ten minutes to defeat a monster. Sure, why not?

I stare at the back of my eyelids playing out scenes from my life but not much springs to mind. Stopping this creature will be the only thing of note and no one will know I did it except Maritza, who is dead.

I feel the monster stretch its way past my lips and I yawn to make room and appear willing. It takes the invitation and gurgles with what sounds like delight.

And that's my cue.

The poison surges through my veins granting me a brief moment of super strength and I bite down with all my might. A terrible screech rips through the void as my jaws become iron gates that crash closed, allowing the poison to flow from me to it. I ball up my hands into fists and hold on as it rolls and screams, terrified of its newly solid form.

I want to smile as the air leaves my lungs and my muscles start to give. It throws me and I soar before crashing on the wood floor of my studio apartment. The tincture with the antidote rolls out of my pocket and disappears into the darkness. The candle is knocked over and its flame travels faster than it should, setting the place ablaze before I can even pull myself up to stand.

Its shrieks pierce my eardrums as it cooks in the heat, too weak to shift back to the shadows. I stay laid out on the floor to avoid its flailing and the room fills with the smell of singed scales and ash. Squinting through the smoke I reach out, hoping that I might get lucky and find the antidote. But the creature starts to bubble over and I vomit from the scent of its death.

I drag my feet under me and manage to make it to the door before stumbling out into the hallway where vague shadows of neighbors run towards the exit. I follow them towards whirling streetlights and sirens.

Having collapsed on the cold wet cement of the sidewalk, I suddenly feel hands lift me towards shapeless halos. There's a stiff mattress at my back and air fills my nostrils as amorphous angels yell over me. I think I'm moving but I can't tell if it's up or forward. The angels open my shirt and something cold spreads across my chest. I can't feel my legs or arms and it's hard to keep my eyes open. Everything keeps getting brighter and all I see is daylight, forever and forever.

I turn my head and Maritza is lying beside me.

"What're you doin' here?"

"I'm not sure," I croak.

"You've come a long way to not be sure. Are you here for me?"

"Okay."

"That doesn't sound very convincing," she says, laughing.

"Where are we?"

"You're in an ambulance. Why are you there?"

"I killed it," I say.

"You killed one of them," Maritza corrects.

"What?"

"You killed one of them. There's more. There's always more."

A wave of sadness and defeat drowns me. So much for doing something of note.

"Don't. That's not why we're talking. I need you to stop dying."

"I'm sorry," I tell her, blinking away tears.

"You're the only sleepwalker we've got, Lo. Think how much ass you could kick."

A smile spreads across her face and I can feel my heart break.

"I didn't save you. I'm sorry."

"You weren't meant to. So stop dying. Sleepwalkers can get close. You can get close," she tells me, tenderly, as she reaches her hand to my cheek.

Her touch sends a pain to my ribs that shoots its way down to the small of my back like a bullet.

"They choose us when we're children."

My throat and eyes start to burn and I try to scream as she continues to hold my face.

"But some children are chosen."

Veins in my arms bulge and stretch forward as if being pulled by magnets.

"You can't stop anything if you're dead."

She leans in towards me and goosebumps spread like a bushfire across my body. Her face is a white-hot blaze of sound and ferocity.

"Live," Maritza echoes before kissing me and making reality pull back.

Suddenly, there are blues and whites looming over me, beeping machines, and someone is screaming. It takes me a full minute to realize it's me.

"She's conscious."

"Hold her down!"

I scream and scream as air sweeps through my lungs and every inch of me explodes in pain.

"Sedate her!"

I gasp as it all goes dark.

* * *

When I manage to come to, Ms. Husky Voice is sitting at the edge of my hospital bed. I try to ask questions but can't find my voice.

"Don't bother. Your vocal cords will be useless for a while due to the poison and, of course, the tentacles."

She moves to my side and the expensive smell of her perfume overwhelms me.

"I'm here to offer you purpose. You are not alone in this purpose and will work in a team to ensure success. You will face many things, Ms. Ives, and you will be ever more successful. Do you know why?"

She leans in and her gaze pins me to the bed.

"Because you know there is no other option."

I wheeze softly and it's clear that she doesn't care.

"You were right to hide, Loretta," she continues, "but now it's time to attack."

She sits up and calmly gazes down at me.

"I'll give you a moment to think about it. When you're ready, press the button for the nurse. She'll make sure you don't run out into the street this time."

She stands, gracefully.

"Oh, if you don't, press the button that is, you'll never see us again. And we won't be able to help you when more come for you," she finishes as she saunters out, leaving me to breathe through the tubes in my nose and consider my survival.

I stare at the clumsy symbols drawn on my chest and remember my sister, my parents' grief, the smile that touched the corners of my mouth as the creature was dying, and Maritza's face near mine.

"Live," I hear her say.

I press the button.

Nacho

Daniel A. Olivas

For Gabino Iglesias

THE TRUTH IS, Abundio Abarca de Jesús had grown accustomed to the lump on his neck. The mass sat just below his right ear but did not cause any pain or discomfort. Three months earlier, on 1 November, his birthday, Abundio had noticed a small, barely perceptible nodule when he slathered on Barbasol shaving cream. Abundio remembered how intriguing he found this new feature – if that was the correct word for it – and eventually anticipated the slow but certain growth he perceived each morning as he commenced his daily ablutions.

When he finally mentioned it to his mother during their once-weekly phone calls, Amaranta Guadalupe de Jesús had exclaimed: "Mijo, you must see the doctor about it!" Since his father had succumbed to lung cancer six years ago, Abundio knew what his mother feared. So he agreed to mention it to his doctor during an upcoming annual checkup. "I promise to show it to the doc, Mamá." And his mother knew that her son's promise was as good as gold.

* * *

Dr. Yesenia Reyes pressed and prodded Abundio's lump as she hummed an indistinct melody that must have sounded quite lovely in her mind's ear but did nothing but annoy her patient, who sat uncomfortably in a backless rough paper robe without anything to shield his skin from the over-active air-conditioning system other than his boxers and argyle socks. Finally she pulled back, looked up into Abundio's wide eyes, and said: "I suspect it's not malignant. But let's do a biopsy to make certain, okay? We can do it here, now."

"Now?"

"Why wait?"

Abundio and Dr. Reyes stared at each other in silence, each waiting for the other to buckle. Abundio lost that battle, as he always did with his doctor.

"Good. Let's get you prepped."

Four days later Abundio received a phone message from Dr. Reyes. He had missed her call because he had taken a wonderful afternoon nap that day, and in order to get the most out of this special time of peace, he had turned off his cell phone. This is what the message said: "Good news. Not cancer. It's what we call a benign lipoma. Nothing to worry about. We can remove it, and you will be as good as new, save for a tiny scar. I have an opening next Thursday. Call my assistant, and we'll take that baby out of you."

Abundio played the message three times, and each time he listened to it he grew a little sadder. He let his mother know, and she was relieved. "¡Maravilloso!" she exclaimed. And then she added: "Is the doctor single?" Abundio ignored this last question and directed his mother to other news about his job, which was not exciting but worked as a perfect deflection. "I got a great annual performance review, Mamá," he said.

"Por supuesto," his mother responded. "They are lucky to have my son!"

* * *

The benign lipoma floated in a small jar that Abundio had set on his nightstand when he came back from the doctor's office. At first, when Dr. Reyes had asked him if he would like to bring it home, Abundio had laughed, thinking this was nothing more than obtuse doctor humor. But Dr. Reyes did not smile and waited for a response to her question. So Abundio said: "Sure."

* * *

Abundio did not like the clinical, somewhat impersonal term of *benign lipoma,* so he renamed the mass of tissue something a bit more friendly: Nacho.

Each night before Abundio turned off his nightstand lamp, he would tap the top of the jar three times and say: "Goodnight, Nacho."

Sometimes Abundio would add: "Sleep tight, and may you have pleasant dreams."

* * *

Not surprisingly, Abundio's kind and thoughtful care of Nacho did not escape Nacho's notice. Over the course of a week Nacho's once pinkish pallor ignited into a vibrant burgundy. Nacho's fleshy mass responded as well, growing just a bit each night while they both slept.

One morning Abundio realized that Nacho was bulging within the tight confines of the little jar, so Abundio retrieved from the attic an old fishbowl that had once served as a lovely home to three guppies he had named Nina, Pinta, and Santa María, but all three were now long deceased and buried at sea with a flush of a low-flow toilet. The fishbowl now had a new purpose. Nacho seemed quite content in his new abode and continued to flourish.

Eventually Nacho outgrew the fishbowl in a somewhat remarkable and astonishing manner. This is what happened one Sunday night: Abundio plumped up his pillow, turned to the fishbowl, tapped it three times, and said, "Goodnight, Nacho. Sleep tight, and may you have pleasant dreams." Abundio then turned off the lamp on his nightstand, snuggled into his plump pillow, and fell into a deep sleep. The next morning, as he slowly awoke, he sensed someone standing over him. Abundio opened his eyes and above him was Nacho, no shorter than five feet eight inches, leaning down to examine Abundio. But since Nacho had no eyes, Abundio was not certain what Nacho perceived.

"Good morning," said Abundio.

Nacho pulled back and stood erect. "Good morning," said Nacho.

At the sound of Nacho's greeting, Abundio thought, *Nacho's voice is much deeper than I would have expected.* And then he wondered, *How does Nacho speak without a mouth?* Many other questions came into his mind, but Abundio decided that they could be saved for later.

"Would you like some breakfast?" asked Abundio.

"Oh, that would be delightful," said Nacho.

Abundio put on a robe and trundled into the kitchen, with Nacho following close behind. He prepared a large pot of coffee and chilaquiles as Nacho sat patiently at the kitchen table. The two new roommates ate their delicious breakfast in contented silence. Nacho eventually drank the last bit of coffee that had cooled at the bottom of his cup.

"Would you like more?" asked Abundio.

"Oh, yes," said Nacho. "You make the best coffee."

This warmed Abundio because no one had ever complimented his coffee before. He poured another cup for Nacho.

"Mil gracias," said Abundio. "I am glad you like it."

"Por nada," said Nacho. "And these chilaquiles are to die for!"

Abundio grinned.

They eventually set up a simple but workable living arrangement. Nacho slept on the living room's foldout couch and Abundio kept his bedroom to himself. Abundio cooked their meals while Nacho eventually got the hang of cleaning house, which he did when Abundio was away at work during the day. On weekends they stayed in, watching movies on the flatscreen, reading magazines and books, playing board games. At first Abundio missed Nacho's nightstand presence, but over time they fell into a placid and fulfilling routine.

* * *

Abundio eventually told his mother about Nacho. When he'd given her as many details as he could think of, she remained silent.

"Mamá, are you still there?"

"Sí, mijo."

"Well?"

"Mijo, I have never heard of such a thing before," his mother ventured. "But you live in a big city, and I know many strange things happen in such big places."

"Strange?"

"Mijo, isn't it strange?" she pressed her son.

"Mamá, what is strange for one person might be very normal for someone else."

"Pues, mijo, most people make friends at school or the office or even at Mass," she said slowly, sensing that perhaps she was pushing her only son a bit too far.

"But this is different, Mamá . . ."

"Sí, diferente, mijo . . ."

"I don't have time to make friends, so I feel lucky I have Nacho."

"Pero, mijo, it is not normal."

"And what is normal?" said Abundio, attempting to control his temper and the conversation.

"Pues, normal is what you see on TV . . ."

"Your telenovelas are normal, Mamá?" said Abundio with a snicker.

"Ay, mijo, never mind," she said, surrendering. "It is your life. And I am sorry."

"Sorry for what, Mamá?"

"I am sorry your father and I could never give you a brother or sister . . ."

"Mamá, don't . . ."

"We tried, but it was not in God's plan."

And with that, mother and son said their goodbyes and ended the conversation.

Eventually during their weekly phone calls, she would ask Abundio about Nacho, and he inevitably would tell some funny story about what Nacho had done or said. His mother could not help but chuckle at these stories, and in the end she was happy her son had a new friend, and she never again questioned Abundio about it.

Then one day everything changed.

On a Wednesday Abundio came home from work and could not find Nacho. He searched each room of the house – he even spied into the attic with a flashlight – but Nacho was not to be found. Abundio started to panic. Should he call the police and report a missing . . . missing . . . a missing what? No, the police must not get involved. So Abundio heated some leftovers, quickly ate his dinner, skipped dessert, and then made a large pot of coffee to keep him fortified as he waited at the kitchen table for Nacho to return from who-knows-where.

After three hours of waiting – and four and a half cups of coffee – Abundio heard the front door open, then shut. Abundio decided to play it cool and to wait for Nacho to come into the kitchen. After a few moments of silence, Nacho slowly sauntered into the room, deliberately retrieved a cup from the cabinet, and poured the last of the coffee. He took a sip, let out an almost imperceptible burp, and sat down across from Abundio.

"So," said Abundio, unable to stop himself from inquiring. "Where were you?"

Silence.

Then Nacho said: "I went to Lake Balboa."

"In Encino?"

"Yes."

"It must be twenty miles away from here."

Silence.

Then, in almost a whisper, Nacho said: "Why didn't you tell me?"

"Tell you what?"

"How beautiful it all is?"

"How beautiful what all is?"

Nacho leaned forward. "All of it."

Abundio was at a loss. He had no idea where this conversation was headed.

Nacho answered: "The strong tree branches that seem to be reaching for the clouds. The rippling lake water with all types of ducks and geese paddling wildly. The people – children, adults, grandparents – of all shapes and sizes and colors speaking a multitude of languages. And the music coming from small portable speakers. I heard Vicente Fernández's buttery baritone for the first time!"

"Ah, yes, my mother called him Chente. She loves his music. Which song was playing?"

"'Tu Camino y el Mío.'"

"My mother's favorite," said Abundio. "It's such a sad song."

"Yes, it made me cry," said Nacho. "Such heartbreak."

"Yes, such heartbreak."

They sat in silence, wrestling with their own thoughts. Finally Nacho said: "Why do you think the man doesn't open the letter?"

"The letter?"

"You know, in the song," said Nacho, leaning in towards Abundio. "The man finds a letter written by his love, but he doesn't open it. He just drinks wine and somehow he knows he's lost her. But we don't really know for sure, right?"

"Well," ventured Abundio, "I guess sometimes we just *know*."

They sat in silence, each pondering the lyrics of Fernández's musical lament.

"It's so sad he passed away," Abundio finally offered.

"What?" said Nacho. "Who passed away?"

"Vicente Fernández. My mother said that she thought he'd live forever."

"So sad."

"Yes."

After a few moments Nacho observed: "But in truth, Vicente Fernández lives forever through his music."

"You are quite a philosopher."

Nacho raised his coffee cup: "To Vicente Fernández."

Abundio raised his coffee cup: "Vicente Fernández."

Nacho added: "¡Presente!"

Abundio echoed: "¡Presente!"

With that, Nacho stood and said: "Time for bed."

Within ten minutes both were in their separate sleeping quarters, snoring softly in unison.

* * *

The next morning Abundio awoke as the morning sun came through his window. He felt refreshed, at peace, knowing that Nacho was safe at home. He got out of bed and went into his bathroom. As Abundio slathered on Barbasol shaving cream, he gently fingered the raised scar on his neck just below his right ear. Abundio smiled. After shaving and showering, he walked through the living room and saw that Nacho had already closed the foldout couch and neatened up. Then the wonderful aromas of coffee and chilaquiles wafted into Abundio's nostrils. This was new! Nacho had never made breakfast – or any other meal – before. Abundio sauntered into the kitchen to welcome the new day.

Abundio beheld a perfectly set kitchen table: a full coffee pot, a skillet brimming with steaming chilaquiles set carefully on a trivet, cloth napkins, a small vase with a single pink rose in the middle.

But something was very wrong.

Nacho was nowhere to be seen.

And Abundio suddenly noticed that there was only one place setting.

Abundio broke into a cold sweat. He scanned the modest kitchen for clues. Then he saw it: a small white piece of paper folded neatly leaning against the gleaming toaster. On the paper was the name "Abundio" written in lovely cursive writing.

Abundio crept up to the note, snatched it, and held the paper, wondering what he should do. He held it for seven seconds before deciding that he should open it. And as he read and reread the note – also written in a beautiful cursive hand – the reality of Abundio's new situation slowly sank into his consciousness. He let the note fall from his fingers, and it floated gently to the tiled floor. Abundio crouched to retrieve it, but then felt himself falling onto his knees. The note looked blurry, and Abundio realized that his eyes brimmed with hot tears.

Abundio's body crumpled, and he shook and trembled. He could feel his chest heave without control. And at that moment Abundio realized that his life had changed forever.

The Ache

Monique Quintana

IN THIS TOWN, there are no deaths by natural causes. As my cousin sparked like a flower, she remembered the grape soap she used that morning. Burning hair that made harpsichord strings. The music blared out of the tiny hospital's speakers. A cornucopia of mothering. A horse's sigh. She had scalded herself, making her family cocido on a blustery morning. While in the hospital to get her scars treated, a disgruntled cafeteria worker came and set the place on fire. That morning, there had been a large flower delivery to the hospital gift shop, and our cousin, taking a walk around the hospital, stopped to remark on the flowers and their beauty. As she struck out her bandaged hand to caress the bluest flower, flames trickled down the hallway, singeing her denim, her entire body like the corn husk doll I had forgotten under a tree as a girl. We mourned her.

My mother's family came from Texas. I grew up hearing stories about how my grandfather Keke, a boy, shined shoes and spent his earnings watching old films on the balcony of the town's movie theater. The balcony was for the Mexicans and had the worst seats in the house. His neck ached, but he never dreamed of leaving the movie early. He walked home rubbing his clavicle so hard that his mother always thought he had flowers blooming from his shoulder when he neared his house. Bright pink. On nights when he went with his brothers to the bonfires they had at Texas A&M University, he threw sweet wrappers in the fire. A celebration, he thought he would never leave that land.

My grandmother Petra came over with her family from Texas when her mother died. Her oak skin was forever trapped in an oil painting that her children commissioned when they had grown up and were old enough to afford it. When her mother, my great-grandmother, got sick, her sisters and cousins and *tías* urged her to go to the doctor, and she always put her hand up to the sky, to its clammy heat and the clouds, and said, "But I have this! My God!" Her God could put a windburn on the moon. She died and left behind children too young to care for themselves. And her widower, leaning against the patched up fence, inhaling the scent of turpentine, contemplated what to do next. His in-laws drove to his house in their beat-up station wagon and invited him and his children to California. And being an orphan, they were the only family he had ever known. So he packed up the little stone children that would grow up and become my elders. They only stopped in places to sleep on the side of the road or urinate in the flowers.

The little girl who became my family's matriarch clutched her butcher paper-wrapped bologna sandwich with the same precocity as if it were a doll. Delicate, made to be broken. It was only years later that she realized the reason they left home was for food. Consumption. A hunger that kept them awake at night. They knew they were in the valley when they saw the grapes. Violent blue. And nearer, they became the color violet. All the children that became my elders held the grapes in their hands like they were removing the organs from their bodies. The land. Their graves. For that fortune, they gave up a natural heart's beating. The right to a natural death. They were so hungry. To live in this town would be to live in abundance and to die from folly.

Alba leans over and speaks to the earth, her dress at her knees like drapes, her legs a theater. These are the legs that will work the land. The ground whispers. It will give them all that they need forever. But they have to give up a natural death. They eat the grapes without even washing the dirt. The pact will apply to all their bloodlines. Their children and their children and their children after that. The grapes offer more than satisfaction. Beauty. Intelligence. Talents. A lack of enemies. Much adoration. After weeks of eating stale sandwiches, the fruits are rich as jewels. The sun leans over the church on the hill.

I used to hear whispering as a child when our families had communal dinners to share food during one-off freezes. Chilling the grapes to oblivion. But they would come back the next morning. As large and magnanimous towards us as ever. When the women in my town worked at the market our elders built, they'd talk about what deaths happened that week, that month, that year. At first, the stories came out in whispers. I used to ask my mother why, and she'd say, Hush, *mijita*. It all came down before I was born. Hush, so the birds won't hear and know the rules.

Sloped nose. Handsome. Daddy. Dark hair like wood around your earlobes. How did you find this town? How did you find your daughter's mother in the vineyards? Was I weeping from fear? Why didn't you just pass through like many others do? Or stop by the market and smile at me while I bagged your fruit? Did you see me walk home from work every night and sit under the old flickering light in the backyard? Smelling my fingertips from cleaning up blood from another lost cousin? A neighbor. An elder. Almost all of our elders are gone. I drink beer under the light and pet our bully dog. Her grey fur is a luxury, like a cheap velvet painting.

An old church on top of the hill cuts off the dusk every night. Sometimes, people come to do photo shoots. That was how I met your father. I'd walk up to that church and around its ruins on long summer nights. Grass grew between the pew and its bookshelves. This wasn't a Catholic church. There were no stained glass images of Christ or his apostles. Instead, there were vacation bible school pamphlets. Rusted bakeware in the kitchen from making bread for the kids and round cookies for communion. The birds that made nests in the old worshipping places mimicked the children's laughter. See, I had been one of those children. I had eaten cookies with the bright-eyed ones whose families had enough money to leave when things got bad. When the deaths were too much for them. We stayed because we had always been here. But yes, we stayed because we had little choice. But then we began to hear that deaths always follow. As long as the pact's been, there's been no escaping them, see?

Your father saw me walking up, my boots dragging tree roots. He had an ice chest filled with store-brand sodas and stone fruit. He invited me for a picnic as the sun went down. Those would have been enough words to fall in love with him. But unlike the white boy drifters in the movies, he resisted silence. He told me his story. He taught the art of our people in a community college. Before that, he worked at his college library, sometimes falling asleep on the shelves when things got so quiet that his thoughts became heavy like a drug. Before that, he had defied his own father. He left their family construction business to go to school and learn things those men thought were useless. His father said he would never be a real man and would never have a place to hang his hat. I immediately interrupted him to point out that we had something in common. His family knew how to build houses, and mine did, too. And we talked about how, as children, we saw the houses rise from lumber. Sawdust. Like animal bones that became snow and then rock. We remembered holding dustpans for our grandmothers when they swept and prepared families to come into the house and live there forever.

The night he came to town, my youngest sister died while hanging clothes on the line. Just as she reached up, it began to rain and thunder. It wasn't the thunder that killed her. It was the falling wire. It came crashing down and severed her arm. The entire family was gone, including myself, as I was still with your father on the hill. My sister lay under the flapping wet clothes for hours. Bleeding out. And she was gone when I came home and found her. There are still nights I sit in front of my long kitchen window and eat regret like a meal. There wasn't even a twitch to her. Just the blue clouds passing over her face in a premonition's stripe.

By the time we had my sister's funeral, your father was mine. There are old Mexican stories from elders that if you go to funerals while a child is still in your body, it could hurt the baby. But again, there are no deaths by natural causes in this town. Your father was so kind that he paid for catering from the local restaurant so my mother and *tías* wouldn't have to cook food. My mother's face must have ached from crying hard at the powdery moon. She sits for hours going through my sister's trinkets. She would nag my sister for her hoarding ways in the past, and now she digs through the remnants. Fabric scraps. Empty perfume bottles. Things she once described as filth are now pristine. As if they belonged in a big city museum. Curated and tagged to mark her little brown daughter's quick and passing existence.

My daughter. The one I can't see yet. I've been waiting for you. In other lives, I may have had daughters. I gave them names that I became ashamed of. I braided their hair in the sunlight, singing do-wop into the tile grout and soda pop bottles. But you will be different. I'll give you a solid name like Opal. Forming an O shape in the way of the grapes. In an old song from Texas.

Alba is the last of the elders. Yet spared and still waiting for her accident. On Thursday nights, in the cantina, she brags that she will have the most beautiful death. Set for her like the booby trap of a delectable soldier, tattooed with a rain of cowboy verses from home. As a child, she taught me how to pull lice from my sister's hair and break the eggs by pressing my two thumbnails with tenderness. Even then, my sister's body was devoured by this town. Alba gives me more condolences for my sister. She says she'd be sorry to see me leave this town. She understands. And she knows how to undo a penance slightly. She knows how to make the measure of the sacrifice. She rubs the grapes into my palms until they become juices. They drip. I make my promise. I rub the soft part of my belly so you can begin to understand me. The wind cools. A dry heat. A different kind of heat than the elders felt as children. The weeds outside her porch scratch my feet goodbye.

Opal. Your daddy has watched you sleep at night. After, he takes pictures of the hills that peek over other towns. The people in those other towns. They don't know us, but they will. Late mornings, I feed you sweet potatoes. I cut butter with an old family knife and salt the vegetables. Some mornings, what you eat becomes a gourd, stewed, and plenty. When your father comes home from work, we trade places and I work nights at the market and snap cherry gum into the moonlight when no one is looking. My mother calls me the most stubborn girl she's ever met as we pack up cardboard in the downtime. Those are my favorite hours. When we turn off the misters that spray over the fruit, it still hangs in resistance. Every night, I look at my hands, dirty from counting the register money. From far away, an observer might think I was working with ink stamps and had a job in an office as a secretary.Taking notes. Leaving thumbprints on the coffee maker for my boss. I predict that it'll be like that. They say the other cities are as dull as us, but I don't believe it.

They say my grandmother Petra saved cash in a jar and buried it in the ground for the most righteous occasion. I cling to these traditions more than you would imagine me, dear. I do the same. I roll the jar on the ground as if rubbing a panther's belly, afraid it might not return the affection and bite me. Make a flower tattoo. Burning. A nostalgia for the humidity because it was all the elders knew back then.

Your father will die by electrocution. Sitting under the old flickering light that has comforted me all my years. The fire sparking, like the night my grandfather Keke danced about in circles, mimicking the hacendado from his matinees that he erroneously longed to be. This house that he made. Faulty old wires. That we thought would be fortified forever. We ate well around this little kitchen table. Mismatched porcelain cups earn the most loving sigh from your father. I can't tell you that I knew how it was coming. I gave a life for a precious life. But yes, I knew it was coming. Like how we never knew when the rain will come down on the vines. Your hair will keep growing long and curly like mine. Your face bones are a graph of your father's skull. I'll help you bless him, see. As I hold these dishes in the soap and the water. Watch the horizon hang its hat on the church and the hill.

In the Black and White Woods: My Personal Experience with Santa Muerte

A.E. Santana

~~~

I ONCE MET Santa Muerte.

Please note, I am speaking as someone outside this closed practice. *Is* working with Santa Muerte a closed practice? Everyone I know who works with her says that it is. So, I am not going to speak on any practices that have been shared with me in confidence.

All I can tell you is my personal experience.

From a young age, I learned that everyone is an energy vampire – waiting to drain you of your vigor and empathy – and if I feed them, I can be given scraps of attention. After years of therapy and learning how to set boundaries, I don't hold true to this thought any longer. But when I first connected with a Santa Muerte practitioner, I had lost so much of my drive and embraced apathy into my already cynical worldview.

At that time, all I knew of Santa Muerte was what I had heard whispered by family and community, from Mexican news outlets when they covered cartel stories, and various *brujas* who spoke highly of her. What I had gathered was that Santa Muerte was not a goddess or deity or the grim reaper. She *is* Death. Depending on who you asked, Santa Muerte was benevolent and harsh, engaged and aloof, supportive and taught hard lessons. If I had been asked what I thought of her then, I would have said: *Can't say. I don't know her.*

When the practitioner offered the opportunity to meet with Santa Muerte on a vision journey, I was going through an emotionally difficult time in my life. I was learning boundaries to keep myself safe from the people who wanted my energy, trying to comprehend that I had to let go of the emotions and tactics that once saved my life but no longer served me, and actively attempting to ignore the resurfacing childhood trauma that I would have rather died than deal with. I wasn't looking to become a practitioner of Santa Muerte. I took the chance to meet her because I wanted to do it. No other reason. That seemed good enough.

* * *

The journey starts with drums. Hands beating taut animal skin create a rhythm that lulls me into a relaxed state. Years before, I volunteered to go on stage with a hypnotist who then proceeded to be unable to hypnotize me. He was upset and sent me back. He then asked for another volunteer, this time saying that if you know you can't be hypnotized, then please don't volunteer. I didn't know that some people couldn't be hypnotized. I had honestly thought that either it was a scam, and no one can be hypnotized, or that everyone could.

The drums the Santa Muerte practitioner plays echo in my ears. I'm told to close my eyes. I no longer see the face of the practitioner who will be guiding me. The world is dusty red through my eyelids until the practitioner begins to speak and my vision is taken over by the setting she paints: a forest.

When I dream, I dream in color. I know a few people who dream in black and white, and only when they're having precognitive dreams. I'm grateful that I don't have premonitions, that my dreams are only ever just dreams and not some other place where our reality and a higher vibrational plane meet to tell me something important. So, when the forest I'm walking through looks like an ink drawing, eerily two-dimensional and devoid of all color, I inwardly groan.

Before this, I wondered whether I was a coward because I never wanted to be called by a deity or higher spirit or the universe. Turns out, I'm just tired. Working with something bigger than yourself that has called to you, and you've accepted, can be exhausting. In the end, all I feared was more work – I feared being drained to nothing.

So, it's telling that the path through the woods is easy, turning this way and that, but level with no loose gravel or other hinderances. The forest is serene, and the deeper I go, the calmer I feel. Although it is black and white – a signal to me that this is an important experience I need to pay attention to – I like the forest. This is a liminal space, and I've always liked liminal spaces. The trees are large oaks, with thick trunks and huge canopies. If there are any creatures in the forest, they're not around. I listen for the sound of birds or maybe footsteps, but all I hear is the distant drumming of the percussion instruments I left behind with my physical body. I no longer hear the voice of the practitioner who is guiding me, but I know she is there with the same visceral understanding that I am in a place between worlds.

Another bend in the path. I make the turn.

My feet stop.

Santa Muerte is usually depicted as a skeletal figure in different colored robes – each color representing a theme her practitioner may be seeking help in – holding a scythe. This is what I expected.

Off the path ahead of me, sitting on a large boulder, is Santa Muerte dressed as La Calavera Catrina. La Catrina is an early 1900s drawing of a female skeletal figure in a European lady's aristocratic outfit first created by illustrator José Guadalupe Posada as a satirical social commentary and later tailored by other artists to become a well-loved depiction of Death, particularly for Día de los Muertos, throughout Latin America.

Why would Santa Muerte be dressed as La Catrina? They are separate from each other and not interchangeable. I know this. One is an illustration that has become a national folk icon – an idea, a representation. The other is the actual incarnation of Death herself, with a mind and will of her own. It would be like saying Santa Claus and Jesus were the same person.

Nonetheless, I am gobsmacked by Santa Muerte's grace and beauty as she appears to me. Inhumanly tall, she wears an intricate maroon gown that is a blend of the traditional bourgeois dress from Posada's images and folklorico skirts with layers of white lace. A matching large-brimmed lady's hat with copious lace and feathers sits elegantly on her skull.

It dawns on me that the reason why Santa Muerte has shown herself in this way is because she's not calling to me. I am not a chosen practitioner of hers. She has dressed for a casual meeting of leisure. Her clothing is the only color in the forest. I recognize this is because it's a costume, not what she would wear when meeting someone who she has called or possibly someone who has been devoutly seeking her.

I am relieved. She seems to laugh at my reaction.

Her deep red skirts spill over the forest floor, creating a blanket that she beckons me to sit upon. She's dazzling and magnificent – and has a presence that is familiar and affectionate. I hesitate, a little confused. Santa Muerte hasn't chosen me but seems delighted to see me.

Suddenly, I am eager to be near her and rush forward. She welcomes me like a mother who hasn't seen her child in ages. And I do feel like she is my mother, and I need her like a child does.

Stepping onto Santa Muerte's skirt is like stepping onto a plush red carpet, luxurious and opulent. This close, I feel dwarfed by her. She's not as tall as the trees, but the trees seem impossibly tall. She tilts her face down to look at me, and although it is a skull I look up to, I feel safe and protected. There is no fear between us. Why would she ever fear me – or anyone – and how could I ever be frightened of such a warm entity?

I am not a practitioner of hers, but she loves me anyway.

Instinctively, I curl up at her feet. I do this of my own accord because I want to. Maybe she's amused by this action – I don't know – but she accepts it. Not as if it was the "correct" action to perform, but rather that she expected no different from me.

Mother, I want to call her, but that doesn't seem to fit – that's for the people who follow her, right? But I want a mother so much it hurts, and she's so open to being my mother. Could Santa Muerte be my mother without me being her practitioner? I'm not her student. I'm more like the child who gets away with not doing chores. She won't ask anything of me and seems to have an ocean of patience. If I wanted to work with her, I get the feeling that she'd accept me. Then I'd be able to see her in robes while she holds a scythe. I also will need to be ready and willing to do the hard work.

Instead, I am content to lie at her feet, feeling like nothing in the universe can harm me. There Santa Muerte lets me doze in the folds of her skirt. She seems to know that I need the rest, that I'm so tired of the world I come from – and there's going to be so much more to do when I get back. That's my destiny, and I hate it. She knows that and consoles me.

This is how I spend the rest of my time with her – quiet, cozy, soothed, and untroubled – until the practitioner's voice that has always been there brings me back to the physical plane where my eyes are closed and the drums are loud in my ears.

I'm sad to leave Santa Muerte's side. I don't have enough time to thank her for watching over me while I rested.

I hope she knows.

* * *

Whenever I feel overworked, I'm able to look back to the time I met Santa Muerte. When I think of her, I think of comfort, a motherly figure, safety, and protection. After being tormented by energy vampires and my own lack of boundaries, Santa Muerte was there without judgement or needing me to learn some lesson. She seemed genuinely pleased to give me a secure respite, to shelter me in an in-between space when I didn't realize how much I needed it.

Recently, I was in a botanica with friends, and there was a larger-than-life statue of Santa Muerte in green robes with money and green candles at her feet. I stopped to stare at her. I wondered if people thought that I was afraid, but all I wanted to do was run up and hug her – it just wasn't the time and place to do so.

Yes, she is Death, and some may say my experience is symbolic of the rest she provides. They're probably right. More importantly, to me, is that she brought me solace without asking for anything in return. Not. A. Thing.

That's love.

Maybe love and death are more linked and intertwined than I originally thought. Either way, I'm grateful to have met her. That small moment we shared changed my heart that, at the time, felt like it was losing passion and compassion. A time when I felt that my two options were either start therapy or never wake up (I started therapy). It's almost as if Santa Muerte, Death incarnate, wanted to tell me: *Don't die. Instead, rest as much as you can.*

I didn't come back from meeting Santa Muerte with a mission or a message. I don't have to tell you this. I want to. Take care of yourself. Death is just around the bend in the path. She is kind and loving but isn't always calling you.

We Cast Our Own Curses

Richard Z. Santos

THIS FAMILY can fake it for a photo here or there, maybe a birthday party or Christmas, but we've never liked each other. We're all too selfish, mean, and stubborn.

Emma, I know I've been a judgmental mother. My mother, Ofelia, was a drunk. Her father was more concerned with the past than her. His father was abusive. It keeps going like that back in time, over and over. We forget their names, thankfully, but they're not gone.

My mother told me a story. I'm recording it not to help you feel closer to your grandmother, but in hope that you and I can shake up the pattern and find happiness. Maybe it's too late for us, but your children have a chance. A generation or two of people who actually like each other might snap this curse.

And don't kid yourself, love. This curse was cast by us on us.

The day of her father's funeral, I *made* my mother tell me about her father. She was sitting in her grandfather's old recliner. It'd been stripped and reupholstered half a dozen times. I thought it felt like cinder blocks but the chair had reformed around my mother, erasing the previous owners.

Her words have been rattling around my brain for thirty years. I remember everything like it was yesterday, sharper than yesterday. I remember the smell of her whisky. I remember the creak of that old chair. I remember being excited to hear something nice for a change. I should have known better.

She never realized she was telling me a ghost story. A family story. A haunting. Same difference. Listen.

* * *

You wrapped those tamales before putting them up, right? God, not like it matters, I hate tamales. You're expected to be grateful someone spent a day making them but hard work can't replace flavor.

Wait, hear that? Head back in there and turn off that faucet. Come on, girl. Yeah, sure, I suppose it turned itself on when you walked in here. Grab that bottle while you're at it.

God, your grandfather would have torn into you for that. He hated a dripping faucet more than anything. I mean *anything*. Break a plate and he'd quietly sweep up. Leave a faucet running and you might as well have built a bonfire on the carpet.

You're sad. Good. What kind of monster wouldn't have a sad granddaughter at their funeral? I tried to be sad, but some people you know too well.

Might as well start in Minnesota because that's when Mom said everything changed. In Texas, he was kinder, more patient. Less caught up in his own ass about everything. You can see it in the McAllen pictures, they're both happy, light, not burdened by much of anything. Then my mom finds a job in Minnesota and it all goes wrong.

Okay, right after we move, I'm starting third grade in a new city and Dad's "getting us settled." That's the phrase my mom used. "Getting us settled." She did the cooking, earned most of the money, but his job was to "get us settled."

We came home one day and he'd been decorating. My jaw dropped open because he'd covered a wall with his grandmother's brass crucifixes. I swear there were a dozen in different sizes. Decades earlier, someone stuffed his grandmother's junk into a box. Well, that box rode to Minnesota in the backseat with me.

We weren't even religious. Barely made it to mass on Easter. He saw my mom's face and shrugs.

"I'm trying a few things," he said. "Besides, they're antiques, right?"

My mom kissed him on the cheek and took one off the wall. "They're brass," she said, "and probably from the 70s."

"Well, I mean, that's antiquey nowadays." He took the cross from her and put it back.

"Yeah, antiques made in old China," she said.

"Calmate, it's not about the origin, it's about the sentiment. They meant something to her so that means something to me."

My mom stepped back and turned her head to the side. "Did you tell me to calm down in Spanish?"

While they were talking I pushed a chair over to see all the junk he'd piled on the mantle. He'd arranged half a dozen little statues and figurines, a photograph of a scowling man, plus some rosaries that had all come out of his grandmother's box of mementoes.

In the center of the mantle was a pile of dust and little pebbles. Something had broken, almost exploded. The shattered pieces weren't big enough to glue back together but I could almost identify the bigger chunks. Maybe a hand or a foot. Possibly the side of a face. I reached out to sift the pile through my fingers but he grabbed my wrist, hard. His parents beat him but he never touched me, so I froze and my eyes filled with tears I didn't even know how to spill.

He shook his head like he was dismissing himself not me and said, "Sorry, just be careful. It could cut you."

My mom pulled me away, all casual like.

"What is that?" she asked.

He straightened some of the junk on the mantle and tried to smile. It was the last time I saw that old him try to come back.

"It broke," he said. "I was unpacking the box and found a beautiful carved rock statue. I mean it was intricate, but

heavy and, you know, not physically heavy but like…
heavy, right?"

He shrugged and put his hands on his head. He looked sadder than I'd ever seen him.

"And then, I don't know. It slipped. I was holding it when a shadow moved towards me and I heard someone talking, so I looked up and…maybe it was the trees outside the window. I don't know. I swept it up and put it there. Couldn't bring myself to throw it away. That thing was ancient. Priceless, I'm sure."

He said it was a statue of an old man holding a bucket with something, probably a fish, flung over his shoulder. What's weird is that his mom was still alive and says she doesn't remember anything like that. She remembers a stone carving but it was of a woman holding a baby. One of his uncles swore it was a man holding a sword. I sifted through the pieces later that night and found a hand holding maybe a flower, but then I got spooked and dropped it. Didn't look again.

Whatever it used to be, that thing was now dust and my mom should have tossed it and asked forgiveness. Instead, that little pile of rubble stayed up there for years. Even after I moved back here to Texas and had you, they never cleared that mantle.

I told you I don't remember my father before he changed and that's true. But I do remember *he* knew he was changing. He'd snap at me or my mom about the dripping faucet, about the music I was listening to, about the fact that all my friends were white – I mean, hello, Minnesota. Then he'd apologize, try to give me a gentle squeeze, but he didn't mean it.

He developed migraines. Never went to the doctor about them. I mean, forty-year-old men don't start getting migraines for no reason, but he suffered alone. I learned to watch TV without sound. My mom learned to cook without filling the house with rich, thick smells. Goodbye beans and enchiladas. Hello flapjacks and baloney sandwiches.

He'd describe each migraine to us. As if giving us some of his pain would make it better next time. I knew how it felt to have your guts scooped out and your brain rattled. First, there's the rainbow auras. It starts as a tiny squiggle. A rainbow worm sparkling like an electric diamond in the corner of your vision. There's nothing actually there, of course, it's just frothing brain chemistry. He told me they were almost beautiful because no one else could see those amazing colors.

Then the auras grow. They turn into rings and get bigger and bigger and the sparkles get brighter and brighter. When the rings overlap, that's when you're fucked. Migraine coming in fast. Then, after they expanded beyond his field of vision, there would always be a few moments of peace. A minute, two, three, where nothing hurt.

He always thought that meant he'd avoided the migraine. Brains are weird and maybe this time would be different. If I was around, watching his shoulders curl up while he sank into a world I couldn't see, he'd look up with a smile. "Close one, mija."

Then it would hit him. Pile of bricks. His face drooped. His eyes unfocused and he went to the back bedroom while Mom and I tried not to disturb the air molecules because he'd remember that door you shut too hard or that spoon clattering on the stove.

He once said that in those moments, when the pain was deep in his bones, deeper, in his soul, he'd gladly blink out of existence if someone gave him the option. Poof. Pain gone. Self gone. Sounds like a heck of a deal.

This is weird. Not as weird as what I'm getting to, but you're not going to like the way this sounds "Miss Biology Major." See, I used to wonder if he took that deal. Blink out. Move on, while your body stays here. If you're vulnerable enough, hurting enough, far enough from home, maybe that's a blessing.

Then he'd emerge. Might be two hours later, might be the next day, but he'd be brimming with pent-up energy. He'd fix things that didn't need to be fixed. He'd turn the water off, double check for leaks, and replace a new faucet with a newer faucet. All because he remembered his own father telling him that spirits enter houses through water and a dripping faucet is asking for someone unwanted to show up.

He'd scrub the house clean while singing along to old Norteño music. He'd make tortillas from scratch and get beans going in a crock pot. He'd vibrate with all the extra energy flooding his system, like his brain had been rebooted and had speed to spare. Those were the fathers I could choose from. Distracted. Writhing with pain. Or hyper.

Then one day he took me to school and didn't come home for twenty-four hours. My mom wasn't in a rush to call the cops or anything because I think she liked having the house to herself.

I was walking into school the next morning when I turned around, God knows why, and saw his car in the faculty parking lot. There he was. Sound asleep in his front seat like he'd been driving all night and was catching some shuteye at a rest stop.

When I knocked on the window he scrambled out of the car. He sat on the ground and cast his eyes around not seeing me or much of anything. When he caught his breath, he smiled at me. A huge smile. Beautiful.

"I saw him," he said. "I saw my grandfather. He was here. I think he...*is* here."

Then he kissed me on the top of my head and drove away.

When my mom got home from work she alternated between blind fury and sheer confusion. He sent me to my room, which of course meant I shut my door then snuck down the hallway to spy on them.

He was so happy and every time my mother tried to get mad at him he'd smile and hold her hands. Finally, he said, "I saw my grandfather."

"Your grandfather died before you were born."

"I saw him. I saw him."

He told the story in a rush, entranced, like he was sharing a favorite childhood memory.

"I dropped Ofelia at school and pulled into the parking lot because a migraine was coming on. Those auras started dancing and I decided to wait until they passed because I can't drive with kaleidoscope vision, you know? So the auras grow and turn into rings, and I turned to make sure Ofe had gone into the building and when I moved my head…I saw him."

He smiled and waited like he was expecting my mom to praise Jesus, but she was gawking like he was a clown or a talking dog or anything other than her cranky husband.

"I looked forward and he disappeared. I turned my head to the right again and it's like I was seeing…another place. The rings changed if I turned, like they were real, and dead center of one that was growing very, very fast was my grandfather's face."

He stood up, picked up the photo that had been on the mantel, and waved it at my mother like proof.

"Right there. Him. Looking at me. Smiling."

"In…during your migraine?"

"Exactly. When I looked again, he was bigger. And, okay, I know how this sounds, but I think he means well."

"He *means* well? Your dead grandfather?"

"And he grabbed the aura with his bare hands and he was pulling it apart, making it wider. It knocked the other auras out of the way and then when he had it big enough he started to climb through."

My father put a hand on his face like he could catch those words, toss them out with the trash. But they were out there. We all heard them. And, to me, that's when Francisco really came through. That was the last moment when my father could have shut up, could have heard himself, could have boxed up that photo, thrown out that pile of dust, and moved on with his life. Instead, he let Francisco in.

"He climbed through."

My father mimicked what he'd seen. He grasped an invisible rainbow aura with two hands and pulled horizontally and then vertically until that invisible aura stretched from over his head down to his waist. I could almost see those vibrating rainbows. Then he put his hands on the bottom of the aura and my father lifted his leg over the side like he was climbing over.

My mother grabbed his shoulders.

"Hospital. Right now. MRI, CAT scan, whatever. We're going."

He shook his head. "I'm fine. I'm fine. He was *smiling*, don't you get it?"

"Hospital," my mother said again. "Now."

"We can't leave Ofe here alone. I'll have some tea. I'll call my mom. Hell, I'll rub an egg on my head. I feel great."

And...yeah, I need another drink. Sure you don't want one too? I'm glad you don't seem to touch this stuff.

Neither did my father, if that's what you're wondering. No, he didn't drink. That was my mother's job. At least it became her job after that night.

I never knew his grandfather, Francisco. That would be my great-grandfather, your great-great. Francisco died after his son was born – your father's father. I know it's getting complicated. So many dead old men. Point is, no one alive had known Francisco.

That box held pots purchased from various reservations. Old crosses. Ancient rosaries. And a big portrait of Francisco in a thin glass case that snapped shut. Maybe it was the style of photos way back then, I mean, more than a hundred years ago, right? But Francisco looked like a monster. Thick eyebrows. Mean little lips. Couldn't imagine his friends calling him Paco and kicking back. That man was serious.

My father became obsessed. Called everyone looking for any information about him. His mother didn't have many stories, a few great uncles and aunts had a couple, but nothing solid. He smoked Chesterfields, some second cousin said. He went to church twice a week. He held his breath when passing cemeteries. He drank too much sometimes. I mean, that's most men in the Valley even now.

Then he found something. Some third cousin dropped something in the mail. My father waited like a kid on Christmas, until this manila envelope showed up.

Inside were a few pieces of typewritten paper held together with an ancient paper clip that had stained the paper. "Lengends and Beliefes in Northern Mexico and Souther Texas by Francisco Alvarado."

I always thought it was some high school writing assignment that Francisco never finished. Typos on every page. Words misspelled, crossed out. But my father acted like it was the goddamn holy grail. I still remember that first paragraph because my father would work it into all his lectures to me.

"The Spaniards of northern Mexico and south Texas believe in a host of legends, spirits, rituals, and myths that fill nearly every part of our day to day lives."

Each paragraph was a few sentences about different... things. I don't want to call them myths, they're stories. La Llorona, of course. La Lechuza. El Mano Negro. A few I hadn't heard about like The Floating Cigarette, the Night Bird, La Rana Infantil.

Every culture has stories, ghosts and whatever. Latinos aren't unique in that, but my father was off to the races. He gathered stories and stories and stories and held onto them. And who was around to listen? Who didn't have a choice?

At first it was a quick story at the table. Or a ghost story before bed. He never lectured me about how to act. He never told me to wear a longer skirt or to take off my makeup. He let my mom deal with all that. Instead, I got folklore lectures. New tales, old ones, it didn't matter as long as some Spanish-speaking sucker believed it. He'd jump from La Llorona and Brujería and Santa Muerte to the fucking Chupacabra. I mean, that's based on a movie from the 90s but if enough Mexicans believed in the Chupacabra then it mattered.

Eventually, I learned how to sit and take it. My mom told me once that *his* father made him kneel on grains of rice for punishment. First few seconds don't hurt. Then after about a minute, it's irritating. Five minutes down the line, you've got lightning bolts running up your legs and you hurt so bad you can't even cry. My father probably learned how to tune out that abuse. I learned how to tune out his.

Soon we started celebrating some new holiday damn near every day. Every Christian saint has a day and a candle. We honored them all and kept digging. Did you know in Brazil they light bonfires on Saint Whoever's Day? Did you know that in Colombia they hang teabags from the tree branches on St. What's His Name's Day? On and on.

Those lessons never ended because even if you worked your way back through all of the twentieth-century urban legends and the nineteenth-century ghost stories and eighteenth- and seventeenth-century myths. Then you get to Mexico City and the Aztecs. Curses and Taino legends and a pantheon of pre-Columbian gods we know hardly anything about. Even then you could keep going back and back. You're through with the Maya and Inca? Fine, let's head over to Spain, Portugal, the Canary Fucking Islands. Muslim stories, Jewish traditions. Or *before* Spain and Portugal when that land belonged to the Goths and the Germanic tribes. Maybe the first curandera was named Theodora and lived in the year 800. Hell, why stop there, my father sure didn't. There's the Romans and the Greeks and then before you know it, you're into the Acadians, the Sumerians, the Babylonians and there's another god, another legend, another belief system connected to yours.

You know why I didn't bury him in a church? You know why I hardly even put up a Christmas tree? Because there's always another angry god, another ritual you're doing wrong, another deity waiting to punish you.

I learned it all in a state bordering the Great Lakes and you know what? There weren't a lot of *brujas* up there so he had to make his own charms and protective bags and *ojo* repellent. House was full of stinking potions and bubbling mud. Goddamn witch of the great lakes.

I would let him tell his stories till he exhausted himself. Till he was sweaty, spent. Done with me, done with himself. I never looked him in the eye. The whole time, however long it was, five minutes, ten minutes, an hour, two hours, I stared past him, at the wall, over his shoulder, just behind his ear.

I could make his face blur while I stared at the air between us. If I let my eyes go a little cross, not too much, too cross and he'd notice. But if I let my eyes go a little cross, my vision go a little fuzzy, I could see someone else.

Someone who looked like him, someone who looked like me, hell, someone who looked like *you*.

This other face was there, on top of my father's face, layered over like wallpaper. And this other person wouldn't move his mouth while my father talked. This person smiled. At me. And it wasn't a scary smile. It was sweet. Fatherly, grandfatherly.

My father was going down the rabbit holes of his mind and obsessing over traditions that nobody cared about anymore, if they even cared about them back then. But this other face, made out of the molecules and electrons between us, that other face was happy, satiated. Alive.

That face disappeared when I blinked. Or I just stopped seeing it.

Okay, fine, there was one story that gripped me. After a few dozen they just slid right off me but this one stuck. It was in an old book of Mexican ghost stories. Typical stuff, you know, spirits of murdered women and children, the Virgin Mary appears, weird animals in the mountains, but one tale was about families. See in this story the ghosts of our ancestors are with us all the time, watching over us. Angry. They're jealous of our warmth, our breath. Not a guardian angel. More of an intruder who keeps knocking and knocking and if you think about them too much, or in the wrong way, then you let them in. They get in through our ears, our eyes, our hands. We're supposed to let people go when they're gone. Live our own lives. But if you give those greedy bastards an opening, they'll grab a hold of you and pull themselves inside.

But you have to want them. My father wasn't swallowed by some spirit. I'm not here to let him off the hook. He let himself be swallowed and my mother and I were crumbs wiped off the table.

That's who your grandfather was.

* * *

Emma played the recording one more time. She used the sleeve of her sweater to wipe at her tears. Her grandmother Ofelia had been dead for years. She'd been a mean, spiteful woman and Emma's mother had always made it clear they would never be close.

Now, Emma's mother was ill and this recording was an attempt to keep communication open between them. Emma poured herself another glass of wine and finished it in two big gulps. She didn't know any of these people. Her grandmother, her great grandfather who'd moved to Minnesota decades ago. But Ofelia's anger moved her.

Emma would apologize to her mother for pushing her away. She hoped to get an apology for all that mothers have to apologize for. If the old woman was lucid. The cancer meds were working but those tumors were deep and her mother slept most of the day, muttering to herself.

Emma poured another glass, told herself it would be the last, and then grabbed the bottle while walking out of the kitchen.

As she went up the stairs she barely heard the dripping kitchen faucet, or the faucet in the hallway bathroom. The dripping kitchen faucet produced a thin metal da-da-da-drip, da-da-da-drip. *The bathroom faucet held a quieter, steady* dot-dot-dot, dot-dot-dot.

Lying in bed she opened her phone and searched "Mexican American folklore."

The sound waves of the dripping faucet crested down the hall, traveled up the stairs, joined with the other dripping faucet. The waves grew louder, multiplied, bounced off the walls, and slipped under Emma's bedroom door. It was a soothing, comforting, almost familiar soundtrack to her dreams.

☼

About the Authors

Hector Acosta is the Edgar and Anthony award-nominated writer and author of the wrestling-inspired novella *Hardway*. His short fiction has appeared in *Mystery Tribune*, *Ellery Queen Mystery Magazine*, *Thuglit* and *The Best American Mystery and Suspense Anthology*. He currently resides in Texas with his wife, dog, and inexplicably, three cats.

Alyssa Alessi is a writer of stories inspired by the unsettling macabre aesthetic of New England. You can find her hiking any trail in the Northeast said to be haunted, roaming old cemeteries with a camera in hand, or thrift shopping anywhere antiques are sold. She resides in Boston, MA with her husband, three children and their mini dachshund. If you'd like to read more from this author, find her middle grade book *Izzy Hoffman Is Not a Witch* anywhere books are sold, or find her stories on The NoSleep Podcast.

Gustavo Bondoni is a novelist and short story writer with over five hundred stories published in fifteen countries, in seven languages. He has published several science fiction novels including two trilogies, six monster books, a dark military fantasy and a thriller. His short fiction is collected in *Thin Air* (2023), *Pale Reflection* (2020), *Off the Beaten Path* (2019), *Tenth Orbit and Other Faraway Places* (2010) and *Virtuoso and Other Stories* (2011). In 2019, Gustavo was awarded second place in the Jim Baen Memorial Contest and in 2018 he received a Judges' Commendation (and second place) in The James White Award. He was also a 2019 finalist in the Writers of the Future Contest. His website is at gustavobondoni.com

David Bowles is a Mexican American author and translator from south Texas, where he works as an associate professor, co-ordinating the English Education Program at the University of Texas Río Grande Valley. Among his forty books are the multiple-award-winning *They Call Me Güero* and its companion *They Call Her Fregona* (Kokila), as well as *My Two Border Towns* (Kokila), *Ancient Night* (Levine Querido), *Secret of the Moon Conch* (Bloomsbury) and *The Prince & the Coyote* (Levine Querido). His work has also been published in multiple anthologies, plus venues such as *The New York Times, Strange Horizons, Apex Magazine, School Library Journal, Rattle, Translation Review*, and the *Journal of Children's Literature*. Additionally, David has worked on several TV/film projects, including *Victor and Valentino* (Cartoon Network), the *Moctezuma & Cortés* miniseries (Amazon/Amblin) and *Monsters and Mysteries in America* (Discovery). In 2017, David was inducted into the Texas Institute of Letters and presently serves as its president. In 2019, he co-founded the hashtag and activist movement #DignidadLiteraria, which has negotiated greater Latinx representation in publishing. In 2021, he helped launch *Chispa*, the Latinx imprint of *Scout Comics*, for which he serves as editor-in-chief.

Arasibo Campeche and **Carra Flowers**: Campeche is originally from Puerto Rico and works as a biochemist. He writes science fiction, fantasy, and horror that's often inspired by scientific principles. His short story collection, *Strained Sigma Bonds*, was published in May 2024 by Water Dragon Publishing. Carra Flowers is originally from Puerto Rico and a chemical engineer who enjoys writing, hiking, reading, and video games. He currently lives in New Jersey with his wife and pets.

Dr. R. Andrew Chesnut is Bishop Walter F. Sullivan Chair in Catholic Studies and Professor of Religious Studies at Virginia Commonwealth University. He is the author of the first academic book in English on the fastest growing new religious movement in the Americas – *Devoted to Death: Santa Muerte, the Skeleton Saint* (OUP, 2012, 2017 & 2025), with translations in six languages, *Competitive Spirits: Latin America's New Religious Economy* (OUP, 2003) and *Born Again in Brazil: The Pentecostal Boom and the Pathogens of Poverty* (Rutgers University Press,1997) as well as numerous book chapters, journal articles and scores of media interviews.

Edited by V. Castro

Angel Luis Colón is the International Latino Book Award-winning author of *Infested* (MTV/Simon & Schuster) and the upcoming *Minecraft: House of Horrors*. His fiction has appeared in multiple web and print publications including *Thuglit*, *Literary Orphans*, and *Great Jones Street*.

Rios de la Luz is the author of the novella, *Itzá* (Broken River Books) and the short story collection, *An Altar of Stories to Liminal Saints* (Broken River Books). She loves writing weird fiction with a mixture of magical realism and a dash of horror. She currently lives in Oklahoma with her partner and son.

Ivette N. Diaz is an author of dystopian sci-fi/fantasy novels that specifically showcase the power of hope even in the darkest of times. Her first published novel *Choices of Power, The I Am Chronicles*, and the prequel *Rise of Power* released in 2024. When not writing, she enjoys reading, being outside, and dancing to the congas of her Latin culture. She secretly loves Kung-Fu movies and takes daily online kickboxing classes in hopes of one day becoming a true ninja. You can also find Ivette on her many adventures throughout Central Florida with her husband and kids.

Laura Diaz de Arce is a South Florida-based writer and author. She's written the speculative collections *MONSTROSITY* and *In Absence* as well as the fantasy romance series, *Curse of the Nobleman*. She draws heavily from her heritage as the daughter of Cuban and Chilean immigrants. You can find her on most social media platforms as @quetaauthor and on her website LauraDiazdeArce.com.

J.F. Gonzalez (1964–2014) was the author of over 30 novels, mostly in the horror and thriller genres, including the seminal *Survivor* and the popular *Clickers* series. He also wrote over 200 short stories, several of which were listed as 'Recommended Reads' in Ellen Datlow's annual *Year's Best Fantasy and Horror* anthologies. Many more Gonzalez novels are slated for posthumous release. For more information please visit www.jfgonzalez.org.

L.P. Hernandez is an author of horror and speculative fiction. He is a regular contributor to The NoSleep Podcast and has released three short story collections, including the recently published *No Gods, Only Chaos*, featured on the Talking Scared podcast. His novellas include *Stargazers* and *In the Valley of the Headless Men*. In 2024, L.P. partnered with fellow military veteran, L.C. Marino to launch Sobelo Books. When not writing, L.P. serves as a medical administrator in the U.S. Air Force. He is a husband, father, and a dedicated metalhead.

Pedro Iniguez is a Mexican-American Bram Stoker and Elgin Award-nominated horror and science-fiction writer from Los Angeles, California. He is the author of *Mexicans on the Moon: Speculative Poetry from a Possible Future*, *Fever Dreams of a Parasite*, *Synthetic Dawns & Crimson Dusks*, and the SF novel *Control Theory*. Apart from leading writing workshops and speaking at several colleges, he has also been a sensitivity reader and has ghostwritten for award-winning apps and online clients. Forthcoming projects include his horror comic *Catrina's Caravan: Blood Cycles*, his SFF collection *Echoes and Embers: Speculative Stories*, and his debut picture book, *The Fib*.

Ruth Joffre is a Bolivian American writer and the author of the story collection *Night Beast*. Her work has been shortlisted for the Creative Capital Awards, longlisted for The Story Prize, and supported by residencies at the Virginia Center for the Creative Arts, Lighthouse Works, and The Arctic Circle. Her writing has appeared or is forthcoming in more than 100 publications, including *Lightspeed*, *Pleiades*, *Nightmare*, *TriQuarterly*, *Reckoning*, *Wigleaf*, and the anthologies *We're Here: The Best Queer Speculative Fiction 2022* and *2022 Best of Utopian Speculative Fiction*.

S. Alessandro Martinez is a Bram Stoker Award® -nominated author of Mexican and Spanish descent who writes horror and fantasy from middle grade to adult. He lives in a haunted manor and loves playing video/board games, practicing necromancy, watching bat videos, collecting skulls, visiting cemeteries, and generally lurking in the dark. The author of the novel *Helminth* and several forthcoming books, his short stories and poetry have also appeared in several magazines, anthologies, and websites.

Juliana Spink Mills was born in England but grew up in Brazil, where they spent their childhood looking for a secret portal to a magic land. Now they live in the suburban wilds of Connecticut, USA, and build their own portals out of words. They like their stories dark adjacent and their tea hot and plentiful. Besides writing speculative fiction, Juliana works as a library assistant and Portuguese/English translator. Find them online at jspinkmills.com or follow them on Instagram @jspinkmills.

Vanessa Molina is a Mexican American writer of speculative horror inspired by her heritage. She is living in Los Angeles and Mexico in alteration and loves scribbling ideas on napkins, Post-its, the backs of gum wrappers, you name it. Her most recent work can be found in Owlcrate's anthology *Monsters in Masquerade*.

Mo Moshaty is a multi-award-winning horror writer, producer, and lecturer. As Founder and Editor-in-Chief of *NightTide Magazine*, she champions marginalized voices in horror. Mo is also the founder of Mourning Manor Media, supporting diverse creatives. Her works include *Love the Sinner* and *Clairviolence: Tales of Tarot and Torment*.

Richie Narvaez is the author of two novels, *Hipster Death Rattle* and *Holly Hernandez and the Death of Disco*, which received an Agatha Award and an Anthony Award, and two short story collections, *Roachkiller & Other Stories* and *Noiryorican*. His work has been published in *Lumina Journal, Latinx Rising: An Anthology of Science Fiction and Fantasy, Mississippi Review,* and *Tiny Nightmares,* among others. He received a Letra Boricuas Fellowship and teaches at Sarah Lawrence College.

Wi-Moto Nyoka (she/her/ella) is an AfroMexican horror & sci-fi writer. She is the founder of Dusky Projects, creating and producing genre projects for young adult and adult audiences. Awards and honors include: Stowe Story Labs selected project, Independent Public Media Foundation grant recipient, Nightmares Film Festival Best Short Screenplay Award Winner, 13 Horror Screenplay Award Winner, Oregon Short Film Festival Best Horror Teleplay Award Winner and more. Published works can be found in Midnight & Indigo's Speculative Fiction collection, *Dread Central, NightTide Magazine, Terror Unleashed: Volume 2,* and *The Last Girls Club* magazine. Follow her on IG & BlueSky @duskyprojects.

Daniel A. Olivas is the author of 12 books including *Chicano Frankenstein* (Forest Avenue Press, 2024), *My Chicano Heart: New and Collected Stories of Love and Other Transgressions* (University of Nevada Press, 2024), and *Crossing the Border: New and Collected Poems* (Pact Press, 2017). He is also a playwright, editor, and book critic. Widely anthologized, Olivas has written on literature for *The New York Times, Los Angeles Review of Books, Los Angeles Times, Zocálo, Latino*

Book Review, *Alta Journal*, and *The Guardian*. He earned his degree in English literature from Stanford University, and law degree from UCLA. By day, Olivas is a senior attorney with the California Department of Justice.

Monique Quintana is the author of *Cenote City* (Clash Books, 2019). Her writing has been supported by Yaddo, The Community of Writers, Storyknife, Sundress Academy for the Arts, and the Kimmel Harding Nelson Center. She lives in Fresno's Tower District. You can find her at moniquequintana.com and @quintanagothic

A.E. Santana writes horror and fantasy. Her works can be found in *The Mirror*, *Latinx Screams*, and other speculative anthologies. She is the moderator for the horror book club, Creepy Story Collective, and is the co-chair of the Colorado Chapter of the Horror Writers Association. She received her MFA in fiction from the University of California, Riverside. Her perfect day consists of a cup of black tea and her cat, Flynn Kermit.

Richard Z. Santos's debut novel, *Trust Me*, was a finalist for the Writer's League of Texas Book Awards and was named one of the best debuts of the year by Crime Reads. He's the editor of the acclaimed anthology *A Night of Screams: Latino Horror Stories*. His fiction has been nominated for The Pushcart, Best of the Net, the International Thriller Writers Awards, and has appeared as a Distinguished Story in Best American Mystery and Suspense. His nonfiction and essays have appeared in *Texas Monthly*, *The Rumpus*, *Los Angeles Review of Books*, and more. A former board member of The National Book Critics Circle, Richard has also judged contests for The Kirkus Prize, The ITW, The NEA, and others. In a previous career, he taught in high schools and before that he worked for political campaigns, consulting firms, and labor unions.

About the Illustrator

Jorge González is an award-winning artist and painter from Buenos Aires, Argentina. He has created editorial illustrations for *The New Yorker* and *Harper's Magazine*, among others, and has illustrated numerous books and graphic novels.

About the Editor

V. Castro is a two-time Bram Stoker Award nominated Mexican American writer from San Antonio, Texas, now residing in the UK. She writes horror, erotic horror, and science fiction. Her books include *Immortal Pleasures*, *The Haunting of Alejandra*, *Alien: Vasquez*, *Mestiza Blood*, *The Queen of the Cicadas*, *Out of Aztlan*, *Las Posadas*, *Rebel Moon* (official Netflix film novelization) and *Goddess of Filth*. Her forthcoming book is *The Pink Agave Motel* from Clash Books. Connect with Violet via Instagram and Twitter @vlatinalondon or www.vcastrostories.com. She can also be found on Bluesky, Goodreads and Amazon. TikTok @vcastrobooks, Pinterest @V. Castro

Acknowledgements

FROM PARTS UNKNOWN © Hector Acosta 2025.

SUCKER © Alyssa Alessi 2025.

SOUTHWARD, THEN UPWARD © Gustavo Bondoni 2025.

WHISPERING SHARDS © David Bowles 2025.

LISTEN TO THIS © Arasibo Campeche and Carra Flowers 2025.

MESTIZA DEATH: HOW THE SPANISH GRIM REAPRESS MORPHED INTO MEXICAN SANTA MUERTE © Dr. R. Andrew Chesnut 2025.

BELINDA MATOS AND THE BRONX RIVER WISHING STONE © Angel Luis Colón 2025.

MATERNAL INSTINCT © Stacey Rios (Rios de la Luz) 2025.

TAÍNO: AN UNTOLD STORY © Ivette N. Diaz 2025.

THE MOTHER OF CANALS IN DADE COUNTY © Laura Diaz de Arce 2025.

EATEN ALIVE © J.F. Gonzalez. Ed. Keith Gouveia and Garrett Peck. Originally published in *Small Bites*, 2004.

EL PUENTE © L.P. Hernandez 2025.

NIGHT OF THE NAGUAL © Pedro Iniguez 2025.

LA DIABLADA © Ruth Joffre 2025.

THE STAINED WALLS © S. Alessandro Martinez 2025.

THE SNAKE GOD'S WAKE © Juliana Spink Mills 2025.

A GUARDIAN OF SALT AND FLESH © Vanessa Molina 2025.

COME BACK © Mo Moshaty 2025.

ISLA DEL ENCANTO PERDIDO © Richie Narvaez 2025.

AND THEN I WAKE UP © Wi-Moto Nyoka 2025.

NACHO © Daniel A. Olivas 2022. Originally published in the literary journal, *The Rumpus* (2022), and featured in *My Chicano Heart: New and Collected Stories of Love and Other Transgressions* (University of Nevada Press, 2024). Reprinted by permission of the author.

THE ACHE © Monique Quintana 2025.

IN THE BLACK AND WHITE WOODS:
MY PERSONAL EXPERIENCE WITH SANTA MUERTE
© Ashley Santana (A.E. Santana) 2025.

WE CAST OUR OWN CURSES © Richard Z. Santos 2025.

Edited by V. Castro

Beyond & Within

THE FLAME TREE Beyond & Within short story collections bring together tales of myth and imagination by modern and contemporary writers, carefully selected by anthologists, and sometimes featuring short stories and fiction from a single author. Overall, the series presents a wide range of diverse and inclusive voices, often writing folkloric-inflected short fiction, but always with an emphasis on the supernatural, science fiction, the mysterious and the speculative. The books themselves are gorgeous, with foiled covers, printed edges and published only in hardcover editions, offering a lifetime of reading pleasure.

FLAME TREE FICTION

A wide range of new and classic fiction, from myth to modern stories, with tales from the distant past to the far future, including short story anthologies, Collector's Editions, Collectable Classics, Gothic Fantasy collections and Epic Tales of mythology and folklore.

•

Available at all good bookstores, and online at flametreepublishing.com